The Sweetness

of

Forgetting

The Sweetness
of
Forgetting

KRISTIN HARMEL

GALLERY BOOKS

New York   London   Toronto   Sydney   New Delhi

Gallery Books
A Division of Simon & Schuster, Inc.
1230 Avenue of the Americas
New York, NY 10020

First Gallery Books trade paperback edition August 2012

GALLERY BOOKS and colophon are registered trademarks of Simon & Schuster, Inc.

For information about special discounts for bulk purchases, please contact Simon & Schuster Special Sales at 1-866-506-1949 or business@simonandschuster.com.

The Simon & Schuster Speakers Bureau can bring authors to your live event. For more information or to book an event contact the Simon & Schuster Speakers Bureau at 1-866-248-3049 or visit our website at www.simonspeakers.com.

Designed by Jaime Putorti

Manufactured in the United States of America

10 9 8 7 6 5 4 3 2 1

Library of Congress Cataloging-in-Publication Data
Harmel, Kristin
  The sweetness of forgetting / Kristin Harmel. — 1st Gallery Books trade paperback ed.
     p. cm.
1. Single-parent families—Fiction. 2. Grandparent and child—Fiction. 3. Family secrets—Fiction. 4. Life change events—Fiction. 5. Alzheimer's disease—Fiction. 6. Domestic fiction. I. Title.
  PS3608.A745S94 2012
  813'.6—dc23   2011051759

ISBN 978-1-4516-4429-6
ISBN 978-1-4516-4431-9 (ebook)

To Grandma and Grandpa from Weymouth

"God hath made of one blood all nations of men."

—ACTS 17:26

"One man's candle is light for many."

—TRACTATE SHABBAT, *ORDER MOED OF THE TALMUD*

"All God's creatures are His family and he is the most beloved of God who doeth most good to God's creatures."

—THE PROPHET MUHAMMAD

The Sweetness
of
Forgetting

Chapter *One*

The street outside the bakery window is silent and still, and in the half hour just before sunrise, as dawn's narrow fingers are just reaching over the horizon, I can almost believe I'm the only person on earth. It's September, a week and a half after Labor Day, which in the little towns up and down Cape Cod means that the tourists have gone home, the Bostonians have boarded up their summer houses for the season, and the streets have taken on the deserted air of a restless dream.

The leaves outside have begun to change, and in a few weeks, I know they'll mirror the muted hues of sunset, although most people don't think to look here for fall foliage. The leaf peepers will head to Vermont, to New Hampshire, or to the Berkshires in the western part of our state, where the oaks and maples will paint the world in fiery red and burnt orange. But in the stillness of the off-season on the Cape, the swaying beach grass will turn golden as the days grow shorter; the birds migrating south from Canada will come to rest in great flocks; the marshes will fade into watercolor brushstrokes. And I will watch, as I always watch, from the window of the North Star Bakery.

I can't remember a time when this place, my family's business, didn't feel more like home to me than the little yellow cottage by the bay that I was raised in, the home I've now had to move back into after the finalization of my divorce.

Divorce. The word rings in my ears, over and over, making me feel like a failure once again as I try to conduct the balancing act of simultaneously opening the oven door with one foot, juggling two industrial-sized trays of miniature cinnamon pies, and keeping an eye on the front of the bakery. It occurs to me yet again as I slide the pies in, pull out a tray of croissants, and push the door shut with my hip that trying to have it all means only that your hands are always full. In this case, literally.

I'd wanted so much to stay married, for Annie's sake. I didn't want my daughter growing up in a home where she had to feel confused about her parents, like I had when I was a kid. I wanted more for her. But life never works out the way you plan, does it?

The front door chimes just as I'm lifting the flaky, buttery croissants from the baking sheet. I glance at the timer on the secondary oven; the vanilla cupcakes need to come out in just under sixty seconds, which will delay me in getting out to the front of the store.

"Hope?" a deep voice calls out from up front. "You back there?"

I sigh in relief. A customer I know, at least. Not that I don't know almost everyone who remains in town after the tourists have gone home.

"Be out in a minute, Matt!" I shout.

I pull on my oven mitts, the bright blue ones with cupcakes embroidered on the edges that Annie bought me for my thirty-fifth birthday last year, and pull the vanilla cakes out of the oven. I breathe in deeply, the sugary scent taking me back to my own childhood for a moment. My *mamie*—French for "grandma"—founded the North Star Bakery sixty years ago, a few years after she moved to Cape Cod with my grandfather.

I grew up here, learning to bake at her knee as she patiently explained how to make dough, why breads rise, and how to turn both traditional and unexpected ingredient combinations into confections that the *Boston Globe* and the *Cape Cod Times* rave about every year.

I put the cupcakes on the cooling rack and slide two trays of anise and fennel cookies into the oven in their place. Beneath them, on the bottom rack, I slide in a batch of crescent moons: almond paste flavored with orange flower water, sprinkled with cinnamon, enclosed in a pastry shell, and shaped into gently curved slivers.

I close the oven door and brush the flour off my hands. Taking a deep breath, I set the digital timer and walk out of the kitchen into the brightly lit front room of the bakery. No matter how overwhelmed I am, it still makes me smile to come through the doors; Annie and I painted the bakery last fall, when business was slow, and she chose princess pink with white piping. Sometimes it feels like we're living inside a giant cupcake.

Matt Hines is sitting in a chair facing the counter, and when he sees me, he jumps up and smiles.

"Hey, Hope," he says.

I smile back. Matt was my high school boyfriend, half a lifetime ago. We broke up before heading off to separate colleges; I came back several years later with a bachelor's degree, the useless half of a law school education, a new husband, and a baby daughter, and Matt and I have been friendly ever since. He's asked me out several times since my divorce, but I've realized, almost with surprise, that we've outgrown each other. He's like a favorite old sweater that no longer fits or flatters. Life changes you, even if you don't realize it while it's happening, and it turns out you can't take back the years that have passed by. Matt doesn't seem to realize that, though.

"Hey, Matt." I try to sound neutral and friendly. "Can I get you a cup of coffee? On the house, since you had to wait." I don't wait for an answer; I'm already pouring. I know exactly how Matt takes it: two sugars and one cream in a to-go cup, so that he can get to the Bank of the Cape, where he's a regional vice president, to get his paperwork started before they open for business. Since he works just two blocks down on Main Street, he stops in once or twice a week.

Matt nods and takes the coffee from me with a smile.

"What else can I get you?" I ask, gesturing to the glass bakery case. I've been here since four, and although I'm not quite done with everything, there are already plenty of fresh pastries. I reach for a miniature pielike confection, which features a phyllolike shell filled with a lemony almond paste and brushed with rosewater and honey. "How about an almond rose tart?" I ask, holding it out to him. "I know they're your favorite."

He hesitates for only a second before reaching for it. He takes a bite and closes his eyes. "Hope, you were born to do this," he says with his mouth full, and although I know it's a compliment, the words hit me hard, because I never intended to do this at all. It wasn't the life I wanted for myself, and Matt knows it. But my grandmother got sick, my mother died, and I no longer had a choice.

I brush the words away and pretend they don't bother me as Matt says, "Hey, listen, I actually came this morning to talk to you about something. Can you sit with me for a sec?"

His smile looks a little frozen, I realize suddenly. I'm surprised I didn't notice it earlier.

"Um . . ." I glance back toward the kitchen. The cinnamon pies need to come out soon, but I have a few minutes before the timer goes off. There's no one else here at this early hour. I shrug. "Yeah, okay, but just for a minute."

I pour myself a cup of coffee—black, my third of the morning—and slide into the chair across from Matt. I lean on the table and brace myself for him to ask me on another date. I'm not sure what to say; focusing on my husband and daughter for all these years has cost me most of the friendships I once had, and selfishly, I don't want to lose Matt too. "What's up?"

From the way he pauses before answering, I have the sense that something's wrong. Maybe it's because I've grown accustomed to bad news lately. My mother's cancer. My grandmother's dementia. My husband deciding he no longer wanted to be my husband. So I'm surprised when what Matt says is, "How's Annie?"

I look at him closely, my heart suddenly racing as I wonder whether he knows something I don't. "Why? What happened?"

"I was just wondering," Matt says quickly. "I'm being nice. Making conversation."

"Oh," I say, relieved that he hasn't come as the bearer of some sort of bad news. I wouldn't have been surprised to hear that my daughter had been caught doing something foolish like shoplifting or spray-painting her middle school. She's been different since her father and I split up: edgy, nervous, and angry. More than once, I've guiltily searched her room, thinking I'd find cigarettes or drugs, but so far, the only evidence of the change in my Annie is the massive chip on her shoulder. "Sorry," I tell Matt. "I keep waiting for something else to go wrong."

He averts his eyes. "How about dinner tonight?" he asks. "Me and you. Annie'll be at Rob's again, right?"

I nod. My ex and I share custody equally, an arrangement I'm not happy about, because I think it makes Annie's life less stable. "I don't know, Matt," I say. "I just think—" I search for words that won't hurt. "I think maybe it's too soon, you know? The divorce was so recent, and Annie's really struggling. I think it's better if we just—"

"It's just dinner, Hope," Matt interrupts me. "I'm not proposing to you."

My cheeks are suddenly on fire. "Of course not," I mumble.

He laughs and reaches for my hands. "Relax, Hope." When I hesitate, he smiles slightly and adds, "You have to eat. How 'bout it?"

"Yeah, okay," I say, and it's at that moment that the front door of the bakery swings open, and Annie comes in, her backpack slung over her shoulder, her dark sunglasses on, even though dawn hasn't yet broken. She stops and stares at us for a moment, and I know instantly what she's thinking. I pull my hands away from Matt, but it's too late.

"Great," she says. She rips her sunglasses off and tosses her long, wavy, dishwater-blonde hair over her shoulder, fixing us with a glare that makes her deep gray eyes even stormier than usual. "Were you going to, like, start making out if I didn't get here?"

"Annie," I say, standing up. "It's not what it looks like."

"Whatever," she mutters. Her new favorite word.

"Don't be rude to Matt," I say.

"What*ever*," she repeats, rolling her eyes for emphasis this time. "I'll be in the back. So you can, like, go back to doing whatever it is you're doing."

I look after her helplessly as she charges through the double doors to the kitchen. I hear her throw her backpack onto the counter, the weight of it rattling the stainless steel bowls I keep stacked there, and I wince.

"Sorry," I say, turning back to Matt. He's staring in the direction Annie disappeared.

"She's really something," he says.

I force a laugh. "Kids."

"Frankly, I don't know how you put up with it," he says.

I smile tightly at him. I'm allowed to feel annoyed with my daughter, but he's not. "She's just going through a hard time," I say. I stand up and glance toward the kitchen. "The divorce has been tough on her. And you remember seventh grade. It's not exactly the easiest year."

Matt stands up too. "But the way you let her talk to you . . ."

Something in my stomach tightens. "Good-bye, Matt," I say through a jaw clenched so tightly it hurts. Before he can reply, I turn away, heading for the kitchen, hoping that he takes the hint to leave.

"You can't be rude to customers," I say to Annie as I come through the double doors into the kitchen. Her back is to me, and she's stirring something in a bowl—batter for red velvet cupcakes, I think. For a moment I think she's ignoring me, until I realize she has earbuds in. That damned iPod.

"Hey!" I say, louder. Still no reply, so I walk up behind her and pull the earbud out of her left ear. She jumps and whirls around, eyes blazing, as if I've slapped her.

"God, Mom, what's your problem?" she demands.

I'm taken aback by the anger in her face, and for a moment, I'm frozen, because I can still see the sweet little girl who used to crawl onto my lap and listen to Mamie's fairy tales, the girl who came to me for comfort after every skinned knee, the girl who made me Play-Doh jewelry and insisted I wear it to Stop & Shop. She's still in there somewhere, but she's hiding behind this icy veneer. When did things change? I want to tell her I love her, and that I wish we didn't have to argue like this, but instead, I hear myself coolly say, "Didn't I tell you not to wear makeup to school, Annie?"

She narrows her overly mascaraed eyes at me and purses her too-red lips into a smirk. "*Dad* said it was fine."

I mentally curse Rob. He seems to have made it his personal mission to undermine everything I say.

"Well, *I'm* telling you it's not," I say firmly. "So get in the bathroom and wipe it off."

"No," Annie says. She puts her hands on her hips defiantly. She glares at me, not yet realizing that she's streaked red velvet batter on her jeans. I'm sure that'll be my fault too when she figures it out.

"This isn't up for debate, Annie," I say. "Do it now, or you're grounded."

I hear the coldness in my voice, and it reminds me of my mother. For a minute, I hate myself, but I stare Annie down, unblinking.

She looks away first. "Whatever!" She rips her apron off and throws it on the floor. "I shouldn't even be working here!" she yells, throwing her hands in the air. "It's against child labor laws!"

I roll my eyes. We've had this discussion ten thousand times. She's not technically working for a paycheck; this is our family business, and I expect her to help out, just like I helped my mom when I was a kid, just like my mom helped my grandmother. "I'm not explaining this to you again, Annie," I say tightly. "Would you rather mow the lawn and do all the chores around the house?"

She stalks out, presumably heading for the bathroom on the other side of the double doors. "I hate you!" she yells back at me as she disappears.

The words hit me like a dagger to the heart, even though I remember screaming them at my own mother when I was Annie's age.

"Yeah," I mutter, picking up the bowl of batter and the wooden spoon she left on the counter. "What else is new?"

By seven thirty, when Annie is about to leave to walk the four blocks to Sea Breeze Junior High, all of the pastries are out and the shop is full of regulars. In the oven is a fresh batch of our Rose's Strudel, filled with apples, almonds, raisins, candied orange peel, and cinnamon, and the scent is wafting comfortingly through the bakery. Kay Sullivan and Barbara Koontz, the two eightysomething widows who live across the street, are gazing out the window, deep in conversation, while they sip coffee at the table closest to the door. Gavin Keyes, whom I'd hired to help me make my mother's house livable again over the summer, is at the table beside them, sipping coffee, eating an éclair and reading a copy of the *Cape Cod Times*. Derek Walls, a widowed dad who lives on the beach, is here with his twin four-year-olds, Jay and Merri, each of whom is licking the icing off a vanilla cupcake, even though it's only breakfast time. And Emma Thomas, the fiftysomething hospice nurse who'd tended to my mom while she was dying, is standing at the counter, trying to choose a pastry to have with her tea.

I'm just about to pack up a to-go blueberry muffin for Emma when Annie strides past me, her coat on and her backpack slung over one shoulder. I reach out and grab her arm before she can get by.

"Let me see your face," I say.

"No," she mumbles, looking down.

"Annie!"

"Whatever," she mutters. She looks up, and I see that she's put on a fresh coat of mascara and reapplied the hideous lipstick. She also appears to have added a layer of fuchsia blush that comes nowhere near the apples of her cheeks.

"Wipe it off, Annie," I say. "Now. And leave the makeup here."

"You can't take it from me," she retorts. "I bought it with my own money."

I glance around and realize that the shop has fallen silent, except for Jay and Merri chattering in the corner. Gavin's looking at me with concern, and the old ladies near the door are just staring. I feel suddenly embarrassed. I know I already seem like the town failure for letting my marriage to Rob end; everyone thinks he's perfect and I was lucky to marry him in the first place. Now I appear to be a failure at parenting too.

"Annie," I say through gritted teeth. "Do it now. And this time, you *are* grounded, for disobeying me."

"I'm staying with Dad for the next few days," she shoots back, smirking at me. "You can't ground me. Remember? You don't live there anymore."

I swallow hard. I won't let her know that her words have

hurt me. "Fantastic," I say brightly. "You're grounded from the moment you step into *my* house."

She curses under her breath, glances around, and seems to realize that everyone's looking at her. "Whatever," she mutters as she heads for the bathroom.

I exhale and turn back to Emma. "I'm sorry," I say. I realize my hands are shaking as I reach for her pastry again.

"Honey, I raised three girls," she says. "Don't worry. It gets better."

She pays and leaves, then I watch as Mrs. Koontz and Mrs. Sullivan, who have been coming here since the bakery opened sixty years ago, get up and hobble out the door, each of them using a cane. Derek and the twins are getting ready to go too, so I come out from behind the counter to pick up their plates. I help button Merri's jacket, while Derek zips Jay's. Merri thanks me for the cupcake, and I wave as they leave.

Annie emerges from the bathroom a minute later, her face blissfully makeup free. She slams a mascara tube, a lipstick, and a pot of blush down on one of the tables and glowers at me. "There. Happy?" she asks.

"Overjoyed," I say dryly.

She stands there for a moment, looking like she wants to say something. I'm steeling myself for some sort of sarcastic insult, so I'm surprised when all she says is, "Who's Leona, anyway?"

"Leona?" I search my memory but come up empty. "I don't know. Why? Where'd you hear that name?"

"Mamie," she says. "She keeps, like, calling me that. And it seems to, like, make her real sad."

I'm startled. "You've been going to see Mamie?" After my mother died two years ago, we'd had to move my grandmother into a memory care home; her dementia had rapidly taken a turn for the worse.

"Yeah," Annie says. "So?"

"I . . . I just didn't know you were doing that."

"Someone has to," she spits back.

I'm sure the guilt plays across my face, because Annie looks triumphant.

"I'm busy with the bakery, Annie," I say.

"Yeah, well, *I* find the time," she says. "Maybe if you were spending less time with Matt Hines, you could spend more time with Mamie."

"*Nothing* is going on with Matt." I'm suddenly acutely conscious of Gavin sitting a few feet away, and I can feel my cheeks turning warm. The last thing I need is the whole town knowing my business. Or lack of business, as the case may be.

"Whatever," Annie says, rolling her eyes. "Anyway, at least Mamie loves me. She tells me all the time."

She smirks at me, and I know that I'm supposed to say *Honey, I love you too,* or *Your dad and I love you very much,* or something along those lines. Isn't that what a good mother would do? Instead, because I'm a horrible mother, what comes out of my mouth is "Yeah? Well, it sounds to me like she's saying 'I love you' to someone named Leona."

Annie's jaw drops, and she stares at me for a minute. I want to reach out, pull her into a hug and say I'm sorry, I didn't mean it. But before I have a chance, she whirls on her heel and strides out of the store, but not before I see the tears glistening at the corners of her eyes. She doesn't look back.

My heart aches as I stare in the direction she disappeared. I sink into one of the chairs the twins vacated a few minutes earlier and put my head in my hands. I'm failing at everything, but most of all at connecting with the people I love.

I don't realize Gavin Keyes is standing above me until I feel his hand on my shoulder. I jerk my head up, startled, and find myself staring directly at a small hole in the thigh of his faded jeans. For an instant, I have the strangest urge to offer to mend it, but that's ridiculous; I'm no better at using a needle and thread than I am at being a mother or staying married. I shake my head and pull my eyes upward, over his blue plaid flannel shirt to his face, which is marked by a thick shadow of dark stubble across his strong jaw. His thick shock of dark hair looks like it hasn't been combed in days, but instead of making him look unkempt, it makes him look really good in a way that makes me uneasy. His dimples, as he smiles gently at me, remind me just how young he is. Twenty-eight, I think, or maybe twenty-nine. I feel suddenly ancient, although I'm only seven or eight years older. What would it be like to be that young, with no real responsibilities, no preteen daughter who hates you, no failing business to save?

"Don't beat yourself up," he says. He pats me on the back and clears his throat. "She loves you, Hope. You're a good mom."

"Yeah, uh, thanks," I say, avoiding his eye. Sure, we'd seen each other nearly every day during the months he was working on my house, and when I returned home from work in the afternoons, I often fixed us lemonade and sat on the porch with him, doing my best to avoid looking at the tanned swell of his biceps. But he doesn't *know* me. Not really. Certainly not well enough to judge me as a mother. If he knew me that well, he'd know what a failure I am.

He pats me awkwardly again. "I mean it," he says.

Then he too is gone, leaving me all alone in my giant pink cupcake, which suddenly feels very bitter.

Chapter *Two*

I close the bakery early that day to run a few errands. Although the sun hasn't set yet when I get home at six fifteen, it feels dark and depressing inside the cottage I'm trying hard to think of as my own.

The silence inside is deafening. Up until last year, when Rob surprised me just before Christmas by announcing he wanted a divorce, I'd looked forward to coming home. I was proud of the life we'd made together in the solid, whitewashed Victorian overlooking Cape Cod Bay, just east of the public beach. I'd painted the interior myself, retiled the kitchen and hall, installed hardwood floors upstairs and in the living room, and planted a garden dominated by blue hydrangeas and pink salt spray roses that looked crisp and beautiful against the sail-white clapboard.

And then, just as I was finally done with everything, finally ready to relax in the dream home, Rob sat me down and announced in a soft voice, without meeting my eyes, that he too was done. Done with our marriage, done with me.

In the space of three months, while still reeling from my mother's death from breast cancer and the decision to put Mamie in a memory care home, I found myself moving back to my mother's place, which I hadn't been able to sell anyhow. A few months later, exhausted and discouraged, I'd signed all the divorce papers, eager only to have it all over and done with.

The truth was, I felt numb, and for the first time, I understood something I'd wondered about my entire life: how my mother had always been able to stay so cold about the men in her life. I'd never known my father; she'd never even told me his name. As she once crisply explained to me, "He left. A long time ago. Never knew you existed. He made his choice." And when I was growing up, she always had boyfriends whom she would spend all her time with, but she never let them get close. Not really. That way, when they'd ultimately leave her, she'd just shrug and say, "We're better off without him, Hope. You know that."

I always used to think she was heartless, even though I admit now that I'd looked forward to those brief periods of time between boyfriends, when I'd have my mom to myself for a few weeks. Now I wish I'd understood sooner, in time to discuss it with her. *I finally get it, Mom. If you don't let them in, if you don't really love them in the first place, they can't hurt you when they leave.* But like so many other things in my life, it's too late for that.

By the time I shower, washing the flour and sugar out of my hair and off my skin, it's a few minutes before seven. I know I should probably call Annie at Rob's and apologize for the way we left things earlier, but I can't bring myself to do it. Besides, she's probably doing something fun with him, and my call would only ruin it for her. Regardless of how I feel about Rob, I have to admit that he's good with Annie most of the time. He seems to get through to her in a way I haven't been able to in a long time. I hate that watching them laughing conspiratorially with each other sometimes makes me jealous first, happy for Annie second. It's like they're forming a new family portrait, and it no longer includes me.

After throwing on a gray cable-knit sweater and slim black jeans, I stare at myself in the mirror as I brush out my shoulder-length dark brown waves, which, blissfully, haven't started to turn gray yet, although they soon will if Annie keeps up this behavior. I search my own face for Annie's features, but as usual, I come up empty. Oddly, she doesn't look a thing like Rob or me, which led him to ask me once, when she was three, "Are you absolutely sure she's mine, Hope?" His words had cut me to the core. "Of course," I'd whispered, tears in my eyes, and he'd left it at that. Unless you counted her skin, which tanned evenly and beautifully, just like Rob's, there was virtually nothing of her tall, brown-haired, blue-eyed father in her.

I examine my features as I put on a coat of nude lipstick and swipe some mascara onto my pale lashes. While Annie's eyes are an uneven gray, just like Mamie's, mine are an unusual sea green flecked with gold. When I was younger, Mamie used to tell me that her looks—everything but the eyes—had skipped a generation and settled on me. While my mother's dark brown, straight hair and brown eyes made her resemble my grandfather, I look like a near carbon copy of some of the old photos I've seen of Mamie. Her eyes, I used to think, were always sad in old photos, and now that mine carry in them the weight of living, we look more alike than ever. My sharply bowed lips—"like an angel's harp," as Mamie used to say—are just like hers were in her younger days, and somehow, I'm fortunate enough to have inherited her milky complexion, although in the last year, I've developed an unfamiliar vertical line between my eyebrows that makes me look eternally concerned. Then again, these days, I *am* eternally concerned.

The doorbell rings, startling me, and I run my brush through my hair once more, then, on second thought, I run a hand through it to mess it up again. I don't want to look like I've made an effort tonight. I don't want Matt to think this is going anywhere.

A moment later, I open the front door, and when Matt leans in to kiss me, I turn slightly so that his lips land on my right cheek. I can smell the cologne on his neck, musky and dark. He's dressed in crisp khakis, a pale blue button-down with an expensive-looking insignia I don't recognize, and slick brown loafers.

"I can go change," I say. I feel suddenly dowdy, plain.

He looks me up and down and shrugs. "You look pretty in that sweater," he says. "You're fine as you are."

He takes me to Fratanelli's, an upscale Italian place on the marsh. I try to ignore it when the maître d' gives my outfit a not-so-subtle once-over before leading us to a candlelit table by the window.

"This is too nice, Matt," I say once we're alone. I glance out the window into the darkness, and as I do, I catch our reflection in the glass. We look like a couple, a nice one, and that thought makes me look quickly away.

"I know you like this place," Matt says. "Remember? It's where we went before senior prom."

I laugh and shake my head. "I'd forgotten." I've forgotten lots of things, actually. I've tried for a long time to outrun the past, but what does it say about me that nearly twenty years later, I'm sitting in the same dining room with the same guy? Apparently, one's history can only vanish for so long. I shake the thought off and look at Matt. "You said you wanted to talk about something."

He looks down at his menu. "Let's order first."

We choose our meals in silence; Matt picks the lobster, and I choose the spaghetti Bolognese, the least expensive item on the menu. Later, I'll offer to pay for my own dinner, and if Matt refuses, I don't want to cost him a fortune. I don't want to feel obligated to him. After we've ordered, Matt takes a deep breath and looks at me. He's about to speak, but I cut him off before he can embarrass himself.

"Matt, you know I think the world of you," I begin.

"Hope—" He cuts me off, but I hold up a hand.

"Let me finish," I blurt out, gaining speed as I go. "I know we have so much in common, and of course we have all this history together, which means a lot to me, but what I was trying to tell you this afternoon was that I don't think I'm ready to date anyone right now. I don't think I will be until Annie goes off to college, and that's a really long time from now."

"Hope—"

I ignore him, because I need to get the words out. "Matt, it's not you; I swear. But for now, if we could just be friends, that would be so much better, I think. I don't know what will happen down the line, but right now, Annie needs me focused on her, and—"

"Hope, this isn't about me and you," Matt interrupts. "This is about the bakery, and your loan. Would you let me talk?"

I stare at him as the waiter brings us a basket of bread and a little plate of olive oil. Red wine is poured for each of us—an expensive cabernet Matt selected without consulting me—and then the waiter disappears and Matt and I are alone again.

"What about my bakery?" I ask slowly.

"I have some bad news," he says. He avoids my gaze, swirls a piece of bread in the olive oil, and takes a bite.

"Okay . . ." I prompt. It feels as if all the air is vanishing from the room.

"Your loan," he says, his mouth full. "The bank is calling it in."

My heart stops. "What?" I stare at him. "Since when?"

Matt looks down. "Since yesterday. Hope, you've been late on several payments, and with the market as it is, the bank has been forced to call in a number of loans with irregular payment records. I'm afraid yours was one of them."

I take a deep breath. This can't be happening. "But I've made every payment this year so far. Yeah, I had some rough months a few years ago when the economy collapsed, but we're a tourist town."

"I know."

"Who didn't have problems then?"

"A lot of people did," Matt agrees. "Unfortunately, you were among them. And with your credit score . . ."

I close my eyes for a moment. I don't even want to think about my credit score. It wasn't exactly helped by my divorce, taking over my mother's mortgage payment after her death, or juggling a large revolving balance between several credit cards just to keep the bakery stocked.

"What can I do to fix this?" I finally ask.

"Not a lot, I'm afraid," Matt says. "You can try other lenders, of course, but the market's tough right now. I can guarantee that you won't get anywhere with another bank. And with your payment history and the fact that a Bingham's just opened down the street . . ."

"Bingham's," I mutter. "Of course." They've been the bane of my existence for the past year. A small New England doughnut chain based in Rhode Island, they've been steadily expanding across the region in an attempt to go head-to-head with Dunkin' Donuts. They opened their sixteenth regional location a half mile from my bakery nine months ago, just when I was climbing out of the financial hole I'd found myself in after the recession.

It was a storm I could have weathered if not for the financial impact of the divorce. But now I'm hanging on for dear life, and Matt knows it; all my loans are with his bank.

"Listen, there's one option I can think of for you," Matt says. He takes a long sip of his wine and leans forward. "There are a few investors I work with in New York. They're always looking for small businesses to . . . help out. I can call in a favor."

"Okay," I say slowly. I'm not sure I like the idea of having strangers invest in what has always been a family business. Nor do I like the thought of Matt calling in favors on my behalf. But I'm also aware that the alternative may be losing the bakery altogether. "How would that work, exactly?"

"They'd basically buy you out," he says. "So they'd assume the loan with the bank. You'd get a cash payout, enough to pay off some of the bills you're facing right now. And you'd stay on to manage the bakery and run the day-to-day operations. *If* they go for it."

I stare at him. "You're telling me that my only option is to entirely sell my family's bakery to some stranger?"

Matt shrugs. "I know it's not ideal. But it would solve your financial problems in the short term. And with some luck, I could persuade them to let you stay on as the bakery's manager."

"But it's my family's bakery," I say in a small voice, aware that I'm repeating myself.

Matt looks away. "Hope, I don't know what else to tell you. This is pretty much your last option unless you have a half million dollars lying around. And with the debt you're in, it's not like you can just pick up and start over in another location."

I can't formulate words. After a moment, Matt jumps back in and adds, "Look, these are good people. I've known them for a while. They'll do right by you. At least you won't wind up closed."

I feel like Matt has just dropped a grenade in my lap, pulled the pin, and then offered to clean up the carnage, all with a smile on his face. "I need to think about this," I say dully.

"Hope," Matt says. He pushes his wineglass aside and reaches across the table. He folds his hands around my much smaller ones in a gesture I know is supposed to tell me I'm safe. "We'll figure it out, okay? I'll help you."

"I don't need your help," I mumble. He looks wounded, and I feel terrible, so I don't pull my hands away. I know he's just trying to be a nice guy. The thing is, it feels like charity. And I don't need charity. I may sink or I may swim, but I'd at least like to do it on my own.

Before either of us can say anything else, I hear my phone ringing from inside my purse. Embarrassed, I pull my hands away and grab for it. I hadn't meant to leave the ringer on. I can see the maître d' glaring at me from across the restaurant as I answer.

"Mom?" It's Annie, and she sounds upset.

"What's wrong, sweetie?" I ask, already half standing up, ready to go to her rescue, wherever she is.

"Where are you?"

"I'm out at dinner, Annie," I say. I avoid mentioning Matt, lest she think it's a date. "Where are you? Aren't you at your dad's?"

"Dad had to go meet a client," she mumbles. "So he dropped me back at your house. And the dishwasher is, like, totally broken."

I close my eyes. I'd filled it with detergent and turned it on a half hour before Matt got there, assuming that the cycle would be nearly over by the time I left. "What happened?"

"I didn't do it," Annie says quickly. "But there's, like, water all over the floor. I mean like lots of inches. Like a flood or something."

My heart drops. A pipe must have burst. I can't even imagine how much it will cost to fix, or how much damage has been done to my old hardwood floors. "Okay," I say in an even tone. "Thanks for letting me know, honey. I'll be right home."

"But how can I stop the water?" she asks. "It's, like, still totally flowing. The whole house is going to be flooded."

I realize I have no idea how to shut off the water to the kitchen. "Let me try to figure it out, okay? I'll call you back. I'm on my way home."

"Whatever," Annie says, and hangs up on me.

I tell Matt what happened, and he sighs and summons the waiter to ask for our meals to be boxed up.

"I'm sorry," I say as we hurry outside to the car five minutes later. "My life is one disaster after another lately."

Matt just shakes his head. "Things happen," he says tightly. It's not until we're driving back toward my house that he speaks again. "You can't put this business thing off, Hope," he says. "Or it's all going to go away. Everything your family's worked for."

I don't reply, both because I know he's right and because I can't deal with it right now. Instead, I ask him whether he knows how to turn off the water supply to the kitchen, but he says he doesn't, so we ride in silence the remainder of the way home.

"Whose Jeep is that?" Matt asks as he pulls up in front of my house. "There's no room for me to park in your driveway."

"Gavin's," I say softly. His familiar dusty-blue Wrangler is parked beside my old Corolla. My heart sinks.

"Gavin Keyes?" Matt says. "The handyman? What's he doing here?"

"Annie must have called him," I say through gritted teeth. My daughter doesn't know that I still haven't paid Gavin in full for the work he did around my house over the summer. Not even close. She doesn't know that one July afternoon on the porch with him, after getting a statement from the bank, I'd broken down in embarrassing tears, and that a month later, when he'd finished his repairs around my house, he'd insisted on letting me pay him in free pastries and coffee from the bakery for the time being. Annie doesn't know that he's the only person in town other than Matt who knows what a mess my life is, or that because of that, he's the last person in the world I want to see right now.

I walk inside, with Matt a few steps behind, carrying my meal from Fratanelli's. In the kitchen, I find Annie with a stack of towels and Gavin bent over with his head under my sink. I blink when I realize my eyes have gone directly to the thigh of his jeans, to see whether the hole I'd noticed this morning is still there. It is, of course.

"Gavin," I say, and he starts, pushes back from the sink, and stands up. His eyes dart back and forth between Matt and me, and he scratches his head as Matt moves past him to put my food in the refrigerator.

"Hey," Gavin says. He glances at Matt again and then back at me. "I came right over when Annie called. I got your water turned off for now. Looks like the pipe that burst is in the wall, behind the dishwasher. I'll come over and fix it for you the day after tomorrow, if you don't mind waiting."

"You don't have to do that," I say softly. I make eye contact with him, hoping that he knows what I'm trying to say: that I still can't pay him.

But he just smiles and goes on as if he hasn't heard me. "Tomorrow's packed, but the next day, I'm wide open," he says. "I just have a small job over at the Foley place in the morning. Besides, this shouldn't take too long to fix. It's just a pipe repair, and you should be good as new." His eyes dart to Matt again and then back to me. "Listen, I've got a wet-vac in the Jeep. Let me go grab it, and I'll help you get some of this water up. We can see if it did any damage once the floors are dry."

I glance at Annie, who's still standing there with a huge pile of towels in her hand. "We can clean all this up ourselves," I tell Gavin. "You don't have to stay. Right?" I add, looking at Annie and then at Matt.

"I guess," Annie says with a shrug.

Matt looks away. "Actually, Hope, I've got an early morning tomorrow. I'm going to have to head home."

Gavin snorts and walks outside without saying another word. I ignore him. "Oh," I say to Matt. "Of course. Thanks for dinner."

By the time I walk Matt to the door, Gavin's reentering with his wet-vac.

"I said you didn't have to do that," I mumble.

"I know what you said," Gavin says, without slowing down to look at me. A moment later, as I watch Matt's shiny Lexus pull away from the curb, I hear Gavin's vacuum turn on in the kitchen. I close my eyes for a minute, and then I turn and begin walking back toward the one mess in my life that can actually be fixed.

The next evening, Annie's at Rob's house again, and as I mop up the remainder of the mess in the kitchen after work, I find myself thinking of Mamie, who always used to know how to fix disasters. It's been two weeks since I last visited her, I realize. *I should be a better granddaughter,* I think with a swell of guilt. *I should be a better person.* Yet one more area in which I seem to be eternally falling short.

With a lump in my throat, I finish mopping, put some lipstick on in the hall mirror, and grab my keys. Annie's right; I need to go see my grandmother. Visiting Mamie always makes me want to cry, because although the home she's in is cheerful and friendly, it's terrible to see her slipping away. It's like standing on the deck of a boat, watching the waves suck someone under, and knowing that there's no life preserver to throw in.

Fifteen minutes later, I'm walking through the doors of Mamie's assisted living facility, a huge home that's painted buttercream yellow and filled with pictures of flowers and woodland creatures. The top floor is the memory care unit, where visitors are required to enter a pass code on a digital pad at the door.

I walk down the hallway toward Mamie's room, which sits at the far end of the west wing. The residents' rooms are all private and apartment-style, although they eat all their meals in the dining room, and staff members all have master keys so that they can check on residents and give them their daily medications. Mamie's on an antidepressant, two heart medications, and an experimental drug for Alzheimer's that doesn't seem to be helping; I meet with the staff doctor once a month to get a status report. He said at our last meeting that her mental faculties have been going sharply downhill in the last few months.

"The worst part is," he'd said, looking over his glasses at me, "she's lucid enough to know it. This is one of the hardest stages to watch; she knows her memory will be all but gone soon, which is very unsettling and sad for patients in this state."

I swallow back a lump as I ring the doorbell beside her name: *Rose McKenna.* I can hear her shuffling around inside, probably getting up from her recliner with some effort, moving toward the door with the cane she's been using since she fell and broke her hip two years ago.

The door opens, and I resist the urge to throw myself into her arms for a hug, the way I used to do when I was a little girl. Up until this moment, I'd thought I'd come here for her, but now I realize it's for me. I need this. I need to see someone who loves me, even if it's an imperfect love.

"Hello," Mamie says, smiling at me. Her hair looks whiter than the last time I saw her, the lines in her face deeper. But as always, she's wearing her burgundy lipstick, and her eyes are rimmed in kohl and mascara. "What a surprise, dear."

Her words are tinged with the hint of a French accent that has all but disappeared. She's been in the United States since the early 1940s, but the traces of her long-ago past still shroud her words like one of the feather-light French scarves she almost always has wrapped around her neck.

I reach forward to hug her. When I was younger, she was solid and strong. Now, as she leans into the embrace, I can feel the bones of her spine, the sharpness of her shoulders.

"Hi, Mamie," I say softly, blinking back tears as I pull away.

She stares at me through gray eyes that are clouded over. "You will have to forgive me," she says. "I get a little forgetful sometimes. Which one are you, dear? I know I should remember."

I swallow hard. "I'm Hope, Mamie. Your granddaughter."

"Of course." She smiles at me, but her gray eyes are foggy. "I knew that. I just need a reminder sometimes. Please, come in."

I follow her inside her dimly lit apartment, where she leads me to the living room window.

"I was just watching the sunset, my dear," she says. "In a moment, we'll be able to see the evening star."

Chapter *Three*

～

North Star Vanilla Cupcakes

CUPCAKES

INGREDIENTS

*1 cup unsalted butter, room
    temperature*
1 ½ cups granulated sugar
4 large eggs
1 tsp. pure vanilla extract

3 cups flour
3 tsp. baking powder
½ tsp. salt
½ cup milk

DIRECTIONS

1. Preheat oven to 350 degrees. Line 24 muffin cups with paper liners.

2. In a large bowl, cream together butter and sugar using electric mixer. Beat until light and fluffy, then beat in eggs one at a time. Beat in vanilla extract and mix well.

3. Sift together flour, baking powder and salt, and add to the butter mixture, about a cup at a time, alternating with milk.

4. Fill muffin cups about halfway. Bake for 15–20 minutes, or just until a knife inserted through the top of a cupcake comes out clean. Cool for 10 minutes in pan, then move to wire rack to cool completely.

5. Wait until they've cooled completely, then frost with pink icing (recipe below).

PINK ICING

INGREDIENTS

*1 cup unsalted butter, slightly
softened*
4 cups confectioners' sugar

½ tsp. vanilla extract
1 tsp. milk
1–3 drops red food coloring

DIRECTIONS

1. Beat the butter in a medium bowl with an electric mixer until light and fluffy.

2. Gradually add the sugar and beat until well blended.

3. Add the vanilla and milk and continue to beat until well blended.

4. Add one drop of red food coloring and beat well to incorporate. If you'd like the icing to be a deeper pink, add one or two drops more, and beat after each drop to incorporate. Spread on cupcakes, as directed above.

Rose

Rose gazed out the window, searching, as she always did, for the first star on the horizon. She knew it would appear, as twinkling and brilliant as an eternal flame, just after the setting sun painted the sky in ribbons of fire and light. When she was a girl, they'd called this twilight *l'heure bleue*, the blue hour, the time when the earth was neither completely light nor completely dark. Rose had always found comfort in this middle ground.

The evening star, which appeared each night during the deep velvet twilight, had always been her favorite, although it wasn't a star at all; it was the planet Venus, the planet named after the goddess of love. She had learned that long ago, but it hadn't changed anything, not really; here on earth, it was hard to tell what was a star and what wasn't. For years, she had counted all the stars she could see in the night sky. She was always searching for something, but she hadn't found it yet. She didn't deserve to, she knew, and that made her sad. A lot of things made her sad these days. But sometimes, from one day to the next, she couldn't remember what she was crying for.

Alzheimer's. She knew she had it. She heard the whispers in the halls. She had watched her neighbors in the home come and go, their memories slipping further with each passing day. She knew that the same thing was happening to her, and it scared her for reasons no one would understand. She dared not speak them aloud. It was too late.

Rose knew that the girl with the glistening brown hair, the familiar features, and the beautifully sad eyes had just told her who she was, but she had already forgotten. A familiar panic rose in her throat. She wished she could grab the memories like lifelines and hold on before she went under. But she found them slippery, impossible to grasp. So she cleared her throat, forced a smile, and hazarded her best guess.

"Josephine, dear, look for the star on the horizon," she said. She pointed to the empty space where she knew the evening star would make its appearance, any second now. She hoped she had guessed right. She hadn't seen Josephine in a long time. Or maybe she had. It was impossible to know.

The girl with the sad eyes cleared her throat. "No, Mamie, I'm Hope," she said. "Josephine isn't here."

"Yes, of course, I know that," Rose said quickly. "I must have misspoken." She couldn't let them know, any of them, that she was losing her memory. It was shameful, wasn't it? It was as if she didn't care enough to hold on, and that embarrassed her, because nothing could be further from the truth. Perhaps if she pretended a little longer, the clouds would go away, and her memories would return from wherever they'd been hiding.

"It's okay, Mamie," said the girl, who looked far too old to be

Hope, her only granddaughter, who couldn't be more than thirteen or fourteen. Yet Rose could see the lines of worry etched around this girl's eyes, far too many lines for a girl that age. She wondered what was weighing on her. Maybe Hope's mother would know what was wrong. Maybe then, Rose would be able to help her. She wanted to help Hope. She just didn't know how.

"Where is your mother?" Rose asked Hope politely. "Is she coming, dear?"

Rose had so many things she wanted to say to Josephine, so many apologies to make. And she feared time was running out. Where would she begin? Would she apologize first for her many failures? For her coldness? For teaching her all the wrong lessons without meaning to? Rose knew she'd had many opportunities to say she was sorry in the past, but the words always caught in her throat. Perhaps it was time to force herself to say them, to make Josephine hear her before it was too late.

"Mamie?" Hope said tentatively. Rose smiled at her gently. She knew Hope would grow up one day to be a strong, kind person. Josephine was that type of woman too, but her character was cloaked in so many layers of defenses, spawned by Rose's mistakes, that it was hard to tell.

"Yes, dear?" Rose asked, for Hope had stopped speaking. Rose suddenly had an inkling of a feeling that she knew exactly what Hope was about to say. She wished she could stop her before the words did their damage. But it was too late. It was always too late.

"My mom—Josephine—died," Hope said gently. "Two years ago, Mamie. Don't you remember?"

"My daughter?" Rose asked, sadness crashing over her like a wave. "My Josephine?" The truth came rolling in with the tide, and for a moment, Rose couldn't catch her breath. She wondered at the tricks of the mind that washed away the unhappy memories, carrying them out to sea.

But some memories, Rose knew, couldn't be erased, even when one has spent a lifetime trying to pretend they are not there.

"I'm sorry, Mamie," Hope said. "Did you forget?"

"No, no," Rose said quickly. "Of course not." Hope looked away and Rose stared at her. The girl reminded her for an instant of something, or someone, but before she could grasp the thought, it fluttered away, just out of reach, like a butterfly. "How could I forget such a thing?" Rose added softly.

They sat in silence for a while, staring out the window. The evening star was out now, and soon after, Rose could see the stars of the Big Dipper, which her father had once told her was the saucepan of God. As her father had once taught her to do, Rose followed the line of the star called Merak to the star called Dubhe and found Polaris, the North Star, who was just beginning to open his sleepy eye for her in the endless sky. She knew the names of so many stars, and the ones she didn't she had named herself, after people she had lost long ago.

How strange, she thought, that she couldn't hold on to the simplest of facts, but the celestial names were written on her memory forever. She'd studied them secretly over so many years, hoping that one day they might provide a pathway home. But she was still here on earth, wasn't she? And the stars were just as far away as ever.

"Mamie?" Hope asked after a while, breaking the silence.

Rose turned to her and smiled at the word. She remembered her own *mamie* fondly, a woman who had always seemed so glamorous to her, a woman whose trademarks were red lipstick, high cheekbones, and a smart, dark bob that had gone out of style in the 1920s. But then she remembered what had happened to her own *mamie*, and the smile faded. She blinked a few times and returned to the present. "Yes, dear?" Rose asked.

"Who is Leona?"

The words stole Rose's breath for a moment, for it was a name she hadn't spoken in nearly seventy years. Why would she? She did not believe in resurrecting ghosts.

"No one," Rose finally replied. But that was, of course, a lie. Leona *was* someone. They all were. By denying them once again, she knew she was weaving the tapestry of deceit a little tighter. She wondered whether one day it would be tight enough to suffocate her.

"But Annie says you've been calling her Leona," Hope persisted.

"No, she is wrong," Rose told her instantly. "There is no Leona."

"But—"

"How is Annie?" Rose asked, changing the subject. Annie, she could remember clearly. Annie was the third generation of American in her family. First Josephine. Then Hope. Now the little one, Annie, the dawn to Rose's twilight. Rose was proud of very few things in her life. But this, this she was proud of.

"She's fine," Hope replied, but Rose noticed that the line of Hope's mouth was set a bit unnaturally. "She's been spending a lot of time with her dad lately. They spent the whole summer going to Cape League games."

Rose searched her memory. "What sort of league?"

"Baseball. Summer league. Like the games Grandpa used to take me to when I was a kid."

"Well, that sounds nice, dear," Rose said. "Do you go with them?"

"No, Mamie," Hope said gently. "Annie's father and I are divorced."

"Of course," Rose murmured. She studied Hope's face when the girl looked down, and she could see in her features the same kind of sadness she saw every time she looked at herself in the mirror. What was she so sad about? "Do you still love him?" she ventured.

Hope looked up sharply, and Rose felt terrible when she realized that it probably was the wrong thing to have asked. She forgot, sometimes, what was polite and what was not.

"No," Hope murmured finally. She didn't meet Rose's eye as she added, "I don't think I ever did. That's a terrible thing to say, isn't it? I think there's something wrong with me."

Rose felt a lump in her throat. So then, the burden had been passed to Hope too. She knew that now. Her own closed heart had repercussions that she had never imagined. She was responsible for all of it. But how could she tell Hope that love did exist, that it had the power to change everything? She couldn't. So instead, she cleared her throat and tried to focus on the present.

"There is nothing wrong with you, dear," she told her granddaughter.

Hope glanced at her grandmother and looked away. "But what if there is?" she asked softly.

"You must not blame yourself," Rose said. "Some things are simply not meant to be." Something lurked at the edges of her memory again. She couldn't remember the name of Hope's husband, but she knew she had never liked him much. Had he been unkind to Hope? Or was it just because he always seemed a little too cold, a little too together? "He has been a good father to Annie, has he not?" she added, because she felt she needed to say something good.

"Sure," Hope said tightly. "He's a great father. Buys her anything she wants."

"But that is not love," Rose said tentatively. "Those are just things."

"Right, well," Hope said. She looked suddenly exhausted. Her hair tumbled in front of her face like a sheet, obscuring her expression. In that moment, Rose was sure she saw tears in her granddaughter's eyes, but when Hope looked up again, her achingly familiar eyes were clear.

"Have you gone out with other men, then?" Rose asked after a moment. "After the divorce?" She thought of her own situation, and the way that sometimes you had to move on, even if you'd already given your heart away.

"Of course not." Hope hung her head and avoided Rose's gaze. "I don't want to be like my mother," she mumbled. "Annie comes first. Not random guys."

And then, Rose understood. In a flash, she remembered bits and pieces of her granddaughter's childhood. She remembered how Josephine had searched endlessly for love in all the wrong places, with all the wrong men, when love was right there, in Hope's eyes, all along. She remembered countless nights when Josephine left her daughter with Rose so that she could go out. Hope, who was just a little girl then, would cry herself to sleep while Rose held her tight. Rose remembered the tearstains in her blouses, and the way they always made her feel empty and alone long after Hope had fallen asleep. "You are not your mother, my dear," Rose said gently. Her heart ached, for this—all of this—was her own fault. Who could have known that her decisions would reverberate for generations?

Hope cleared her throat, looked away, and changed the subject. "So you're sure you don't know a Leona?" she asked.

Rose blinked a few times as the name pierced another hole in her heart. She pressed her lips together and shook her head. Maybe the lie wasn't as wrong if it wasn't uttered aloud.

"Weird," Hope murmured. "Annie was so sure you'd called her that."

"How unusual." Rose wished she could give the girl the answers she sought, but she wasn't ready, for to speak the truth would be to open a floodgate. She could feel the water surging up behind the dam, and she knew it would spill over soon. For now, the rivers, the tides, the floodwaters were still hers, and she sailed them alone.

Hope looked for a moment like she wanted to say something else, but instead, she stood and hugged Rose tightly, promising to return soon. She left without looking back. Rose watched her go, noting that darkness hadn't entirely fallen yet; Hope hadn't even stayed for the entire *heure bleue*. This made Rose sad, although she did not blame the girl. Rose knew that this, like so many other things, was her own fault.

Some time later, after all the stars were out, Rose's favorite nurse, a woman whose skin shone like the *pain au chocolat* Rose used to bring home for her brother David and her sister Danielle so long ago, came to make sure she'd taken her evening doses of medicine.

"Hi, Rose," she said, smiling into her eyes as she poured a small glass of water and opened Rose's pillbox. "Did you have a visitor tonight?"

Rose puzzled this over, trying hard to remember. There was a flash of something, glinting in the background of her memory, but then it was gone. She was certain that she'd watched the sunset alone, as she did every night. "No, dear," Rose told her.

"Are you sure, Rose?" the nurse prodded. She handed Rose her pills in a Dixie cup and watched as Rose swallowed and washed them down. "Amy at the desk downstairs said your granddaughter was here. Hope."

Rose smiled, for she loved Hope, who must be thirteen or fourteen by now. *How quickly time flies,* she thought. *Before I know it, she will be all grown up.* "No," she told the nurse. "There was no one here. But you must meet her one day. She is a very nice girl. Maybe she will come visit with her mother."

The nurse squeezed Rose's arm gently and smiled. "All right, Rose," she said. "All right."

Chapter *Four*

~

I never intended to come back here, to the bakery, to the Cape, to any of this.

At thirty-six, I wasn't supposed to be the mother of a teenager, the owner of a bakery. When I was in school, I dreamed of moving somewhere far away, traveling the world, becoming a successful attorney.

Then I met Rob, who was in his last year of law school just as I'd started my JD. If I thought the magnetic pull of the Cape was strong, it didn't compare to being pulled into his orbit. When something went wrong with my birth control midway through my first year of law school, and I had to tell him I was pregnant, he'd proposed the next week. It was, he said, the right thing to do.

We'd decided together that I'd take a year off to have the baby before returning to school. Annie was born that August; Rob got a job with a firm in Boston and suggested I stay home with our daughter for a while longer now that he was making more money. At first, it seemed like a good idea. But after the first year, the gulf between us had opened so wide that I no longer knew how to cross it. My days, filled with diapers, breast-feeding, and

Sesame Street, held little interest for him, and I was admittedly jealous of him going out into the world each day and doing all the things I'd once dreamed of. Not that I regretted having Annie; I'd never felt that way for a second. I just regretted that I'd never had a chance to live the life I'd thought I was supposed to.

When my mother was diagnosed with breast cancer for the first time, nine years ago, Rob agreed, after many nights of arguments, to relocate to the Cape, where he'd realized he could set up shop and be one of the only personal injury lawyers in the area. Mamie watched Annie at the bakery during the day while I worked as Rob's legal assistant, which wasn't exactly what I'd dreamed of, but it was close enough. By the time Annie was in first grade, she was frosting cupcakes and fluting piecrusts like a pro. For a few years, the whole arrangement was almost perfect.

Then my mother's cancer returned, Mamie's memory began to ebb at the edges, and there was no one to save the bakery but me. Before I knew what had happened, I had become the keeper of a dream that wasn't mine, and in the meantime, I'd lost my hold on everything I'd ever dreamed of.

It's nearly five in the morning, and dawn is still two hours away. When I was in grade school, Mamie used to tell me that each new morning was like unwrapping a gift from God. This used to confuse me, because she wasn't a big churchgoer. But in the evenings, when my mother and I would visit for dinner, we'd sometimes find her on her knees at the back window, praying softly as the light fell from the sky. "I prefer to have my own relationship with God," she told me once when I'd asked her why she prayed at home instead of at Our Lady of the Cape.

This morning, the smells of flour, yeast, butter, chocolate, and vanilla dance through the kitchen, and I breathe in deeply, relaxing into the familiarity of it all. From the time I was a little girl, these scents have always reminded me of my grandmother, for even when the bakery was closed, even after she'd showered and dressed at home, her hair and her skin still carried the perfume of the kitchen.

As I roll out piecrusts and add more flour to the industrial mixer, my mind isn't on the tasks at hand. I'm thinking about Mamie's words last night as I methodically go through the motions of the morning preparations. Check the timer for the chocolate chip meringues in oven 1. Roll out the dough for the almond rose tarts Matt Hines likes so much. Layer the baklava and slide it into oven 2. Put the softened cream cheese for the lemon-grape cheesecake into my second bowl mixer. Fold the layers of croissant around little squares of dark French chocolate for the *pains au chocolat*. Braid the long ropes of whole wheat challah, sprinkle it with raisins, and set it aside to rise again.

There is nothing wrong with you, dear, Mamie had said, but what does she know? Her memory is all but gone, her senses completely off. Yet there are times when her eyes look as clear as ever, and when I'm sure she's looking directly into my soul. Although I never doubted that she and my grandfather loved each other, theirs always seemed to be a relationship of function more than romance. Had I had that with Rob and thrown it away because I believed there was more out there? Perhaps I'd been a fool. Life isn't a fairy tale.

The timer on oven 1 goes off, and I move the meringues to a baking rack. I turn the oven on and prepare to slide the *pains au chocolat* in. I've started making a double batch of those in the mornings; they go more quickly now that it's autumn and the air has turned cool. Our fruit tarts and pastries are more popular in the spring and summer months, but the denser, sweeter confections seem to bring people comfort as winter approaches.

I started helping Mamie in the bakery, the way Annie helps me now, when I was eight. Every morning, just before the sun came up, Mamie would stop what she was doing and lead me to the side window that looked due east, over the winding ribbon of Main Street. We'd watch the horizon in silence until dawn broke, and then we'd go back to our baking.

"What are you always looking at, Mamie?" I'd asked her one morning.

"I am looking at the sky, my dear," she'd said.

"I know. But why?"

She'd pulled me close, hugging me against her faded pink apron, the one she'd been wearing for as long as I could remember. I was a little scared by how tightly she was holding on.

"*Chérie,* I am watching the stars disappear," she said after a minute.

"Why?" I asked.

"Because even though you cannot see them, they are always there," she said. "They are just hiding, behind the sun."

"So?" I asked timidly.

She released me from the hug and bent down to look me in the eye. "Because, my dear, it is good to remember that you do not always have to see something to know that it is there."

Mamie's words from almost three decades earlier are still echoing in my head when I hear Annie's voice in the doorway to the kitchen, startling me out of my fog.

"Why are you crying?" she asks.

I look up, surprised to realize that she's right; there are tears rolling down my cheeks. I swat them away with the back of my hand, streaking wet, sticky dough across my face in the process, and force a smile.

"I'm not," I say.

"You don't have to, like, lie."

I sigh. "I was just thinking about Mamie."

Annie rolls her eyes and makes a face at me. "Great, *now* you decide to show some emotion." She throws her backpack down in the corner, where it lands with a decisive thud.

"What's that supposed to mean?" I ask.

"*You* know," she says. She rolls up the sleeves of her pink long-sleeved shirt and grabs an apron from a hook on the wall, just to the left of the racks where I store the trays.

"No, I *don't* know," I tell her. I stop what I'm doing and watch as she gets a carton of eggs and four sticks of butter out of the stainless steel refrigerator and grabs a measuring cup. She moves as fluidly through the kitchen as Mamie once did.

Annie doesn't answer until after she has creamed the butter in the stand mixer, added four cups of sugar, and cracked the eggs in, one at a time. "Maybe if you'd been, like, capable of feeling anything when you were married to Dad, you wouldn't be divorced right now," she says finally, over the whir of the mixer.

My breath catches in my throat and I stare at her. "What are you talking about? I showed emotion."

She turns the mixer off. "Whatever," she mutters. "Only to, like, send me to my room and stuff. When did you ever act like you were happy to be with Dad?"

"I was happy!"

"Whatever," she says. "You couldn't even tell Dad you loved him."

I blink at her. "Did he say that to you?"

"What, like I'm not old enough to figure things out on my own?" she asks, but from the way she avoids my gaze, I know I've hit the nail on the head.

"Annie, it's not appropriate for your father to be saying bad things about me to you," I say. "There are a lot of things about our relationship that you don't understand."

"Like what?" It's a challenge, and she gazes at me coolly.

I weigh my options, but in the end, I know it's not appropriate to drag our daughter into an adult battle that isn't hers to fight. "That's between me and your dad."

She laughs at that and rolls her eyes. "*He* trusts me enough to talk to me," she says. "And you know what? You ruin everything, Mom."

Before I can reply, the front door to the bakery chimes. I

glance at my watch. It's a few minutes before six, our official opening time, but Annie must not have locked the door behind her when she came in.

"We'll continue this later, young lady," I say sternly.

"Whatever," she mutters under her breath. She turns back to the batter she's mixing, and I watch for a second as she adds some flour and then some milk, then a dash of vanilla.

"Hey, Hope, you back there?" It's Matt's voice, from the front of the store, and I snap out of it.

I hear Annie say "Of *course* it's him" under her breath, but I pretend not to as I make my way up front.

Mrs. Koontz and Mrs. Sullivan come in at 7:00 a.m. as usual, and for once, Annie rushes out to wait on them. Usually, she's happier to be in the kitchen, baking cupcakes and miniature pies with her iPod on, effortlessly ignoring me until she has to go to school. But today, she's sunshine and smiles, whisking into the main room and pouring their coffee before they even have a chance to order.

"Here, let me help you to your seats," she says, juggling two coffee mugs and a little pitcher of cream as they trail behind her, exchanging glances.

"Why, thank you, Annie," Mrs. Sullivan says as Annie puts the coffees and cream down and pulls out her chair for her.

"You're welcome!" Annie replies brightly. For a moment, she sounds exactly like the girl who inhabited her body before the divorce. Mrs. Koontz murmurs a thank-you too, and Annie chirps, "Yes, ma'am!"

She hovers while they each take their first sips of coffee, and she's practically hopping from foot to foot by the time Mrs. Sullivan takes a bite of her blueberry muffin and Mrs. Koontz picks up her cinnamon-sugar doughnut.

"Um, can I, like, ask you a question?" Annie asks. I'm tidying up behind the counter, and I pause, straining to hear what she wants to know.

"You may, dear," Mrs. Koontz says. "But you mustn't use *like* in the middle of a sentence that way."

"Huh?" Annie asks, confused. Mrs. Koontz raises an eyebrow, and Annie's smart enough to correct herself. "I mean, *excuse me,*" she amends.

"The word *like* is not a space holder in a sentence," Mrs. Koontz tells my daughter seriously. I duck behind the counter to hide my smile.

"Oh," Annie says. "I mean, I know." I peek over the counter and see her face flaming red. I feel bad for her; Mrs. Koontz, who'd been my tenth-grade English teacher years ago, is a tough cookie. I think about coming to Annie's defense, but before I have a chance, Mrs. Sullivan jumps in.

"Oh, Barbara, give the child a break," she says, swatting her friend on the arm. She turns to Annie and says, "Ignore her. She simply misses being able to boss children around, now that she's retired." Mrs. Koontz starts to protest, but Mrs. Sullivan swats her again and smiles at Annie. "Did you say you had a question for us, dear?"

Annie clears her throat. "Uh, yeah," she says. "I mean, yes, ma'am. I was just wondering . . ." She pauses, and the women wait. "Well, you knew my great-grandma, right?"

The women glance at each other, then back at Annie. "Yes, of course," Mrs. Sullivan finally replies. "We've known her for years. How is she?"

"Fine," Annie says instantly. "I mean, not totally fine. She's having some—problems. But, um, mostly fine." Her face is flaming again. "Anyways, I was just wondering, do you, um, know who Leona is?"

The women exchange looks again. "Leona," Mrs. Sullivan says slowly. She mulls it over for a moment and shakes her head. "I don't think so. It doesn't sound familiar. Barbara?"

Mrs. Koontz shakes her head. "No," she says. "I don't think we know a Leona. Why?"

Annie looks down. "It's just something she keeps calling me. I was just wondering, like, who she is." She looks horrified for a second and mumbles, "Sorry for saying 'like.' "

Mrs. Sullivan reaches out and pats Annie's hand. "Now you've gone and scared the child, Barbara," she says.

Mrs. Koontz sighs and says, "I'm just trying to correct her grammar."

"Yes, well, this isn't the time or place," Mrs. Sullivan replies. She winks at Annie. "Why is this so important to you, dear? The question of who this Leona is?"

"My great-grandma seems sad," Annie replies after a minute, in a voice so low I have to strain to hear her. "And I don't know that much about her, you know? My great-grandma, I mean. I want to help her, but I don't know how."

A pair of customers come in then, a gray-haired man and a young blonde woman I don't know, and I miss what Annie and the women are talking about while I help them. The blonde orders a piece of carrot cake, after asking if we have anything diet—we don't—and her male companion, who looks a few decades too old to be squeezing her hand and kissing her ear, orders an éclair. By the time they leave and I glance back at Annie, she's seated with the two older women.

I glance at my watch and consider reminding Annie that if she doesn't leave in the next few minutes, she'll be late to school, but the look on her face is so earnest that instead, I freeze for a minute and just look at her. I'm used to her sneering and rolling her eyes lately every time she's around me, but in this moment, she just looks innocent and interested. I swallow the lump in my throat.

I walk into the dining room with a rag and a spray bottle so that I can eavesdrop under the pretense of cleaning up. The women, I realize, are telling Annie the story of how Mamie came to live in Cape Cod.

"All the girls in town used to be in love with Ted, your great-grandfather," Mrs. Koontz is telling her.

"Oh my." Mrs. Sullivan fans herself with her newspaper. "I used to scribble his name and mine in a notebook every day during our senior year of high school."

"He was older than us," Mrs. Koontz says.

"By four years," Mrs. Sullivan agrees. "He was off at college—Harvard, you know—but he'd come home every few weeks to visit. He had a car, a nice one, which was a big deal out here in those days. And the girls would just swoon."

"He was so kind," Mrs. Koontz agrees. "And like so many others, he joined the army the day after Pearl Harbor."

The women pause in tandem and look down at their hands. I know they're thinking about other young men they'd lost, so long ago. Annie shifts in her seat and asks, "So then what happened? He met my great-grandma in the war, right?"

"In Spain, I believe," Mrs. Koontz says, looking to Mrs. Sullivan for confirmation. "He was shot down somewhere in northern France or Belgium, I think. I never heard the whole story; everyone here spent months believing he was missing in action. I was sure he was dead. But he somehow escaped to Spain, and your great-grandmother was there too."

Annie nods solemnly, like she knows this story by heart, although my grandfather died twelve years before she was born.

"She's French of course, your great-grandmother Rose. But the way I understand it, her parents died when she was young, and she wanted to leave France because the country was at war, right?" Mrs. Sullivan picks up the thread of the story, glancing at Mrs. Koontz.

Mrs. Koontz nods. "We never found out exactly how they met, but yes, I think Rose was living in Spain. But it was, what, 1944 when we heard he was back in America, and he'd married a girl from France?"

"Late 1943," Mrs. Sullivan corrects. "I remember it exactly. It was my twentieth birthday."

"Oh yes, of course. You cried into your birthday cake." Mrs.

Koontz winks at Annie. "She had a silly schoolgirl crush on your great-grandfather. But your great-grandmother stole him away."

Mrs. Sullivan makes a face. "She was two years younger than us, and she had that exotic French accent. Boys are very easily swayed by accents, you know."

Annie nods again, solemnly, as if this is something she knows instinctively. I hide a smile as I pretend to concentrate on a particularly tough spot to wipe up. I've never heard my grandmother talk about how she and my grandfather met. She rarely talks about the past at all, so I'm interested to hear what the women know.

"Ted got some sort of job in New York, at a secondary school, after he received his doctoral degree," Mrs. Koontz says. "And then he and your grandmother moved back to the Cape. That's when he took the job at the Sea Oats."

My grandfather, whose PhD was in education, had been the first headmaster of the Sea Oats School, a prestigious private school one town over. It used to serve grades K through twelve, but now it's only a high school. It's where Annie will go from ninth grade on, on a legacy scholarship.

"And, um, my grandma was there too?" Annie asks. "When Mamie and my great-grandpa moved here?"

"Yes, your grandmother Josephine must have been what, five years old? Six years old when they moved?" Mrs. Sullivan says. "They moved back to the Cape in 1950. I remember clearly, because it's the year I got married."

Mrs. Koontz nods. "Yes, Josephine started first grade when they moved here, if I remember right."

"And Mamie founded the bakery then?" Annie asks.

"I think it was a few years later," Mrs. Koontz says. "But your mother would probably know." She calls to me. "Hope, dear?"

I pretend I haven't been listening to their whole conversation. "What's that?" I ask, looking up.

"Annie here was wondering when your grandmother founded the bakery."

"In 1952," I say. I glance at Annie, who's staring at me. "Her parents had owned a bakery in France, I think." I've never heard any more about Mamie's past than this. She never talked about her life before she met my grandfather.

Annie ignores me and turns back to the two women. "But you don't know anyone named Leona?" she asks.

"No," Mrs. Sullivan says. "Maybe she was a friend of your great-grandmother's from France."

"She never really had any friends here," Mrs. Koontz says. Then she shoots me a guilty look and amends hurriedly, "Of course, she's very nice. She just kept to herself, that's all."

I nod, but I wonder whether that was all Mamie's fault after all. She's quiet and reserved, certainly, but it doesn't seem as if Mrs. Koontz, Mrs. Sullivan, and the other women of the town exactly welcomed her with open arms. I feel a pang of sadness for her.

I look at my watch again. "Annie, you'd better get going. You're going to be late for school."

Her eyes narrow, and the brief glimpse of the old Annie is gone; she's back to hating me.

"You're not the boss of me," she mutters.

"Actually, young lady," Mrs. Koontz says, shooting me a look, "she is. She's your mother, which makes her the boss of you until you turn eighteen, at the very least."

"Whatever," Annie says under her breath.

She gets up from the table and stomps into the kitchen. She emerges a moment later with her backpack.

"Thank you," she says to Mrs. Koontz and Mrs. Sullivan on the way out the door. "I mean, thanks for telling me about my great-grandma." She doesn't even look at me as she strides through the front door, onto Main Street.

Gavin comes by as I'm closing to drop off the spare keys I'd given him two days earlier. He has on the same pair of jeans with the hole in the thigh, which seems to have gotten marginally bigger since I last saw him.

"Your pipe's fixed," he tells me as I pour him the last of the afternoon's coffee. "Dishwasher's running good as new."

"I don't even know how to thank you."

Gavin smiles. "Sure you do. You know my weaknesses. Star Pie. Cinnamon strudel. Hours-old coffee." He looks into his coffee cup and arches an eyebrow, but he takes a sip anyhow.

I laugh, despite my embarrassment. "I know I should be paying you in something other than baked goods, Gavin. I'm sorry."

He looks up. "You have nothing to be sorry for," he says. "You're obviously underestimating my addiction to your baking."

I give him a look, and he laughs. "Seriously, Hope, it's fine. You're doing your best."

I sigh as I place the last of the day's remaining almond rose tarts into a flat Tupperware container that I'll store overnight in the freezer. "Turns out my best isn't good enough," I mutter. Matt had brought me a bunch of paperwork that morning, and I haven't begun to read it yet, although I know I need to. I'm dreading it.

"You're not giving yourself enough credit," Gavin says. Before I can reply, he adds, "So Matt Hines has been around a lot." He takes another sip of his coffee.

I look up from packing away the pastries. "It's just business," I tell him, although I'm not sure why I feel like I have to explain myself.

"Hmm," is all Gavin replies.

"We dated in high school," I add. Gavin grew up on the North Shore of Boston—he'd told me all about his high school in Peabody one afternoon on the porch—so I assume he doesn't know about my past with Matt.

I'm surprised when he says, "I know. But that was a long time ago."

I nod. "That was a long time ago," I repeat.

"How's Annie holding up?" Gavin changes the subject again. "With the stuff between you and your ex and everything?"

I look up at him. No one has asked me this recently, and I'm surprised by how much I appreciate it. "She's okay," I tell him. I pause and correct myself. "Actually, I don't know why I said that. She's not okay. She seems so angry lately, and I don't know what to do about it. It's like I know the real Annie's in there somewhere, but right now, she just wants to hurt me."

I don't know why I'm confiding in him, but as Gavin nods slowly, there's not a bit of judgment on his face, and for that I'm grateful. I begin to wipe down the counter with a wet rag.

"It's rough when you're that age," he says. "I was just a few years older than her when my parents got a divorce. She's just confused, Hope. She'll come out of it."

"You think so?" I ask in a small voice.

"I *know* so," Gavin says. He stands and crosses to the counter, where he puts his hand on mine. I stop wiping and look up at him. "She's a good kid, Hope. I saw that this summer with all that time I spent at your house."

I can feel tears in my eyes, which embarrasses me. I blink them away. "Thanks." I pause and pull my hand away.

"If there's ever anything I can do . . ." Gavin says. Instead of completing the sentence, he looks at me so intensely that I look away, my face burning.

"You're really nice to offer, Gavin," I say. "But I'm sure you've got better things to do than worry about the old lady who runs the bakery."

Gavin arches an eyebrow. "I don't see any old ladies around here."

"That's nice of you to say," I murmur. "But you're young, you're single . . ." I pause. "Wait, you're single, right?"

"Last time I checked."

I ignore the unexpected feeling of relief that sweeps through me. "Yeah, well, I'm thirty-six going on seventy-five; I'm divorced; I'm sinking financially; I've got a kid who hates me." I pause and look down. "You've got better things to do than worry about me. Shouldn't you be out doing something . . . I don't know, something young, single people do?"

"Something young, single people do?" he repeats. "Like what, exactly?"

"I don't know," I say. I feel foolish. I haven't felt young in ages. "Clubbing?" I venture in a small voice.

He bursts out laughing. "Yeah, I moved to the Cape because of the wild club scene. In fact, I'm just on my way back from a rave now."

I smile, but my heart's not in it. "I know I'm being dumb," I say. "But you don't have to worry about me. I have a lot on my plate. But I've always handled everything before. I'll figure things out."

"Letting someone in once in a while wouldn't kill you, you know," Gavin says softly.

I look at him sharply and open my mouth to respond, but he speaks first.

"Like I said the other day, you're a good mom," Gavin goes on. "You've got to stop doubting yourself."

I look down. "It's just that I seem to screw everything up," I say. I feel the color rise to my cheeks and I mumble, "I don't know why I'm telling you this."

I hear Gavin take a deep breath, and a moment later, he has come around the counter and wrapped his arms around me. My heart thuds as I hug him back. I try not to notice how solid his chest is as he pulls me close, and instead focus on how nice it feels to be held. There's no one left to comfort me this way anymore, and I hadn't realized until this moment how much I've missed it.

"You don't screw everything up, Hope," Gavin murmurs into

my hair. "You've got to cut yourself a break. You're the toughest person I know." He pauses and adds, "I know things have been hard on you lately. But you never know what will happen tomorrow, or the next day. One day, one week, one month can change everything."

I look up sharply and take a step away. "My mother used to say that. Those exact words."

"Yeah?" Gavin asks.

"Yeah."

"You never mention her," he says.

"I know," I murmur. The truth is, it hurts too much to think about her. I'd spent my childhood hoping that if I behaved a little better or thanked her a little more profusely, or did more chores around the house, she'd love me a little more. Instead, she seemed to drift farther and farther away with every passing year.

When she was diagnosed with breast cancer, and I came home to help her, the same cycle took over; I expected that she'd see how much I loved her as she lay dying, but instead, she continued to keep me at a distance. When she told me, on her deathbed, that she loved me, the words didn't feel real; I want to believe that she felt that way, but I knew it was more likely that she was hazy and delusional in her final moments and thought she was talking to one of her countless boyfriends. "I was always a lot closer to my grandmother than to my mom," I tell Gavin.

Gavin puts a hand on my shoulder. "I'm sorry you lost her, Hope," he says. I'm not sure whether he means my mother or Mamie, because in a lot of ways, they're both gone.

"Thanks," I murmur.

As he leaves a few minutes later with a box of strudel, I stare after him, my heart thudding hard in my chest. I don't know why he seems to believe in me when I don't believe in myself anymore. But I can't think about that now; I have to tackle the more pressing issue: the bank's plans to foreclose. I rub my temples, plug in the electric tea kettle, and sit down at one of my café tables to read the paperwork Matt gave me.

Chapter *Five*

I need to talk to you."

It's a week and a half later, and I'm standing on Rob's doorstep—my old doorstep—my arms crossed over my chest. I look at my ex-husband now, and all I see is hurt and betrayal; it's as if the person I fell in love with has disappeared entirely.

"You could have called, Hope," he says. He doesn't invite me in; he stands in the doorway, a guard at the door to a life left behind.

"I *did* call," I say firmly. "Twice to the house, and twice to your office. You haven't called me back."

He shrugs. "I've been busy. I would have gotten back to you eventually." He shifts his weight to his left side, and for a moment, I have the distinct feeling he looks sad. Then, all the emotion is gone from his face and he says, "What is it you need?"

I take a deep breath. I hate arguing with Rob; I always have. He once told me that it was a good thing he was the one who became a lawyer, while I dropped out to raise the baby. *You don't know how to fight,* he'd said. *You have to have that killer instinct if you're going to make it in the courtroom.* "We need to talk about Annie," I say.

"What about her?" he asks.

"Well, for one thing, we need to be in agreement about the ground rules. She's twelve. She shouldn't be wearing makeup to school. She's a kid."

"Christ, Hope, is that what this is about?" He laughs, and I'd be insulted if I didn't know this is just part of the strategy he employs regularly against opposing attorneys and witnesses for the other side. "She's almost a teenager, for God's sake. You can't keep her a little girl forever."

"I'm not trying to," I tell him. I take a deep breath and struggle to stay collected. "But I'm trying to set some boundaries. And when I set them, and you undermine them, she doesn't learn a thing. And she winds up hating me."

Rob smiles, and perhaps I'd feel patronized if I hadn't spent endless nights during our marriage watching him practice his strategic smirk in the mirror. "So *that's* what this is about," he says. Ah yes, Rob Smith Argument Tactic Number Two: Pretend that you know exactly what the other person is thinking—and that you're already way ahead of her.

"No, Rob." I pinch the bridge of my nose and close my eyes for a second. *Relax, Hope. Don't get sucked into this.* "This is about our daughter growing up to be a decent young woman."

"A decent young woman who doesn't hate you," he amends. "Maybe you should just give her some space to be herself, Hope. That's what I'm doing."

I glare at him. "No, it's not," I say. "You're trying to be the cool parent so I'm stuck being the disciplinarian. That's not fair."

He shrugs. "So you say."

"Furthermore," I continue as if I haven't heard him, "it's totally inappropriate for you to be saying bad things about me to Annie."

"What have I said?" he asks, holding up his hands in mock surrender.

"Well, for one thing, you've apparently told her that I was

never capable of telling you I loved you." I feel my throat close up a little, and I take a deep breath.

Rob just looks at me. "You can't be serious."

"That's a stupid thing to say to her. I told you I loved you."

"Yeah, Hope, what, once a year?"

I look away, not wanting to have this conversation again. "What are you, an insecure teenage girl?" I mumble. "Did you want me to get you a BFF necklace too?"

He doesn't look amused. "I just don't want our daughter blaming *me* for our divorce."

"So the divorce had *nothing* to do with the affair you had with the girl from the Macy's in Hyannis?"

Rob shrugs. "If I'd felt emotionally fulfilled at home . . ."

"Ah, so you were seeking *emotional* fulfillment when you began sleeping with a twenty-two-year-old," I say. I take a deep breath. "You know, I've never felt that it's appropriate to tell Annie about your affair. That's between you and me. She doesn't know that you cheated, because I don't think she should have to see her father in that light."

"What makes you think she doesn't know?" he asks, and for a moment, I'm stunned into silence.

"You're saying she knows?"

"I'm saying that I try to be honest with her. I'm her dad, Hope. That's my job."

I stop for a minute and process what he's saying to me. I'd thought I was protecting her—and her relationship with her father—by not dragging her into it.

"What did you say to her?" I ask.

He shrugs. "She's asked about the divorce. I've answered her questions."

"By blaming it on me."

"By explaining that not everything is as simple as it appears on the surface."

"Meaning what? That I drove you to cheat?"

He shrugs again. "Your words, not mine."

I clench my fists. "This is between you and me, Rob," I say, my voice shaking. "Don't drag Annie into it."

"Hope," he says, "I'm just trying to do what's best for Annie. I have some real concerns that she's going to turn out like you and your mother."

The words physically hurt. "Rob . . ." I begin. But no other words come.

He shrugs after a moment. "We've had this conversation a thousand times. You know how I feel. I know how you feel. That's why we're divorced, remember?"

I don't acknowledge his words. What I want to say is that the reason we're divorced is he got bored. He got insecure. He got emotionally needy. He got flirted with by a stupid twenty-two-year-old with legs up to her neck.

But I know there's a grain of truth to what he's saying. The more I felt him slipping away, the more I retreated into myself instead of hanging on. I swallow back the guilt.

"No makeup," I say firmly. "Not at school. It's inappropriate. And so is sharing the details of our divorce with her. That's too much for a twelve-year-old."

Rob opens his mouth to reply, but I hold up my hand. "I'm done here, Rob," I say, and this time, I really am. We look at each other in silence for a minute, and I wonder whether he's thinking, as I am, about how we don't even know each other anymore. It seems a lifetime ago that I promised him forever. "This isn't about me and you," I say. "It's about Annie."

I walk away before he can reply.

I'm driving home when my cell phone rings. I look at the caller ID and see Annie's cell number, the one she's supposed to use only in emergencies, even though I'm fairly sure Rob lets her text and call her friends with abandon. That is, after all, what cool parents do. Something in my stomach tightens.

"Why aren't you at work?" Annie asks when I pick up. "I called you there first."

"I had to go"—I search for an explanation that doesn't involve her father—"run some errands."

"At four on a Thursday?" she asks. The truth is, the bakery had been slow all day, and I hadn't had a customer since one o'clock, which left me plenty of time to think about Rob, Annie, and all the damage that was being done while I stood idly by, baking my way into oblivion. I knew Annie was planning to see Mamie after school, which meant I'd get Rob alone.

"Business was slow," is all I tell her.

"Well, anyways," she says, and I realize she's calling because she wants something. I steel myself for an absurd request—money, concert tickets, maybe the new four-inch heels I saw her gazing at in my copy of *InStyle* last night—but instead, she sounds almost shy as she asks, "Can you, like, come over to Mamie's?"

"Is everything okay?" I ask instantly.

"Yeah," she says. She lowers her voice. "Actually, it's really weird, but Mamie is acting normal today."

"Normal?"

"Yeah," she whispers. "Like she did before Grandma died. She's acting like she didn't lose her memory."

My heart lurches a little, as I remember what the nurse told me when I was last there, on my way out. *There will be times she's as clear as day. She'll remember everything, and she's just as lucid as you or me. Those are the days you'll have to seize, because there's no guarantee there will be more of them.*

"Are you sure?" I ask.

"Totally," Annie says, and I don't hear any of the sarcasm or anger I've been hearing in her voice lately. I wonder suddenly whether part of her attitude problem is that she's hurt that her great-grandmother is forgetting her. I make a mental note to have a real talk with her about Alzheimer's. Then again, that means I'll have to face it myself.

"She's been, like, asking me about school and stuff," Annie continues. "It's weird, but she knows exactly who I am and how old I am and everything."

"Okay," I say, already checking my rearview mirror to make sure it's safe to do a U-turn. "I'm on my way."

"She says she wants you to bring one of the miniature Star Pies from the bakery," Annie adds.

Those have always been Mamie's favorites; filled with a blend of poppy seeds, almonds, grapes, figs, prunes, and cinnamon sugar and topped with a buttery star-shaped lattice crust, they're our signature item. "Okay," I tell her, "I'll be there as fast as I can." And for the first time in a while, I feel a sliver of hope. I didn't realize, until that moment, how very much I missed my grandmother.

"I would like to go to the beach," is the first thing Mamie says to me when she answers her door fifteen minutes later.

For a moment, my heart sinks. It's late September, and there's a chill in the air. The memory cloud must be back, for it makes no sense for my eighty-six-year-old grandmother to suddenly want to go out and sunbathe. But then she smiles at me and pulls me into a hug. "I am sorry," she says. "Where are my manners? It is nice to see you, Hope, dear."

"You know who I am?" I ask hesitantly.

"Well, of course I do," she says, looking insulted. "Do not tell me you think I am old and senile?"

"Er . . ." I stall for time. "Of course not, Mamie."

She smiles. "Do not worry. I am not a fool. I know I am forgetful at times." She pauses. "You brought me the Star Pie?" she asks, glancing at the white bakery bag in my hand. I nod and hand it to her. "Thank you, dear," she says.

"Sure," I say slowly.

She tilts her head to the side. "Today, Hope, everything feels clear. Annie and I have just been having a lovely talk."

I glance at Annie, who's perched on the edge of Mamie's sofa, looking nervous. She nods in agreement.

"But now you want to go to the beach?" I ask Mamie hesitantly. "It's, um, a little chilly for a swim."

"I am not planning on a swim, of course," she says. "I want to see the sunset."

I look at my watch. "The sun doesn't go down for almost two hours."

"Then we will have plenty of time to get there," she says.

Thirty minutes later, after Annie and I help Mamie to bundle up in a jacket, the three of us are headed for the beach at Paines Creek, which was my favorite place to watch the sun sink into the horizon when I was in high school. It's a quiet beach on the western edge of Brewster, and if you walk carefully out on the rocks jutting out where the creek empties into Cape Cod Bay, you have a great view of the western sky.

We stop on the way, at Annie's suggestion, to get lobster rolls and french fries at Joe's Dockside, a tiny restaurant that's been on the Cape even longer than our family bakery. People drive from miles away and wait in forty-five-minute lines during the summer for takeout lobster rolls, but fortunately, at five o'clock on a Thursday during the off-season, we're the only ones here. Annie and I listen in disbelief as Mamie, who orders a grilled cheese—she has never liked lobster—tells us a completely lucid story about the first time she and my grandfather took my mother here, when my mother was a little girl, and Josephine asked why lobsters would be silly enough to swim up to Joe's if they knew they might be made into sandwiches.

We get to the beach just as the edges of the sky are beginning to burn. The sun hangs low on the western horizon above the bay, and the wispy clouds in the sky promise a beautiful sunset. Arms linked, the three of us make our way slowly down the beach, Annie on Mamie's left side, and me on her right with a folding chair tucked under my arm.

"You okay, Mamie?" Annie asks gently, once we're about halfway down the beach. "We can stop and rest for a bit, if you want."

My heart lurches as I glance at my daughter. She's staring at Mamie with a look of concern and love so deep that I realize, suddenly, that whatever's going on with her now is truly just a phase. This is the Annie I know and love. It means I haven't screwed up entirely. It means my daughter is still the same decent person she's always been underneath, even if she hates me for the time being.

"I am fine, dear," Mamie replies. "I want to be up on the rocks by the time the sun goes down."

"Why?" Annie asks softly after a pause.

Mamie is silent for so long that I begin to think she didn't hear Annie's question. But then, finally, she replies, "I want to remember this day, this sunset, this time with you girls. I know I do not have many days like this left."

Annie glances at me in concern. "Sure you do, Mamie," she says.

My grandmother squeezes my arm, and I smile gently at her. I know what she's saying, and it breaks my heart that she's aware of it.

She turns to Annie. "Thank you for your faith," she says. "But sometimes, God has another plan."

Annie looks wounded by the words. She looks away, staring off into the distance. I know that the truth is finally beginning to sink in for her, and it makes my heart hurt.

We finally reach the rocks, and I set up the chair I'd grabbed from the trunk of the car. I help Annie lower Mamie into it. "Sit with me, girls," she says, and Annie and I quickly settle down on the rocks on either side of her.

We stare in silence toward the horizon as the sun melts into the bay, painting the sky orange, then pink, purple, and indigo as it disappears.

"There it is," Mamie says softly, and she points just above the horizon, where a star twinkles faintly through the fading twilight. "The evening star."

I'm reminded suddenly of the fairy tales she used to tell me about a prince and a princess in a faraway land, the ones where the prince had to go fight the bad knights, and he promised the princess he'd come find her one day, because their love would never die. So I'm surprised when it's Annie who murmurs, " 'As long as there are stars in the sky, I will love you.' That's what the prince in your stories always said."

When Mamie looks at her, there are tears in her eyes. "That's right," she says.

She reaches into the pocket of her coat and withdraws the Star Pie she asked me to bring from the bakery. It's smooshed now, and the star-shaped lattice crust on top is crumbling. Annie and I exchange looks.

"You brought the pie with you?" I ask. My heart sinks; I'd thought she was entirely lucid.

"Yes, dear," she replies quite clearly. She stares down at the pie for a moment as the light continues to fade from the sky. I'm just about to suggest we start heading back before it gets too dark out when she says, "You know, my mother taught me to make these pies."

"I didn't know that," I say.

She nods. "My mother and father had a bakery. Very near the Seine, the river that runs through Paris. I worked there as a girl, just like you do now, Annie. Just like you did when you were a girl, Hope."

"You've never told us about your parents before," I say.

"There are a lot of things I have never told you," she says. "I thought I was protecting you, protecting myself. But I am losing my memories now, and I fear that if I do not tell you these things, they will be gone forever, and the damage I have done will not be reversed. It is time you know the truth."

"What are you talking about, Mamie?" Annie asks, and I can hear worry in her voice. She looks at me, and I know she's thinking the same thing I am. Mamie's mind must be clouding over again.

Before I can say anything, Mamie begins breaking off pieces of the Star Pie and throwing them into the ocean. She's whispering something under her breath, speaking so softly that I can barely hear her over the roll of the tide into the rocks below.

"Um, what are you doing, Mamie?" I ask as gently as possible, trying to keep the worry from creeping into my voice.

"Shhh, child," she says. Then she goes back to throwing pieces into the water.

"Mamie, what are you saying?" Annie asks. "It's not French, is it?"

"No, dear," Mamie replies calmly. Annie and I exchange confused looks as Mamie throws the final piece of the pie into the water. She reaches for our hands. "Who is like unto You, O God," she says in English, "and You will cast all their sins into the depths of the sea."

"What are you saying, Mamie?" Annie asks again. "Is it from the Bible?"

Mamie smiles. "It is a prayer," she replies.

She stares at the evening star for a moment while Annie and I watch her in silence. "Hope," she finally says. "There is something I need you to do for me."

Chapter *Six*

〜

Rose's Strudel

STRUDEL

INGREDIENTS

3 Granny Smith apples, peeled, cored, and sliced into narrow slivers

1 Granny Smith apple, peeled, cored, and shredded

1 cup raisins

½ cup chopped candied orange peel (see recipe below)

1 cup brown sugar

2 tsp. cinnamon

½ cup slivered almonds

1 sheet frozen puff pastry, thawed

1 egg, beaten

Cinnamon sugar for sprinkling (3 parts sugar mixed with 1 part cinnamon)

DIRECTIONS

1. Mix apples, raisins, candied orange peel, brown sugar, and cinnamon in large bowl. Let sit for 30 minutes.

2. Preheat oven to 400 degrees.

3. Spread slivered almonds in a thin layer on a baking sheet and toast in oven for 7–9 minutes, until slightly browned. Remove and set aside for 5 minutes until cool enough to touch. Mix into the apple mixture.

4. Spoon apple mixture into a colander lined with cheesecloth and press down with another piece of cheesecloth, to eliminate extra moisture in

the mixture. Leave in cheesecloth-covered colander to drain while you place puff pastry sheet on a greased baking sheet. Roll lightly to expand area of pastry without breaking through the dough.

5. Spread apple mixture down the middle of the pastry lengthwise and fold the pastry around the mixture, sealing on all sides by using a bit of water on your fingers and pressing edges firmly together.

6. Brush top of pastry with beaten egg, cut 5 or 6 narrow slivers in the top, and sprinkle liberally with cinnamon sugar.

7. Bake for 35–40 minutes, until golden brown.

CANDIED ORANGE PEEL

INGREDIENTS

Four oranges   *2 cups granulated sugar*
14 cups water, divided

DIRECTIONS

1. Peel all four oranges, taking care to remove the peels whole or in two pieces, if possible.

2. Cut the peels into thin strips

3. Boil 6 cups of water, and add the peels to the boiling water. Boil 3 minutes, drain, and rinse the peels, then repeat the same process again. (This gets rid of some of the bitterness of the orange peels.)

4. Mix remaining 2 cups water with 2 cups sugar and bring to a boil. Add the peels, reduce heat, and cover pot. Simmer for 45 minutes.

5. Remove from sugar water with a slotted spoon, and lay peels on a rack to dry. Wait at least two hours before using them in the recipe above. Dip the remainder in dark chocolate and enjoy as a snack.

Rose

When Rose had awoken that morning, she knew. It was just like the old days, when she'd known things deep in her bones before they happened. Those days were far in the past, but lately, as the Alzheimer's had stolen more of the in-between, it was like the timeline of her life had become an accordion, folding in on itself, bringing the past ever closer to the present by bending and contracting the years that had gone by.

But on this day, Rose remembered everything: her family, her friends, the life she'd once had. For a moment, she had closed her eyes and wished to drift back into the oblivion from which she'd come. The Alzheimer's terrified her some days, but other days, it was a comfort. She was not ready for this clear window into the past. But then she opened her eyes and looked at the calendar that sat on her bedside table. Each night before closing her eyes, she crossed off the day she'd just completed. She was losing everything else, but knowing the day of the week was something she could still control. And according to the red X's on the calendar, today, the twenty-ninth of September, was a special day. Rose knew in an instant that the fact she'd been granted a reprieve of clarity on this day, of all days, was a sign from above.

And so she'd spent the morning writing it all down, as best she could, in a letter addressed to her granddaughter. Someday, Hope would read it and understand. But not yet. There were still pieces missing. When Rose closed the envelope, just before lunch, she felt empty and sad, as if she had just sealed off a piece of herself. In a way, she supposed, she had.

She carefully wrote out the address of Thom Evans, the attorney who'd drawn up her will, and she asked one of the nurses to please stamp and post the letter. Then she sat down and wrote out a list, forming each name carefully and clearly in big block writing, despite her shaking hands.

Later that day, as she drove to the beach with Hope and Annie, she checked the pocket of her skirt three times, just to make sure the list was still there. It was everything to her, and soon, Hope would know the truth too. It was impossible to hold back the tide any longer. In fact, Rose was no longer sure she wanted to. Being a one-woman dam against a surging flood was exhausting.

Now, as she stood on the piled rocks, her granddaughter on one side and her great-granddaughter on the other, in the fading *heure bleue*, she looked up at the sky and breathed in and out, in tune with the ocean, as she held the Star Pie in her hands. She threw the first piece into the water and recited the words so softly that she couldn't hear them herself over the rhythmic rushing of the waves.

"I am sorry for leaving," she whispered into the wind.

"I am sorry for the decisions I have made." A piece of the crust landed on an incoming wave.

"I am sorry for the people I have hurt." The wind carried her words away.

As she threw piece after piece of the pie into the ocean, she glanced at Hope and Annie, both of whom were staring at her in confusion. She felt a pang of guilt for scaring them, but they would understand soon enough. It was time.

She looked back to the sky and spoke to God softly, using words she hadn't said aloud in sixty years. She did not expect forgiveness. She knew she didn't deserve it. But she wanted God to know that she was sorry.

No one knew the truth. No one but God, and of course Ted, who had died twenty-five years earlier. He'd been a good man, a kind man, Papa to her Josephine and Grandpa to her Hope. He'd shown them love, and she would be forever grateful for that, because she had not known how. Still, she wondered whether he would have loved her the way he did if he'd known the whole truth. He'd guessed at it, she knew, but to tell him, to say it aloud, would have been to crush his soul.

Rose took a deep breath and looked into the eyes of Hope, the granddaughter she knew she'd failed. Hope's mother, Josephine, had suffered from Rose's mistakes, and so too had Hope. Even now, Rose could see it in her granddaughter's eyes and in the way she lived her life. Then, she looked to Annie, the one who brought all the memories rushing back in. She hoped for a better future for her. "I need you to do something for me," Rose said at long last, turning to her granddaughter.

"What do you need?" Hope asked softly. "I'll do whatever you want."

Hope didn't know what she was agreeing to, but Rose had no choice.

"I need you to go to Paris," Rose said calmly.

Hope's eyes widened. "Paris?"

"Paris," Rose repeated firmly. Before Hope could ask any questions, she went on. "I must know what happened to my family." Rose reached into her pocket and withdrew the list, the one that felt like it was on fire, along with a check she'd carefully made out for a thousand dollars. Enough for a plane ticket to France. Her palm burned as Hope took them from her. "I must know," Rose repeated softly. The waves crashed against the dam of her memories, and she braced herself for the flood.

"Your . . . family?" Hope asked tentatively.

Rose nodded, and Hope unfolded the slip of paper. Her eyes quickly scanned the seven names.

Seven names, Rose thought. She looked upward, to where the stars of the Big Dipper were beginning to appear. *Seven stars in the sky.* "I must know what happened," she told her granddaughter. "And so, now, must you."

"What's going on?" Annie interrupted. She looked scared, and Rose longed to comfort her, but she knew she was no better at comfort than she was at truth. She never had been. Besides, Annie was twelve. Old enough to know. Just two years younger than Rose had been when the war began.

"Who are these people?" Hope asked, looking down at the list again.

"They are my family," Rose said. "*Your* family." She closed her eyes for a moment and traced their names on her own heart, which, astoundingly, had gone on beating for all these years.

Albert Picard. b. 1897

Cecile Picard. b. 1901

Helene Picard. b. 1924

Claude Picard. b. 1929

Alain Picard. b. 1931

David Picard. b. 1934

Danielle Picard. b. 1937

When Rose opened her eyes, Hope and Annie were staring at her. She took a deep breath. "Your grandfather went to Paris in 1949," she began. Her voice was strained, for the words were hard to say aloud, even now, even so many years later. Rose closed her eyes again and remembered Ted's face the day he came home. He'd been unable to meet her eye. He'd spoken slowly as he delivered the news of the people she'd loved more than anything in the world.

"They all died," Rose continued after a moment. She opened her eyes again and looked at Hope. "It was all I needed to know then. I asked your grandfather to tell me no more. My heart could not bear it."

Only after he'd delivered the news had she finally agreed to return with him to the Cape Cod town where he'd been born and raised. Until then, she had been determined to remain in New York, just in case. It was where she'd always believed she'd be found, in the meeting place they'd spoken of years before. But now, there was no one left to find her. She was lost forever.

"All these people?" Annie asked, breaking the silence, bringing Rose back to the moment. "They all, like, died? What happened?"

Rose paused. "The world fell down," she said finally. It was all she could explain, and it was the truth. The world had collapsed upon itself, writhing and folding into something she could no longer recognize.

"I don't understand," Annie murmured. She looked scared.

Rose took a deep breath. "Some secrets cannot be spoken without undoing a lifetime," she said. "But I know that when my memory dies, so too will the loved ones I have kept close to my heart all these years."

Rose looked at Hope. She knew that her granddaughter would do her best to explain it to Annie one day. But first, she would need to understand it herself. And for that, she needed to go to the place it had all begun.

"Please go to Paris soon, Hope," Rose urged. "I do not know how much time I have."

And then, she was done. The toll was too high. She had said more than she'd said in sixty-two years, since the day Ted had returned with the news. She looked up at the stars and found the one she had named Papa, the one she had named Maman, the ones she had named Helene, Claude, Alain, David, Danielle. There was still one star missing. She could not find him, no matter how much she searched. And she knew, as she'd always known, that it was her fault he wasn't there. A piece of her wanted Hope to find out about him, on her journey to Paris. She knew the discovery would change Hope's life.

Hope and Annie were asking questions, but Rose could no longer hear them. Instead, she closed her eyes and began to pray.

The tide was coming. It had begun.

Chapter *Seven*

~~~

"D o you, like, have any idea what she was talking about?" Annie says as soon as we get back in the car after dropping Mamie off.

She's fumbling with her seat belt as she tries to buckle it. It's not until I notice that her hands are shaking that I realize mine are too.

"I mean, like, who *are* those people?" Annie finally clicks the belt closed and looks at me. There's confusion etched across her smooth brow, along with her smattering of freckles that are fading more the farther we get from the summer sun. "Mamie's maiden name wasn't even Picard. It was Durand."

"I know," I murmur.

When Annie was in fifth grade, her class did a basic family tree project. She'd tried to use a website to trace Mamie's roots, but there'd been so many immigrants with the last name Durand in the early 1940s that she'd gotten stuck. She'd sulked about it for a week, upset at me that I hadn't thought to research Mamie's past before her memory began to vanish.

"Maybe she got the name wrong," Annie says finally. "Maybe she wrote Picard but she meant Durand."

"Maybe," I say slowly, but I know that neither of us quite believes it. Mamie was as lucid as we'd seen her in years. She knew exactly what she was saying.

We drive the rest of the way home without speaking. But for once, it's not an uncomfortable silence; Annie isn't sitting in the passenger seat resenting me with her every breath; she's thinking about Mamie.

The light in the sky has almost entirely gone out now; I imagine Mamie at her window, searching the stars as twilight finally gives way to the blackness of night. Out here on the Cape, especially when the summer tourists have all snuffed out their porch lights until the next season, the nights are dark and deep. The larger streets are lit, but as I turn onto Lower Road and then Prince Edward Lane, the faint glow of Main Street vanishes behind us, and ahead of us, the last vestiges of Mamie's *heure bleue* disappear into the dark void that I know is the west side of Cape Cod Bay.

I feel like we're in a ghost town as I make the last turn onto Bradford Road. Seven of the ten homes on our street are summer homes, and now that the season's over, they're deserted. I pull into my driveway—the same driveway where I spent summer nights as a little girl catching fireflies and winter days helping my mom shovel snow so she could get her old station wagon out—and turn off the ignition. We're still in the car, but now that we're a block from the beach, I can smell salt in the air, which means that the tide is coming in. I have a sudden urge to hurry down to the beach with a flashlight and dip my toes in the frothy surf, but I quell it; I have to get Annie ready to go to her father's for the night.

She doesn't seem to be any more ready to get out of the car than I am.

"Why did Mamie want to leave France so bad anyway?" she finally asks.

"The war must have been pretty bad for her," I say. "Like

Mrs. Sullivan and Mrs. Koontz said, I think her parents had died. Mamie would have only been seventeen when she left Paris. Then I think she met your great-grandpa and fell in love."

"So she, like, left everything behind?" Annie asks. "How could she do that without being sad?"

I shake my head. "I don't know, honey."

Annie's eyes narrow. "You never *asked* her?" She looks at me, and I can tell that the anger, which had gone into hibernation temporarily, is back.

"Sure I did," I say. "When I was your age, I used to ask her about her past all the time. I wanted her to take me to France and show me all the things she did when she was a kid. I used to imagine her riding the Eiffel Tower elevator up and down all day with a poodle, while eating a baguette and wearing a beret."

"Those are stereotypes, Mom," Annie says, rolling her eyes at me. But I'm fairly sure I can see the hint of a smile tugging at the corners of her mouth as she gets out of the car.

I get out too and follow her across the front lawn. I forgot to turn the porch light on before I left the house earlier, so it looks like the darkness is swallowing Annie whole. I hurry to the door and turn the key in the lock.

Annie lingers in the hallway for a long moment, just looking at me. I'm sure she's about to say something, but when she opens her mouth, no sound comes out. Abruptly, she turns on her heel and strides toward her bedroom in the back of our small cottage. "I'll be ready in five!" she yells over her shoulder.

Since "five" usually means at least twenty minutes in Annie-speak, I'm surprised to see her in the kitchen just a few minutes later. I'm standing at the refrigerator with the door open, willing dinner to materialize out of thin air. For someone who works around food all day, I do a lousy job of keeping my own fridge stocked.

"There's a Healthy Choice meal in the freezer," Annie says from behind me.

I turn and smile. "Guess it's time I go to the grocery store."

"Nah," Annie says. "I wouldn't recognize our fridge if it was full. I'd think I'd accidentally gone into the wrong house."

"Ha-ha, very funny," I say with a grin. I shut the refrigerator door and open the freezer, which contains two trays of ice cubes, a half bag of miniature Reese's Peanut Butter Cups, a bag of frozen peas, and, as Annie promised, a Healthy Choice frozen meal.

"We already ate, anyways," Annie adds. "Remember? The lobster rolls?"

I close the door to the freezer and nod. "I know," I say. I look over at Annie, who's standing by the kitchen table, her duffel bag propped against the chair beside her.

She rolls her eyes at me. "You're so weird. Do you just sit here and eat junk food every time I go to Dad's?"

I clear my throat. "No," I lie.

Mamie used to deal with stress by baking. My mother used to deal with stress by getting furious about little things, and usually sending me to my room after telling me what a lousy daughter I was. I, apparently, deal with stress by stuffing my face.

"All right, honey," I say. "Got everything?" I cross the kitchen toward her, moving absurdly slowly, as if I can prolong her time with me. I pull her into a hug, which seems to surprise her as much as it surprises me. But she hugs back, which makes the pain in my heart temporarily disappear.

"I love you, kiddo," I murmur into her hair.

"I love you too, Mom," Annie says after a minute, her voice muffled against my chest. "Now could you let me go before you, like, smother me?"

Embarrassed, I release her. "I'm not sure what to do about Mamie," I say as she reaches for her duffel bag and swings it over her shoulder. "Maybe she's talking nonsense."

Annie freezes. "What are you talking about?"

I shrug. "Her memory's gone, Annie. It's awful, but that's what Alzheimer's is."

"It wasn't gone today," she says, and I can see the inner corners of her eyebrows beginning to point sharply downward as she furrows her brow. Her tone is suddenly icy.

"No, but talking about these people we've never heard of . . . You have to admit it doesn't make any sense."

"Mom," Annie says flatly. Her eyes burn a hole in me. "You *are* going to Paris, right?"

I laugh. "Sure. Then I'll go shopping in Milan. And skiing in the Swiss Alps. Then maybe I'll take a gondola around Venice."

Annie narrows her eyes. "You *have* to go to Paris."

I realize she's serious. "Honey," I say gently, "that's just not practical. I'm the only one here to run the bakery."

"So close it for a few days. Or I'll help out after school."

"Sweetheart, that's not going to work." I think about how close I am to losing everything.

"But Mom!"

"Annie, who's to say that Mamie will even remember the conversation later?"

"That's why you *have* to go!" Annie says. "Didn't you see how important it was to her? She wants you to find out what happened to those people! You can't just let her down!"

I sigh. I'd thought that Annie understood this better, that she realized how often her great-grandmother speaks nonsense. "Annie—" I begin.

But she cuts me off. "What if this is her last chance? What if this is our last chance to help her?"

I shrug. I don't know what to say. I can't possibly explain to her that we're teetering on the edge.

When I'm silent for a moment, Annie seems to make up her mind without me. "I hate you," she hisses. Then she turns on her heels and stalks out of the kitchen, her duffel bag bobbing behind her. A few seconds later, I hear the front door slam. I take a deep breath and follow her outside, steeling myself for a silent drive to her father's.

The next morning, after a mostly sleepless night, I'm at the bakery alone, sliding a tray of giant sugar cookies into the oven, when there's a rattling knock on the glass-paned front door. I put the oven mitts on the counter, set the timer on the oven, dust off my hands on my apron, and check my watch: 5:35 a.m. Twenty-five minutes before I open.

As I cross from the kitchen to the sales floor, through the swinging, slatted door, I see Matt, his hand shading his eyes as he presses his face against the glass and peers in. He sees me and backs up quickly, then waves casually as if he hasn't just left his nose print on my window.

"Matt, we're not open yet," I say after I've turned the three locks and cracked open the front door. "I mean, you're welcome to come in and wait, but the coffee's not on yet, and—"

"No, no, I'm not here for coffee," Matt says. He pauses and adds, "But if you get some going, I'll take a cup."

"Oh," I say, checking my watch again. "Yeah, okay." It shouldn't take more than two minutes to grind the beans, scoop them into the coffeemaker, and push the Brew button. I hurry to do that, mentally ticking off all the other things I need to do before we open, as Matt follows me inside and pulls the door closed behind him.

"Hope, I came over to ask what you're going to do," Matt says while the coffeemaker gurgles and spits its first sizzling drops into the pot.

For an instant, I wonder how he knows about what Mamie said, but then I realize he's talking about the bakery and the fact that the bank is apparently ready to begin proceedings to take it away from me. My heart sinks.

"I don't know, Matt," I say stiffly without turning around. I pretend I'm busy with the coffee preparation. "I haven't had a chance to work through things yet."

In other words, I'm in denial. That's my general approach when things are going wrong; I simply bury my head in the sand and wait for the storm to pass. Sometimes it does. Most of the time, I only wind up with sand in my eyes.

"Hope—" Matt begins.

I sigh and shake my head. "Look, Matt, if you've come here to try to persuade me to sell to these investors of yours, I've already told you that I don't know what to do yet, and I'm not ready to—"

He cuts me off. "You're running out of time," he says firmly. "We need to talk about this."

Finally, I turn. He's standing at the counter, leaning forward. "Okay," I say. My chest feels tight.

He pauses and picks an invisible speck from his lapel. He clears his throat. The smell of coffee is wafting through the air now, and because he's making me nervous, I turn and busy myself with pouring him a cup before the maker has finished. I stir in his cream and sugar, and he takes the cup from me with a nod.

"I want to try to persuade the investors to make you a partner," he finally blurts out. "*If* they'll take the bakery on, which we still don't know. They need to come in, view your operations, and run your numbers. But I'm talking you up."

"A partner?" I ask. I decide not to mention how much it hurts to have it presented to me like a gift that I could have a share in my own family's business. "Does that mean I'd have to come up with the money to cover a percentage of the purchase from the bank?"

"Yes and no," he says.

"Because I don't have it, Matt."

"I know."

I stare and wait for him to go on.

He clears his throat. "What if you borrowed some money from me?"

My eyes widen. "What?"

"It would be more of a business arrangement, Hope," he says quickly. "I mean, I have the credit. So what if we went into this, say, seventy-five twenty-five. Seventy-five percent ownership for you. Twenty-five for me. And you just pay me what you can every month. We could keep a piece of the bakery in your family . . ."

"I can't," I say, before I've even had a chance to consider it. The invisible strings attached would strangle me. And as much as I hate the idea of strangers owning the majority of my bakery, it's even worse to think of Matt having an ownership interest in it too. "Matt, it's such a nice offer, but I can't possibly—"

"Hope, I'm just asking you to consider it." He's speaking quickly. "It's not a big deal. I have the money. I've been looking for something to invest in, and this place is an institution in this town. I know you'll turn things around soon, and . . ."

His voice trails off, and he looks at me hopefully.

"Matt, that means a lot to me," I say softly. "But I know what you're doing."

"What?" he asks.

"Charity," I say. I take a deep breath. "You feel sorry for me. And I appreciate that, Matt, I really do. It's just—I don't need your pity."

"But—" he begins, but I cut him off again.

"Look, I'm going to sink or swim on my own, okay?" I pause and swallow hard, trying to believe I'm doing the right thing. "And maybe I'll sink. Maybe I'll lose everything. Maybe the investors will decide this place isn't worth it anyhow." I take a deep breath. "But if that happens, maybe that's what's meant to be."

His face falls. He taps his fingers on the counter a few times. "You know, Hope, you're different," he says finally.

"Different?"

"Than you used to be," he says. "Back in high school, you wouldn't let anything get you down. You always bounced back. That was one of my favorite things about you."

I don't say anything. There's a lump in my throat.

"But now, you're ready to give up," he adds after a moment. He doesn't meet my eye. "I just . . . I thought you would feel differently. It's like you're just letting life *happen* to you."

I press my lips together. I know I shouldn't care what Matt thinks, but the words still wound me, largely because I know he's not trying to be cruel. He's right; I *am* different than I used to be.

He regards me for a long moment and nods. "I think your mother would be disappointed."

The words hurt, because they're meant to. But at the same time, they help, because he's dead wrong. My mother never cared about the bakery the way my grandmother did; she looked at it as a burden. She probably would have been happy to see it fail while she was still around, so that she could have washed her hands of it.

"Maybe, Matt," I say.

He pulls out his wallet and takes out two dollar bills. He puts them on the counter.

I sigh. "Don't be silly. The coffee's on the house."

He shakes his head. "I don't need your charity, Hope," he says. He half smiles at me. "Have a good one," he adds. He grabs his coffee and strides quickly out the front door. As I watch the darkness wrap itself around his disappearing silhouette, I shiver.

Annie comes and goes that morning, and once again, she's barely speaking to me, other than to ask tightly whether I've had a chance to look into booking flights to Paris. By eleven in the morning, the bakery is empty, and I'm staring out the front panes at the changing leaves of Main Street. There's a breeze today, and every once in a while, oak leaves in fiery red or maple leaves in burnt orange waft by, reminding me of graceful birds.

At eleven thirty, with no customers, nothing left to do, and a batch of Star Pies in the oven, I log on to the old laptop that I keep behind the register—I "borrow" WiFi from Jessica Gregory's gift shop next door—and I slowly type in www.google.com. Once there, I pause. What am I looking for? I chew my lip for a moment and enter the first name on Mamie's list. *Albert Picard.*

A second later, the search results are up. There's an airport in France named Albert-Picardie, but I don't think that has anything to do with Mamie's list. I read the Wikipedia entry, nonetheless, but it's clear that this is something else altogether; it's a regional airport that serves a community called Albert in the Picardie region of northern France. Dead end.

I click back and scan the other search results. There's a Frank Albert Picard, but he's an American attorney who was born and raised in Michigan and died in the early 1960s. That can't be the person she's looking for; he has no ties to Paris. A few other Albert Picards come up when I add the word *Paris* to my search string, but nothing seems to fit with the time Mamie lived in France.

I bite my bottom lip and clear the search field. I type in *White Pages, Paris,* and after a few click-throughs, I wind up on a page titled *Pages Blanches,* which asks for a *nom* and a *prénom.* I know from my limited high school French that this is surname and first name, so I type in *Picard* and *Albert,* and under the blank asking *Où?,* I enter *Paris.*

One listing comes up, and my heart skips a beat. Will it really be this easy? I jot down the number, then I erase *Albert* and fill in the second name on Mamie's list: *Cecile.* There are eight matches in Paris, including four people listed as *C. Picard.* I jot down those numbers too and repeat the search with the rest of the names. *Helene, Claude, Alain, David, Danielle.*

I finish with a list of thirty-five numbers. I return to Google to figure out how to call France from the United States and jot down those instructions too; I work out the overseas number for the first Picard and reach for the phone.

I pause before I pick it up. I have no idea what international calls cost, because I've never had to make one before. But I'm sure it's something just short of a fortune. I think about the check for a thousand dollars Mamie wrote to me and resolve to take the long-distance charges out of that and deposit the rest of the money back into her checking account. It'll still be a lot cheaper than buying a ticket to Paris.

I glance at the door. Still no customers. The street outside is empty; there's a storm brewing, and the sky is darkening, the wind picking up. I glance back at the oven. Thirty-six minutes left on the timer. The smell of cinnamon is wafting through the bakery as I breathe in deeply.

I dial the first number. There are a few clicks as the call connects, and then a pair of almost buzzerlike pulses. Someone picks up on the other end.

"Allo?" a woman's voice says.

It suddenly occurs to me that I don't speak more than rudimentary French. "Um, hello," I say nervously. "I'm looking for the relatives of someone named Albert Picard."

There's silence on the other end.

I search my memory desperately for the correct French words. "Um, *je chercher* Albert Picard," I attempt, knowing that's not quite right but hoping that it conveys my point.

"There is no Albert Picard here." The woman speaks clear English with a heavy French accent.

My heart sinks. "Oh. I'm sorry. I thought that—"

"There is no Albert Picard here because he is a useless bastard," the woman continues calmly. "He cannot keep his hands from touching all the other women. And I am done with it."

"Oh, I'm sorry . . ." I say, my voice trailing off because I'm not sure what else to say.

"You are not one of these women, are you?" she asks, suddenly sounding suspicious.

"No, no," I say quickly. "I am looking for someone my grandmother once knew, or maybe was related to. She left Paris in the early 1940s."

The woman laughs. "This Albert, he is only thirty-two. And his father is Jean-Marc. So he is not the Albert Picard you search for."

"I'm sorry," I say. I glance down at the list. "Do you know a Cecile Picard? Or a Helene Picard? Or a Claude Picard? Or . . ." I pause. "Or a Rose Durand? Or Rose McKenna?"

"No," the woman says.

"Okay," I say, disappointed. "Thank you for your time. And I hope, um, that you work things out with Albert."

The woman snorts. "And I hope he gets run over by a taxi."

The line clicks, and I'm left holding the phone in surprise. I shake my head, wait for the dial tone, and try the next number.

Chapter *Eight*

~

By the time Annie comes in just before four, the Star Pies have cooled, I have tomorrow's blueberry muffins in the oven, and I've called all thirty-five numbers on my list. Twenty-two of them answered. None of them knew the people from Mamie's list. Two of them had suggested that I try calling the synagogues, which might have records of their members from that time period.

"Thank you," I told both of them, puzzled, "but my grandmother is Catholic."

Annie barely meets my gaze as she tosses her backpack behind the counter and stalks into the kitchen. I sigh. Great. We're going to have one of *those* afternoons.

"I already cleaned all the bowls and trays!" I call to my daughter as I start pulling cookies from the display case in preparation for closing in a few minutes. "We had a slow day today, so I had some extra time," I add.

"So did you book your trip to Paris?" Annie asks, appearing in the doorway to the kitchen with her hands on her hips. "With all this extra time you had?"

"No, but I—" I begin, but Annie holds up her hand to stop me.

"No? Okay. That's all I need to hear," she says, clearly borrowing phrasing from her father in an attempt to sound like a miniature adult. Just what I need.

"Annie, you're not listening," I say. "I called all the—"

"Look, Mom, if you're not going to help Mamie, I don't know what we have to talk about," she says sharply.

I take a deep breath. I've been walking on eggshells around her for the last several months, because I've been worried about how she's handling the divorce. But I'm tired of being the bad guy. Especially when I'm not. "Annie," I say firmly. "I'm doing everything I can to keep us afloat here. I understand that you want to help Mamie. I do too. But she has Alzheimer's, Annie. The request she's making isn't logical. Now if you'll just listen to me, I—"

"Whatever, Mom," she cuts me off again. "You don't care about anyone."

She strides back into the kitchen, and I start to follow her, my hands clenched into fists as I struggle to control my temper. "Young lady, don't you walk away from me in the middle of an argument!"

Just then, the door chime dings, and I spin around to see Gavin, dressed in faded jeans and a red flannel shirt. He meets my gaze and rakes a hand through his unruly brown curls, which I distractedly realize need to be cut.

"Um, am I interrupting something?" he asks. He glances at his watch. "Are you still open?"

I force a smile. "Of course, Gavin," I say. "Come in. What can I do for you?"

He looks uncertain as he approaches the counter. "You sure?" he asks. "I can come back tomorrow if—"

"No," I cut him off. "I'm sorry. Annie and I were just having a . . . talk."

Gavin pauses and smiles at me. "My mom and I used to have lots of talks when I was Annie's age," he says in a low voice. "I'm sure my mom always enjoyed them."

I laugh, despite myself. Just then, Annie emerges from the kitchen again. "I brought you coffee," she announces to Gavin before I can say anything. "On the house," she adds. She shoots a glance at me, as if daring me to challenge her. Little does she know that I haven't charged him for anything since he completed his work on our cottage.

"Well, thank you, Annie. That's generous," Gavin says, taking the coffee from her. I watch as he closes his eyes and breathes in the aroma. "Boy, this smells great."

I arch an eyebrow at him, because I suspect he knows as well as I do that the coffee's been on the burner for approximately the last two hours and is anything but fresh.

"So, Mr. Keyes," Annie begins. "You, like, help people and stuff, right?"

Gavin looks surprised. He clears his throat and nods. "Sure, Annie, I guess so." He pauses and glances at me. "And you can call me Gavin, if you want. Um, do you mean I help people by being a handyman? By fixing things?"

"Whatever," she says dismissively. "You help people because it's the right thing to do, right?" Gavin shoots me another look, and I shrug. "So anyways," Annie continues, "if something was lost, and it was really bothering someone, you'd probably want to help them find it, right?"

Gavin nods. "Sure, Annie," he says slowly. "No one likes to lose things." He shoots me another look.

"So, like, if someone asked you to help them find some of their relatives who they'd lost, you'd help them, wouldn't you?" she asks.

"Annie," I say in warning, but she isn't paying any attention.

"Or would you, like, totally ignore them when they ask for your help?" she goes on. She looks at me pointedly.

Gavin clears his throat again and looks at me. I know he realizes he's been dragged unwittingly into our fight, despite the fact that he has no idea what we're arguing about. "Well, Annie," he says slowly, turning his gaze back to her, "I suppose I'd try to help find them. But it really depends on what the situation is."

Annie turns to me with a triumphant look on her face. "See, Mom? Mr. Keyes cares, even if you don't!" She whirls around and disappears back into the kitchen. I close my eyes and listen to the sound of a metal bowl slamming into the counter. I open them again to see Gavin looking at me with concern. Our eyes meet for a moment, and then we both turn to look as Annie reemerges from the back.

"Mom, all the dishes are clean," she says, without looking at me. "I'm walking to Dad's now. Okay?"

"Have a nice time," I say flatly. She rolls her eyes, grabs her backpack, and strides out without looking back.

When I look up and meet Gavin's gaze again, the concern in his eyes makes me uncomfortable. I don't need him—or anyone—worrying about me. "Sorry," I mutter. I shake my head and try to look busy. "So, what can I get you, Gavin? I have some muffins in back that just came out of the oven."

"Hope?" he says after a pause. "Are you okay?"

"I'm fine."

"You don't look fine," he says.

I blink and continue to avoid his eyes. "I don't?"

He shakes his head. "You're allowed to be upset, you know," he says.

I must give him a harsh look without meaning to, because his cheeks suddenly flush and he says, "I'm sorry. I didn't mean—"

I hold up a hand. "I know," I say. "I know. Look, I appreciate it."

We're silent for a moment, and then Gavin says, "So what was she talking about? Is there something I can help you with?"

I smile at him. "I appreciate the offer," I say. "But it's nothing."

He looks like he doesn't believe me.

"It's a long story," I clarify.

He shrugs. "I've got time," he says.

I glance at my watch. "But you were going somewhere, weren't you?" I ask. "You came in for pastries."

"I'm not in a rush," he says. "But I *will* take a dozen cookies. The ones with cranberries and white chocolate in them. If you don't mind."

I nod and carefully arrange the remaining Cape Codder cookies in the display case in a robin's egg–blue box with *North Star Bakery, Cape Cod* written on it in swirly white letters. I tie it with a white ribbon and hand it across the counter.

"So?" Gavin prompts as he takes the box from me.

"You really want to hear this?" I ask.

"If you want to tell me," he says.

I nod, realizing suddenly that I *do* want to tell another adult what's going on. "Well, my grandmother has Alzheimer's," I begin. And for the next five minutes, as I pull miniature pies, croissants, baklava, tarts, and crescent moons out of the display case and pack them into airtight containers for the freezer or boxes for the church's women's shelter, I tell Gavin about what Mamie said last night. Gavin listens intently, but his jaw drops when I tell him about Mamie throwing pieces of miniature Star Pies into the ocean.

I shake my head and say, "I know, it sounds crazy, right?"

He shakes his head, a strange expression on his face. "No, actually, it doesn't. Yesterday was the first day of Rosh Hashanah."

"Okay," I say slowly. "But what does that have to do with anything?"

"Rosh Hashanah is the Jewish New Year," Gavin explains. "It's customary for us to go to a flowing body of water—like the ocean—for a little ceremony called a *tashlich*."

"You're Jewish?" I ask.

He smiles. "On my mom's side," he says. "I was kind of raised half Jewish, half Catholic."

"Oh." I just look at him. "I didn't know that."

He shrugs. "Anyhow, the word *tashlich* basically means 'casting out.'"

I realize suddenly that the phrase rings a bell. "I think my grandmother said something like that last night."

He nods. "The ceremony involves throwing crumbs into the water to symbolize the casting out of our sins. Usually bread crumbs, but I guess pie crumbs would work too." He pauses and adds, "Do you think that might have been what your grandmother was doing?"

I shake my head. "It can't be," I say. "My grandmother's Catholic." As the words leave my mouth, I'm suddenly struck by the fact that two of the people I'd reached in Paris today suggested I call synagogues.

Gavin arches an eyebrow. "Are you sure? Maybe she wasn't always Catholic."

"But that's crazy. If she was Jewish, I would know."

"Not necessarily," he says. "My grandmother on my mom's side, my nana, lived through the Holocaust," he says. "Bergen-Belsen. She lost both her parents and one of her brothers. Because of her, I got started volunteering with survivors when I was about fifteen. Some of them say that for a while, they abandoned their roots. It was hard for them to hang on to who they'd been when everything was taken away. Especially those who were kids taken in by Christian families. But all of them eventually came back to Judaism. Kind of like coming home."

I just stare at him. "Your grandmother was a Holocaust survivor?" I repeat, trying to piece together a whole new side to Gavin. "You used to work with survivors?"

"I still do. I volunteer once a week at the Jewish nursing home in Chelsea."

"But that's a two-hour drive," I say.

He shrugs. "It's where my grandmother lived until she died. The place means something to me."

"Wow." I don't know what else to say. "What do you do there? When you volunteer?"

"Art classes," he says simply. "Painting. Sculpture. Drawing. Things like that. I bring them cookies too."

"That's where you're always going with the boxes of cookies you pick up here?"

He nods. I just stare at him. I'm realizing there are more layers to Gavin Keyes than I'd ever appreciated. It makes me wonder what else I'm missing. "You do . . . art?" I ask finally.

He looks away and doesn't answer. "Look, I know this thing with your grandmother, it's probably a lot to take in. And I may be totally off base here. But you know, some people who escaped before they were sent to concentration camps were snuck out of Europe with false papers that identified them as Christians," he says. "Is it possible your grandmother could have come here under an assumed identity?"

I shake my head immediately. "No. No way. She would have told us." But, I realize suddenly, this could explain why everyone on the list she gave us had the last name Picard, while I'd always believed her maiden name to be Durand.

Gavin scratches his head. "Annie's right, Hope. You have to find out what happened to your grandmother."

We talk for another hour, Gavin patiently explaining all the things I don't understand. If Mamie is indeed from a Jewish family in Paris, I ask, why can't I just call the synagogues in Paris? Or aren't there Holocaust organizations that help you track down survivors? I'm sure I've heard of places like that, although I've never had reason to look into them before.

Gavin explains that it's worth trying Holocaust organizations as a first step, but that he thinks it's unlikely I'll find all my answers there. At most, even if I can find the names on a list somewhere, I'll only get a date and place of birth, maybe a date of deportation, and if I'm lucky, the name of a camp where they were taken.

"But that won't tell you the whole story," he adds. "And I think your grandmother deserves to know what really became of the people she loved."

"*If* she even is who you're saying she is," I interject. "I think this sounds crazy."

Gavin nods. "I don't blame you. But you have to go find out."

I'm not convinced, and I look away as he explains that the synagogues might have better records, that they might be able to point me to other survivors who remember the Picard family. Besides, he says, even though the Holocaust happened seventy years ago, some of the record keepers are reluctant to give out information over the phone. While there had been many efforts made over the years to open things up, for many of the people who'd been alive during the war, giving away names was like giving away lives.

"Plus," Gavin concludes, "your grandmother obviously wants you to go to Paris. There must be a reason."

"But what if there isn't a reason at all?" I ask in a small voice. "She's sick, Gavin. Her memory's gone."

Gavin shakes his head. "My grandpa had Alzheimer's too," he says. "It's awful, I know. But I remember his moments of clarity. Especially about the past. And from what you said, it sounds like your grandmother was completely lucid when she gave you the names."

"I know," I admit finally. "I know."

By the time I lock up and we walk out, daylight is waning, the blue of the sky starting to deepen. I shiver as I pull my denim jacket a little tighter around me.

"You okay?" Gavin asks, pausing before he turns to the left. I can see his Jeep parked along Main about a block down.

I nod. "Yeah. Thanks. For everything."

"It's a lot to take in," he says. "*If* it's true," he adds as an afterthought, and I know the words are for my benefit, not his.

I nod again. I feel numb, as if the things he explained to me this afternoon completely overloaded my system. I simply can't bring myself to believe that my grandmother has a past she's never spoken of. But I have to admit that everything he said made sense. That chills me to the bone.

"Well," Gavin says, and I realize I've been standing on the street, staring blankly into space.

I shake my head, force a smile, and stick out my hand. "Listen, thank you again. So much."

Gavin looks surprised by my extended hand, but he shakes it after a moment and says, "My pleasure."

His hand is calloused and warm, and it takes me an instant longer than it should to let go. "I hope you enjoy those cookies," I say, nodding to the box in his left hand.

He smiles. "They're not for me," he says.

I feel suddenly awkward. "Well, take care," I say.

"Take care," he repeats. And as I watch him walk away, a sense of loss rolls in from nowhere.

Chapter *Nine*

～

I toss and turn all night, and when I do fall asleep, I have nightmares of people being rounded up in the streets, right outside my bakery, and marched off toward train cars. In my dream, I'm running through the crowd, trying to find Mamie, but she's not there. I awake in a cold sweat at two thirty in the morning, and although I don't normally leave for work until three forty-five, I get out of bed anyhow, pull on some clothes, and head out into the crisp air. I know I won't be able to sleep another wink.

The tide must be low, because as I walk to my car, I can smell the muddy salt from the bay two blocks away. In the stillness of the early morning, I can hear the faint sound of waves rolling into shore. Before I get into the driver's seat, I stand there for a moment, breathing in and out. I've always loved the smell of salt water; it reminds me of my childhood, when my grandfather would come over after a day of fishing, the scent of the sea still on his skin, and swing me high into the air.

"Who's my favorite girl in the world?" he'd ask while he flew me, Supergirl-style, around the room.

"Meeeee!" I would reply with a giggle, delighted anew each time. I'd already figured out, even at that age, that my mother could be cold and moody, and my grandmother terribly reserved. But my grandfather smothered me in kisses, read me bedtime stories, taught me how to fish and play baseball, and called me his "best pal."

I find myself missing him terribly as I start my car engine. He'd know what to do about Mamie. I wonder suddenly whether he knew the secrets that she kept. If so, he'd never let on. I'd always thought they had a decent marriage, but can a relationship really survive if there are lies wrapped around its roots?

It's a few minutes past three by the time I walk into the bakery. I mechanically pull out yesterday's frozen muffins, cookies, and cupcakes, which will go into the bakery cases once they're defrosted. Then, I sit down to spend an hour online before I need to start the day's baking.

I log on to my e-mail and am startled to see a message from Gavin, sent to the bakery's online orders address just past midnight. I click to open it.

> *Hey Hope,*
>
>   *Thought I'd send you the links to the organizations I told you about. www.yadvashem.org and www.jewishgen.org are the best places to start your search. Then you might want to try the Mémorial de la Shoah, the Holocaust memorial, in Paris. They have good records for French victims of the Holocaust, I think. Let me know if I can help.*
>
>

Good luck,
Gavin

I pause and take a deep breath, bracing myself, then I click on the first link, which takes me to a database of Holocaust victims' names. Below the search box, it's explained that the database includes records of half of the six million Jews murdered during World War II. My stomach lurches suddenly; I've heard the figure before, but now it feels more personal. *Six million. My*

God. I remind myself that Gavin's probably wrong about Mamie anyhow. He has to be.

The text on the main page also explains that millions of victims remain unidentified. I wonder how this can be the case, seven decades later. How can so many people be lost forever?

I take a deep breath, enter *Picard* and *Paris,* and click Search.

Eighteen results are returned, and my heart pounds as I scan the list. None of the first names match the names Mamie gave me, and I don't know whether to be relieved or disappointed about that. But there's an Annie on the list, which makes me feel suddenly ill. I click on her name, not realizing until I do so that my hand is trembling. I read the scant text; the girl was born in December 1934, it says. She lived in Paris and Marseille and died on July 20, 1943, at Auschwitz. I do the math quickly. She didn't even live to see her ninth birthday.

I think about my Annie. On her ninth birthday, Rob and I took her and three friends into Boston for an afternoon tea party at the Park Plaza. They dressed up like princesses and giggled about the little tea sandwiches with the crusts cut off. The picture I took of Annie, in her pale pink dress, her hair long and loose as she blew out the candle atop a pink cupcake, is still one of my favorites.

But little Annie Picard from Paris never had a ninth birthday party. She didn't become a teenager, fight with her mother about makeup, worry about homework, fall in love, or live long enough to figure out who she really wanted to be.

I realize suddenly that I'm crying. I'm not sure when I started. I quickly close the page, wipe my eyes, and walk away. It takes fifteen minutes of pacing the kitchen before the tears stop.

I spend another thirty minutes clicking around the first site Gavin sent me, horrified by nearly everything I find. I remember reading Anne Frank's diary in school and studying the Holocaust in history classes, but there's something about reading about it as an adult that has a completely different impact.

The staggering numbers and facts swim before my eyes. Two hundred thousand Jews lived in Paris in 1939 when war broke out. Of those, fifty thousand perished. The Nazis began arresting Parisian Jews in May 1941, when they rounded up 3,700 men and sent them to internment camps. In June 1942, all Jews in Paris were made to wear yellow Stars of David marked with *juif,* the French word for *Jew.* A month later, on July 16, 1942, there was a massive roundup of twelve thousand Jews—mostly foreign born—who were taken to a stadium called the Vélodrome d'Hiver, then deported to Auschwitz. By 1943, the Nazis were going into orphanages, retirement homes, and hospitals, arresting those who were the most defenseless. The thought makes my stomach lurch.

I enter *Picard* into the second database Gavin sent me. I find three surviving Picards listed in a Munich newspaper, and three others—including another Annie Picard—listed as survivors living in Italy. There are three Picards listed in the death book of the Mauthausen concentration camp in Austria, another eleven listed at Dachau in Germany. There are thirty-seven Picards on a list of 7,346 French female deportees who perished. I find the eight-year-old Annie Picard again on this list, and the tears return. My sight is so blurred that I almost don't notice when two familiar names come up on the screen. Cecile Picard—the second name on Mamie's list—and Danielle Picard—the last.

Heart thudding, I read the details listed for the first name.

Cecile Picard. Born Cecile Pachcinski on May 30, 1901, in Krakow, Poland. From Paris, France. Deported to Auschwitz, 1942. Died autumn 1942.

I swallow hard a few times. Cecile Picard would have been forty-one when she died. Just five years older than I am now. Mamie, I know, was born in 1925, so she would have been seventeen in 1942. Could Cecile have been her mother? My great-grandmother? If that's true, how is it that we've never spoken of this before?

I blink a few times and as I read the details of Danielle, my heart catches in my throat.

Danielle Picard. Born April 4, 1937. From Paris, France. Deported to Auschwitz. Died 1942.

She was only five.

I close my eyes and try to breathe evenly again. After a moment, I google the third organization Gavin suggested, the Mémorial de la Shoah. I click on the link and enter the first name on Mamie's list, Albert Picard, into the search box. My eyes widen as I find him.

Monsieur Albert PICARD né le 26/03/1897. Déporté à Auschwitz par le convoi n° 58 au départ de Drancy le 31/07/1942. De profession médecin.

I quickly cut and paste the entry into an online translator and stare at the results. Albert Picard. Born March 26, 1897. Deported to Auschwitz in convoy number 58 from Drancy on July 31, 1942. He was a doctor.

Numb, I enter the other family names. It doesn't say what happened to them, only the dates of their deportations. They'd all been taken to Auschwitz in convoys 57 or 58, in late July 1942. I find all of the names except Alain, who, according to Mamie's list, would have been eleven when it appeared his whole family was taken away. I stare at the screen, puzzled.

I check my watch. It's five thirty in the morning here. France is six hours ahead of us, so it's likely that there will be someone at the memorial's offices now. I take a deep breath, try not to think of my phone bill, and dial the number on the screen.

On the sixth ring, a machine answers in French. I hang up and redial, but once again, a machine picks up. I look at my watch again. They should be open by now. I dial a third time, and after a few rings, a woman answers in French.

"Hello," I say, exhaling in relief. "I'm calling from America, and I'm sorry, but I don't really speak French."

The woman switches immediately to heavily accented English.

"We are closed," she says. "It is a Saturday. We close every Satur-day. For the Sabbath. I am here completing some research."

"Oh," I say, my heart sinking. "I'm sorry. I didn't realize." I pause and ask in a small voice, "Is it possible to answer a question for me quickly?"

"It is not our policy." Her tone is firm.

"Please," I say in a small voice. "I'm trying to find someone. Please."

She is silent for a moment, then she sighs. "Fine. Quickly."

I hastily explain that I'm looking for people who may be my grandmother's family, and that I've found some of their names, but I'm missing one. She sighs again and tells me that the memo-rial has some of the best records in Europe because the depor-tations were recorded meticulously by the French police, who carried them out.

"Through Europe," she says, "half of the records are miss-ing. But in France, we know the names of almost every person deported from our country."

"But how can I find out what happened to them after the deportations?" I ask.

"In many cases, you cannot, I am afraid," she says. "*Mais,* well, in certain cases you can. We have here the written records, the census documents, and some other things. Some of the depor-tation cards have notes on them about what happened to the peo-ple."

"What about finding Alain? The name that's not in your database?"

"That is more difficult," she says. "If he was not deported, we would not have a record of him. But you can feel welcome to come here and look through our records. There is a librarian who will help you. Maybe you will find him."

"Come to Paris?" I ask.

"*Oui,*" she says. "It is the only way."

"Thank you," I murmur. "*Merci beaucoup.*"

"De rien," she replies. "Maybe we will see you soon?"

I hesitate for only a moment. "Maybe you will see me soon."

I'm so shaken by the results of the search, and by the conversation with the woman at the memorial, that I'm late in getting the Star Pies in the oven and the almond rose tarts prepped. This is very unlike me; sticking rigidly to the morning schedule is what keeps me sane most days. So when the alarm clock in the kitchen goes off, alerting me to the fact that it's 6:00 a.m. and time to unlock the front door, I'm in an uncharacteristic state of disarray.

I hurry out front and am surprised to see Gavin patiently standing outside. When he sees me through the glass, he smiles and raises a hand in greeting. I unlock the door. "Why didn't you knock?" I ask as I push it open toward him. "I would have let you in."

He follows me inside and watches as I flip the switch on the Open sign. "I haven't been here long," he says. "Besides, you open at six. Didn't seem right to bother you before that."

I gesture for him to follow me. "I have pies in the oven. Sorry; I'm running a little late this morning. Coffee?"

"Sure," he says.

He pauses at the counter, and I gesture again for him to follow me back into the kitchen. "Can I do anything to help?" he asks, rolling up his sleeves like he's already prepared to dive in.

I shake my head and smile. "No, I'm okay," I say. "Unless you can turn back time so that I'm running on schedule."

I grind a cup of coffee beans and am surprised to turn around and see Gavin filling the coffeemaker with water and lining the basket with a filter, as if he's entirely at home here.

"Thanks," I say.

"Rough morning?" he asks.

"Weird morning. I got your e-mail. Thanks."

"Did it help?"

I nod. "I spent some time on those sites."

"And?"

"And I found all but one of the names from my grandmother's list." I pour the coffee grinds into the filter, and Gavin flicks the switch to Brew. We're silent for a moment as the coffee begins to gurgle and spit. "I couldn't find Alain. But the others, they were all deported. In 1942. The youngest one was five. The mother wasn't much older than I am now."

I inhale deeply and feel my chest tremble as I do. "I'm still not convinced they're my grandmother's family."

"How come?"

I feel suddenly embarrassed and avoid his eye. "I don't know. It would change everything."

"What would it change?"

"Who my grandmother is," I say.

"Not really," he says.

"It changes who I am," I add in a small voice.

"Does it?"

"It makes me half Jewish. Or a quarter Jewish, I guess."

"No," Gavin says. "It would just mean you've had that piece of her past in you all along. It would mean you've always been a quarter Jewish. It wouldn't change anything about who you really are."

I suddenly feel like I'm talking to a therapist, and I don't like it. "Never mind," I say. The coffee pot is only half full, but I reach out abruptly to pour Gavin a cup as I change the subject. "You're earlier than usual this morning."

I realize as soon as the words are out of my mouth that it sounds like I'm keeping track of him. My cheeks heat up, but Gavin doesn't seem to notice.

"I couldn't sleep. And I wanted to see how your search was going."

I nod and take this in as I pour a cup of coffee for myself.

"Are you going to Paris?" Gavin asks.

"Gavin, I can't."

The timer on the oven goes off, and I can feel Gavin watching me as I slip oven mitts on and remove two trays of Star Pies. I set the temperature fifty degrees lower for the croissants I've already rolled out and shaped, and I head out to the front of the bakery to see whether anyone has come in without me hearing the door chimes. The shop is empty. Gavin waits until I've slid the croissants into the oven before he speaks again.

"Why can't you go?" he asks.

I bite my lip. "I can't afford to close the bakery."

Gavin takes this in, and I sneak a glance at him to see if there's judgment on his face. There isn't. "Okay," he says slowly. I realize he hasn't asked why, and I'm glad. I don't want to have to explain my situation to anyone.

"Can't someone run it for you for a few days?" he asks after a moment.

I laugh and realize the sound is bitter. "Who? Annie's not even old enough, technically, to work here. I don't have enough money to hire someone."

Gavin looks thoughtful. "I'm sure you have friends who can step in."

"No," I say, "I don't." *Yet another one of my many failures in life,* I add in my head.

We're interrupted by the front-door chime, and I head out to help my first customer of the day. It's Marcie Golgoski, who has been running the town's library since I was a little girl. As I pour her a cup of coffee in a to-go cup and package a blueberry muffin—her usual—I hope Gavin stays in the kitchen. I know how it will look to her if he's in back with me, and I don't like anyone in town making assumptions about my personal life. As much as I love it here, this town is as gossipy as a high school.

The timer on the oven goes off just as I'm ringing Marcie up, and I hurry back to the kitchen after she leaves, afraid that I've slightly overdone the croissants. I'm surprised to see Gavin setting the tray of croissants gently on a cooling rack.

"Thanks," I say.

He nods and slips the pot holders off. "I have to get going," he says. "But you're wrong."

"About what?" I ask, because if I'm going to be honest with myself, I'm sure I'm wrong about lots of things.

"About not having friends," he says. "You have me."

I don't know what to say, so I don't say anything. My heart is suddenly racing, though, and I can feel heat rising to my cheeks.

"I know you think I'm just the guy who fixes pipes and stuff," he adds after a moment.

I can feel my face heat up. "I'm a mess," I say finally. "Why would you want to be my friend?"

"For the same reason anyone wants to be anyone's friend," Gavin says. "Because I like you."

I stare after him as he disappears out the front door.

Annie is miraculously pleasant when she arrives in the afternoon; she's in such a seemingly good mood that I don't bring up the Internet search I did or my conflicted thoughts about Paris, because I can't bear the thought of another argument. She's heading back to her father's for the evening, and as we wash dishes side by side in the kitchen after closing, she breaks our companionable silence with a question.

"So are you, like, dating Matt Hines or something?" she asks.

I shake my head vigorously. "No. Absolutely not."

Annie looks skeptical. "I don't think he knows that."

"Why do you say that?"

"The way he looks at you," she says. "And talks to you. All possessive-like. Like you're his girlfriend."

I roll my eyes. "Well, I'm sure he'll figure out that I'm not."

"How come you never, like, date?" Annie asks after a pause, and from the way she's staring into the sink instead of meeting my eye, I get the sense that she's uncomfortable with the conversation. I wonder why she's bringing it up.

"Your dad and I haven't been divorced for that long," I reply after a moment.

Annie gives me a strange look. "So what, you want to get back together with Dad or something?"

"No!" I say instantly, because that's not it at all. "No. I think it's just that I didn't expect to be single again. Besides, you're my priority now, Annie." I pause and ask, "Why?"

"No reason," Annie says quickly. She's silent for a moment. I know her well enough to know that if I don't press her, she'll say what's on her mind—or at least a version of it. "It's just weird is all."

"What's weird?"

"That you don't have a boyfriend or anything."

"I don't think it's weird, Annie," I say. "Not everyone has to be in a couple." I don't want Annie growing up to be one of those girls who feels incomplete without a relationship. It hasn't occurred to me before this moment that those kinds of thoughts might be swirling in her head.

"Dad's in a couple," she mumbles. Again, she's staring straight into the sink, and I'm not sure what hurts me more initially—the sudden realization that Rob has moved on from me so quickly, or the fact that it's clearly bothering Annie. Either way, I feel like someone has punched me in the gut.

"Is he?" I ask as evenly as possible. "And what do you think about that?"

"It's fine."

I don't say anything, waiting for her to go on.

She breaks the silence again. "She's around all the time, you know. His girlfriend. Or whatever."

"You haven't mentioned her before."

Annie shrugs and mumbles, "I thought it would make you feel bad."

I blink a few times. "You don't have to worry about that, Annie. You can tell me anything."

She nods, and I can see her looking at me sideways. I pretend to be absorbed in the dishwashing. "So what's her name?" I ask casually.

"Sunshine," she mumbles.

"Sunshine?" I stop what I'm doing and stare at her. "Your dad's dating a woman named Sunshine?"

Annie cracks a smile for the first time. "It's a pretty dumb name," she agrees.

I snort and go back to washing off a baking tray. "So, do you like her?" I ask carefully after a pause.

Annie shrugs. She turns off her faucet, grabs a towel, and begins drying a stainless steel mixing bowl. "I guess," she says.

"Is she nice to you?" I try again, because I feel like I'm missing something here.

"I guess," she repeats. "Anyways. I'm glad you're not dating anyone, Mom."

I nod and make an attempt at humor. "Yeah, well, available men aren't exactly beating down the door."

Annie looks confused, like she hasn't gotten the self-deprecating jab. "Anyways," she says. "It's better when we're a family. Without strangers."

I resist the urge to agree, which would be the selfish thing to do. But I'm supposed to do the right thing, aren't I? And the right thing here is to help her to understand that eventually, her father and I have to move on. "We can still be a family, Annie," I say. "Your dad having a girlfriend doesn't change how he feels about you."

Annie narrows her eyes at me. "Whatever."

"Sweetheart, your father and I both love you very much," I say. "That'll never change."

"Whatever," she repeats. She places the mixing bowl in the drying rack. "Can I go now? I have a lot of homework."

I nod slowly and watch as she takes off her apron and hangs it carefully on the hook near the larger refrigerator. "Sweetie?" I venture. "Are you okay?"

She nods. She grabs her backpack and crosses the room to give me a quick, unexpected peck on the cheek. "Love you, Mom," she says.

"I love you too, honey. You're sure you're fine?"

"*Yes,* Mom." Her annoyed tone has returned, and she rolls her eyes.

She's gone before I can say anything more.

I go to see Mamie that night, after I've closed the bakery. On the drive over, my insides are swimming with a mixture of trepidation, sadness, and dread that I can't quite understand. In the space of a year, I've become the divorced owner of a failing bakery, whose daughter hates her. Now I might be Jewish too. It's like I don't know who I am anymore.

My grandmother is sitting at her window, gazing out to the east, when I let myself in.

"Oh dear!" she says, turning around. "I did not hear you knock!"

"Hi, Mamie," I say. I cross the room, kiss her on the cheek, and sit down beside her. "Do you know who I am?" I ask hesitantly, because this conversation will ride on how lucid she is.

She blinks. "Of course, dear," she says. "You are my grand-daughter. Hope."

I sigh in relief. "That's right."

"That is a silly question," she says.

I sigh. "You're right. Silly question."

"So how are you, my dear?" she asks.

"I'm okay, thanks," I say. I pause, struggling with how to bring up the things I need to know. "I was just thinking about what you told me the other night, and I had some questions."

"The other night?" Mamie asks. She tilts her head to the side and stares at me.

"About your family," I say gently.

Something flickers in her eyes, and her gnarled fingers are suddenly in motion, kneading the tasseled ends of her scarf.

"At the beach the other night," I continue.

She stares at me. "We did not go to the beach. It is autumn."

I take a deep breath. "You asked Annie and me to take you. You told us some things."

Mamie looks more confused. "Annie?"

"My daughter," I remind her. "Your great-granddaughter."

"Of course I know who Annie is!" she snaps. She looks away from me.

"I need to ask you something, Mamie," I say after a moment. "It's very important."

She's staring out the window again, and at first, I don't think she's heard me. But finally, she says, "Yes."

"Mamie," I say slowly, enunciating every syllable so that there's no chance of her misunderstanding, "I need to know if you are Jewish."

She whips her head toward me so quickly that I shift back in my seat, startled. Her eyes bore into mine, and she's shaking her head violently. "Who told you that?" she demands, her voice sharp and brittle.

I'm surprised to feel my heart sink a little. As much trouble as I'm having believing in what Gavin has said, I realize I've been buying into the possibility.

"N-no one," I say. "I just thought—"

"If I were Jewish, I would be wearing the star," my grandmother goes on angrily. "It is the law. You do not see the yellow star on me, do you? Do not make accusations you cannot prove. I am going to America to see my uncle."

I stare at her. Her face has turned pink, and her eyes are flashing. "Mamie, it's me," I say gently. "Hope."

But she seems not to hear me. "Do not harass me, or I will have you reported," she says. "Just because I am alone does not mean you can take advantage of me."

I shake my head, "No, Mamie, I would never—"

She cuts me off. "Now if you will excuse me." I watch, open-mouthed, as she stands with surprising agility and walks quickly toward her bedroom. She slams the door.

I stand up and take a step after her, but then I freeze. I don't know what to say or do. I feel terrible that I've made her upset. The violence of her response confuses me.

After a moment, I follow after her and rap lightly on her door. I can hear her get up from the bed, the springs of her old mattress creaking in protest. She pulls open the door and smiles at me. "Hello, dear," she says. "I did not hear you come in. Forgive me. I was just reapplying my lipstick."

Indeed, she has a fresh coat of burgundy on. I stare at her for a moment. "Are you okay?" I ask hesitantly.

"Of course, dear," she says brightly.

I take a deep breath. She seems to have no recollection of her explosion just moments before. This time I reach for her hands. I need an answer.

"Mamie, look at me," I say. "I'm your granddaughter, Hope. Remember?"

"Of course I remember. Do not be foolish."

I hold her hands tightly. "Look, Mamie, I'm not going to hurt you. I love you very much. But I need to know if your family is Jewish."

Her eyes flash again, but this time, I hold on and make sure she doesn't look away. "Mamie, it's me," I say. I feel her hands tighten around mine. "I'm not trying to hurt you. But I need you to answer me."

She stares at me for a moment then pulls away. I follow her as she strides back to the window in the living room. I'm just beginning to think that she's forgotten my question when finally she speaks, in a voice so soft it's almost a whisper.

"God is everywhere, my dear," she says. "You cannot define him in any one religion. Do you not know that?"

I put a hand on her back, and I'm heartened when she doesn't flinch. She's staring at the oyster sky as the blue seeps into the ground along the horizon.

"No matter what we think of God," she continues in the same soft, even tone, "we all live under this same sky."

I hesitate. "The names you gave me, Mamie," I say softly. "The Picards. Are they your family? Were they taken away during World War Two?"

She doesn't answer. She continues to stare out the window. After a moment, I try again. "Mamie, was your family Jewish? Are you Jewish?"

"Yes, of course," she says, and I'm so startled at the immediacy of her reply that I take a step back.

"You are?" I ask.

She nods. Finally, she turns to look at me. "Yes, I am Jewish," she says. "But I am also Catholic." She pauses and adds, "And Muslim too." My heart sinks. For a moment, I'd thought she was speaking with clarity.

"Mamie, what do you mean?" I ask, trying to keep the tremor out of my voice. "You're not Muslim."

"It is all the same, is it not? It is mankind that creates the differences. That does not mean it is not all the same God." She turns to look out the window again. "The star," she murmurs after a moment, and I follow her gaze to the first pinprick of light against the sunset. I watch with her for a moment, trying to see what she sees, trying to understand what makes her sit at this window every night, searching for something she seems never to find. After a long while, she turns toward me and smiles.

"My daughter Josephine will come to visit one day soon," she tells me. "You should meet her. You would like her."

I shake my head and look down at the floor. I decide not to tell her that my mother has long since died. "I'm sure I would," I murmur.

"I think I will rest," she says. She looks at me without a glint of recognition. "Thank you for coming. I have enjoyed our visit. I will show you out now."

"Mamie," I try.

"No, no," she says. "My *mamie* does not live here. She lives in Paris. Near the tower. But I will tell her you say hello."

I open my mouth to reply, but no words come out. Mamie is herding me toward the door.

I'm over the threshold and the door has almost closed on me when Mamie suddenly cracks it open once more and stares at me, long and hard. "You must go to Paris, Hope," she says solemnly. "You must. I am very tired now, and it is nearly time for me to sleep." And then the door is closed, and I'm staring at a characterless palette of pale blue paint.

I stand there for so long, dumbstruck, that I don't even notice the nurse, Karen, approach me.

"Miss McKenna-Smith?" she says.

I turn and look at her blankly.

"Are you okay, ma'am?" she asks.

I nod, slowly. "I think I'm going to Paris."

"Well . . . that's nice," Karen says hesitantly. She obviously thinks I've lost it, and I don't blame her. "Um, when?"

"As soon as I can," I tell her. I smile. "I need to go."

"Okay," she says, still looking bewildered.

"I'm going to Paris," I repeat to myself.

Chapter *Ten*

Cape Codder Cookies

INGREDIENTS

1 stick butter, softened
2 cups packed brown sugar
2 large eggs
½ tsp. vanilla extract
2 Tbsp. heavy cream

3 cups flour
2 tsp. baking soda
½ tsp. salt
1 cup dried cranberries
1 cup white chocolate chips

DIRECTIONS

1. Preheat oven to 375 degrees.

2. In a large bowl, cream together butter and brown sugar using electric mixer. Beat in eggs, vanilla, and cream.

3. Sift together flour, baking soda, and salt, and add to the butter mixture, approximately one cup at a time. Beat just until combined.

4. Add cranberries and chocolate chips. Stir to distribute evenly.

5. Drop heaping teaspoons onto a greased cookie sheet with room to spread. Bake 10–13 minutes. Cool for 5 minutes on baking sheet, then move to a wire rack.

MAKES APPROXIMATELY 50 COOKIES

Rose

The sunset that night was brighter than usual, and as Rose watched the eastern horizon, she thought about how the vivid illumination of the sky was one of God's most marvelous tricks. She remembered, with a clarity that surprised her, sitting at the window of her family's apartment on rue du Général Camou, watching the sun set in the west, over the Champ-de-Mars. It had always seemed to her that the view at sundown was the most beautiful blend of the magic of God and the magic of man; a beautiful light show surrounding a glittering, mysterious tower of steel. She used to imagine that she was a princess in a castle, and that this light show was being put on just for her. She was sure that hers was the best window in the city, perhaps the best view in all the world.

But that was back when she was still terribly proud of her country, proud to be Parisian. The Eiffel Tower seemed to be a symbol of everything that made her beloved city great.

Later, she would hate what it stood for. She marveled at how quickly love and pride could transform into something dark and inescapable.

Rose watched the Cape Cod sky flame orange and then fade to pink, and finally to the brilliant blue that made her feel at home, so far away here from the place where she'd begun her journey. Although the sunset itself looked different here than it did in Paris—a trick of the atmosphere, she supposed—the deep cerulean twilight was just the same as it had been all those years ago. It brought her comfort to know that while everything else in the world could change, the ending to God's light show remained eternally the same.

Rose had the sense, as she sat at the window, that something important was happening. She was having trouble placing the feeling, though. It seemed that someone had told her something vital, but who? And when? She couldn't recall having any visitors.

The doorbell rang, interrupting her wisps of thoughts, and

with one last, reluctant look at the North Star above the crest of the horizon, she moved slowly to her front door. She wondered when this body had begun to fail her; she could remember moving on her feet, light as air, graceful as a breeze. It felt like just yesterday. But now, her body felt to her like a sack of bones that she had to drag, with effort, everywhere she went.

At the door, she found herself staring at the kind nurse, the one whose name she found impossible to remember. But she had a face that could be trusted, Rose knew.

"Hi, Rose," the nurse said, in a gentle voice that reminded Rose that people here felt sorry for her. She didn't want their pity. She didn't deserve it. "Are you coming down to dinner? The other three ladies at your table miss you in the dining room."

Rose knew this wasn't true. She couldn't, for the life of her, remember the names or even the faces of the three women she ate three meals a day with.

"No, I will stay here," Rose told the nurse. "Thank you."

"How about I bring you a tray in your room?" the nurse asked. "We're having meat loaf tonight."

"That would be fine," Rose said.

The nurse hesitated. "So you had a visit from your granddaughter today?"

Rose struggled to remember. "Why yes, I did," she said quickly, because the nurse seemed so sure of it, and of course she didn't want anyone to know that she was losing her memory.

The nurse seemed encouraged by Rose's reply, and Rose, for a moment, felt a little guilty for deceiving her.

"How nice," the nurse said. "She's been coming more often lately. That's wonderful."

"Yes, of course," Rose said, wondering when her granddaughter had been there. She supposed the nurse would have no reason to lie to her, and she felt a sudden, instant pang of regret that she could not bring to mind the visits. She would have loved to remember a visit with Hope.

The nurse patted Rose on the shoulder and continued in the

same gentle voice. "It sounds like she has an exciting trip planned," the nurse said.

"A trip?" Mamie asked.

"Oh yes, didn't she tell you?" the nurse said, brightening. "She's going to Paris."

And suddenly, Rose remembered. Hope coming to see her. Annie's confusion when Rose handed Hope the list of names earlier in the week. The concern etched in Hope's face just this afternoon. She closed her eyes for a moment, the revelations washing over her, until she heard the nurse's voice, far away, calling her back.

"Rose? Mrs. McKenna? Are you all right?"

Rose forced her eyes open and feigned a smile. She had become skilled at faking happiness over the years. It was, she thought, a terrible talent to have.

"I am sorry," Rose said. "I was just thinking about my granddaughter and her trip."

The nurse looked relieved. Rose knew that the real explanation—that her mind was suddenly back in 1942—would frighten the woman, whose kind eyes gave away the fact that she'd never had to endure the kind of loss that shatters one's soul forever. Rose recognized that kind of loss in other people because she saw it in her own eyes every time she gazed at her reflection.

The nurse left to go prepare a dinner tray, and Rose closed the door behind her and drifted to the window. She stared into the eastern sky, dotted with a sprinkling of twilight's first stars, but the sky looked different to her now than it had before. Beyond the darkness at the horizon, across the vast ocean, somewhere to the east, lay Paris, the city where it all began, the city where it would all end. Rose would never return there, but for the past to be completed, she knew that Hope had to go.

The end was coming, Rose knew. She felt it in her bones, just like she'd felt it that summer of 1942, before *they* came. When she'd arrived on American shores late that year, gliding into New York past the Statue of Liberty, she'd made herself a promise to put the past behind her forever. But the Alzheimer's nibbling at her brain, twisting her timeline, had brought it raging back, uninvited.

Now, when Rose awoke each morning, she had trouble holding on to the present. Some days, she woke up in 1936, or 1940, or 1942 again. Things were as clear to her as if they'd just happened, and for scant, frozen moments in time, her life lay ahead of her, rather than behind. She imagined tucking them away in the beautiful jewelry box her own *mamie* had given her for her thirteenth birthday, turning the lock, and throwing the key into the endless depths of the Seine.

But now that the present was blurred and uneven, it seemed that that beautiful box of memories, closed now for nearly seventy years, contained the only moments of clarity Rose could find in this life. She sometimes wondered whether the willful forgetting had, in fact, caused the recollections to survive entirely intact, the way that storing a document in an airtight, darkened container for years could keep it from disintegrating.

To her surprise, Rose realized that she found comfort in the moments she'd hidden from for so many years. Slipping into the past was like watching a slow-motion picture show of the life she knew she would soon leave behind. And because of the gaps in her recollection, there were days when she could bask in the past without immediately feeling the crushing blow of its inevitable outcome.

She loved seeing her mother, her father, her sisters, and her brothers in those brief journeys into the past. She loved feeling her *mamie*'s hand wrapped around hers; she loved hearing her baby sister's tinkling laughter; she loved breathing in the sweet, yeasty scent of her parents' bakery. Now she lived for the days when she could slip back in time and see the ones she had vowed never to speak of again. For that's where her heart remained; she had left it behind, on those foreign shores, so long ago.

She knew now, as her own twilight closed in around her, that she was very wrong to have tried so hard to forget, for it was the key to who she was. But it was too late. She had left everything behind in that terrible, beautiful past. And there it would forever remain.

Chapter *Eleven*

~

As I drive home in silence that night, my mind is spinning. *I'm going to Paris.*

At the traffic light on Main, I pull out my cell phone and, before I can stop myself, dial Gavin's cell number.

I let it ring once before I realize how foolish I'm being. I quickly hit End. Why would Gavin care that I'm going to Paris? He's been helpful, but I'm being presumptuous in assuming that my plans matter to him at all.

The light turns green, and as I put my foot on the gas, my phone rings, startling me. I look at the caller ID and can feel my cheeks heating up as I realize it says *Gavin Keyes.*

"Um, hello?" I answer tentatively.

"Hope?" His voice is deep and warm, and I'm annoyed at myself for feeling instantly comforted.

"Um, yeah, hi," I say.

"Did you just call?"

"It was nothing." I can feel my cheeks grow even hotter. "I don't even know why I was calling," I mumble.

He's silent for a moment. "Did you go see your grandmother?"

"How did you know?"

"I didn't." He pauses and adds, "Are you going to Paris?"

"I think so," I reply in a small voice.

"Good," he says immediately, as if he was expecting me to say this. "Listen, if you need someone to help you keep the bakery open while you're gone—"

I cut him off. "Gavin, that's so kind, but there's no way that would work."

"Why not?"

"Well, for one thing, you've never run a bakery before, have you?"

"I'm a quick learner."

I smile. "And besides, you have your own job."

"It wouldn't be a problem to take a few days off. If there are any emergencies, I can always take care of them after the bakery closes."

I'm not accustomed to people caring, people helping me. It makes me uneasy, and I'm not sure how to reply. "Thanks," I finally say. "But I could never ask you to do that."

"Hope, you okay?" Gavin asks.

"I'm okay," I tell him, but I'm pretty sure I'm lying.

A week later, wondering whether I'm mad to be doing such a thing, I board an Aer Lingus flight from Boston to Paris, via Dublin, the cheapest flight I could find on such short notice.

Annie was so thrilled that I'd decided to go that she didn't even give me a hard time about her having to spend an extra few days at her father's house. She'd asked to come along to Paris, of course, but she had seemed to understand when I'd told her that I could only afford one ticket.

"Besides, Mamie only asked *you* to go," Annie had mumbled, looking at her feet.

"Because she needs you here with her," I'd told my daughter.

I'd decided to leave on a Saturday night so that I'd only have to close the bakery a total of three days; we're closed every Monday anyhow. Still, it feels like an eternity to be gone, especially with the financial storm brewing. I don't know if and when the investors are coming to check out the bakery, because I haven't talked to Matt since I turned down his offer to loan me money. I know he was hurt, but I can't deal with that now. It's possible I'm making a huge mistake, but I know I couldn't refuse this trip.

We have two orders to fill while I'm gone—both regular weekly orders for two hotels by the beach—and I'd reluctantly accepted Gavin's offer to drive Annie to deliver the muffins, which I'd baked in advance and frozen. She would need to defrost them before school on Monday morning, and after school, Gavin would take her to complete the deliveries and then drop her at Rob's house.

Eleven hours after taking off from Boston and connecting through Dublin, I watch from the window as we break through the blanket of clouds covering the Paris sky and descend over the city. I can't make out any landmarks—I suppose I'll see them from the ground soon enough—but I can see the sapphire ribbon of the Seine River snaking across the terrain, as well as alternating patches of green grass and fiery-hued trees stretching across the countryside beyond the urban area.

This was once Mamie's home, I think as we come in for a landing. How strange it must have been to leave all of this behind, never to return.

On the ground, I breeze through the tubular glass halls of Charles de Gaulle International, go through customs, and wait in the line for taxis, which I'm surprised to realize are mostly luxury cars in France. I wait my turn, climb into a Mercedes, and hand the driver the address of the hotel I booked on Travelocity; I don't trust myself to correctly pronounce it aloud.

It takes us thirty minutes to emerge from a series of industrial suburbs into the outskirts of Paris itself. We pass by a huge sports complex, and I'm struck suddenly by the recollection of what I'd read online, about the massive roundup in 1942, where thousands of Jews were taken to a sports stadium before being deported to concentration camps. I doubt this is that stadium—it appears too modern—but the dark image stays with me as my driver weaves expertly around traffic, takes a harrowing left on a street called rue de la Verrerie, and screeches to a halt in front of a white building with big block letters identifying it as the Hôtel de Mille Etoiles. I look up at the wrought-iron balconies surrounding french doors on the second floor and smile. Somehow, Paris is exactly as I'd pictured it. I also have the sense that in this neighborhood at least, it hasn't changed much in the last century. It makes me wonder whether Mamie ever walked by this same building, marveled at these same balconies, wished she could see through the wispy curtains draping the same french doors. It's strange for me to think of her here, as a girl not much older than Annie.

After checking in, I take a quick shower and throw on jeans, flat boots, and a sweater. Armed with directions from the concierge, I walk the few blocks toward rue Geoffroy-l'Asnier, where I know the Mémorial de la Shoah is located.

Paris in October is crisp and beautiful, I realize. I've never been here before, of course, so there's little to compare it against, but the streets seem quiet and peaceful. I'm fascinated by the way the old mixes with the new here; cobblestone meets cement at some corners, and on others, stores selling electronics or high fashion inhabit buildings that look like they're hundreds of years old. Having spent most of my life in Massachusetts, I'm accustomed to history being naturally interwoven with modern life, but it feels different here, perhaps because the history is much older, or perhaps because there's so much more of it.

I can smell baking bread, and changing autumnal leaves, and the faint odor of fire, as I walk along, and I breathe in deeply, because it's a blend I'm not used to. Little arched doorways, bicycles propped against stone walls, and nearly hidden gated gardens remind me that I'm in a place foreign to me, but there's something about Paris that feels very familiar. I wonder for the first time if a sense of place can be passed down through the blood. I dismiss the thought, but despite the fact that the streets are unfamiliar and winding, I easily find my way to the Holocaust museum.

After going though a metal detector outside the stout, somber building, I cross through an open-air, gray courtyard, past a monument with the names of the concentration camps, beneath a metal Star of David, and enter the museum through the doors ahead. The woman at the front desk, who fortunately speaks English, suggests that I first try the computers opposite the desk, which are the first stop for guests seeking family members. On these too, as expected, I find the same information I found on the Internet. The names on my grandmother's list, minus Alain.

I return to the desk and explain to the woman that I'm looking for a person whose name doesn't appear in the records, and for information about what actually happened to the people whose names I have found. She nods and directs me to the elevator down the hall.

"Take that to the fourth level," she says. "There, you will find a reading room. Ask at the desk for help."

I nod, thank her, and follow her directions upstairs.

The reading room is home to computers and long tables on the lower level and rows of books and files on the second level, beneath a high ceiling that lets light pour in. I approach the desk, where a woman greets me in French and switches to English as soon as I ask, "Can you help me find some people, please?"

"Of course, madame," she says. "How can I help you?"

I give her the names from Mamie's list, along with their years of birth, and I explain that I can't locate Alain. She nods and disappears for a few minutes. She returns with several pages of loose records.

"Here is all we have on these people," she says. "Like you said, we cannot find Alain on any list of the deported."

"What could that mean?" I ask.

"There could be many reasons for this. As complete as our records are, there are occasionally people who have not been properly recorded, especially children. They were lost in the chaos."

She hands me the documents she has, and I sit down to read over them. For the next few minutes, I try to read the notations, some handwritten, some typed, all of them in French. It's not until I flip to the third document she's given me, a census page, that my eyes widen.

There, in tilted handwriting, on a list stamped with the word *recensement,* is a 1936 listing of the Picard family of Paris, and among their children is a daughter, Rose, born 1925.

As caught up as I'd been in finding out the fate of the names on Mamie's list, and as much as I'd begun to believe that they were indeed her family, it's not until I see my grandmother's first name and her birth year scrawled in indelible ink that it finally sinks in.

My heart pounds as I stare at the page.

I read over the scant details. It appears that, like the deportation information I'd found online said, the man who may be Mamie's father, Albert, was a doctor. His *femme,* his wife, Cecile, is listed *sans profession*. She must have stayed home with the children. The children—the *fils* and *filles*—including Rose, are listed, all but Danielle, the youngest, who wasn't born until 1937, the year after the census. Alain's name is on the list too. He was just as real as the rest of them.

I go through all the documents, which take me a long time to read, both because my eyes keep tearing up and because I need to keep referring to the English-French dictionary I've brought with me. At the end, I'm no closer to finding out what happened to Alain than I was before, nor am I any closer to finding out what happened after the family was deported. None of the copies of deportation documents are annotated with any additional information. The last record of everyone in the family—except for Rose and Alain, for whom no records exist—is that they were all deported on convoys bound for Auschwitz.

I take the documents back to the desk, where the woman who had helped me earlier looks up and smiles at me.

"Did you have luck?"

I nod and feel my eyes fill with tears. "I think it's my grandmother's family," I say softly. "But I can't tell what happened to them after they were deported."

She nods solemnly. "Of the seventy-six thousand taken in France, only two thousand survived. It is very likely that they perished, madame. I am sorry."

I nod, and it's not until I draw in a deep breath that I realize I'm trembling.

"Did you find the name you were looking for?" she asks after a moment.

I shake my head. "Only on the census form. There's no record of an Alain Picard being arrested or deported."

She chews her lip for a moment. "*Alors.* There is another person who may be able to help you. She is a researcher here, and she speaks some English. Let me see if she is available."

After a few brief phone calls in French, she tells me that Carole, from the research library, will help me in thirty minutes. She suggests waiting in the museum itself, where I'm welcome to browse the permanent exhibition.

I walk down the stairs into the nearly deserted exhibit hall and am immediately struck by the number of photographs and documents lining the long, narrow room. In the middle of the room, a big screen plays a film in French, and as I listen to a man's voice talking about what I assume is the Holocaust, I drift to the first wall on the left and am heartened to realize that all the exhibits are captioned in English as well as French. At the end of the room, an eerie image of train tracks to nowhere is projected on a big, blank wall, and I'm reminded of the dream I had just after Mamie gave me the list.

For a half hour, I'm lost in my own thoughts as I read testimony after testimony of the beginning of the war, the loss of Jewish rights in France and across Europe, and about the first deportations out of the country.

Not only did these things happen in my grandmother's lifetime, but they may very well have happened to the people she loved most in the world. I close my eyes and realize I'm breathing hard. My heart is still thudding double time in my chest when I hear a woman's voice in front of me.

"Madame McKenna-Smith?"

I snap my eyes open. The woman standing there is about my age, with brown hair pulled into a bun, and blue eyes rimmed with expression lines. She's wearing dark jeans and a white blouse.

"Yes, that's me," I say. I hastily add, "Sorry, I mean, *Oui, madame.*"

She smiles. "It is all right. I speak some English. I am Carole Didot. Would you like to come with me?"

I nod and follow her through the rest of the exhibit, where we walk briskly past another series of videos, and more walls full of documents and information. She leads me out through a hall filled with photos of children; they go on as far as the eye can see. I stop and lean forward to read one of the captions at eye level.

Rachel Fournier, 1937–1942, it reads. In the photograph, a dark-haired little girl grins into the camera, her hair done up in pigtails tied with ribbons. She's clutching a big rubber ball and smiling directly at the camera.

"These are the French children whose lives were lost," Carole says softly.

"My God," I murmur. This hall hits me even harder than the chilling photographs of death I'd seen in the other room. As I gaze dazedly at the photos, I can't help but think of my own daughter. Had fate placed us in a different country, in a different time, she could have been one of these little girls on the wall.

"Nearly eleven thousand children from France died in the Shoah," Carole said, reading my expression. "This hall always reminds me of all that could have been and never was."

Her words ring in my ears as I follow her to an elevator, where she pushes the button for the fourth floor. We ride up in silence as I think about Mamie's family and all that was lost.

Carole leads me into a modern office with two chairs facing a desk piled high in books and papers. Out the window, I can see a church tower over a series of apartments, and on the wall are pictures drawn by children that say *Mama*. Carole gestures to one of the chairs and takes a seat behind her computer.

"So what makes you come all the way to Paris?" she asks as she jiggles her mouse and hits a few keys on her keyboard.

I briefly tell her Mamie's story and that I think the names she's given me were family members who'd been lost in the Holocaust. I explain that I've found all but Alain, for whom no records seem to exist. I also explain that I can't figure out what happened to my grandmother; there's no record of a Rose Picard in the deportation documents either.

"But your grandmother, you say she escaped Paris before arrest, no?" Carole asks.

I nod. "Yes. I mean, I think so. She's never explained. And now she has Alzheimer's."

Carole shakes her head. "So the past, it is nearly lost for her."

I nod. "I just want to know what happened. She wanted me to find out what became of her family. If I go home without an answer about Alain, I'm afraid it will break her heart."

"I am sorry we cannot be more help, but if he is not in the records, he is not in the records."

My heart sinks. "So that's it?" I ask in a small voice. "I may never find out what happened to him?"

Carole hesitates. "There is one more chance," she says.

"There is?"

"There is a man," she says, but her voice trails off and she doesn't finish her thought. Instead, she flips through an old-fashioned Rolodex, pauses, and picks up her handset to dial a number. After a moment, she says something in rapid French, glances at me, says something else, and then hangs up.

"Voilà," she says. She jots something down on a piece of paper. "Take this."

I take the piece of paper from her and glance down to see a name, an address, and a series of four numbers and the letter *A*.

"This is Olivier Berr," she says. She smiles slightly. "He is a legend."

I look at her questioningly.

"He has ninety-three years," she goes on. "He is a survivor of the Shoah, and he has made it his life's work to make a listing of all the Jewish people of Paris who were lost, and all those who returned."

I stare in disbelief. "His lists are different than yours?"

"*Oui,*" she replies. "They are from the people themselves, the people who were in the camps, the people who came to the synagogues after the war, the people who walk around still with the scars of loss. Our records are the official ones. His records are the verbal ones, which sometimes are more revealing."

"Olivier Berr," I repeat softly.

"He says you may come now. The number there is the code to his front door. He says to come in."

I nod, my heart thudding. "How do I get there?"

She gives me walking directions, explaining that it may take less time to go there by foot than to find a taxi. "Plus, you will see the Louvre and cross the Seine at the Pont des Arts," she says. "You should see some of Paris on your mission."

I smile at this, suddenly aware that I haven't even bothered to look for the Eiffel Tower yet. "Thank you," I say. I stand, not sure whether to feel disappointed about the lack of records here, or hopeful because this Olivier Berr might be able to help.

"Bonne chance," Carole says with a smile. She reaches out to shake my hand. "Good luck," she says, looking me in the eye.

Carole Didot's walking directions take me through a few side streets, onto the crowded rue de Rivoli. I pass the Gothic facade of the Hôtel de Ville on my left and continue down a strip of storefronts—H&M, Zara, Celio, Etam—that would be at home on Newbury Street in Boston. Several French flags whisper in the breeze, their crisp red, white, and blue blocks of color saluting as I walk by. The few trees that dot the sidewalk have blushed deep red with the coming of autumn and have begun to drop their leaves on the sidewalks, where a steady stampede of people tramples them.

I do as Carole directed and turn left just as I begin passing the enormous Louvre museum on my left. I emerge into a sprawling square surrounded on all four sides by the walls of the museum itself, and for a moment, I stop in my tracks, breathless. I don't know much of the history of France, but I remember reading that the Louvre used to be a palace, and as I look around me, I can almost imagine a seventeenth-century monarch striding through the square, trailed by his attendants.

Emerging on the other side, I see the pedestrian bridge Carole told me about. She had explained that the rails of the bridge are lined with padlocks, put there by lovers to declare the sealing of their relationships. It's a romantic thought, but I know that padlock or not, relationships are temporary, even when you believe in them with all your heart.

I look to the right as I cross the bridge and smile to see the tip of the Eiffel Tower soaring over rooftops in the distance on the other side of the river. I've seen it in photographs a thousand times, but seeing it in person for the first time that reminds me that I'm really, truly here, thousands of miles away, across an ocean from home. I miss Annie terribly at that moment.

It's not until I'm halfway across the wooden bridge that I'm struck with a sudden sense of déjà vu, as if I've been here before. It takes me a moment to realize why, and when I do, I stop in my tracks so abruptly that the woman behind me runs directly into me. She mumbles something in French, shoots me a withering glance, and makes an exaggerated, wide loop around me. I ignore her and turn in a slow circle, my eyes wide. To the right, beyond the glittering Seine, the tip of the Eiffel Tower slices through the blue of the sky in the distance. Behind me, the Louvre museum looms, palatial and enormous, on the river's bank. To my left, I can see an island connected to two bridges. I quickly count the arches. Seven on the left bridge; five on the right bridge. And ahead, the building Carole had called the Institut de France looks a lot like a second palace, as if it and the Louvre were once halves of the same royal kingdom.

My heart pounds, and I can hear Mamie's voice in my ears, telling me the fairy tale she repeated so often that I knew it by heart by the time I was Annie's age.

"Every day, the prince walked across the wooden bridge of love to see his princess. The great palace lay behind him, and ahead of him was the domed castle at the entrance to the princess's kingdom. He had to cross a great moat to get to his one true love, and to his left, there were two bridges leading to the heart of the city—one with seven arches, and one with five. To his right, a giant sword cut through the sky, warning him of the danger that lay ahead. Still, he came each day and braved that danger because he loved the princess. He said that all the danger in the world could not keep him away from her. Every day, the princess sat at her window and listened for his footsteps, because she knew he would never disappoint her. He loved her, and when he promised he would come for her, he always kept his word."

I'd always thought that Mamie's stories were simply fairy tales she'd heard as a little girl, but for the first time, I find myself wondering whether she'd made them up herself and set them in her beloved Paris. I shake my head and begin walking again, but my knees feel wobbly beneath me. I imagine my grandmother as a teenage girl, walking across this same bridge, taking in the same buildings, the same current beneath her, imagining that a prince was coming for her one day. Had her footsteps fallen where mine fall now, in this very same place, some seventy years earlier? Had she stood on this bridge and looked for the stars to appear to the east, over the island in the middle of the Seine, the way she waits for them to appear now from her window each night? Had she regretted leaving it behind forever?

As I walk on, I think of my favorite of her tales, the one in which the prince tells the princess that as long as there are stars in the sky, he will love her.

"One day," the prince said to the princess, "I will take you across a great sea to see a queen whose torch illuminates the world, keeping all of her subjects safe and free."

When I was a girl, I used to cling to those words, to imagine that one day, I too would find a prince who would rescue me from my mother's coldness. I used to imagine climbing on this prince's white horse with him—because of course in my imagination, the prince had a white horse—and going away forever to that fairy-tale kingdom with the queen who kept everyone safe.

But now I'm thirty-six, and I know better. There are no dashing, heroic princes waiting to save me. There is no magical queen to protect me. In the end, you can only rely on yourself. I wonder how old Mamie was when she learned those same truths.

Suddenly, although I have the sense I'm being cradled by my grandmother's past, I feel more alone than ever.

Rue Visconti is dark and narrow, more a long alleyway than a proper street. The sidewalks are slender ribbons on each side, and a lone bicycle propped against a black doorway makes me think of an old-fashioned postcard. I pass a few storefronts and make my way down nearly to the end, where I finally see number 24, a pair of huge black double doors under an arch. I enter the code Carole gave me—48A51—on the keypad to the right, and when the door buzzes, I push it inward. When I make it from the cool darkness of the arched courtyard up to the second floor of the building, the door is already open. I rap lightly against the doorframe anyhow, and from the depths of the apartment, a deep, froggy voice calls, *"Entrez-vous! Entrez-vous, madame!"*

I walk in, close the door lightly behind me, and make my way through a narrow hallway lined by bookcases, all of which are overflowing with old, leather-bound volumes. I emerge into a sunlit room where I see a white-haired, stoop-shouldered man standing near the window, gazing out at the street below. He turns as I enter, and I'm surprised at how lined his face is; it appears as if he's lived through hundreds of years of history, instead of just the ninety-three years Carole Didot had promised. I approach to shake his hand, and he looks at me oddly.

"Ah, an American," are the first words he says to me. He smiles then, and I'm struck by how bright his green eyes seem; they're the eyes of a young man and appear out of place housed in his sunken features. "Madame Didot did not tell me you are American. In Paris, we greet with *deux bisous,* two kisses on the cheek, my dear." He demonstrates, leaning forward to kiss me lightly on each cheek. I can feel myself blushing.

"I'm sorry," I mumble.

"There is nothing to be sorry about," he says. "Your American customs are quite charming." He gestures to a small table with two wooden chairs, which is situated near the window. "Come, sit," he says. He waits until I'm seated, offers me a cup of tea, and when I decline, he sits down with me. "I am Olivier Berr."

"I'm Hope McKenna-Smith. Thank you for having me here on such short notice," I say slowly. I'm trying to be conscious of both his age and the fact that English isn't his first language.

"It is no trouble," he says. "It is always a pleasure to have a visit from a pretty girl." He smiles and pats my hand. "I understand you search for some information."

I nod and take a deep breath. "Yes, sir. My grandmother is

from Paris. I just learned recently that her family may have died in the Holocaust. I think they were Jewish."

He looks at me for a moment. "You learned this only recently?"

Embarrassed, I struggle to explain. "Well, she never spoke of it."

"You were raised in another religion." It is a statement, not a question.

I nod. "Catholicism."

He nods slowly. "This is not entirely unusual. Leaving the past behind in this manner. *Mais,* in her heart, I suspect, your grandmother may still consider herself *juive.*"

I tell him briefly what happened on Rosh Hashanah, with the crusts of the Star Pie.

He smiles. "*Judaïsme* is not just a religion, but a state of the heart and of the soul. I suspect perhaps all religions are this way, for those who truly believe in them." He pauses. "You have come here today for answers."

"Yes, sir."

"About what became of her family."

"Yes, sir. She'd never spoken of them before."

Again, he nods knowingly. "You have with you their names?"

"Yes," I say. I pull out a copy of Mamie's list and hand it to him. As his clear eyes scan the page, I add quickly, "But Alain, her brother, isn't in any Holocaust registry."

He looks up and smiles. "Ah yes. But my registries are different." He stands, trembling a little on his feet, and then he gestures with a crooked finger. He moves slowly, one foot in front of the other in a shuffle, toward the hallway lined with books. "I was twenty years of age when the Second World War began, twenty-two years of age when they began taking us away, right from the streets of France. More than seventy-six thousand *juifs* were taken from France, most never to return."

I shake my head, suddenly mute.

"I was at Auschwitz," he continues, and suddenly, he stops

his slow shuffle to the hall, pausing as if the memory itself holds him back. After a moment, he moves again. "More than sixty thousand were sent there from France. Did you know?" He stops speaking again for a moment, and then he coughs. "After *la libération,* I returned to find everyone gone. All my friends. My neighbors."

"What about your family?" I ask.

"All of them, dead." His voice is flat. "My wife. My son. Mother. Father. Sisters. Brother. Aunts. Uncles. Cousins. Grandparents. Everyone. When I came home to Paris, I came home to nothing. To no one."

"I'm so sorry," I murmur. The enormity of it begins to hit me. I've never met a concentration camp survivor before, and as the images from the Mémorial de la Shoah play themselves over again in my mind, I blink a few times, feeling numb. The atrocities in the pictures had actually happened to this kind man before me. I can feel tears in my eyes. I blink them away before he notices.

He waves a hand, dismissing my words. "It is the past. Not for you to be sorry about, mademoiselle. The world you live in today is very different, and I am glad." He shuffles a little farther and regards his wall of books solemnly. He touches a gnarled finger to one book spine, then another. "The only place I knew to go when I returned was to the synagogue I had attended as a boy. But it had been destroyed. It was a shell, no longer a place."

I'm frozen as I watch him scan the books. He pulls one out, reads something inside, and then returns it to the shelf.

"When I realized that the ones I loved were never coming home, I began to think about the great tragedy, not just of their deaths but of the loss of their legacies," he continues. "For when you take away an entire family, and they all perish, who will tell their stories?"

"No one," I murmur.

"*Précisément.* And when that occurs, it is as if their lives have been lost twice over. That is when I began creating my own records." He reaches for another book, and this time, his eyes light up and he smiles. He flips through a few pages and stops at one. He's silent for a moment as he reads.

"Your own records?" I ask.

He nods and shows me the page he's stopped on. I see a cursive scrawl across neat, lined pages that are yellowed at the edges. "My lists of the lost." He smiles and adds, "And of the found. And of the stories that go with them."

I take a step back and look in awe at his bookshelves. "All of these books are your lists?"

"Yes."

"You compiled them yourself?" I look around in disbelief.

"It filled my time in those early days," he says. "It was how I stopped living in the sadness. I began visiting synagogues every day, looking at their records, talking to every person I could meet."

"But how did you put together so much information?"

"To everyone I met, I asked them for the names of anyone they knew who had been lost, and anyone they knew who had survived. Family, friends, neighbors, it did not matter. No piece of information was small or *insignifiant*. Each one represented a life lost or a life saved. Over the years, I have written and rewritten their memories, organized them into volumes, followed the leads they gave me, and sought out the people who survived."

"My God," I murmur.

"Each person who survived a camp," he continues, "has many stories to tell. Those people are often the key to who was lost, and how. For others, the only key we have is that they never returned. But their names are here, and what details we do know."

"But why aren't these lists in the Mémorial de la Shoah?" I ask.

"These are not the kind of records they keep," he says. "They keep official records, the ones made by the governments. These are not official. And for now, I want my lists with me, because I am always finding new names, and it is important to keep up my life's work. When I die, these books will go to the memorial. It is my hope that they too will keep them alive and, in doing so, keep the people who live in these pages alive forever."

"This is amazing, Monsieur Berr," I say.

He nods, smiles slightly. "It is not so amazing. Amazing would be to live in a world where there was no need to make lists of the dead." Before I can reply, he puts a finger on the page of his open book and says calmly, "I have found them."

I look at him, confused.

"Your family," he clarifies.

My eyes widen. "Wait, you found the names? Already?"

He chuckles. "I have lived inside these lists for many years, madame. I know my way." He closes his eyes for a moment and then focuses on the page before him. "The Picard family," he says. *"Dix, rue du Général Camou, septième arrondissement."*

"What does that mean?"

"It was your grandmother's address," he says. "Number ten on the street of Général Camou. I tried to include addresses wherever I could." He smiles slightly and adds, "Your grandmother, she must have lived in a nice place, in the shadow of the Tour Eiffel."

I swallow hard. "What else does it say?"

He reads ahead for a moment before speaking. "The parents were Albert and Cecile. Albert, he was a doctor. The children were Helene, Rose, Claude, Alain, David, Danielle."

"Rose is my grandmother," I whisper.

He looks up from the book with a smile. "Then I will have to change my list."

"Why?"

"She is listed as presumed dead, the fifteenth of July, 1942, in Paris." He squints at something on the page. "She went out that night and never returned, according to my notations. The next day, her family was all taken."

I can't seem to muster words. I just stare at him.

"The sixteenth of July, 1942," he continues. His voice has softened now. "The first day of the Vel' d'Hiv roundup."

My throat is dry. It's the massive arrest of thirteen thousand Parisians that I'd read about online.

"I was there too," he adds softly. "My family was taken that day."

I stare. "I'm so sorry."

He shakes his head. "It was the end of the life I once knew," he says softly. "The beginning of the life I now live."

Silence descends. "What happened?" I ask finally.

He looks into the distance. "They came for us before dawn. I did not know to expect them. I did not know it could happen. As I look back, I realize I should have. We all should have. But sometimes in life, it is easier to believe things will be all right. We were blind to the truth."

"But how could you have known?" I ask.

He nods. "It is easy to look back and question, but you are correct; it would have been impossible to know what was coming. For us, for my wife and my son, just three years old, we were taken with many others to the Vélodrome d'Hiver in the *quinzième,* just near the Eiffel Tower and very near the Seine. There were maybe seven thousand, maybe eight thousand people there. It was hard to count them all. It was a sea of people. There was no food. Hardly any water. We were packed together like fish in a can. Some people killed themselves. I saw a mother smother her baby, and I thought she was crazy, but by the end of the third day, I understood that she was merciful. Later, as she wailed, I watched a guard shoot her. I remember thinking quite clearly, *She is lucky.*"

His voice is flat, but his eyes are watery as he goes on. "We stayed there for five days before they moved us. On the fourth day, my son, my Nicolas, he died in my arms. And before we were taken away to Drancy, and then to Auschwitz, my wife and

I were separated, but I could see in her eyes that she was already gone. Losing Nicolas had taken her will to live. I was told later that she did not pass the initial selection at Auschwitz when she arrived, and that she did not cry, not once, as they led her away."

"I'm so sorry," I murmur, but he waves dismissively.

"It was long ago," he says. I watch as he turns back to his book, studying the page that he said contained the records I was looking for.

"*Alors,*" he says. He blinks a few times. "Your family. The Picards of rue du Général Camou. The youngest two, David and Danielle, they died at Auschwitz. Upon arrival. David was eight years of age. Danielle was five."

"God," I breathe. "They were just babies."

Monsieur Berr nods. "Most of the young ones never returned. They were taken to the gas chamber immediately because the Germans considered them useless." He swallows and continues reading. "Helene, age eighteen, and Claude, age sixteen, died at Auschwitz, in 1942. So too did the mother, Cecile. The father, Albert, died in Auschwitz at the end of 1943." He pauses and adds softly, "It says here that he worked in the crematorium, until he became ill in the winter. That must have been terrible. He knew his own fate."

I feel tears in my eyes, and this time, it's too late to blink them back. Monsieur Berr is silent as the rivers run down my cheeks. It takes a few moments for his words to fully settle into my soul. "All of them died there?" I whisper. "At Auschwitz?" He meets my eye and nods slowly, a look of pity on his face. "What about Alain? How did he die?"

For the first time today, Monsieur Berr looks surprised. "Die? But he is the one who gave me this information."

I stare at him. "I don't understand."

He squints at the page again. "Yes, this interview is dated the sixth of June, 2005. I remember him. A very nice man. Kind eyes. You can always know a person by his eyes. He was playing chess with another survivor, a man I knew. That is how I came upon him."

"Wait," I say. My heart is thudding as I struggle to understand what he's saying. "You're telling me that Alain Picard, my grandmother's brother, is still alive? And that you talked to him?"

Monsieur Berr looks concerned. "*Bien sur,* he *was* alive in 2005. I do not know what became of him after that. He was never deported, but he suffered during the war. Everyone did. He told me that he went into hiding, and for nearly three years, he had very little food. A man, his old piano teacher, gave him a place to sleep on the coldest winter nights, but the man was afraid of putting his own family in danger. So Alain, he slept on the streets, and sometimes, the nuns at the church would give him meals. He would be eighty now, if he is still alive. Then again, I am ninety-three, my dear. And I am not giving up anytime soon."

He smiles at this. I'm too stunned to reply.

"My grandmother's brother," I murmur. "Do you know where he is?"

Monsieur Berr reaches for a pad of paper. "Do you have a pen?" he asks. I nod and fumble in my purse. He jots something down on a piece of paper, rips it off, and hands it to me. "This is the address he gave me in 2005. It is in the Marais, the Jewish quarter, near the Place des Vosges. That is where I found him playing chess."

"That's near my hotel," I tell him. I look at the address he's handed me: 27, rue du Foin, no. 2B. I feel a chill run down my spine.

"Well then," Monsieur Berr says. "You should go now. The past waits on no one."

Chapter *Twelve*

I'm in stunned disbelief as I bid Monsieur Berr adieu and hurry
downstairs. My feet carry me back toward the Seine, where I
hail a cab on the main street and hand the driver the slip of paper
Monsieur Berr has just given me. The driver grunts in reply and
pulls away from the curb. He veers across lanes of traffic, takes a
bridge over the Seine, and cuts back to the east, where he paral-
lels the river as I watch the twin towers of Notre-Dame grow
closer and closer out the right window. Finally, he turns left and,
after a series of twists and turns, screeches to a halt in front of a
gray stone building with a pair of massive, dark wooden doors. I
pay the driver, and as he pulls away, I approach the call box.

There, in black and white, is the name *Picard, A.* I take a deep
breath and push the buzzer next to the now familiar last name.
Only then do I realize my hands are shaking.

My heart pounds wildly as I wait. There's no reply. I push the
buzzer again, but there's still no response. My heart sinks. What
if it's too late; what if he's dead? I remind myself that it's equally
possible he's merely out; it's midafternoon on a lovely fall day.
Perhaps he's gone for a walk, or to the store. I linger outside the
building for a few minutes, in hopes that someone will come in

or out and I'll be able to ask about him, but the street is quiet, and there's no one coming or going.

I check my watch. Perhaps he's in the Place des Vosges, playing chess, like Monsieur Berr said. I pull out my map, flip to the correct page, and realize the park is less than a block away. I turn and walk in that direction.

On the way, I stop at a pay phone, and after spending a few minutes trying to get an English-speaking operator, I use my Visa to make a call to Annie's cell. I realize she's probably asleep and won't answer, but I'm suddenly dying to tell her what I've found. The call goes to voice mail, and although I'd expected that, my heart still sinks. I consider telling her about Alain, but instead, I say, "I was just thinking about you, honey, and I wanted to say hi. It's beautiful here in Paris. I think I might have found something, but I'm trying not to get my hopes up. I'll call you later. I love you."

Five minutes later, I enter the Place des Vosges through the middle of three stone arches beneath a building. The whole square is surrounded by uniform brick and stone buildings, with graying roofs, french doors, and narrow balconies. Nearly twenty soaring trees with kelly-green leaves surround a statue on horseback in the middle of the rectangular park, while four two-level fountains hold up the four grassy corners, inside the frame of the sandy footpaths.

I look around for anyone who matches Alain's general description, but so far the oldest man I've seen—a man walking a little black dog—couldn't be much older than sixty. I quickly walk the length of the park, staring into the faces of those who pass by, but there is no one here who might be Alain. My heart heavy in my chest, I sigh and walk out the way I came. It is beginning to dawn on me that I might not encounter him, here or anywhere. I fight off a feeling of crushing disappointment—I can't admit defeat yet.

I wander east to kill a little time before I return to the address

Monsieur Berr gave me. I turn a few corners, passing apartment buildings and storefronts, until I find myself on a narrow street filled with people ducking in and out of designer stores. Rue des Rosiers, I read from a street sign. I wander down the street, staring up at a disconcerting mix of ancient-looking butcher shops, bookstores, and synagogues, blended with modern clothing stores.

I come to a stop outside a small storefront marked with the Star of David and the word *synagogue,* which is apparently the same in French as it is in English. My heart is thudding, and I reach out a shaking hand to touch the outer wall. I wonder how long it's been here, and whether my grandmother might have worshipped here at some point.

As I stand there, lost in thought about the past, a familiar scent tugs me back to the present. The air smells ever so faintly like the buttery, cinnamon-scented, fig-and-prune-filled Star Pies I bake every day in my own bakery.

I turn, slowly, and find myself facing a deep red storefront with big picture windows overflowing with breads and pastries. A bakery. I blink a few times and, as if drawn forward by an invisible magnet, float across the street and through the doors.

Inside, the store is packed with people. To the right is a long deli case with meats and prepared salads; to the left is a seemingly endless display of bagels, cheesecakes, pies, tarts, and pastries, all with little signs announcing their names in French and their prices in euros.

I'm frozen in place as my eyes roam over the familiar selection. I see the lemon-grape cheesecake that's one of the North Star's specialties. There's a delicate-looking strudel that looks just like the one that always sells out at my bakery; I take a step closer and realize it's practically identical: it has apples, almonds, raisins, candied orange peel, and cinnamon, just like I use. There's even a sourdough rye bread like the one I earned top honors with two years ago in the *Cape Cod Times*'s "Best Breads of the Cape" poll.

And there, in the window, are slices of something they call Ronde des Pavés. I'm accustomed to seeing them baked into little individual pies with star-shaped lattice crusts, but as I bend to look at the slices, the filling is unmistakable. Poppy seeds, almonds, grapes, figs, prunes, and cinnamon sugar. Just like Mamie's beloved Star Pies.

"Que puis-je pour vous?" There's a high-pitched French voice behind me, and I turn slowly, as if in a fog.

"Um, I don't speak French," I stammer. "I'm sorry." My heart is still pounding a mile a minute.

The woman, who looks about my age, smiles. "No problem," she says, switching seamlessly to accented English. "We have a lot of tourists here. What would you like?"

I point shakily to one of the pieces of Ronde des Pavés. She begins to bag it for me, but I reach out to stop her. I realize my hand is trembling when it makes contact with her arm. She looks up in surprise.

"Where do these recipes come from?" I ask her.

She frowns and looks suspicious. "They're old recipes of my family, madame," she says. "We do not give them out."

"No, no, that's not what I mean," I say quickly. "It's just that I have a bakery in the States, in Massachusetts, and I make the same things. All these recipes that I thought were my grandmother's family recipes . . ."

The suspicion fades from her expression, and she smiles. "Ah. Your grandmother, she is Polish?"

"No, she's from here. Paris."

The woman tilts her head to the side. "But her parents are from Poland, no?" She bites her lip. "This bakery, it was opened by my great-grandparents, just after the war. In 1947. They were from Poland. These recipes, they have much influence of Eastern Europe."

I nod slowly.

"Everything we bake was developed in the *tradition ashké-*

naze of my family's past. We keep to those traditions today. Your grandmother, she is *juive*? Um, Jewish?"

I nod slowly. "Yes. I think. But what's the *tradition ash . . .* whatever you said?"

"It's the, how you say, *le judaïsme traditionnel* in Europe," she explains. "It began in Germany, but hundreds of years ago, these *juifs* moved to other countries of Europe in the east. Before the war, most *communautés juives,* em, communities of *juifs,* in Europe were *ashkénaze,* like my great-grandparents. Before Hitler destroyed them."

I nod slowly and look at the pastries again. "My grandmother always said her family had a bakery here in Paris," I say quietly. "Before the war." I look around and realize how many of Mamie's favorite pastries are missing. "Do you have pistachio cakes?" I ask.

She shakes her head, looking at me blankly, and I go on to describe Mamie's sweet crescent moons and her almond rose tarts. Again, the woman shakes her head. "Those do not sound familiar," she says. She looks around, seeming to suddenly realize how crowded the shop is. "I am sorry," she says. "I must go now. Unless you want a pastry."

I nod and point to one of the Ronde des Pavés, which I know will taste just like one of our Star Pies. "I'll take one of those, please," I say.

She nods, wraps it in wax paper, and places it in a little white bakery bag for me. "There is no charge," she says, handing it to me with a smile. "Maybe you will give me a pastry if I come to Massachusetts someday."

I smile back. "Thank you. And thanks for all your help."

She nods and turns away. I'm already walking toward the door when I hear her call out, "Madame?"

I turn around.

"Those other things you mentioned," she says. "I do not think they are of the Eastern European *tradition ashkénaze*." She waves and disappears into a crowd of waiting customers. I frown and stare after her in confusion.

I eat my Ronde des Pavés as I retrace my steps back to the address Monsieur Berr gave me. It's not exactly like one of our Star Pies, but it's close enough. The one I make is heavier on the cinnamon—Mamie has always loved cinnamon—and our crust is a little denser and more buttery. The raisins in the Ronde are golden, while I use traditional dark raisins. But it's clear the recipes originate from the same place.

I've finished the pastry, but not my swirling questions, by the time I reach Alain's door again. I take a deep breath and close my eyes for a moment, steeling myself for the feeling of disappointment I know will flood through me if he doesn't answer. I open my eyes and press the buzzer.

At first, I'm greeted by silence. I buzz again and am about to turn away when suddenly, there's a crackling sound and a muffled male voice on the other end.

"Hello!" I practically shout into the call box, my heart suddenly pounding. "I'm trying to find Alain Picard."

There's a pause and then more crackling and a muffled male voice.

"I'm sorry, I can't understand you," I say. "I . . . I'm trying to reach Alain Picard."

The speaker crackles again, the voice says something, and then, to my relief, I hear the front door buzz.

I push it open and hurry into a tiny, beautiful courtyard, where vines creep up old stone walls framed by red roses and yellow daffodils. I cross quickly and make my way into the building. He's in apartment 2B, Monsieur Berr said. I climb the flight of stairs in the corner and am momentarily surprised to see that the two apartments in front of me are labeled 1A and 1B. Then I remember that the French think of the ground floor as 0 instead of 1, and I ascend a second flight of stairs.

Heart pounding, I knock on the door marked 2B. The moment it opens and I find myself face-to-face with an old, slightly stooped man with thick white hair, I know for sure. He has Mamie's eyes, the slate-gray, slightly almond-shaped eyes that she passed on to my mother. I've found my great-uncle. Mamie *is* part of this mysterious, lost Picard family after all, and therefore, so am I. I take a deep breath.

"Alain Picard?" I manage when I've found my voice.

"Oui," he says. He's staring at me. He shakes his head and says something in rapid French.

"I . . . I'm sorry," I say. "I only speak English. I'm sorry."

"Forgive me, mademoiselle," he says, switching seamlessly to English. "It is just that you look like someone I used to know. It is like seeing a ghost."

My heart thuds. "Do I remind you of your sister?" I ask. "Rose?"

The color drains from his face. "But how did you . . . ?" His voice trails off.

"I think I'm your great-niece," I tell him. "I'm Rose's grand-daughter. Hope."

"No," he says, his voice nearly a whisper now. "No, no. That is impossible. My sister died seventy years ago."

I shake my head. "No," I say. "She's still alive."

"Non, ce n'est pas possible," he murmurs. "It is not possible."

"She always believed *you* had died," I tell him softly.

He stares. "She is alive?" he whispers after a long pause. "You are certain?"

I nod, the words stuck behind the sudden lump in my throat.

"But how . . . how are you here? How did you find me?"

"She asked me to come to Paris to find out what happened to her family," I say. "Your name was nowhere in the records." I quickly explain about how the people at the memorial sent me to Olivier Berr.

"I remember him," he says softly. "He spoke to Jacob too. A long time ago. Right after the war."

"Jacob?" I ask.

His eyes widen. "You do not know of Jacob?"

I shake my head. "Is he another of your brothers?" I wonder why Mamie didn't put his name down on the list.

Alain shakes his head slowly. "No," he says. "But he was more important to Rose than anyone else in the world."

I follow Alain into his apartment, which is small and filled with books. Dozens of teacups sit with their matching saucers on shelves and atop cabinets, a few even framed on the walls.

"My wife collected those," Alain says, following my gaze and nodding to a shelf filled with cups and saucers, as he shuffles down the hall toward a sitting room. "I never liked them. But after she died, I could not bring myself to throw them away."

"I'm sorry," I say. "When did she . . . ?"

"A very long time ago," he says, looking down. We enter the sitting room, and he gestures to one of two high-backed chairs, upholstered in red velvet. I sit, and he shakily sinks into the seat opposite me. "My Anne, she was one of the few who survived Auschwitz. We used to say how lucky she was. But she could never have children, because of what they had done to her. She died at forty with a broken heart."

"I'm so sorry," I murmur.

"Thank you," he says. He leans forward eagerly and stares at me with eyes that are achingly familiar. "Now, please, tell me about Rose. Forgive me; I am in shock."

So I quickly tell him what I know: that my grandmother came to the United States in the early 1940s after marrying my grandfather, that they had one daughter, my mother. I tell him about the bakery Mamie opened on Cape Cod and how just an hour earlier, I'd stumbled upon the *ashkénaze* Jewish bakery on rue des Rosiers and realized how familiar so many of the pastries were.

"I always knew Rose had baking in her blood," Alain says softly. "Our mother, she was from la Pologne. Her parents brought her here to Paris when she was just a little girl. They had a bakery, and before our mother married our father, she worked there every day. Even after our mother had children, she would still help at the bakery on the weekends and on busy evenings. Rose, she loved to go there with her. Baking is our family's legacy."

I shake my head. It's incredible, I think, that I've been surrounded by Mamie's family history for all my life and never known it. Every time I baked a strudel or a Star Pie, I was following a tradition that had been in our family for generations.

"But how did she escape Paris?" Alain asks, leaning forward even farther, so far that I'm beginning to fear he might fall from his chair. "We always believed she died somehow, just before the roundup."

My heart sinks. "I don't know," I say. "I was hoping you would know."

He looks confused now. "But she is still alive, you say? Can you not ask her?"

I hang my head. "She has Alzheimer's disease," I say. "I don't know how to say it in French."

I look up and Alain nods, sadness sweeping his features. "It is the same word. So she does not remember," he whispers.

"She has never talked about the past before," I say. "In fact, I didn't know until just a few days ago that she was even Jewish."

Now he looks confused. "But of course she is Jewish."

I shake my head. "For my whole life, she's been Catholic."

Alain looks puzzled. "But . . ." He stops there, as if unsure of what to ask me next.

"I don't understand either," I say. "I never knew until just a few days ago that our family was Jewish. I never even knew her maiden name had been Picard. She'd always said it was Durand. My daughter even did a family tree project a few years ago, and it's Durand in every piece of documentation we could find. There's no record of her being a Picard."

Alain looks at me for a long moment and sighs. "Rose Durand is probably the identity she escaped under. To have gotten out of France at that time, she would have had to get new identity papers, probably in unoccupied France. And to get new papers, she likely would have had to claim to be someone else. She probably had help from the *résistance*. They would have given her false papers."

"False papers that listed her as a Christian? That listed her as Rose Durand instead of Rose Picard?"

"Much easier to escape as a Catholic than as a Jew, of course, during the war." Alain nods slowly. "If she believed she had lost all of us, perhaps she wanted to forget. Perhaps she lost herself in her new identity, because it was the only way to maintain her *santé d'esprit*. Her sanity."

"But why would she think you were dead?" I ask.

"After the liberation, everything was very confused," Alain says. "Those of us who were left came to the Hôtel Lutetia on the boulevard Raspail. It was where all the survivors came after. Some to heal, to receive medical care. For the rest of us, it was the place to find each other. To seek our families that had been lost."

"You went there?" I ask.

He nods. "I was never deported," he says softly. "After the war, I came to the Hôtel Lutetia to find my family. I wanted so badly to believe they had survived, Hope. We would arrive and put the names of the family members on a board. '*I am looking for Cecile Picard. Mother. Age forty-four. Arrested July 16, 1942. Taken to Vel' d'Hiv.*' People would come to you and tell you, 'I knew your mother at Auschwitz. She died in her third month, of pneumonia.' Or, 'I worked with your father in the crematorium at

Auschwitz. He became sick and was sent to the gas chamber, just before the liberation of the camp.' "

I stare at him. "You found out that they all died."

"All of them," Alain whispers. "Grandparents, cousins, aunts, uncles. Rose was listed as dead too. Two people swore they had seen her shot in the streets during the roundup. I left without giving my name, because there was no one left to find me. That is what I believed. It is why there is no record of me. I wanted only to disappear."

"How did you escape being captured?"

"I was eleven years old when they came for us. My parents, they did not believe all the rumors we were hearing. But Rose believed. She could not convince my parents. They thought that she was crazy, that she was a fool for accepting the predictions of Jacob, whom they viewed as a young rebel who knew nothing."

There it was again. That name. "You never told me who Jacob is."

Alain searches my face for a moment. "Jacob was everything," he says simply. "Jacob was the one who told me to run if the police came. Jacob was the one who told me to try to convince my family. Jacob was the one who saved me, for when the police came for us, to take us away, I climbed out the back window, fell to the ground from three floors above, and ran."

He looks down at his hands for a long moment. They're gnarled and scarred. Finally, he draws a deep breath and continues. "I let my family die, because I was scared," he says. He looks up at me and there are tears in his eyes. "I did not try hard enough to persuade them. I did not take Danielle and David, the younger ones, with me. I was frightened, very frightened, and because of that, they are all gone."

A tear runs down his cheek. Before I can even consider what I'm doing, I've crossed the room to hug him. He stiffens for a moment, and then I feel his arms encircle my shoulders. His whole body is shaking. "You were eleven," I murmur. "You are not to blame."

I pull away, and he sighs. "No matter who holds the blame, my family was all murdered, and I am still here, seventy years later. I have lived with that all my life. It is heavy in my heart."

I can feel tears in my own eyes as I sit back down. "How did this Jacob know? How did he know to tell you to run?"

"He was part of an underground movement against the Nazis," Alain says. "He believed the rumors of the death camps. He believed they were exterminating us systematically. He was in the minority. But Rose believed him. And Jacob was my hero, so I believed him too. He must have saved her."

"How?" I ask softly.

Alain looks at me for a long moment. "I do not know. But she was the love of his life. He would have done anything to protect her. Anything."

I blink. "She loved him too?"

He nods. "With a strength I'd never known she had," he says. He looks off into the distance for a long time. "That is why, for all these years, I've always firmly believed that she died. For if she had lived, I know she would have come back for him."

"She must have believed that he was dead too," I murmur. "Was his name at the Hôtel Lutetia?"

Alain looks perplexed. "Yes, it was," he says. "He was hoping beyond hope that she had made it out, that she had survived, despite the rumors we had heard. His name was always there, so if she came back, she would find him."

"But my grandfather came back," I tell him. "In 1949. To find out what happened to her family. That's what my grandmother said."

"There were no records of me," Alain says. "That is surely why he did not find me. But Jacob did everything to be listed, just in case Rose had somehow survived."

I swallow hard and wonder what this means. Had Mamie

not given Jacob's name to my grandpa? Or had my grandfather found Jacob's name on survivor lists after all and told Mamie otherwise, because he realized how much she apparently loved him and wanted to protect the life he'd already begun with her? I shudder involuntarily.

"Did this Jacob escape, like you and my grandmother did?" I ask Alain. "Before the roundup?"

Alain shakes his head and draws a deep breath. "Jacob was at Auschwitz," he says simply. "He survived because he was so sure Rose was safe somewhere, and he had vowed he would find her. He told me, when I last saw him, that he could not believe she was dead, because he would have felt it in his soul. It was that hope of reuniting with her that kept him alive in that hell on earth."

Chapter Thirteen

Lemon-Grape Cheesecake

INGREDIENTS

1½ cups ground graham cracker
    crumbs
1 cup granulated sugar, divided
1 tsp. cinnamon
6 Tbsp. unsalted butter, melted

2 eight-ounce blocks of cream cheese
¼ cup white grape juice
Juice and zest of one lemon
2 eggs

DIRECTIONS

1. Preheat oven to 375 degrees. Mix graham cracker crumbs, ½ cup sugar, cinnamon, and melted butter until well blended. Press evenly into an 8-inch pie pan.

2. Bake for 6 minutes. Remove from oven and cool.

3. Reduce oven temperature to 300 degrees.

4. In a medium bowl beat cream cheese until smooth using an electric mixer. Gradually beat in remaining ½ cup sugar. Gradually add grape juice, lemon juice, lemon zest, and eggs, and beat until just smooth and lump-free.

5. Place cooled crust on a cookie sheet. Pour cream cheese mixture into crust.

6. Bake for 40 minutes, or until center of crust no longer jiggles.

⌒

Rose

Annie had been to see Rose earlier that day; Rose was sure of it. But she couldn't quite make sense of what the girl had said.

"Mom's in Paris right now," Annie had declared, her gray eyes flashing with excitement. "She left me a message! She said she might have, like, found something!"

"How nice, my dear," Rose had replied. But she couldn't quite place who Annie's mother was. Was she a relative of Rose's? Or maybe one of her customers at the bakery? But she couldn't tell the girl that she didn't remember her mother. So instead, she said, "Did your mother find something nice at a boutique? A scarf or some shoes, perhaps?" Paris was, after all, known for its shopping.

Annie had laughed then, a bright sound that reminded Rose of the birds that used to sing outside her window on the rue du Général Camou, so very long ago. "No, Mamie!" she had exclaimed. "She went to the Holocaust museum! You know, to find out what happened to those people you told us about!"

"Oh," Rose had murmured, all of the breath suddenly gone from her lungs.

Annie had departed soon after, and Rose had been left alone with her thoughts, which were closing in on her. The girl's words had triggered a tornado of memories that threatened to lift Rose off her feet and take her away, into the past, where she found herself dwelling more and more frequently now. Most days, the memories rolled in uninvited, but this day, it was the mentions of Paris and the Holocaust, the Shoah, that sent Rose spinning backward to that terrible day in 1949 her dear Ted had come home and confirmed her worst fears.

She loved her husband. And because she loved her husband, she had told him about Jacob, because she knew she was supposed to be honest with the people she loved. And she *had* been honest—to a point. She had told Ted that there was a man she had loved very much in Paris. It had hardly needed to be said; she knew it was already clear.

But when he'd asked her if she loved the man in Paris more than she loved him, she hadn't been able to meet his eye. And so he had known. He had always known.

She wished she felt differently. Ted was a wonderful man. He was a wonderful father to Josephine. He was trustworthy and loyal. He had built her a life she never could have dreamed of all those years ago in the land of her birth.

But he wasn't Jacob. And that was his only flaw.

For the first few years after the war, she hadn't wanted to know. Not officially, anyhow. When she'd first been married to Ted and they'd been living in New York, in an apartment not far from the Statue of Liberty, there had been bits and pieces of news from other immigrants who drifted in from France. Survivors, they called themselves. Rose thought that, instead, they looked like ghosts, already dead. Pale, washed out, hollowed eyes, floating through rooms like they didn't quite belong there.

I knew your mother, one of the ghosts would say. *I watched her die at Auschwitz.*

I saw sweet little Danielle at Drancy, another would say. *I don't know if she made it to the transport.*

And the bit of news that shattered her soul, from a ghost named Monsieur Pinusiewicz, whom she'd known in a former life. He was the butcher whose shop was just down the street from her grandparents' bakery.

That boy you were running around with? Jacob?

Rose had stared at him. She hadn't wanted him to go on, because she could see the truth written in his eyes. She couldn't bear to hear it. She made a muffled sound, for it was all she could muster, and he took it as a signal to go on.

He was at Auschwitz. I saw him there. And I saw him the day they led him to the gas chamber.

And that was it. He was gone. The ghost of Monsieur Pinus-iewicz, as well as the last shred of hope she had that she could somehow find her past again.

By the time she left New York, she knew they were all gone. The ghosts had told her. One had watched her father get sick while working at Auschwitz's crematorium. One had held her mother's hand as she died. Another had worked alongside Helene and had one day returned from the field, a day that Helene had been too sick to rise from her bed, to find her on the floor, beaten to death by the guards, her lovely brown hair matted with blood. The fates of the others were less clear, and Rose didn't ask questions. What mattered was that they were all dead. All of them.

And so, when Ted had promised her a life far away from these hollow-eyed ghosts, far away from New York, in a magical place called Cape Cod, where he said the waves washed up on sandy beaches, and cranberry bogs grew, she said yes. Because she loved him. And because she needed to finish becoming someone else. She needed to concentrate on building a family, because the one she'd had was gone forever.

But by 1949, seven years after she'd left Paris, she had needed to know for sure. She knew she could not bury Rose Picard without the certainty that could only come from the official records. What if one of the ghosts was wrong? What if little Danielle had survived and was in an orphanage somewhere, believing there was no one in the world who loved her? What if Helene hadn't died on that floor but had escaped and was waiting for her, wondering where she was? What if the ghost who said she'd held Rose's mother's hand had been mistaken about the identity of the woman she'd watched die?

But Rose couldn't go. It had been nothing short of miraculous that her falsified papers had gotten her into the United States in the first place. She knew it was likely that the immigration people had looked the other way only because she had married Ted, a war hero. She had made her bargains; now her life was here, and she had a little girl who needed her. She didn't trust France. She didn't trust that she could get out again. And she feared her heart wouldn't be able to bear going back anyhow.

And so she asked Ted to go. And because he loved her, and because he was a good man, he said yes.

He left on a shining summer Monday. She waited, the seconds ticking by like minutes, the minutes feeling like hours. Time stretched like the taffy she, Ted, and little Josephine had eaten on their trip to Atlantic City the summer before.

When he finally came home, very late that Friday, he sat her down in the still, damp heat of the Cape Cod night and told her everything.

He had been to the synagogue Rose had grown up in. It pained her deeply when he told her the synagogue had been destroyed during the war, but that they had rebuilt it, as good as new. She knew then that he didn't understand that when things were rebuilt, they weren't the same. You could never get back the things that had been destroyed.

"They all died, Rose," he told her gently, looking into her eyes and holding her hands tightly, as if he were afraid she'd float away, like a helium balloon bound for the heavens. "Your mother, your father, your sisters, your brothers. All of them. I am so sorry."

"Oh," was all she could muster.

"I spoke to the rabbi there," Ted said softly. "He showed me where to find the records. I am so sorry."

She didn't say anything.

"Do you want to know what happened to them, Rose?" Ted asked.

"No." She shook her head, looked away. She could not hear it. She feared it would break her heart in a million pieces. Would she die right here, in front of her husband, with her daughter upstairs, when it shattered? "It is my fault," she whispered.

"No, Rose!" Ted exclaimed. "You can't feel that way. None of this is your fault." He took her in his arms, but her body was stiff, unwilling.

She shook her head slowly against his chest. "I knew," she whispered. "I knew they were coming for us. And I did not try hard enough to save them."

She knew she would have to live with that forever. But she didn't know how. It was why she couldn't be herself anymore. It was why she had found solace in Rose Durand, and then Rose McKenna. It was impossible to be Rose Picard. Rose Picard had died in Europe with her family long ago.

"It's not your fault," Ted said again. "You have to stop blaming yourself."

She nodded, because she knew it was what was expected of her. She pulled away from him. "And Jacob Levy?" she asked in a flat voice, looking up at long last to meet Ted's eye.

This time, it was he who looked away. "My dear Rose," he said. "Your friend Jacob died at Auschwitz. Just before the liberation of the camp."

Rose blinked a few times. It was as if someone had pushed her head underwater. All of a sudden, she couldn't see, couldn't breathe. She gasped for breath. "You are certain?" she asked after a very long while, when air filled her lungs again.

"I'm sorry," Ted said.

And that had been that. The world became very cold for Rose that day. She nodded and looked away from her husband. She would not cry. She could not cry. She had already died inside, and to cry would be to live. And how could she live without Jacob?

Jacob had always told her that love would save them. And she had believed him. But he'd been wrong. She had been saved, but what good was she without him? What meaning did her life have?

It was at that moment that Josephine appeared from around the corner, wearing the long pink cotton nightgown Rose had sewn for her, clutching her Cynthia doll.

"What's wrong, Mama?" Josephine asked from the doorway, blinking sleepily at her parents.

"Nothing, my dear," Rose said, standing and crossing the room to kneel beside her daughter. She looked at the little girl and reminded herself that this was her family now, that the past was in the past, that she owed it to *this* life to keep going.

But she felt nothing.

After she'd tucked Josephine back into bed, singing her a lullaby her own mother had sung to her so many years before, she had lain beside Ted in the dark until his chest rose and fell in slumber and she could feel him slipping away into his dreams.

She rose softly, silently, and moved toward the hall. She climbed the narrow staircase to the small widow's walk atop their house, and she emerged into the still night.

The moon was full, and it hung heavy over Cape Cod Bay, which Rose could see over the rooftops. The pale lunar light reflected on the water, and if Rose looked down, she could almost believe that the sea was lit from within. But she wasn't looking down. Tonight, she was searching the heavens for the stars she had named. *Mama. Papa. Helene. Claude. Alain. David. Danielle.*

"I am sorry," she whispered to the sky. "I am so sorry."

There was no answer. She could hear, in the near distance, the waves lapping at the shore. The sky was silent.

She searched the sky, murmuring apologies, until dawn began to break on the eastern horizon. Still, she could not find him. Was this her fate? Was he lost to her forever?

"Jacob, where are you?" she cried out to the sky.

But there was no reply.

Chapter *Fourteen*

⟋⟍

The air in Paris becomes very still as darkness falls. First, the sky begins to deepen, from the pale, hazy periwinkle of late afternoon to the deepening cerulean of evening, streaked with tangerine and gold at the horizon. As the stars begin to poke holes in the blanket of dusk, the wispy clouds hold on to the disappearing sunset, turning shades of ruby and rose. Finally, as sapphire fades to night, the lights of Paris come on, as twinkling and endless as stars. I stand on the Pont des Arts with Alain, watching in awe as the Eiffel Tower begins to sparkle with a million tiny white lights against the velvet sky.

"I've never seen anything so beautiful," I murmur. Alain had suggested a walk, because he needed a break from speaking about the past. I'm eager to hear the story of Jacob, but I don't want to push him. I have to keep reminding myself that Alain is eighty, and these must be painful, long-buried memories.

We're leaning against the railing of the bridge, looking west, and as he folds his hand gently over mine, I can feel it trembling. "Your grandmother used to say the same thing," he says softly. "She would take me here when I was a boy, before the occupation, and tell me that the sunset over the Seine was God's show, put on just for us."

I feel tears in my eyes and shake my head, trying to rid myself of them, for they blur the perfect view.

"Whenever I feel alone," Alain says, "I come here. I've spent years dreaming that Rose was with God, lighting the sky for me. I never imagined that all this time, she's been alive."

"We have to try to call her again," I say. We had tried her number before leaving for a walk, but there'd been no answer; she was likely napping, something she seemed to be doing more of lately. "We have to tell her that I've found you. Even though she might not understand or remember."

"Of course," Alain says. "And then I will come with you. Back to Cape Cod."

I turn and stare at him. "Really? You'll come with me?"

He smiles. "I've spent seventy years without a family," he says. "I do not want to waste another moment. I must see Rose."

I smile into the darkness.

When the last rays of the sun have seeped into the horizon and the stars are all out, Alain loops his arm through mine and we begin to walk slowly back the way we came, toward the palatial Louvre, which is aglow in muted light, reflecting on the river beneath us.

"I will tell you about Jacob now," Alain says softly as we begin to cross through the courtyard of the Louvre, toward the rue de Rivoli.

I look at him and nod. I realize I'm holding my breath.

Alain takes a deep breath and begins, his voice slow and halting. "I was with Rose when she met him. It was the end of 1940, and although Paris had already fallen to the Germans, life was still normal enough that we could believe it would all be okay. Things were beginning to get bad, but we never could have imagined what was in store."

We turn right on the rue de Rivoli, which is still crowded with people although the stores have closed. Couples stroll through the darkness, holding hands, whispering to each other, and for a moment, I can imagine Mamie and this Jacob walking the same street seventy years ago. I shiver.

"It was love at first sight, something I have never seen before or since," Alain continues. "I would not believe in it if I had not seen it for myself. But from the very first moment, it was as if they had found the other half of their souls."

As corny as it sounds, there's something in the gravity of Alain's voice that makes me believe him.

"Jacob was with us always from that first moment," Alain continues. "My father did not care for him, for he was from a lower class. My father was a doctor, while Jacob's father was a factory laborer. But Jacob was kind, polite, and intelligent, so my parents tolerated him. He was always taking the time to teach me things, and to play with David and Danielle."

Alain pauses, and I imagine he's thinking about his little brother and sister, lost so long ago. We stroll in silence for a while, and I wonder what it's like to entirely lose one's innocence at such a young age, to never be able to retrieve it. We pass the Hôtel de Ville, Paris's palatial city hall, which is bathed in pale light. Alain takes my hand as we cross the street, and as we make our way north into the Marais, he doesn't let go. I realize I don't want him to. I've been missing a family too, now that my mother is gone and my grandmother's memory has all but vanished.

"When the anti-Jewish laws began being imposed, and as things became worse for us, Jacob began to become more vocal about his opposition to the Nazis, and my parents were concerned," Alain continues. "My father, you see, wanted to believe that we would be immune, because we were wealthy. He wanted to believe that people were blowing everything out of proportion, that the Nazis did not truly intend us harm. Jacob, on the other hand, understood exactly what was happening. He was part of an underground movement. He believed the Nazis were coming to erase us all from the face of the earth. He was right, of course.

"I look back now, and I wonder why my parents could not see things more clearly," Alain says. "I think they didn't *want* to believe that our country could turn its back on us. They wanted to believe the best. And when Jacob spoke the truth, they would not hear it. My father was outraged and accused him of bringing lies and propaganda into our home.

"Rose and I were the only ones who believed him." Alain's voice is hollow, almost a whisper. "And that is what saved us both."

We walk in silence for a little while more. Our footfalls echo off the stone walls around us.

"Where's Jacob now?" I ask finally.

Alain stops in his tracks and looks at me. He shakes his head. "I do not know," he says. "I do not know if he is still alive."

My heart drops in my chest.

"The last time we spoke was 1952, when Jacob set off for America," Alain says.

I stare at him. "He moved to America?"

Alain nods. "Yes. I don't know where in America. But of course that was nearly sixty years ago. He would be eighty-seven now. It's very possible he is not alive anymore. Remember, he spent two years in Auschwitz, Hope. That takes a toll."

I don't trust myself to speak until we arrive back at Alain's building. I can't fully wrap my mind around the idea that my grandmother and the apparent love of her life have been living in the same country for sixty years and never knew the other had survived. But if Jacob had found her during the war, my mother might never have been born, and of course I wouldn't have been either. So had things worked out the way they were supposed to? Or was my very existence a slap in the face of true love?

"I have to try to find him," I say as Alain punches his code into the keypad to the right. He holds the door open for me.

"Yes," he agrees simply.

I follow him up to his apartment. I feel like I'm in a fog.

"Shall we call Rose again now?" he asks once he's locked the door behind us.

I nod again. "But remember, she has good days and bad ones," I remind him. "It's very possible that she won't understand who you are. She's different than she used to be."

He smiles. "We're all different than we used to be," he says. "I understand."

I check my watch. It's nearly ten, so it would be nearly four on the Cape, late enough in the day that Mamie is probably sundowning; it's common for dementia patients to be less lucid as the day wears on. "You sure you don't mind if I call from your phone?" I ask. "It's expensive."

Alain laughs. "If the cost were a million euros, I would still say yes."

I smile, pick up the receiver, and punch in 001, then Mamie's number. I listen to the line ring six times before I hang up. "That's strange," I say. I check my watch again. Mamie doesn't participate in the social activities at her home—she says bingo is for children—so there's no reason she shouldn't be in her room. "Maybe I dialed wrong."

I try again, and this time, I let it ring eight times before I hang up. Alain is frowning at me, and although there's a bad feeling in the pit of my stomach, I force a smile. "She's not answering, but maybe my daughter took her out for a walk or something."

Alain nods, but he looks concerned.

"Do you mind if I try her?" I ask. "My daughter?"

"Of course," Alain says. "Please."

I dial 001 and then Annie's cell number. She picks up after half a ring. "Mom?" she asks, and I can tell from her voice that something's wrong.

"What is it, honey?" I ask.

"It's Mamie," she says. Her voice is trembling. "She . . . she had a stroke."

My heart stops, and I look up at Alain, stunned. I know he can read everything on my face.

"Is she . . . ?" I ask. I don't complete the sentence.

"She's in the hospital," Annie says. "But she's not doing good."

"Oh my God." I look up at Alain, who looks panicked.

"What has happened?" he asks.

I cover the receiver with my hand and say, "My grandmother had a stroke. She's in the hospital."

Alain puts a hand over his mouth as I turn my attention back to my daughter. "Honey, are you okay?" I ask. "Who's with you?"

"Mr. Keyes," she mumbles.

"Gavin?" I ask, confused. "But where's your dad?"

"Still at work," she says. "I—I tried to call him. But his assistant said he was in the middle of an important case. She said he'd call me when court was in recess."

I close my eyes and try to breathe. "I'm so sorry I'm not there with you, honey. I'm coming home as soon as I can. I promise."

"I tried calling you at your hotel," Annie says in a small voice. "Where were you?"

I look up at Alain, who has tears in his eyes.

"I have a lot to tell you, Annie," I say. "I'll tell you as soon as I get home, okay?"

"Okay," she says in a small voice.

"Can I talk to Gavin for a minute?"

She doesn't answer, but I hear a rustling as she passes the phone to him. "Hello?" he says a moment later, and it's not until I hear his voice that I release a breath I didn't realize I'd been holding.

"Gavin, what happened?" I ask right away. I know I should begin by thanking him for once again coming to my rescue, but all I can think about is Mamie, and how Annie is coping.

"Hope, your grandmother had a stroke, but they've stabilized her," he says, and his voice is all business, but there's a gentleness there that soothes me. "She hasn't regained consciousness, but they're monitoring her. It's too soon to tell how much damage there's been."

"How . . . what . . . ?" My voice trails off, because I don't know what I'm trying to ask. I look up at Alain helplessly again. He's sunk into a chair opposite me and is watching with watery eyes. His gnarled hand is still over his mouth. "How did you know?" I finally ask.

"Annie called," Gavin explains quickly. "She was at her father's house. I guess your grandmother's assisted living place still had your old home number as one of the emergency contacts, so a nurse called there, and Annie answered. She couldn't reach anyone to take her to the hospital, so she called me."

"I'm sorry," I mumble. "I mean, thank you."

"Hope, don't be silly," Gavin says. "I was happy to help Annie out. I'm glad she called. I was just down the street, actually, finishing up a repair job at Joan Namvar's cottage, so I was able to come get her right away."

I close my eyes. "Thank you, Gavin. I don't even know how to thank you enough."

"It's fine," he says dismissively.

"Is she okay?" I ask. "Annie?"

"She's okay," he says. "Shaken up, but okay. Don't worry; I'll stay with her until your ex gets out of work."

"Thank you," I whisper. "I'll make it up to you, Gavin."

"Don't worry," he repeats.

I take a deep breath. "I'll be on the next available flight." I'm not good at accepting favors from people, and I know that the guilt from this one will weigh on me for a long time.

"Hope, are *you* okay?" Gavin asks.

I blink a few times. No one ever asks me that. "Yeah," I say, but it's a lie. "Can I talk to Annie again?"

"Sure," Gavin says. "Hang in there. See you soon."

I hear a rustling again, and then Annie's on the line. "Mom?" she asks.

"Listen, I'm sorry about your dad," I say. "I'm going to call him right now and make sure that—"

"I'm fine, Mom," Annie interrupts. "Mr. Keyes is with me."

I sigh and pinch the bridge of my nose. "I'll be there as soon as I can, sweetheart," I say.

"I know," Annie says.

"I love you, honey."

There's a pause. "I know," Annie says again. But then she adds, "I love you too."

It's only then that I begin to cry.

Alain calls all the airlines while I struggle to get myself under control. I pace his apartment, feeling like a caged animal. For the thousandth time, I visualize Annie crying in the waiting room with no one there to comfort her except Gavin Keyes. He's been wonderful to us these last few months, but still, she doesn't know him that well and she must be scared about Mamie. Her father should be there with her, not Gavin. As soon as Alain gets off the phone, I plan to call Rob and give him a piece of my mind.

"I switched your ticket," Alain tells me when he finally hangs up, "and I bought one for myself. The earliest nonstop I could get for us was 1:25 p.m., arriving in Boston just after three. There were early flights from Paris, but with the stops, they would have gotten us into Boston later."

I blink and nod; 1:25 p.m. tomorrow feels like an eternity from now. "Thank you," I say. "How much do I owe you?" I know I shouldn't be thinking about money now, but I'm aware that the cost will be much more than the thousand-dollar check Mamie gave me. I have no idea how I'll pay for this.

Alain looks confused. "Do not be crazy," he says. "This is not a time to talk about such things. We must get to Boston quickly to see Rose."

I nod. I'll insist later. I don't have the energy right now. "Thank you," I say softly.

I ask Alain whether I can use his phone once more, and he watches me carefully as I speak first to Rob's assistant and then, after I persuade her to put me through, to Rob, my voice taut with tension.

"Jesus, Hope, I'll get there as soon as I can," Rob says. "I'm in the middle of an important hearing. It's not like Annie's life is in danger or something."

"Your *daughter* is at the hospital, *alone and scared,*" I say through gritted teeth. "That doesn't matter to you?"

"I *said* I'll get there as soon as I can," he repeats.

"Yeah, I heard you the first time," I retort. "And it sounded just as selfish then."

As I place the receiver down, I realize I'm shaking. Alain crosses the room and hugs me. I hesitate for a moment, then hug back.

"You are not married to the father of Annie?" Alain asks after a moment, and I realize that for all the talking we've done about Mamie, I've barely told him anything about myself.

"No," I say. "Not anymore."

"I am sorry," Alain says.

I shrug. "Don't be," I say. "It's for the best." I'm trying to sound more lighthearted and casual about it than I feel. But I can tell, from the look on Alain's face, that he sees right through my nonchalance. I'm grateful that he doesn't ask anything else.

"You are welcome to stay here tonight if you wish," Alain says. "But I think you have things at your hotel that you need to retrieve."

"Yeah, I have to pack," I say numbly. "And check out."

"I will not sleep tonight," Alain says. "There are too many things in my mind. So please return when you would like in the morning. There is no time too early. We will have breakfast together before we leave for the airport."

I nod. "Thank you," I murmur.

"Thank *you*," Alain says. He squeezes my hands and kisses me on both cheeks. "You have given me my family back."

I can't sleep that night either, although I try. I feel ashamed to be crawling under the covers while my daughter is alone and scared thousands of miles away. I try Annie twice more, but she doesn't answer; her phone goes straight to voice mail, and I wonder whether the battery has run out. Around four in the morning Paris time, I reach Gavin on his cell, and he tells me that he left when Rob got to the hospital around seven in the evening. As far as he knows, there's been no change in Mamie's condition since then.

"Try to get some rest, Hope," Gavin says softly. "You're coming home as soon as you can. And you're not helping anyone by lying there awake right now."

I mumble a thank-you and hang up. The next thing I know, I'm staring at a clock that tells me it's five forty-five in the morning. I don't remember falling asleep.

I'm at Alain's by seven, after showering, shoving the remainder of my things into my duffel bag, checking out, and hailing a cab outside the hotel.

Alain is already dressed for our trip, in slacks and a button-down shirt with a navy tie, when he greets me at his door. He kisses me on both cheeks and embraces me. "You did not sleep much either, I see," he says.

"Barely."

"Come in," he says, stepping aside. "My friend Simon is here. He knew our family before the war. And my friend Henri. He is a survivor too. They want to meet you."

My heart is in my throat as I follow Alain into his apartment. In the sitting room, two men are sipping tiny cups of espresso by the window, while sunlight streams in, lighting their matching snow-white heads of hair. Both stand and smile at me as I enter,

and I note that they look even older than Alain and are both sig-
nificantly stooped.

The one closest to me speaks first. His green eyes are watery.
"Alain is right. You look just like Rose," he whispers.

"Simon," Alain says, stepping into the room behind me. "This
is my niece. Hope McKenna-Smith. Hope, this is my friend
Simon Ramo. He knew your grandmother."

"You look just like her," he says. He takes a few steps forward
to meet me in the middle of the room. As he leans forward to kiss
me on both cheeks, I notice two things: that he is trembling, and
that he has a number tattooed on the inside of his left forearm.

He sees me staring at it. "Auschwitz," he says simply. I nod
and look quickly away, embarrassed.

"For me, the same," says the other man. He holds up his left
arm, and I see a similar tattoo, the letter *B* followed by five dig-
its. He steps forward to kiss me on both cheeks too and backs
away smiling. "I never knew your grandmother," he says. "But
she must have been very beautiful, for you are very beautiful,
young lady."

I smile weakly. "Thank you."

"I am Henri Levy."

My heart skips, and I look at Alain. "Levy?"

"A common last name," Alain explains quickly. "He is no
relation to Jacob."

"Oh," I say, feeling oddly deflated.

"Shall we sit down?" Henri motions to the chairs. "Your
uncle forgets I am ninety-two. He is, how do you say in English?
A spring chicken?"

I laugh, and Alain smiles. "Yes, a spring chicken," Alain says.
"I am sure that is just what young Hope sees when she looks at
me."

"Hope, do not listen to these old men," Simon says. He totters
back to his chair. "We are only as old as we feel. And today, I feel
like I am thirty-five."

I smile, and after a moment, Alain offers me a cup of espresso, which I gladly accept. The four of us settle into seats in the living room, and Simon leans forward.

"I know I have said this," he begins. "But you bring me back in time. Your grandmother was—*is*—a wonderful woman."

"He always had a crush on her," Alain interjects with a grin. "But he was eleven, like me. She was his babysitter."

Simon shakes his head and shoots Alain a look. "Oh, she had a crush on me too," he says. "She just did not know it yet."

Alain laughs. "You are forgetting Jacob Levy."

Simon rolls his eyes. "My great foe for Rose's affection."

Alain looks at me. "Jacob was only Simon's foe in Simon's own mind," he says. "To everyone else, Jacob was Prince Charming, and Simon was a miniature toad with sticks for legs."

"Hey!" Simon exclaims. "My legs developed very nicely, thank you." He points to his legs and winks at me.

I laugh again.

"Now," Henri says after a moment, "perhaps Hope can tell us a little about herself. Not that we are not very interested in the legs of Simon."

The three men look at me expectantly, and I clear my throat, suddenly nervous to be put on the spot.

"Um, what would you like to know?"

"Alain says you have a daughter?" Henri asks.

I nod. "Yes. Annie. She's twelve years old."

Simon smiles at me. "So what else, Hope?" he asks. "What do you do for work?"

"I have a bakery." I shoot a look at Alain. "My grandmother started it in 1952. It's all her family recipes, from back here in Paris."

Alain shakes his head and turns to his friends. "Incredible, isn't it? That she has kept our family's tradition alive all these years?"

"It would be more incredible," says Henri, "if she had brought us some pastries this morning. Since you, Alain, did not bother to get any."

Alain holds up his hands in mock defeat and Simon tilts his head to the side. "Perhaps Hope can tell us about some of her pastries," he says. "So that we can imagine eating them."

I laugh and begin to describe some of my favorites. I tell them about the strudels we make, and the cheesecakes. I tell them about Mamie's Star Pies, and how they're virtually identical to the slices of pie I found at the *ashkénaze* bakery the day before. The men are smiling and nodding enthusiastically, but something changes when I begin listing some of our other specialties: the orange flower-tinged crescent moons, the savory anise and fennel cookies, the sweet pistachio cakes drenched in honey.

Henri and Alain are staring at me in confusion, but Simon looks like he's just seen a ghost. All the blood has drained from his face.

I half laugh, uneasily. "What?" I ask.

"Those aren't pastries from any traditional Jewish bakery I've ever heard of," Henri says. "Your grandmother wouldn't have gotten those from her family."

I watch as Henri and Simon exchange looks.

"What?" I ask again.

It's Simon who speaks first. "Hope," he says softly, all trace of jest gone from his voice. "I think those are Muslim pastries. From North Africa."

I stare back. "Muslim pastries?" I shake my head. "What?"

Henri and Simon glance at each other again. Alain looks like he understands what they're talking about now too. He asks something in French, and when Simon replies, Alain murmurs, "It cannot be true. Can it?"

"What are you talking about?" I ask, leaning forward. They're making me nervous. The men ignore me and exchange a few more words in rapid French. Alain checks his watch, nods, and stands up. The other two men stand too.

"Come, Hope," Alain says. "There is something we must do."

"What?" I ask, completely baffled. "Do we even have time?"

Alain looks at his watch again, and I check mine too. It's nearly eight.

"We will find the time," he says. "This is important. Let us go. Bring your things."

I grab my duffel bag and follow behind the men as we silently leave the apartment.

"Where are we going?" I demand once we get to the rue de Turenne and Henri puts his arm up to hail a cab.

"To the Grand Mosquée de Paris," Simon says. "The Grand Mosque."

I stare at him. "Wait, we're going to a mosque?"

Alain reaches out and touches my cheek. "Trust us, Hope," he says. His eyes are sparkling, and he smiles at me. "We will explain on the way."

Chapter *Fifteen*

～～

We never knew whether to believe the rumors," Alain begins once we've piled into a cab and are hurtling south toward the river. Outside, the streets are just coming alive with people as the sun begins to warm the earth and bathe the buildings in lemon light.

"What rumors?" I ask. "What are you talking about?"

Alain and Simon exchange looks.

Henri speaks first. "There have been rumors that the Muslims in Paris saved many Jews during the war," he says flatly.

I stare at him, then I look at Alain and Simon, who are nodding. "Wait, you're telling me that Muslims saved Jewish people?"

"We never heard about it during the war," says Simon. He glances at Alain. "Well, almost never."

Alain nods. "Jacob said something once that made me think . . ." His voice trails off and he shakes his head. "But I never really believed it."

"There was a time," Henri says, "that we viewed each other as brothers, in a way. The Jews and the Muslims. The Muslims were not persecuted during the war as we were, but they were always made to feel as outsiders, just like the Jews. I would guess

that to some Muslims, seeing Jews being persecuted felt very personal. Who was to say that the country wouldn't turn its back on
them next?"

"And so the rumor was that they helped us," Simon says. "I
never knew if it was true."

"What do you mean?" I ask.

"The rumors have always said that they gave housing and
shelter to many children whose parents had been deported, and a
few adults too," Alain says. "And that eventually, they sent those
people through underground channels to the free zone, in some
cases helping them to get false papers."

"You're telling me Muslims smuggled Jews out of Paris?" I
ask. I shake my head; it's difficult to believe.

"The leader of the Grand Mosque of Paris was, at that time,
the most powerful Muslim in Europe," Henri says. He glances at
Alain. "Si Kaddour Beng—*Comment s'est-il appelé?*"

"Benghabrit," Alain says.

Henri nods. "Yes, that is it. Si Kaddour Benghabrit. The
French government was afraid to touch him. And it is possible
he used that power and influence to save many lives."

I shake my head and stare out the window at Paris rolling
by. The towers of Notre-Dame are silhouetted in the distance
against the sky to the right as we cross over a bridge and hurtle
toward the Left Bank. Far away, I can hear church bells striking
the hour. "So you're saying that might be how my grandmother
got out of Paris? That Muslims from the Grand Mosque may
have gotten her out?"

"It would explain where she learned to bake Muslim pastries," Alain says.

"It would answer a lot of questions," Henri adds. "It is doubt-
ful that there are any records. No one speaks of it. The secrets of
that time have died with that time. Today, there is much tension
between the religious groups. It is impossible to know whether
it is true."

"But what if it is?" I whisper. And then I remember, suddenly, Mamie's words for me just before I left for Paris, when I was pressing her for an answer about whether or not she was Jewish. *Yes, I am Jewish,* she had said. *But I am also Catholic. And Muslim too.* A shiver of realization runs through me and my eyes widen.

The cab pulls up to the curb alongside a white building with deep green tiles on its roof, ornate arches, and glistening domes. A green-trimmed minaret rises from the building, and although it's decidedly Moroccan in its details, it looks a lot like one of the towers of Notre-Dame that we just passed. Something else Mamie said echoes in my head. *It is mankind that creates the differences,* she'd told me last week. *That does not mean it is not all the same God.*

Henri pays the driver, and we get out of the cab. I give both Henri and Simon a hand as they straighten their legs and step out onto the sidewalk.

"There was a time I used to be able to do that myself," Henri says with a smile. He winks at me, and the four of us head toward an arched entrance at the corner of the building.

"If no one here ever speaks of what happened," I whisper to Alain as we cross into a small courtyard, "what are we doing here?"

He links his arm through mine and smiles. "Looking at pastries," he says.

The courtyard is dappled in patches of sunlight that filter through the trees and throw shadows on the tiled white ground. Small blue-and-white-tiled tables are set up in the middle of the courtyard and along the walls, and all of them are framed by wooden chairs with seats and backs of woven bright blue. Deep green plants with yellow flowers creep up the walls, and sparrows hop from table to table. It's peaceful, tranquil, and so empty that I'm certain it's not open yet.

A middle-aged Arab man dressed all in black approaches and says something in French. Alain replies and gestures to me, and for the next minute, the four men talk in rapid French I can't understand. The man shakes his head at first, but finally, he shrugs and gestures for us to follow him up a small stairway into the main building.

There's a dark-haired, olive-skinned younger man, maybe twenty-five, inside the doorway filling a clear bakery case with pastries, and my heart stops as I look inside. There, in the case, are numerous baked goods, nearly half of which are exactly the same as the pastries I make at my own bakery. There are delicate crescent moons dusted in snow-white powdered sugar; small, pale green cakes in white pastry wrappers, topped with tiny pieces of pistachios; honey-drenched slices of baklava; and sticky almond pastries topped with single cherries in their middles. There are thin rolls of phyllo dough rolled in sugar; thick slices of a sugary almond cake rolled in almonds; and even the small, dense rings of cinnamon and honey that have been Annie's favorites since she was a little girl.

My heart is thudding as I look up at Alain.

"They are the same?" he asks.

I nod slowly. "They are the same," I confirm.

He smiles, his eyes suddenly watery, and turns to the older man, who is frowning at us. They exchange a few sentences in French, and then Alain turns to me. "Hope, would you tell this man about your pastries? I've told him what we think might have happened with Rose."

I smile at the man, who looks skeptical. "The things you make here," I say. "They are the same as my grandmother taught me to make. They're the same things we sell in our bakery in Cape Cod."

The man shakes his head. "But that means nothing. These are common pastries. And there are many Jews who came from northern Africa. The pastries are not just Muslim, you see. Your grandmother, she could have learned to make them anywhere. She probably learned them from another Jew."

My heart sinks. It's silly for us to be staking our whole idea of the past on a collection of pastries. "Of course," I murmur. "I'm sorry." I nod slowly and turn away.

Alain puts a hand on my arm. "Hope?" he asks. "Are you all right?"

I nod again, but I don't mean it. I can't find words, because I feel like I'm about to cry, and I can't quite understand why. I don't know why it feels so important to me to be able to explain what happened to Mamie, but it does. I'm sure now that she wanted me to come here to learn about her past. But now we may never know how she made it out alive during the war.

"Let's go," I finally muster. The man in black nods curtly at us and walks away, while Henri and Simon begin making their way back out the way we came in. Alain and I start to follow, but suddenly, I catch the scent of something familiar, and I come to an abrupt halt. I turn slowly around and look at the young man behind the pastry counter, who is sliding a tray of rectangular, sugar-powdered pastries into the display case. I walk back up to the counter.

"Excuse me," I say. "Do you, by any chance, have, um"—I struggle to remember the name of the pastry from the bakery in the Marais—"Ronde des Pavés?"

The man looks at me. "Ronde des Pavés?" he repeats. "I no speak good the English. *Mais, non,* I do not know what this is, Ronde des Pavés."

"Um." I look around for Alain. He joins me at the counter. "Can you tell this man that Ronde des Pavés is a pie made of poppy seeds, almonds, grapes, figs, prunes, and cinnamon sugar? Can you ask if that sounds familiar?"

I know I might be losing my mind, but I swear, I can smell Star Pie wafting through the air. Before Alain translates, he gives me a strange look. "That was my mother's recipe," he says.

I nod. "It's our bakery's specialty," I tell him. "And my grandmother's favorite thing."

Alain blinks at me a few times, turns back to the young man, and quickly translates. I watch as the young man nods and says something in return. Alain turns to me. "He says yes. He says that here, though, they make the pies individually, and each crust has the pattern of a star."

My mouth falls open. "That's how Mamie taught me to make them," I say softly. "She calls them Star Pies."

Alain scratches his head. Beside me, Simon and Henri are silent. We all stare at the young man as Alain explains the Star Pies in French. The man's eyes widen, and he looks quickly at me and then back to Alain. He says something in rapid French, and then Alain turns to look at me.

"He says there is a man who lives in the sixth," Alain says. "Not so very far away. His family has a Muslim bakery. The recipe came from him. He might be able to explain where it originated."

I nod and glance at the young man. "Thank you," I say. *"Merci beaucoup."*

"De rien." The man nods at me and smiles. *"Bonne chance."*

As I follow Alain and his two friends back through the courtyard toward the street, my heart is pounding. "Do you think the pies have something to do with my grandmother?" I ask him.

"There is no way to tell," Alain says. But from the sparkle in his eyes and the quickening of his step, I can tell he's hopeful, and that gives me hope too.

We hail a cab and ride in silence for fifteen minutes, until our driver pulls up in front of the address the young man at the bakery gave us. It's a small bakery that looks typically French, except for its sign, which is in both Arabic and French. Inside, the smell of yeast is heavy, and the walls are lined with baguettes standing vertically. The display case in front is an endless array of pastries dotted with fruits and crystallized sugar. I recognize the large Star Pies immediately, with their signature crisscrossed crust pattern that I've been making for years, and my heartbeat picks up; surely this is a sign that we're on the right path.

We ask the young woman behind the counter whether we can speak with the owner, and a moment later, a tall, middle-aged man with caramel skin and jet-black hair graying at the temples emerges from a back room. He's wearing a stark white baker's apron over perfectly pressed khaki slacks and a pale blue button-down shirt.

"Ah yes, Sahib telephoned from the mosque and told me you would be coming," the man says after greeting the four of us. "I am Hassan Romyo, and you are most welcome here. But I am afraid I may not be able to help you."

My heart sinks. "Sir, do you know where the recipe for the pies with the star lattice crust comes from?" I ask in a small voice, pointing to the pies in the display case.

He shakes his head. "I have owned this bakery for twenty years now," he tells me, "and the recipe has been here as long as I can remember. My mother before me made it too, but she died long ago. I thought always that it was a family recipe."

"It's a Jewish recipe," Alain interjects softly. Monsieur Romyo looks at him with raised eyebrows. "It comes from my grandmother's mother, in Poland, many years ago."

"Jewish?" Monsieur Romyo asks. "And Polish? Are you quite certain?"

Alain nods. "It is the exact same recipe my grandparents made in their bakery, before World War Two. We believe there is a chance my sister may have taught your family how to make this pie, during the war."

Monsieur Romyo looks at Alain for a long time and then nods. "*Alors.* My parents have both died, but they were young in the war. Just children. They would not remember. But my mother's uncle, he may know."

"Is he here?" I ask.

Monsieur Romyo laughs. "No, madame. He is very old. He is seventy-nine."

"Seventy-nine is not old," Henri mutters under his breath behind me, but Monsieur Romyo doesn't seem to hear him.

"I will telephone him now," he says. "But he is nearly deaf, you understand? It is difficult to talk with him."

"Please try," I say in a small voice.

He nods. "Now I admit I am curious too."

He crosses behind the counter, picks up a cell phone, and scrolls through the phone's address book. He pushes Send a moment later and lifts the phone to his ear.

It's not until I hear him say *"Hallo? Oncle Nabi?"* that I realize I've been holding my breath. I exhale slowly.

I listen without understanding as he speaks loudly into the phone in French, repeating himself several times. Finally, he puts his hand over the mouthpiece and addresses me. "This tart of stars," he says, "my uncle Nabi says his family learned it from a young woman."

Alain and I exchange glances. "When?" I ask urgently.

Monsieur Romyo says something else into the phone, then he repeats himself more loudly. He puts his hand over the receiver once more. "During *l'année mille neuf cents quarante-deux,*" he says. "Nineteen forty-two."

I gasp. "Is it possible . . . ?" I ask Alain, my voice trailing off. I turn to Monsieur Romyo. "Does your uncle remember anything about this woman?"

I watch as he repeats my question, in French, over the phone. A moment later, he looks up at us again. "Rose," he says. *"Elle s'est appelée Rose."*

"What?" I ask Alain in a panic.

Alain turns to me with a smile. "He says that the woman's name was Rose."

"That's my grandmother," I murmur, looking at Monsieur Romyo.

He nods, then he says something else into the phone and listens for a moment. He hangs up and scratches his head. "This is all very unusual," he says. He glances at Alain and then back at me. "All of these years, I had no idea . . ." His voice trails off and he clears his throat. "My uncle, Nabi Haddam, would like you to visit him right away. *D'accord?*"

"Merci. D'accord," Alain agrees instantly. He glances at me. "Okay," he translates. "We will go now."

Five minutes later, Simon, Henri, Alain, and I are in a cab heading south, toward an address on the rue des Lyonnais, which Monsieur Romyo assured us was close by. I check my watch again. It's 8:25. We'll barely make our flight, but right now, this feels like something we have to do.

I'm shaking by the time we pull up to Nabi Haddam's apartment building. He's already waiting outside for us. I know from what Mr. Romyo told us that he's just a year younger than Alain, but he looks like he's from a different generation entirely. His hair is jet-black and his face isn't nearly as lined as my uncle's. He's dressed in a gray suit, and his hands are clasped together. As we step out of the car, he stares at me.

"You are her granddaughter," he says haltingly, before we've had a chance to introduce ourselves. "You are the granddaughter of Rose."

I take a deep breath. "Yes."

He smiles and strides quickly over. He kisses me on both cheeks. "You are a mirror image," he says. There are tears in his eyes as he pulls away.

Alain introduces himself as Rose's brother, and Henri and Simon say hello too. I tell Monsieur Haddam that my name is Hope.

"It is right, this name," he murmurs. "For your grandmother, she survived because of hope." He blinks a few times and smiles. "Please, come in."

He gestures to the door of the building, punches in a code, and leads us into a dark hallway. A door to the left is ajar, and he pushes it open farther for us. "My home," he says, gesturing around. "You are welcome here."

Once we're seated, in a dimly lit room lined with books and photographs of who I'm guessing are Monsieur Haddam's family members, Alain leans forward. "How did you know my sister? Rose?"

"Pardon?" he says. He blinks a few times and says, "I am nearly *sourd*. Deaf. I am sorry."

Alain repeats the question loudly, and this time, Monsieur Haddam nods.

He smiles and leans back in his chair. He looks at Alain for a long time before answering. "You are her younger brother? You had eleven years in 1942?"

"Oui," Alain says.

"She talked of you often," he says simply.

"She did?" Alain asks in a whisper.

Monsieur Haddam nods. "I think it is one reason why she was so kind to me. I had just ten years old that year, you see. She told me often that I made her think of you."

Alain looks down, and I know he's struggling not to cry in front of the other men.

"She thought you were all lost," Monsieur Haddam says after a moment. "I think her heart, it was broken, because of this. She often cried herself to sleep, and she said your names as she wept."

When Alain looks up again, there's a single tear rolling down his right cheek. He brushes it away. "I thought she was lost too," he says. "All these years."

Monsieur Haddam turns to me. "You are her granddaughter," he says. "And so, she lived?"

"She lived," I say softly.

"Still, she is alive?"

I pause. "Yes." I'm about to tell him that she's had a stroke, but I swallow the words. I'm not sure whether it's because I'm not ready to acknowledge the fact or because I don't want to ruin Monsieur Haddam's happy ending. "How . . . What happened?" I finally ask.

Monsieur Haddam smiles. "Can I get any of you a cup of tea?" he asks.

We all shake our heads. The men are as eager as I am to hear the story.

"Very well," Monsieur Haddam says. "I will tell you." He takes a deep breath. "She came to us in July of 1942. The night those terrible roundups began."

"The Vel' d'Hiv," I say.

Monsieur Haddam nods. "Yes. Before that, I think many people were blind to what was happening. Even after that, many people remained blind. But Rose, she knew it was coming. And she came to us for sanctuary.

"My family, we took her in. She told the officials at the mosque that her mother's family were bakers. So they asked us if we could provide her refuge for a time. That was a time in the world when a shared profession meant more than different religions.

"I looked up to Rose, in a way that concerned my father at first, because she was different, and I was not supposed to have such admiration for a young woman from a different world," he continues. "But she was kind and gentle and taught me many things. And in time, I think my parents understood that she was not so different from us after all."

He pauses for a moment, his head bent. Finally, he sighs and continues. "She lived with us, as a Muslim, for two months. Every morning and every night, she said our prayers with us, which made my parents happy. But she still prayed to her God too; I heard her every night, long into the night, asking for the protection of the people she loved. It seems that in you, God answered her prayers." He smiles at Alain, who covers his face with his hands and looks away.

"We taught her many things, about Islam and about baking," Monsieur Haddam continues. "And in turn, she taught us many things. She worked in our bakery. She and my mother spent many hours in the kitchen, whispering to each other. I do not know what about; my mother would always say it was woman talk. But Rose, she taught us the *tarte des étoiles,* the star pie that brought you here to me today. It was her favorite, and it was my favorite too, because Rose told me the story."

"What story?" I ask.

Monsieur Haddam looks surprised. "The story of why she made the crust of stars."

Alain and I exchange looks. "Why?" I ask. "What's the story?"

"You do not know?" Monsieur Haddam asks. When Alain and I shake our heads, he continues. "It was because it made her think of her true love's promise to love her as long as there were stars in the sky."

I look at Alain. "Jacob," I whisper. He nods. All these years that I've been making Star Pies, I realize, I've been baking a tribute to a man I never knew existed. A small noise rises from the back of my throat as I choke back a sob that seems to come from nowhere.

"There were many nights when it was not safe to be outside, or when the clouds covered the city, or when smoke hung thick in the air," Monsieur Haddam continues. "On those nights that Rose could not see the stars, she said she needed comfort in something. And so she began putting the stars in her tarts. Years later, when I was a young man, my mother used to bake me these same pies and remind me that true love is worth everything. It was not a common concept in those days; there were many arranged marriages. But she was right. And I waited. I married the love of my life. And so for the rest of my days, I have made the *tartes des étoiles* in honor of Rose. And I taught my children, and my cousins, and the next generation, to do the same, to remember to wait for love, like Rose did. Like I did."

"So then, did Rose reunite with the man she loved?" Monsieur Haddam asks after a moment. "After the war?"

Alain and I exchange looks. "No," I say, feeling the weight

of the loss pressing against my chest. Monsieur Haddam looks down and shakes his head sadly.

Beside me, Henri clears his throat. I'd become so enraptured by Monsieur Haddam's story that I'd almost forgotten that he and Simon were still here. "So how did she get out of Paris?" he asks.

Monsieur Haddam shakes his head. "It is impossible to know for sure. Part of the reason that the mosque was able to save many people was that everything was shrouded in secrecy. The Koran teaches us to give to those in need and to do it quietly, for God will know your deeds. For that reason, and because of the danger involved, no one talked of these things, even then. Certainly not to a ten-year-old boy. But from what I have learned since that time, I believe many of the Jews we sheltered were brought through the catacombs to the river Seine. Perhaps she was smuggled onto a barge that took her down the river to Dijon. Or taken with false papers across the line of demarcation."

"Was that not expensive?" Henri asks. "Getting false papers? Getting across the line?" He turns to me and adds, "My family could not get out, because of the expense."

"Yes," Monsieur Haddam replies. "But the mosque helped with papers. That much I know. And the man she loved, Jacob? He left her with money. She sewed it into the lining of one of her dresses. My mother helped her.

"Once she was in the unoccupied zone, it would have been easier for her to get out of the country," Monsieur Haddam continues. "Here in Paris, she lived as a Muslim with false papers. But in Dijon, or wherever she went, she likely filled out a census form with the *gendarmerie*. Because she was French, she was likely able to pay a small bribe and obtain papers listing her as Catholic. From there, she could have made it to Spain."

"She met my grandfather in Spain," I say.

"Your grandfather is not Jacob?" Monsieur Haddam asks

with a frown. "It seems impossible that she loved another so soon."

"No," I say softly. "My grandfather's name was Ted."

He bows his head. "So she married another." He pauses. "I always assumed Rose perished," he says. "So many did in those days. I always believed she would have made contact after the war, if she had lived. But perhaps she wanted only to forget this life."

I think of what Gavin said about some Holocaust survivors wanting to start over when they believed they'd lost everything.

"But why are there no records of any of this?" I ask after a moment. "It's so brave and heroic what your family did. What other people at the Grand Mosque did."

Monsieur Haddam smiles. "At the time, we could not keep any sort of written record," he says. "We knew we were tying our fate to that of the people we saved. If the Nazis, or the French police, had raided the mosque and found even one piece of evidence, it could have been the end of us all.

"So we helped quietly," he concludes. "It is the thing I am proudest of in all my life."

"Thank you," Alain whispers. "For what you did. For saving my sister."

Monsieur Haddam shakes his head. "There is no need to thank me. It was our duty. In our religion, we are taught, 'Whoever saves one life, saves the entire world.' "

Alain makes a strange strangled sound. "In the Talmud, it is written, 'If you save one life, it is as if you have saved the world,'" he says softly.

He and Monsieur Haddam look at each other for a moment and smile.

"We are not so different, then," Monsieur Haddam says. He looks at Henri and Simon, then back at Alain. "I never understood the war between our religions, or the war with Christianity. If there is one thing I learned from the time young Rose spent with us, it is that we are all speaking to the same God. It is not religion that divides man. It is good and evil here on earth that divides us."

The words sink in as we look at one another in silence.

"Your sister," Monsieur Haddam continues, turning to Alain, "she suffered every day, because she left her family. She never believed she did enough to save you. But you understand, of course, she did what she had to do. She had to save her baby."

In the silence that follows, you could hear a pin drop. "Her baby?" Alain finally asks, his voice an octave higher than it should be. My mouth is suddenly dry.

"Yes, of course," says Monsieur Haddam. He blinks at us. "It is why she came here. She was with child. You did not know?"

Alain turns to stare at me. "Did *you* know this?"

"Of course not," I say. "It's . . . it's not possible. My mother wasn't born until 1944." I turn back to Monsieur Haddam. "And my mom didn't have any siblings. My grandmother couldn't have been pregnant in 1942."

He pauses and stands up. "Excuse me for a moment," he says. He disappears into his bedroom, while Alain and I go back to staring at each other.

"How could she have been pregnant?" Alain asks.

"Well, she and Jacob were in love . . ." Henri says, his voice trailing off.

Alain shakes his head. "No, absolutely not. She was very religious," he says. "She would never have done such a thing." He glances at me and adds, "Things were different in those days. People did not have relations before marriage. Certainly not Rose."

"Maybe Monsieur Haddam is remembering wrong," I say.

But when he emerges from his bedroom a moment later, he's carrying a photograph, which he hands to me. I recognize my grandmother immediately; she looks just like I looked when I was sixteen or seventeen, and her head is wrapped in a scarf. She has one arm around a dark-haired, smiling boy and the other around a middle-aged woman.

"That is my mother and me," Monsieur Haddam says softly. "And your grandmother. The day she left. The last time I ever saw her."

I nod, but I can't seem to speak, because I can't look away from the bulging belly in the photograph. There's no doubt that my grandmother is pregnant. She gazes into the camera with wide eyes that broadcast extraordinary sadness, even in grainy black and white. Alain sinks down beside me on the couch and stares at the photo too.

"She knew that if she was taken to one of the camps, she would be killed as soon as they found out she was with child," Monsieur Haddam says softly after a moment. "She knew she had to protect herself in order to protect the baby. It was the only reason she let Jacob separate her from her family."

"My God," Alain murmurs.

"But what happened to the baby?" I ask.

Monsieur Haddam frowns at me. "You are certain that the baby was not your mother?"

I nod. "My mother was born a year and a half later to my grandfather, Ted, not Jacob." I turn to Alain. "The baby must have died," I say softly. Even saying the words aloud horrifies me.

Alain hangs his head. "There is so much we do not know. What if she does not wake up?" he murmurs.

His words send me hurtling back from a past we can't understand to a present we can't control. But we *can* control whether we leave for the airport on time. I look at my watch and stand up.

"Monsieur Haddam, I'm sorry, but we have to leave," I say. "I don't know how to thank you."

He smiles. "Young lady, you do not have to," he replies. "Knowing that Rose lived, and went on to have a happy life, is thanks enough for a million years."

I wonder, in that moment, whether my grandmother's life

was happy. Had she ever let go of the sadness she must have felt when she believed she'd lost Jacob and her family forever?

"Please," Monsieur Haddam says, "tell your grandmother that I think of her often. And that I thank her for helping me to believe in finding love. She changed my life. I will never forget her."

"Thank you so much, Monsieur Haddam," I murmur. "I'll tell her."

He kisses me on both cheeks, and as I follow Alain, Henri, and Simon back out to the street to hail a cab to the airport, I find myself wondering whether this is why Mamie sent me here. I wonder whether somewhere deep down, she wanted me to hear the story of her first love, and of the lost child she gave everything to protect. I wonder whether I'm supposed to learn something about love from all of this.

Or perhaps it's too late for me. Alain and I are silent on the way to the airport, both of us lost in our own worlds.

Chapter *Sixteen*

Anise and Fennel Cookies

INGREDIENTS

2 cups sugar

4 eggs

2 tsp. anise extract

3 cups flour, plus extra for rolling

3 tsp. baking powder

1 tsp. salt

1 tsp. anise seed

2 cups confectioners' sugar

1 Tbsp. fennel seed

DIRECTIONS

1. Preheat oven to 350 degrees.

2. In a medium bowl, using a hand mixer, beat sugar, eggs, and anise extract until well blended.

3. Sift together 3 cups flour, baking powder, and salt, then add to the egg mixture, approximately one cup at a time, beating after each addition.

4. Add anise seed and make sure mixture is well blended.

5. In a separate, shallow bowl, mix together confectioners' sugar and fennel seed.

6. Flour hands lightly and roll tablespoon-sized lumps of dough into balls. Roll each ball in confectioners' sugar mixture, making sure it's well-coated, and place on greased cookie sheets.

7. Bake for 12 minutes. Cool for 5 minutes on baking sheets, then remove to wire racks.

Rose

Something was terribly wrong, and Rose knew it. All afternoon, she had been sitting in front of her television, watching daytime reruns of programs she knew she had seen before. But it didn't matter; she couldn't remember the plots anyhow. She had grown very tired, and back in her room, she realized she could no longer feel her body. Then, everything had gone black.

The world had still been dark as night when they came for her, the people from the home. She heard them saying *unconscious* and *stroke* and *barely hanging on*, and she wanted to tell them that she was fine. But she found that she could no longer use her tongue, nor could she open her eyes, and it was in this way that she realized her body was failing her, just like her mind was. Perhaps it was time.

And so she let go and drifted further into the past. As the ambulance sirens sounded in the distance, as the doctors shouted and gave orders from very far away, as the small voice of a child cried near her bed, she released her grip on the present and let herself float, like jetsam on a wave, back to a time just before the world fell apart. There were voices then too, in the darkness, just as there were now. And as the present disappeared, the past came into focus, and Rose found herself in her father's study, in the apartment on rue du Général Camou. She was seventeen again, and she felt as if she had a crystal ball and no one believed her.

"Please," she was begging her father, her voice hoarse from endless hours of fruitless persuasion. "If we stay, we will die, Papa! They are coming for us!"

The Nazis were everywhere. German soldiers filled the streets, and the French police followed along like lemmings. Jews were no longer permitted to go out without the yellow Star of David sewn over their left breast, a brand marking them as different.

"Nonsense," said her father, a proud man who believed in his country and in the goodness of his fellow man. "Only criminals and cowards run."

"No, Papa," Rose whispered. "It's not just criminals and cowards. It's people who want to save themselves, who don't want to blindly follow, hoping that everything will be okay."

Her father closed his eyes and rubbed the bridge of his nose. Beside him, Rose's mother rubbed his arm comfortingly and looked at her daughter. "You are upsetting your father, Rose," she said.

"But, Maman!" Rose exclaimed.

"We are French," her father said tersely, opening his eyes. "They are not deporting French."

"But they *are*," Rose whispered. "And Maman is not French. To them, she is still Polish. In their eyes, that makes her—and us—foreigners."

"You are talking nonsense, child," her father said.

"This roundup is going to be different," Rose said. She felt like she'd said it a thousand times before, but her father wasn't hearing her because he didn't want to. "They are coming for all of us this time. Jacob says—"

"Rose!" her father interrupted, slamming his fist on the table. Beside him, Rose's mother jumped, startled, and shook her head sadly. "That boy has a runaway imagination!"

"Papa, it's not his imagination!" Rose had never spoken against her parents before, but she had to make them believe her. This was life and death. How could they be so blind? "You're our father, Papa. You have to protect us!"

"Enough!" her father roared. "You will not tell me how to run my family! That boy, Jacob, will not tell me how to run my family! I *am* protecting you children, and your mother, by following the rules. Do not tell me how to be a parent! You know nothing of such things."

Rose fought back the tears in her eyes. She put her right hand on her belly, without intending to, and she quickly moved it back to her side when she saw her mother look at her curiously and frown. She wouldn't be able to hide it from them for much longer, and then they would know. Would they forgive her? Would they understand? Rose thought not.

She wished she could tell them the truth. But now wasn't the time. It would only complicate matters. Before she did anything, she needed to save them.

"Rose," her father said after a moment. He stood and walked over to where she sat. He knelt beside her, the way he used to when she was a little girl. She remembered, in that moment, the way he'd been so patient with her when he'd taught her to tie her shoelaces, the way he'd comforted her the first time she skinned her knee, the way he'd pinched her cheeks when she was just a little girl and called her *ma filfille en sucre,* my little girl made of sugar. "We will do what they say. If we follow the rules, everything will be fine."

She looked into his eyes and knew in that moment that she would never change his mind. And so she wept, for she had already lost him. She had already lost them all.

When Jacob came for her later that night, she wasn't ready. How could she ever be ready? She gazed into his gold-flecked green eyes, which had always reminded her of a magical ocean, and thought about how she could get lost there forever. Her own eyes filled with hot, stinging tears as she realized she might never sail those seas again.

"Rose, we must go," he whispered urgently. He took her in his arms and tried to absorb her sobs with his body.

"But how can I leave them, Jacob?" she whispered into his chest.

"You must, my love," he said. "You must save our baby."

She looked up at him. She knew he was right. There were tears in his eyes too. "Will you try to protect them?" she asked.

"With every ounce of my being," Jacob vowed. "But first I must protect you."

Before they left, she slipped into the room Alain and Claude shared. Claude was sleeping soundly, but Alain was wide awake.

"You're leaving now, aren't you, Rose?" Alain whispered when she drew close.

She sat down on the side of his bed. "Yes, my dear," she whispered. "Will you come with us?"

"I must stay with Maman and Papa," Alain said after a moment. "Maybe they are right."

"They are not," Rose said.

Alain nodded. "I know," he whispered. He paused for a moment and then wrapped his arms around her. "I love you, Rose," he whispered.

"I love you too, my little man," she replied, pulling him tightly to her. She knew Alain didn't understand why she was leaving him. She knew it seemed to him as if she was choosing Jacob over her family. But she couldn't tell him about the baby growing within her. He was eleven, too young to understand. She hoped that someday, he would realize that she felt as though her heart were being ripped in two.

Thirty minutes later, Jacob led her through an alleyway, where his friend Jean Michel, who was part of the resistance movement, waited outside a darkened doorway.

Jean Michel kissed Rose hello on both cheeks. "You are very brave, Rose," he said simply.

"I am not brave; I am frightened," she replied. She did not want anyone to think she was brave. To think that it was brave to leave her family behind was absurd. She felt, in that moment, like the worst human being on the earth.

"May we have a moment alone?" Jacob asked Jean Michel.

Jean Michel nodded. "But quickly, please. There isn't much time." He slipped through the doorway, leaving Rose and Jacob alone in the darkness.

"You are doing the right thing," Jacob whispered.

"It does not feel that way anymore," Rose said. She took a deep breath. "You are completely sure? About this roundup?"

Jacob nodded. "I'm certain. It's beginning in a few hours, Rose."

She shook her head. "What has happened to us?" she asked. "To this country?"

"The world has gone mad," Jacob murmured.

She took a deep breath. "You will come back for me?"

"I will come back for you," Jacob said immediately. "You are my life, Rose. You and our baby. You know that."

"I know," she whispered.

"I will find you, Rose," Jacob said. "When all of the horrors are over, and you are safe, I will come for you. I give you my word. I will not rest until I am beside you again."

"Nor will I," Rose murmured.

He pulled her to him, and she breathed in the scent of him, memorized the feel of his arms around her, pressed her head against his chest, and wished she never had to let go. But then Jean Michel was back, and he was gently pulling her away from Jacob, softly telling her that they had to go now, before it was too late. She knew only that Jean Michel, a Catholic, was taking her to another man who was part of a resistance, a man named Ali, who was a Muslim. It was the sort of thing that would have made her smile—Catholics, Jews, and Muslims working together as one—had the world not been falling down around them.

Jacob pulled her to him once more, for one more long kiss good-bye. As Jean Michel led her away, she pulled away from him. "Jacob?" she called softly into the darkness.

"I'm here," he said. He reappeared from the shadows.

She took a deep breath. "Go back for them. Please. My family. I can't lose them. I can't live with myself if they perish because I did not try hard enough."

Jacob stared into her eyes, and for a moment, Rose wanted to take the words back, because she knew what she was asking. But there wasn't time. He nodded and said simply, "I will go back. I promise. I love you."

And then he was gone into the inky darkness. Rose stood paralyzed, rooted to the spot, for what felt like an eternity but was only a few seconds. "No," she murmured to herself. "What have I done?"

She took a step after Jacob, meaning to stop him, meaning to warn him. But Jean Michel wrapped his arms around her and held tight.

"No," he said. "No. It is in God's hands now. You must come with me."

"But . . ." she protested, trying to pull away.

"It is in God's hands," Jean Michel repeated as sobs began to rack Rose's body. He held her more tightly and whispered into the darkness, "For now, all we can do is pray and hope that God can hear us."

It was torture, after that, to live in Paris in secret, knowing that within a mile or two, her family or Jacob might also be in hiding. Knowing that she could not reach out to find them, that her one responsibility now was protecting the child within her, made her weep with helplessness every night.

The people who took her in, the Haddams, were kind, although she knew the mother and the father did not want her there. She was, after all, a liability; she knew her very presence put them in danger. If not for the baby she had vowed to protect, she would have left long ago, out of politeness. Still, they were hospitable, and over time, they seemed to accept her. Their boy, Nabi, reminded Rose of Alain, and this was what kept her sane most days; she could talk to him the way she had once talked to her little brother, and in that way, this new home felt a little more like the one she'd left behind.

She and Madame Haddam spent many hours in the kitchen, and after a while, Rose had the courage to offer Madame Haddam some of the recipes from her own family's *ashkénaze* bakery. Madame Haddam, in turn, taught Rose to make many delicious pastries that she'd never heard of before.

"You should know how to cook with rosewater," Madame Haddam had told her one day. "It is only fitting for a girl named Rose."

And so Rose fell in love with the almond crescents and the orange blossom baklava and the rosewater cookies that crumbled in her mouth like magic, and these were the foods that nourished the baby within her. Her father had often said negative things about the Muslims, but Rose knew now that he'd been just as wrong about religion as he had been about the intentions of the Nazis. The Haddams had put their own lives at risk to save hers. They were some of the best people she had ever known.

Furthermore, Rose knew that in order to make pastries like the ones the Haddams made, one had to be good and kind. One's heart always came out in the baking, and if there was darkness in your soul, there would be darkness in your pastries too. In the Haddams' pastries, though, there was light and goodness. Rose could taste it, and she hoped the baby growing inside her could too.

Sometimes, Madame Haddam would let Rose accompany her to the market, as long as Rose vowed not to speak and veiled herself with a scarf. She liked the anonymity it gave her, and at the market, even though the Haddams shopped in a Muslim neighborhood, Rose would scan the crowd desperately, hoping for a glimpse of someone from her old life. One day on the street, she saw Jean Michel, but she couldn't yell for him because of the sudden lump in her throat. By the time she could make a sound again, he was long gone.

One evening, after saying the Salah in Arabic with the Haddams, Rose was in her own room praying in Hebrew when she turned around and saw Nabi watching her. "Come, Nabi," she said to the boy. "Pray with me."

He knelt beside her while she finished her prayers, and then they sat together in silence. "Rose?" he asked after a long while. "Do you think God speaks Arabic or Hebrew? Can he hear your prayers or mine?"

Rose considered this for a moment and realized that she did not know the answer; she had begun to doubt recently that God could hear her at all, no matter what language she spoke. For if he could hear her, how could he allow her family and Jacob to vanish from her life? "I do not know," she said finally. "What do you think, Nabi?"

The boy thought about this for a long time before replying. "I think God must speak all the languages." His tone was confident. "I think he can hear all of us."

"Do you think we are all praying to the same God?" Rose asked after a moment. "Muslims and Jews and Christians and all the people who believe in other things?"

Nabi appeared to be considering this question quite seriously too. "Yes," he finally told Rose. "Yes. There is one God, and he lives in the sky, and he hears all of us. It is just that here on earth, we are confused about how to believe in him. But what does it matter, as long as we trust he is there?"

Rose smiled at that. "I think perhaps you are right, Nabi," she said. She thought of the words Jean Michel had spoken to her the last time she saw Jacob. "For now," she said softly to the young boy, reaching out to ruffle his hair, "all we can do is pray and hope that God can hear us."

Chapter *Seventeen*

⌒

After persuading the gate agent to take us after the required check-in time, rushing through security, and running to our gate, Alain and I make it onto our flight five minutes before they close the cabin doors.

I'd used Alain's cell phone to call Annie from the taxi, but she didn't answer. Nor did Gavin or Rob, both of whom I tried. Mamie's home had no new information about her condition, and the nurse I reached at the hospital said that my grandmother was stable, but that it was impossible to tell how long she'd stay that way.

As we taxi down the runway and take off over Paris, I watch the Seine disappear beneath us, a ribbon cutting through the land, and I imagine Mamie hiding on a barge at the age of seventeen, slowly snaking down the same topaz river to the unoccupied zone. Is that how she'd gotten out of Paris? I wonder whether we'll ever really know.

"What do you think happened to the baby she was carrying?" Alain asks me softly as we climb higher into the sky. We're above the clouds now, with sunlight filtering down all around us, and I can't help but wonder whether this is a bit like what heaven looks like.

I shake my head. "I don't know."

"I should have guessed that she was with child," Alain says. "It explains why she left us. That never made sense to me. It would not have been in her nature to run and leave us behind. She would have stayed to try to persuade us, to try to protect us, even if it meant risking her own life."

"But she believed it was more important to protect the baby," I murmur.

Alain nods. "And it was. She was right. That is what it means to be a parent, is it not? I think it was the same with my parents. They truly thought that following the rules would protect us all. Who could have known that their best intention would lead where it did?"

I shake my head, too sad to speak. I can't imagine the feeling of horror my great-grandmother must have felt when Danielle and David were torn from her. Had she been able to stay with the oldest, Helene, after they separated the men and the women? Had she lived long enough to suffer the anguish of realizing that all her children had been lost? Had my great-grandfather regretted not listening to his daughter's words of warning? What would it feel like as a parent to realize too late that you'd made a terrible, irreversible mistake and that your children were going to die for it?

I stare out the window for a long moment and turn back to Alain. "Maybe my grandmother couldn't care for the baby. Maybe the baby was born and she put it up for adoption." I don't really believe the words, but it feels better to say them.

"Impossible, I think," Alain says. He frowns. "If the baby was a piece of her and Jacob, I cannot imagine there is any way she would have parted with the child." He looks at me sideways and adds, "You are absolutely certain there is no chance the baby was your mother?" he asks.

I shake my head. "When my mother died a couple of years ago, I had to get her estate in order," I say. "I remember looking at her birth certificate. It clearly said 1944. Plus, she looked a lot like my grandfather."

Alain sighs. "The baby must have died, then."

I look away. I can't imagine anything sadder. "But to think she would get pregnant again so soon after . . ." I add, my voice trailing off. I can't understand that piece of the puzzle.

"That is not as unusual as it sounds," Alain says softly. He sighs again and turns to look out the window. "After the war, many Shoah survivors married and tried to have babies right away, even the ones who were malnourished and had no money."

I look at Alain, surprised. "But why would they do that?"

"To create life when everything around them was death," he says simply. "To be a part of a family again, after they'd lost everyone they'd ever loved. By the time Rose met your grandfather, she must have thought that all of us, including Jacob, were dead, and if she had lost the baby too, she must have felt very, very alone. Maybe she just wanted to create a family so that she'd have a place in the world again."

It takes an eternity to get our bags, get through customs, and retrieve my car from the parking garage, but eventually, we're on our way to the Cape. We're out of Boston just before rush hour hits, and as we hurtle south on Route 3, I take my chances, weaving in and out of traffic at twenty miles over the speed limit.

I call Annie on the way, and this time, she answers. Her voice sounds hollow, but she tells me she's at the hospital, and that there hasn't been any change in Mamie's condition.

"Is your dad with you?" I ask.

"No," she says without elaborating.

I can feel my blood pressure rising. "Where is he?"

"Don't know," she says. "Maybe at his office."

"Did you ask him to go with you to the hospital?"

Annie hesitates. "He was here earlier. But he had to leave to get some work done."

It physically hurts my heart to hear her say that. I want nothing more than to protect my daughter, and it seems that the last place in the world I should be looking for potential harm is from her other parent.

"I'm sorry, honey," I say. "I'm sure your dad must be very busy. But he should have stayed with you."

"It's fine," Annie mumbles. "Gavin's here."

My heart lurches. "Again?"

"Yeah. He called to see if I was okay. And I told him Dad had left. I didn't ask him to come, but he just came."

"Oh," I say.

"You wanna talk to him?"

I'm about to say yes, but I realize we'll be there in an hour. "Just tell him I said hi. And thank you. We'll be there soon."

Annie is silent for a minute. "Who's *we*? You got a boyfriend now too or something?"

I laugh despite myself. "No," I say. I glance at Alain, who's watching Pembroke roll by outside his window. "But I do have a surprise for you."

An hour later, we're in Hyannis, hurrying through the sliding front doors of Cape Cod Hospital. The nurse at the front desk directs us to the third floor, and I see Annie sitting in the waiting room, her head hung low. Beside her, Gavin is flipping through a magazine. They both look up at the same time.

"Mom!" Annie exclaims, apparently forgetting for a moment that she's recently become too cool to greet me with enthusiasm. She jumps up from her chair and hugs me. Gavin gives me a little wave and a crooked half smile. I mouth *thank you* over Annie's head.

Annie finally pulls back and notices Alain for the first time. He's standing beside me, frozen to the spot, staring at her.

"Hi," Annie says. She reaches out her hand. "I'm Annie. Who are you?"

Alain shakes her hand slowly, then opens and closes his mouth without saying anything. I put a hand on his back, smile at my daughter, and say gently, "Annie, this is Mamie's brother. He's your great-great uncle."

Annie looks up at me with wide eyes. "Mamie's brother?" She looks back at Alain. "You're really Mamie's brother?"

Alain nods, and this time, he finds words. "You look so familiar, my dear," he says.

Annie looks at me, and then back at Alain. "Do I, like, look like Mamie looked when she was my age?"

Alain shakes his head slowly. "Perhaps a little. But that is not who you resemble."

"Is it someone named Leona?" Annie asks eagerly. "'Cause Mamie keeps calling me that."

Alain furrows his brow and shakes his head. "I do not think I know a Leona."

Annie frowns, and I look up to realize Gavin has crossed the room and is standing a few steps behind my daughter. For a split second, I have a powerful urge to throw my arms around him, but I blink and take a step back instead. "Gavin," I say, "this is Alain. My grandmother's brother. Alain, this is Gavin." I pause, and as an afterthought, I add, "My friend."

Gavin's eyes are wide. He reaches out and shakes Alain's hand. "I can't believe you and Hope found each other," Gavin says.

Alain glances at me and then back at Gavin. "I understand that she had some help and encouragement from you, young man."

Gavin shrugs and looks away. "No, sir. She did it on her own. I just told her a few things I knew about Holocaust research."

"Do not take away the importance of what you did," Alain says. "You helped reunite our family." He blinks a few times and asks Gavin, "Can we see her now? My sister?"

Gavin hesitates. "Technically, visiting hours are over. But I know a few of the nurses here. Let me see what I can do."

I watch as Gavin approaches a pretty blonde nurse who looks like she's in her early twenties. She laughs and twirls her hair while she talks to him. I'm surprised to realize that watching them together makes me feel a little jealous. I blink a few times, turn away, and put a hand on Alain's arm.

"Are you okay?" I ask. "You must be exhausted."

He nods. "I just need to see Rose."

Annie launches into a rapid-fire series of questions—"When did you last see Mamie?" "How come you thought she died?" "How did you escape those Nazis?" "What happened to your parents?"—which Alain answers patiently. As Annie bends her head toward his and continues to babble excitedly, I smile.

After a moment, Gavin returns and puts a hand on my arm, and as he does, a strange jolt of something shoots through me. I pull away quickly, like I've been burned.

Gavin frowns and clears his throat. "I talked to Krista. The nurse. She says she can sneak us back. But only for a few minutes. They're pretty strict about visiting hours here."

I nod. "Thank you," I say. Oddly, I can't bring myself to thank Krista as she leads the four of us down a narrow hallway, her blonde ponytail bobbing perkily behind her as her narrow hips swish back and forth exaggeratedly. I could swear she's walking that way for Gavin's benefit, but he doesn't seem to notice; he has a hand on Alain's shoulder and is guiding the older man gently toward a doorway at the end of the hall.

"Five minutes," Krista whispers as we stop in front of the last door on the right. "Or I'll get in trouble."

"Thank you so much," Gavin says. "I owe you."

"You can take me out to dinner sometime?" Krista says. The end of the statement rises like a question, and as she bats her eyes at him, she reminds me of a cartoon character. I don't wait to hear his reply; I tell myself it's not important. I follow Annie and Alain into the room, and I gasp at the sight of the still figure lying in the hospital bed, seemingly swallowed by a mound of sheets.

Mamie looks tiny, pale, and shrunken, and beside me, I can feel Alain flinch. I want to tell him that the last time I saw her, she didn't look like this. In fact, I hardly recognize her without her signature burgundy lipstick and kohl eyeliner. But I'm as dumbstruck as he is. We both approach, Annie trailing behind us.

"She looks real bad, doesn't she?" Annie murmurs. I turn and put my arm around her, and she doesn't pull away. I put my right hand on top of Mamie's left hand, which feels cold. She doesn't move.

"They apparently found her slumped over her desk when she didn't come down for dinner," Gavin says softly. I turn and see him standing in the doorway. "They called 911 right away," he adds.

I nod, too choked up to speak. Beside me, I can feel Annie trembling a little, and I look down to see her blinking back tears. I pull her closer and she wraps both arms around me for a hug. We watch as Alain approaches the bed and kneels down so that his face is even with Mamie's. He murmurs something to her, and then he reaches out and strokes her face gently. Tears are glistening in his eyes.

"I thought I would never see her again," he whispers. "It has been nearly seventy years."

"Is she gonna be okay?" Annie asks Alain. She's staring at him as if his answer determines everything.

Alain hesitates and nods. "Annie, I do not know. But I can't believe that God would reunite us, only to take her away without a good-bye. I have to believe there's a reason in all this."

Annie nods vigorously. "Me too."

Before we can say anything more, the perky nurse reappears at the doorway. "Time's up," she says. "My supervisor is on her way."

Gavin and I exchange looks. "Okay," Gavin says. "Thanks, Krista. We'll get out of here." He nods at me, and I slowly lead

Annie away from Mamie. I glance back over my shoulder as I near the door, and I see Alain with his head bent over Mamie's again. He kisses her on the forehead, and when he turns, there are tears rolling down his face.

"I am sorry," he says. "This is difficult."

"I know," I say. I reach for his hand, and together, Annie, Alain, and I walk out of the room, leaving Mamie behind in the darkness.

Gavin and I part at the doorway to the hospital. He has to work at seven the next morning, and I have to open the bakery. Life has to go on. Annie takes my keys from me, and she and Alain go wait in the car.

"I don't know how to thank you," I tell Gavin, looking down at my feet.

"I didn't do anything," he says. I look up in time to see him shrug. He smiles at me. "I'm really glad you found Alain."

"I found him because of you," I say softly. "And Annie was okay while I was gone because of you."

He shrugs again. "Nah. I just did what anyone would do." He pauses and adds, "Maybe this is out of line, but that ex-husband of yours is a real piece of work."

I swallow hard. "Why do you say that?"

He shakes his head. "He barely seemed concerned about Annie, you know? She was so upset about your grandmother. She really needed someone."

"And you were there for her," I say. "I don't even know what to say."

"Yeah, well, say you'll spot me a cup of coffee on my way to the porch repair job I'm doing at Joe Sullivan's place tomorrow," he says. "And we'll be even."

I laugh at this. "Yeah, sure, a cup of coffee is definitely equal to taking care of my daughter and helping reunite my family."

Gavin looks at me for a long time, so intently that my heart starts thudding. "I did those things because I wanted to help," he says.

"Why?" I ask, realizing before I can stop myself that I sound rude and ungrateful.

He stares at me again and shrugs. "Stop selling yourself short, Hope," he says. And with that, he's gone. I watch him get into his old Wrangler and wave to Annie as he pulls out of the parking lot.

"Mom, we have to find Jacob Levy," Annie announces the next morning when she and Alain show up at the bakery together, arms linked. Concerned that he was overexerting himself, I'd suggested that Alain sleep in, but he and Annie have been inseparable since meeting at the hospital the night before, so I should have suspected that she'd bring him to the bakery with her. "Alain told me all about him," she adds proudly.

"Annie, honey," I say, glancing at Alain, who is rolling up his sleeves and glancing around the kitchen, "we don't even know if Jacob is still alive."

"But what if he *is,* Mom?" Annie asks, her voice taking on a desperate edge. "What if he's out there somewhere and he's been looking for Mamie all these years? What if he could come here, and that would make her wake up?"

"Sweetheart, that's unlikely."

Annie glowers at me. "C'mon, Mom! Don't you believe in love?"

I sigh. "I believe in chocolate," I say, nodding to the *pains au chocolat* waiting to go into the oven, "and I believe that if I don't pick up the pace here, we're not going to be ready to open at six."

"What*ever,*" Annie grumbles. She puts on a pair of pot holders and slides the chocolate croissants into the oven. She sets the timer and then turns around to roll her eyes at Alain. "See? I told you she's mean in the morning."

Alain chuckles. "I do not think your mother is being unkind, my dear," he says. "I think she's trying to be realistic. And also perhaps to change the subject."

"Why are you changing the subject, Mom?" Annie demands, putting her hands on her hips.

"Because I don't want you to get your hopes up," I tell her. "There's a huge chance Jacob Levy isn't even alive. And even if he *is,* there's no guarantee we'll find him."

There's also no guarantee that he has waited around for my grandmother all these years. I don't want to tell Annie that even if we do somehow miraculously locate him, he'll probably be married to wife number four or something. He most likely moved on from Mamie seventy years ago. That's what men do. Besides, it appears my grandmother wasted no time in moving on from him.

Alain is looking closely at me, and I avert my gaze, because I have the uneasy feeling he can read exactly what I'm thinking. "Can I help you with anything, Hope?" he asks after a pause. "I used to work in my grandparents' bakery when I was a boy."

I smile. "Annie can show you how to prep the batter for the blueberry muffins," I say. "But don't feel like you have to help. I'm perfectly fine on my own."

"I didn't say that you were not," Alain says. I raise an eyebrow at him, but he has already turned around to let Annie help him tie on an apron.

"So, like, if Mamie was so in love with Jacob, how come she married my great-grandpa?" Annie asks Alain once he turns back around. He grabs a bag of sugar and the flat of plump blueberries that Annie has pulled out of the refrigerator. "She couldn't have loved him too, right?" Annie adds. "Not if Jacob was her one true love."

I roll my eyes, but truth be told, I wish I still believed in the concept of one true love too. Alain seems to be considering the question as he pulls out a big bowl and a wooden spoon and begins mixing sugar and flour. I watch as he measures in salt and baking powder. Annie hands him four eggs, and he sets to work cracking them in.

"There are all different kinds of love in this world, Annie," he says finally. He glances at me and then back at my daughter. "I have no doubt that your great-grandmother loved your great-grandfather too."

Annie stares at him. "What do you mean? If Mamie was in love with Jacob, how could she also, like, be in love with my great-grandpa?"

Alain shrugs and adds some milk and sour cream to the bowl. He mixes vigorously with the wooden spoon, and then Annie helps him fold in the blueberries. "Some kinds of love are more powerful than others," Alain finally replies. "It doesn't mean they aren't all real. Some loves are the kind we try to make fit but are never quite right." He glances at me, and I look away.

"Others are the loves between good people who admire each other's souls and grow to love each other over time," he continues.

"Is that what you think Mamie and my great-grandpa had?" Annie asks.

Alain begins carefully lining muffin tins. "Perhaps," he says. "I do not know. There is also, Annie, the love that all of us have the chance to have, but that few of us are wise enough to see or brave enough to seize. That's the kind of love that can change a life."

"Is that how Jacob and Mamie loved each other?" Annie asks.

"I believe it is," Alain says.

"But what do you mean you have to be wise enough to see it?" Annie asks.

Alain glances at me again, and I pretend to be busy filling a tray full of miniature Star Pies. My fingers shake a little as I form the lattice crusts into star shapes.

"I mean that love is all around us," Alain says. "But the older we get, the more confusing it becomes. The more times we've been hurt, the harder it is to see love right in front of us, or to accept love into our hearts and truly believe in it. And if you cannot accept love, or cannot bring yourself to believe in it, you can never really feel it."

Annie looks confused. "So you mean Mamie and Jacob fell in love because they were young?"

"No, I believe your great-grandmother and Jacob fell in love because they were meant for each other," Alain replies. "And because they did not run from it. They were not scared of it. They did not let their own fears get in the way. Many people in this world never fall in love that way, because their hearts are already closed, and they do not even know it."

I slide a tray of Star Pies into the smaller oven on the left and wince as I carelessly smash my hand against the oven door. I curse under my breath and set the timer.

"Mom?" Annie asks. "Did you love Dad that way?"

"Sure I did," I say quickly, without looking at her. I don't want to tell her that if she hadn't been conceived, I never would have married her father. It wasn't a love for him that made me create a family; it was a love for the life growing inside me.

But what had Mamie been thinking when she met my grandfather? She'd believed, apparently, that she'd already lost Jacob, and somewhere along the way, she'd lost the child she was carrying. Her life must have felt tremendously empty. Had loneliness driven her into the arms of my grandfather? How had she been able to lie beside him at night, knowing that she'd already had—and lost—the love of her life?

"So how come you got a divorce then?" Annie asks. "If you loved Dad like that?"

"Sometimes, things change," I reply.

"Not Mamie and Jacob," Annie says confidently. "I bet they always loved each other. I bet they still love each other."

In that moment, I feel terrible sadness for my grandfather, a kind, warm man who was endlessly devoted to his family. I wonder whether he realized that his wife had apparently given her heart away long before she met him.

I look up to see Alain gazing at me thoughtfully. "It's never too late to find true love," he says, locking eyes with me. "You just have to keep your heart open."

"Yeah, well," I say, "some of us just don't get that lucky."

Alain nods slowly. "Or sometimes, we *are* that lucky, and we are too frightened to see it."

I roll my eyes. "Oh yes, there are men coming out of the woodwork, wanting to woo me."

Annie glances at me and then at Alain. "She's right. No one asks her out. Except Matt Hines, but he's, like, weird."

I can feel myself blushing, and I clear my throat. "Okay, Annie," I say brusquely. "Let's get moving. I need you to prep the strudel, okay?"

"Whatever," she mutters.

Our open goes better than I'd expected that morning; with Alain's help, we're ready for customers by six. Gavin comes in at about six forty, but the shop is busy, so we hardly have a chance to talk as I hand him his coffee, thank him again for his help, and wish him a good day on the job at Joe Sullivan's place.

Alain stays with me when Annie heads off to school, and after the morning rush is over, and I've tersely answered questions from a dozen nosy customers about where I'd vanished to for the last three days, we're alone in the bakery.

"Whew!" Alain explains. "You do a good business, my dear."

I shrug. "It could be better."

"Perhaps," Alain says. "But I think you should be thankful for what you do have."

What I *do* have is a situation of mounting debt and a mortgage that will soon be yanked out from under me, leaving me without a business. But I don't tell him that; no reason to burden Alain with my problems. I'd imagine they pale in comparison to the worries of his lifetime anyhow. It makes me feel as if there must be something terribly wrong with me if I get so easily overwhelmed by the little things.

The day flies by, and Annie arrives after school with a big stack of papers in her hand.

"When are we going to see Mamie?" she asks as she hugs Alain hello.

"Just as soon as we close up," I tell her. "Why don't you get started on the dishes in the back? We might be able to close a little early today."

Annie frowns. "Can you do the dishes? I have some phone calls I gotta make."

I stop pulling slices of baklava from the display case and frown at her. "Phone calls?"

Annie holds out the sheaf of papers she's been clutching and rolls her eyes. "To Jacob Levy. Duh."

My eyes widen. "You found Jacob Levy?"

"Yeah," Annie says. She looks down. "Well, okay, so I found a whole lot of people named Jacob Levy. And, like, that doesn't even count the ones who are listed as J. Levy. But I'm gonna call them all until we find the right one."

I sigh. "Annie, honey . . ." I begin.

"Stop, Mom!" she snaps. "Don't be negative. You're always negative! I'm going to find him. And you can't stop me."

I open and close my mouth helplessly. I hope she's right, but it looks like she has hundreds of numbers in front of her. It's no wonder; I'm sure Jacob Levy is a very common name.

"So? Can I use the phone in the back?"

I pause and nod. "Yeah. As long as they're all U.S. numbers."

Annie grins and skips into the kitchen.

Alain smiles at me and rises to follow her. "I miss being young and hopeful," he says. "Don't you?"

He disappears into the kitchen behind my daughter, and I'm left standing there, feeling like Ebenezer Scrooge. When had I stopped being young and hopeful? I hadn't been trying to rain on Annie's parade; I simply want to help her manage her expectations. Expecting good things leads to getting hurt, I've found.

I sigh and go back to packaging the bakery items in airtight cases for freezing overnight. The baklava I'd made late this morning will last another couple of days, the muffins and cookies will freeze, and I should be able to recycle at least one of the strudels tomorrow morning. Our homemade doughnuts stay fresh for only a day, which is why I usually make only one variety each morning; today's sugar-cinnamon doughnuts are nearly gone, and the remaining three will likely wind up in my daily pickup basket for the women's shelter if I don't have another customer in the next few minutes.

I can hear Annie in the next room chattering away into the phone, probably asking person after person whether they know a Jacob Levy who came from France after World War II. In between calls, I can hear Alain murmuring to her, and I wonder what he's saying. Is he telling her stories of Jacob to keep her inspired? Or is he being responsible and reminding her that this might be an impossible task and that she shouldn't get her hopes up?

I finish emptying the bakery cases and begin carrying pastries back to the industrial freezer. I set to work washing baking sheets, muffin tins, and miniature pie molds in the back, as Annie talks more loudly to be heard over the running water.

"Hi, my name is Annie Smith," I hear her chirp into the phone. "I'm looking for a Jacob Levy who'd be, like, eighty-seven now. He's French. Is there a Jacob Levy there like that? . . . Oh, okay. Thanks anyhow. Yeah, bye."

She hangs up, and Alain murmurs something to her. She giggles, picks up the phone, and repeats the exact same words on the next call.

By the time I'm ready to leave the bakery and head to the hospital—after serving one last-minute customer, Christina

Sivrich from the local theater group, who begged for two and a half dozen cookies she could bring in for a class party for her six-year-old, Ben, tomorrow—Annie has made three dozen calls.

"You ready?" I ask, drying my hands off on a towel and grabbing my keys off the hook by the kitchen door.

"Can I make one more call, Mom?" Annie asks.

I look at my watch and nod. "One more. But then we have to get to the hospital while visiting hours are still going on. Okay?"

I lean against the counter and listen as Annie repeats her spiel once more. Her face looks pained as she hangs up. "Another dead end," she murmurs.

"Annie, you're only on the third page," Alain reminds her. "We have many more Jacob Levys to try tomorrow. And then look at all the J. Levys on your list."

"I guess," Annie says. She sighs and hops off the counter, leaving the list sitting beside the phone.

"Annie, don't worry," I say, trying to share in her optimism. "Maybe you'll find him."

From the withering look she gives me, I realize she's beginning to lose hope. "Whatever," she says. "Let's go see Mamie."

Alain and I exchange concerned looks and follow her out the door.

Chapter *Eighteen*

For the next several days, nothing changes. Mamie doesn't stir. Gavin comes in every morning for a cup of coffee and a pastry and asks about my grandmother's condition. Alain tags along with Annie in the morning, helps me out during the day, and huddles with her in the afternoon while she embarks on a series of fruitless phone calls. After we close for the day, the three of us trek the thirty minutes to the hospital in Hyannis to spend ninety minutes at Mamie's bedside. The one saving grace of the whole routine is that, thankfully, the tourist season is over, so there's relatively little traffic on Route 6 as we cross to the southwest side of the Cape and back.

In the hospital room, Alain holds Mamie's hand and murmurs to her in French, while Annie and I sit in chairs facing her bed. Annie gets up sometimes and scoots in beside Alain, stroking Mamie's hair while he speaks quietly. I can't bring myself to participate; I feel strangely empty. The last person I can rely on is slipping away, and there's nothing I can do to stop it.

On Sunday, I close early at noon, and Alain requests a ride to the hospital.

"Do you want to go too?" I ask Annie.

She shrugs. "Maybe later. But I want to call more Levys from my list today. Can I stay home while you take Uncle Alain?"

I hesitate. "All right. But don't answer the door for anyone."

"God, Mom, I'm not a kid anymore," Annie says, reaching for the phone.

In the car on the way down to Hyannis, Alain tells me about a restaurant he and Mamie used to like in Paris, before the war. He was just a little boy then, and Mamie wasn't even a teenager yet. The owner would always come over to the table after the meal and make special crepes for the kids, with chocolate and brown sugar and bananas. Mamie and Alain would giggle and point as the owner set the crepes flaming in front of them and then pretended he couldn't put them out.

"Those were beautiful days," Alain says. "It was before one's religious preferences mattered. Before everything changed." He pauses and adds, "The night they took my family away, I ran by that restaurant. And the owner, he was outside, watching all the people being marched down the street toward their death. And you know what? He was smiling. Sometimes, that smile still haunts my nightmares."

He stares out the window for the rest of the ride.

At the hospital, I sit with Alain for a little while at Mamie's bedside as he whispers to her.

"Do you think she can hear you?" I ask before we leave.

He smiles. "I do not know," he says. "But doing something feels better than doing nothing. And I am telling her stories of our family, stories I have not let myself think of in seventy years. If anything will bring her back, I believe this will. I want her to know that the past is not lost, not forgotten, even if she came here and tried to erase it."

When I get home an hour later, after dropping Alain at the library at his request, Annie is sitting in the middle of the living room floor with her legs crossed, holding the portable phone to

her ear and saying, "Uh-huh . . . Uh-huh . . . Uh-huh . . . Fine."
For a moment, my eyes light up; has she found Jacob Levy? After
all, the words on her end aren't following the typical sorry-I've-
called-the-wrong-Levys script. But then she turns and I see the
look on her face.

"Yeah, fine," I hear her say. "Whatever." She presses the End
button on the phone and slams it down on the ground.

"Honey?" I ask tentatively. I've stopped in the doorway
between the kitchen and living room and am staring at her in
concern. "Was that one of the Levys?"

"No," she says.

"Was it one of your friends?"

"*No,*" she says, and this time, her voice is tighter. "It was Dad."

"Okay," I say. "Is there anything you want to talk about?"

She's silent for a long time as she looks down at the carpet,
which I realize I haven't vacuumed in eons. Housekeeping is not
one of my fortes. But when she looks up at me, she looks so angry
that I take a step back without meaning to.

"Why did you get us into this, anyways?" Annie demands.
She scrambles to her feet, her fists clenched beside her long,
skinny legs that have yet to develop from those of a child into
those of a young woman.

I blink at her in surprise. "Get us into what?" I ask before
it occurs to me that as her mom, I should be telling her that it's
unacceptable to talk to me this way. But she's already on a roll.

"Everything!" she screams.

"Honey, what are you talking about?" I ask carefully.

"We're never going to find him! Jacob Levy! It's impossible!
And you don't even care!"

My heart sinks a little. I've failed her once again by not pre-
paring her better for the likelihood that this is a wild goose chase,
that Jacob has already died, or that he's disappeared because he
doesn't want to be found. I know Annie wants to believe in true
love that lasts forever—probably as an antidote to the front-row

seat she had to the crumbling of my marriage—but I'd hoped that I wouldn't have to burst her bubble yet and tell her the truth. When I was twelve, I'd believed in true love too. It wasn't until I was older that I realized it was all a sham.

I swallow hard. "Of course I care, Annie," I begin. "But it's possible that Jacob isn't—"

She cuts me off before I can get the words out of my mouth. "It's not just that!" she exclaims. She waves her long, skinny arms around some more and hardly seems to notice when her pink watchband snags her hair and gets stuck for a minute. She simply rips it free and winces momentarily before going on. "It's everything! You ruin everything!"

I take a deep breath. "Annie, if this is about me going to Paris for a few days, I've already told you how much I appreciate you being responsible when I was gone."

She rolls her eyes and stomps her left foot on the ground. "You don't even know what I'm talking about!" she says, shooting me a withering look.

"Fine, I guess I'm an idiot!" I say. I can finally feel my temper rising. There's a fine line between feeling sorry for my daughter and feeling annoyed by her behavior, and I can feel myself floating over that line right now. "What is it that I've done wrong this time?"

"It's *everything*!" she screams. Her face is turning red, and for a split second, I have a weird, fleeting flashback to holding her in my arms when she was a colicky infant, trying to calm her in the middle of the night so that Rob, who always had an important case that he had to rest up for, could sleep. Why did I let him do that to me? I don't think I slept more than two hours at a stretch for the first three months, while he always seemed to get at least six hours of sleep. I shake my head and zero back in on my daughter.

"Everything?" I ask carefully.

"Everything!" she repeats immediately. "You didn't care

enough about Daddy to make your marriage work! You didn't love him like Mamie and Jacob loved each other! And now my life is ruined! Because of you!"

I feel like she's punched me in the stomach, and for a moment, I can't catch my breath. I stare at her. "What are you talking about?" I ask once I can find my voice. "Now you're blaming the divorce on me?"

"Of course I am!" she shrieks. She puts her hands on her hips and stomps her foot again. "Everyone knows it's your fault!"

I'm unprepared once again for how hard her words hit me. "What?"

"If you had just loved Daddy, he wouldn't be living on the other side of town now, and he wouldn't have a dumb girlfriend who hates me!" Annie says. And suddenly, I understand. This isn't about me and Rob. This is about the way Rob's new girlfriend is making Annie feel. And despite the fact that Annie is wounding me to the core right now, I'm more hurt for her than I am for myself.

"What do you mean his girlfriend hates you?" I ask quietly.

"What do you care?" Annie mumbles, suddenly deflating. Her back arches inward, and she crosses her arms over her chest as she slumps her shoulders. She looks at the ground.

"I care because I love you," I say after a moment. "And your father loves you. And whoever this woman is, if she's acting like she doesn't like you, she's obviously completely nuts."

"Whatever," Annie mutters. "Dad doesn't think she's nuts. Dad thinks Sunshine's perfect."

I take a deep breath. That sounds just like Rob. He's like a little kid; he gets entranced for a while by shiny, new things. Cars. Houses. Clothes. Boats. And, once upon a time, me. But I know the truth. I know that his infatuations are always temporary. But Annie is the one thing in his life that's supposed to be permanent. "I'm sure your dad doesn't think this woman is perfect," I say. "He loves you, Annie. If she's doing something that bothers you, tell your dad about it. He'll make it right." I don't expect much of Rob these days, but at least I expect that.

But Annie just stares at the ground. "I *did* tell him," she says softly. The anger has gone out of her voice now, and her limbs look limp and lifeless. She hangs her head and doesn't meet my eye.

"What did he say?" I ask.

"He said I need to learn to respect my elders better," Annie says. She takes a deep breath. "And that I need to learn to get along better with Sunshine."

My blood boils and I clench my fists. Annie's not perfect, and I wouldn't put it past her to be giving her father's new girlfriend a hard time. But there's no excuse for Rob taking his girlfriend's side over his daughter's, especially when Annie is probably confused by him moving on so quickly.

"What exactly does Sunshine do to make you think she doesn't like you?" I ask carefully.

Annie guffaws, making her sound much older and tougher than she is. "What *doesn't* she do?" she asks. She sniffs and looks away. When she speaks again, she just sounds sad. "She doesn't ever talk to me. She talks to Dad like I'm invisible or something. Sometimes, she laughs at me. She told me my outfit the other day was stupid."

"She told you your outfit was stupid?" I repeat, incredulous. "She actually said it was *stupid*?"

Annie nods. "Yeah. And when she was gone the other day, and I tried to talk to Dad about it, I thought he understood. I thought he, like, got it. But that night, when I got home after the bakery, I went into the bathroom, and right there on the counter—in *my* bathroom—was a silver necklace he'd bought for Sunshine and a note he'd written her that said, *'I'm sorry Annie made you feel bad with the things she said. I'll take care of it. I don't want you hurting.'*"

I stare at her. "He told her about the conversation you had with him?" I ask.

Annie nods. "And then bought her a *present,*" she says, spitting the last word out like it tastes bad. "A *present.* To make her feel better. And then what does she go and do? She leaves the present in *my* bathroom, like it's some kind of a mistake. But I know what she was doing. She was, like, trying to show me that Dad would always choose her over me."

"I'm sure that's not true," I murmur. But of course it is. Sunshine sounds like a manipulative shrew. And that's fine if she wants to manipulate my ex-husband. I'm done looking out for him, and to be honest, he deserves to be the one manipulated and used for once. But I draw the line at a woman who goes out of her way to hurt a twelve-year-old girl. And when that twelve-year-old girl is mine, I see red. "What did your dad say?" I ask Annie. "Did you tell him about finding the necklace?"

She nods slowly. She looks down. "He said I shouldn't be looking through Sunshine's things," she says. "I tried to tell him she left it sitting out in *my* bathroom, but he didn't believe me. He thought I was, like, going through her purse or something."

"I see," I say tightly. I take a deep breath. "Okay. Well, first of all, honey, your father has obviously lost his mind. There's no reason in the world to put *anyone* ahead of your child. And particularly not a bitch named Sunshine."

Annie looks shocked. "You just called her a bitch?"

"I just called her a bitch," I confirm. "Because she obviously is one. And I will have a talk with your father about this. I know this is hard for you to understand, but this isn't about you. This is about your father being insecure and foolish. Six months from now, I guarantee you, Sunshine isn't going to be in the picture anymore. Your dad's interests are fleeting, trust me. But in the meantime, there's no excuse for him treating *you* this way, or letting some bimbo treat you this way. And I'm going to take care of it. Okay?"

Annie stares at me, as if she's not sure whether to believe me or not. "Okay," she says finally. "You're really going to talk to him?"

"Yes," I say. "But what's with blaming everything on me, Annie? That's got to stop. I know you're upset. But I'm not your punching bag."

"I know," she mutters.

"And the divorce *wasn't* my fault," I say. "Your dad and I just fell out of love. It was pretty equal. Okay?" Actually, it didn't feel equal at all. It felt like I'd been used as a doormat for a decade, and I'd finally realized it and decided to stand up for myself. And it turned out that the person walking all over me hadn't particularly liked it when his doormat developed some self-respect. But Annie doesn't need to know all that. I want her to keep loving her father, even if I don't anymore.

"That's not what Dad says," Annie mutters, looking down. "Dad and Sunshine."

I shake my head in disbelief. "And what is it that Dad and Sunshine say?"

"Just that you changed," she says. "And that you weren't the same person anymore. And that when you changed, you stopped loving Dad."

Of course her father's right in a way; I *did* change. But that still doesn't mean the divorce is my fault. But I don't say any of this to Annie. Instead, I just say, "Yeah, well, believing a couple of idiots is pretty idiotic, don't you think?"

She laughs. "Yeah."

"Fine," I say. "I'll talk to your dad. I'm sorry that he and his girlfriend are hurting you. And I'm sorry you're upset about Mamie right now. But Annie, none of those things give you the right to say hateful things to me."

"Sorry," she mumbles.

"I know," I say. I take a deep breath. I hate being the bad guy, especially when she's getting it from all sides, but as her mom, I also can't let that kind of behavior stand. "Kiddo, I'm afraid you're grounded for the next two days. No phone either."

"You're *grounding* me?" She's incredulous.

"You know better than to talk to me like that," I say, "or to take things out on me. The next time you're upset about something, just come talk to me, Annie. I've always been here for you."

"I know." She pauses and looks at me in anguish. "Wait, does this mean I can't call any more Levys?"

"Not for the next two days," I say. "You can start again Tuesday afternoon."

Her jaw drops. "You are *so* mean," she says.

"So I've heard," I say.

She glares at me. "I hate you!" she tells me.

I sigh. "Yeah, and you're a real peach too," I reply. "Go to your room. I'm going to go have a talk with your dad."

As I pull up to the house I used to live in, the first thing I notice is that the pink salt spray roses in the front garden, the ones that I carefully and lovingly tended for eight years, are gone. All of them. They were here just weeks ago when I was here last.

The second thing I notice is that there's a woman in the garden wearing a pink bikini top and denim cutoff shorts, despite the fact that it can't be more than fifty-five degrees out. She's at least a decade younger than I am, and her long, blonde hair is gathered into a high ponytail that looks like it should be giving her a massive headache. I *hope* it's giving her a headache. I can only assume that she's Sunshine, recent torturer of my daughter. I suddenly want, more than anything in the world, to gun the engine and flatten her against the soil. Thankfully, I am not actually a murderess, so I refrain. But at the very least, I sure would like to pull her perky ponytail until she screams.

I put the car in Park and take the keys out of the ignition. She stands up and looks at me as I step out of the car. "Who are you?" she asks.

Wow, an A plus for manners, I think. "I'm Annie's mother," I reply crisply. "You must be, what is it, Raincloud?"

"Sunshine," she corrects.

"Ah, of course," I say. "Is Rob in?"

She tosses her ponytail over her right shoulder and then her left. "Yeah," she says finally. "He's, like, inside."

Well, she talks like a twelve-year-old. No wonder she feels as if she has to compete with my daughter; they're obviously at the same maturity level. I sigh and head for the door.

"Aren't you even going to say thank you?" she calls after me.

I turn and smile at her. "No. No, I'm not."

I ring the doorbell, and Rob comes to the door a moment later, wearing only a pair of swim trunks. What is this, naked day? Do they not realize the temperatures are dipping into the low forties tonight? To his credit, he looks somewhat flustered when he realizes it's me.

"Oh, hey, Hope," he says. He takes a few steps back and grabs a T-shirt from the basket of laundry that sits beside the laundry room off the front hall. He pulls it on quickly. "I wasn't expecting you. How's, uh, your grandmother?"

His concern, feigned or otherwise, surprises me momentarily. "She's fine," I say quickly. Then I shake my head. "No, she's not. I don't know why I just said that. She's still in a coma."

"I'm sorry to hear that," Rob says.

"Thanks," I say.

We stand there for a moment, staring at each other, before Rob remembers his manners. "Sorry, you want to come in?"

I nod and he steps aside to let me pass. Walking into my old house feels like entering a *Twilight Zone* version of my former life. Everything's the same, but different. Same view of the bay out the back picture windows, but different curtains hanging from the windows. Same curving staircase up to the second floor, but another woman's purse sitting on the landing. I shake my head and follow him into the kitchen.

"Want some iced tea or a soda or something?" he offers.

"No, thanks." I shake my head. "I'm not staying. I need to go see Mamie. I just need to talk to you about something first."

Rob sighs and scratches his head. "Look, is this about the makeup again? I think you're overreacting, but I've been trying to be strict about it, okay? She came home the other day with lipstick on, and I made her wipe it off and give me the tube."

"I appreciate that," I say. "But that's not what this is about."

"Then what?" he asks, spreading his arms wide. We stand there for a moment and stare at each other, neither of us making a move to sit down or relax.

"Sunshine," I say flatly.

He blinks a few times, and I know, just from that simple reaction, that he realizes what I'm about to say, and he knows I'm right. It's funny how spending a dozen years with a person lets you learn all their tells.

He laughs uneasily. "Hope, c'mon, it's over between me and you," he says. "You can't be jealous that I've moved on."

I just stare at him. "Rob, seriously? That's what you think I'm here about?"

He smirks at me for a moment, but when I don't drop my gaze, the smarmy expression falls from his face and he shrugs. "I don't know. What are you here about?"

"Look," I say, "I don't care who you date. But when it impacts Annie negatively, that's when I get involved. And you're dating a woman who apparently feels like she has to compete with Annie for your affections."

"They're not competing for my affections," Rob says, but from the tiny upturn of his mouth at the corners, I wonder for a moment whether, in fact, he's completely aware of what's going on and is getting some sort of sick egotistical rush out of it. I wish for the zillionth time that I'd realized in my early twenties that having a baby with a selfish man meant that my child would always have to deal with that selfishness too. I'd been too naive to realize then that you can't change a man. And my daughter is paying for that mistake.

I close my eyes for a moment, trying to summon some

patience. "Annie told me about the silver necklace," I say, "which she found sitting out on the counter in *her* bathroom, where Sunshine obviously left it—along with your note—to rub it in Annie's face that you're choosing her."

"I'm not choosing anyone," Rob protests, but he looks embarrassed.

"Yeah," I say, "and that's the problem. You're Annie's father. And that counts for so much more than whatever you are to the girl you've been dating for thirty-five seconds. You should be choosing Annie. Always. In every situation. And when Annie's wrong, yes, you have to let her know, but not in a way that makes her feel like you're picking someone else over her. You're her father, Rob. And if you don't start acting like it, you're going to crush her."

"I'm not trying to hurt her," he says. And from the slight whine to his voice, I know he means it, for whatever that's worth.

"You also have to be aware of how the people you let into your life treat her," I continue. "If you're dating someone who's going out of her way to hurt your daughter, don't you think there's maybe something wrong with that? On a few different levels?"

Rob looks down and shakes his head. "There's no way for you to know the whole situation." He scratches the back of his neck and turns to look out the picture window for a long time. I follow his gaze to a gaggle of white sailboats bobbing on the perfectly blue horizon, and I wonder whether he's thinking, as I am, about the days early in our marriage, when he and I used to take the boat out on the water near Boston without a care in the world. Then again, it occurs to me that I was pregnant at that time, and very apt to get seasick, and Rob would just look away as I threw up over the side of the boat. He always got what he wanted—his pliable, willing wife alongside him, creating a picture-perfect couple—and I always pasted a smile on and made it work. Had that been the nature of our whole marriage? Could it be summed up that easily, in the image of me vomiting off the side of a sailboat while Rob pretended not to notice?

We turn back to each other at the same moment, and I wonder whether, on some level, he's aware of what I'm thinking. He surprises me by bowing his head and saying, "I'm sorry. You're right."

I'm so startled that I can't even find the words to respond. I'm not sure he's conceded to anything in the entire time I've known him. "Okay," I say finally.

"I'll take care of it," he says. "I'm sorry I hurt her."

"Okay," I say, and I really am grateful. Not to him, because he's the one who screwed up and inflicted harm on my daughter in the first place. But I'm grateful for the fact that Annie won't have to suffer anymore, and that she still has a father who cares at least a little bit, even if he has to be nudged in the right direction in order to do the right thing.

I'm also grateful, more so than I'd previously realized, to be out of this life with my ex-husband. My mistake wasn't in letting the marriage end; it was in fooling myself into believing that marrying him was a good idea in the first place.

I think suddenly of the stories Alain has told me about Mamie and Jacob, and I realize, with a crushing clarity, that I've never had anything even close to that. Not with Rob, not with anyone. I'm not sure I even believed in it before, so it never felt like I was missing anything. Alain's stories are making me sad, not just for Mamie but for myself.

I smile at Rob, and as I do, I realize I'm grateful for something else too. I'm grateful that he let me go. I'm grateful that he felt it necessary to have an affair with a twenty-two-year-old. I'm grateful that he took it upon himself to end our marriage. Because that means that there's a tiny chance, however small, that it's not too late for me after all. Now I just have to find a way to believe in the kind of love Alain's talking about.

"Thank you," I say to Rob. And without another word, I turn and head for the door. Sunshine is standing in the front garden, her hands on her hips, looking pissed, as I walk out the front door. I wonder whether she's been standing there the entire time, trying to string together words to say to me. If so, I must remember to congratulate Rob on his pick of an intellectual superstar.

"You know, you can't be rude to me at my own house," Sunshine says, again tossing her long ponytail back and forth in a way that makes her look like a stubborn horse with a twitchy tail.

"I'll bear that in mind if I ever come to your house," I tell her brightly. "But since this is *not* your house, but rather the house I lived in for the last decade, I'd suggest you keep your comments to yourself."

"Well, it's not like you live here anymore," she says, and then she wiggles her hips oddly and smirks at me, like she's just said something deeply devastating. In fact, she's just reinforced my newfound feeling of tremendous freedom, and I smile.

"You're right," I reply. "I absolutely don't. Thank God." I cross the garden, stepping across the ground where my beloved roses used to be, until I'm standing face-to-face with her. "One more thing, Sunshine," I say calmly. "If you do *anything* to hurt my daughter, and I mean *anything,* I will spend the rest of my life making sure you regret it."

"You're crazy," she mutters, taking a step back.

"Is that right?" I ask cheerfully. "Well, push me the wrong way, and I guess you'll find out."

As I walk away, I can hear her muttering behind me. I climb into my car, start the engine, and back onto the main road. I head west, toward Hyannis, for I plan to spend the rest of the day with Mamie, beginning to understand the lessons in love that I didn't realize I was missing until right about now.

Chapter *Nineteen*

⁓

North Star Blueberry Muffins

MUFFINS

INGREDIENTS

Streusel topping (see recipe below)
½ cup butter
1 cup granulated sugar
2 large eggs
2 cups flour
2 tsp. baking powder
½ tsp. salt
¼ cup milk
¼ cup sour cream
1 tsp. vanilla extract
2 cups blueberries

DIRECTIONS

1. Preheat oven to 375 degrees. Line 12 muffin cups with paper liners.

2. Prepare streusel as directed below. Set aside.

3. In a large bowl, using a hand mixer, cream together the butter and sugar. Add eggs, beating well.

4. In a separate bowl, combine flour, baking powder, and salt. Gradually add the dry ingredients to the butter-sugar mixture, alternating with the milk, sour cream, and vanilla. Mix until just fully combined.

5. Gently fold in the blueberries.

6. For oversized muffins, fill each muffin cup nearly to the top. Sprinkle generously with streusel topping.

7. Bake for 25–30 minutes, or until a knife inserted in the center of a muffin comes out clean. Cool for 10 minutes in pan, then move to wire rack to cool completely.

STREUSEL TOPPING

INGREDIENTS

½ cup granulated sugar   *2 tsp. cinnamon*
¼ cup flour
¼ cup very cold butter, chopped into
*   small cubes*

DIRECTIONS

Combine all ingredients in a food processor and process with quick pulses, until mixture has consistency of thick crumbs. Sprinkle over unbaked muffins, as directed above.

Rose

For years, in the darkness of the night in this idyllic Cape Cod town so far from where she'd come, the mental pictures always came back to Rose. Unbidden. Unwanted. Images she had never seen in person but that were burned into her memory nonetheless. Sometimes, imagination was a stronger painter than reality.

Crying children being torn from their dead-eyed mothers.

Filthy huddles of people being hosed down in piles while they screamed.

The terror on parents' faces at the very moment they realized there was no going back.

Children in long lines being herded systematically to their deaths.

And always, in those images that played like an endless picture show across her mind, the people had the faces of her family, her friends, the people she loved.

And Jacob. Jacob, who had loved her. Jacob, who had saved her. Jacob, whom she'd foolishly, horribly sent back to die.

And now, in the dark netherworld of her coma, the images of those she'd loved were floating before her like a picture show. She had imagined so many times what might have happened to them that she could see it now just as if she had witnessed it with her own eyes.

As she drifted through this dark, underwater world between life and death, she could see Danielle and David being ripped from her mother, their little faces streaked with tears, their eyes wide with confusion, their screams vivid in her ears. She wondered how they had died. Right there in the Vel' d'Hiv, just blocks from the Eiffel Tower, in whose shadow they had lived their whole short lives? Or later, in the crowded, airless train cars on the way to camps like Drancy or Beaune-la-Rolande or Pithiviers? Or did they make it all the way to Auschwitz, only to be led in a neat, orderly line into a gas chamber, where they surely would have gasped in terror for their final breaths? Did they cry out? Did they understand what was happening to them?

Maman and Papa. Had they been separated in the Vel' d'Hiv, or not until they were taken away from France? How had Papa borne being ripped from the family he had always so fiercely protected? Had he fought back? Had he been struck by the guards, beaten for his obstinacy? Or had he gone willingly, already resigned to the futility of it all? Had Maman been left alone, with the children huddled around her, knowing the terrible truth that she could no longer protect them? How would it feel to realize you were no longer in control of your fate, no longer able to protect the children you would gladly die to save?

Helene. It broke Rose's heart every time she thought of her older sister. What if she had tried harder to reason with her? Could she have saved her if only she'd managed to convince her that the world had lost all logic and had gone mad? Had Helene regretted, in her final moments, not believing Rose? Or had she held out hope until the end that perhaps they were only being sent away to work, and not to die? Somehow, Rose always imagined her slipping away in her sleep, peaceful, alone, although she knew from the ghosts that her end had likely been much different. Each time she thought of how Helene had reportedly been beaten to death, simply for being too ill to work, Rose had to run to the bathroom to throw up, and for days afterward, she couldn't hold down a meal.

Claude. Just thirteen, he had tried so hard to be grown up, to pretend to understand the things that adults understood. But he was a child the last time Rose saw him. Had he become the adult he'd always wanted to be in the few days inside the Vel' d'Hiv? Had he been forced to understand things he shouldn't have known for years? Did he try to protect the younger ones, or his sister, or his mother? Or had he remained a child, terrified of what was happening? Had he made it onto a transport to Auschwitz? Had he survived there for a while, or had he been drawn out of line upon his arrival, judged to be too young or too small to work, and sent immediately to the gas chamber? What had he said with this last breath? What had been his last waking thought?

Alain. The one Rose loved the best. And the one who understood everything, although he was only eleven. Her heart ached most of all for him, because without the cloak of denial that the others had managed to wrap themselves in, there was no way to dull the pain. He would have felt every moment of it, because he understood it all, understood what was happening, believed Jacob's urgent warnings. Had he been frightened? Or had he grown up in those moments and decided to meet his fate with brave resilience?

He was tougher than Rose was, tougher than all of them. Had he used that bravery to rise above the terror? Rose felt sure that he hadn't lived long; he was much smaller than Claude, very small for his age, and no guard in his right mind would have selected such a little boy for work duty. When Rose closed her eyes at night, she often saw Alain's little face, his eyes somber, his rosy cheeks sallowed, his beautiful blond hair shaved, as he awaited the fate he knew was coming in the midst of a thousand other children in the cold darkness of a gas chamber somewhere in Poland.

And then there was Jacob. It had been nearly seventy years since she'd last seen him, and still, his face was as clear in Rose's mind as if they'd parted just yesterday. She often imagined him as she'd seen him the first time she met him, in the Jardin du Luxembourg in the winter. His dancing green eyes, his thick brown hair, the way they had looked at each other and known in that very first instant what they'd found. She could imagine, in her darkest moments, his face, resolute and brave, as he endured the torture of the Vel' d'Hiv, or as he was thrown aboard a transport to a transit camp, or as he entered Auschwitz. But unlike the others, she couldn't visualize him dying. It was strange, she thought, and she wondered whether it was her mind's way of protecting her, even though she did not want to be protected. She wanted to feel the pain of his death, because she deserved it.

But those weren't the only moments of her life that Rose returned to as she drifted farther and farther away from the world. She thought also of the moments that had come since then, the few happy times over the years, when her heart had filled up with love and joy, the way it once had when she was a girl. And here in the depths of her coma as she floated through the darkness, she thought back to a cold morning in May 1975, one of her favorite memories.

That morning, Rose had woken to find Ted gone to work already. Usually, she was up long before the dawn, but her nightmares had sucked her in that night, as they sometimes did, and held her captive until nearly six in the morning. When she slept in like this, Ted

let her rest and called Josephine to open the bakery in her mother's
stead. He didn't understand that she wasn't resting but reeling in
the terror that she could never find a way out of. And because she
loved her husband, she didn't tell him this. He thought that in marrying her, and in giving her a good life, he had helped the past to
disappear, as she wanted it to. She could not bear to tell him that in
the thirty-three years since she'd last seen those she loved most, the
memories, both real and imagined, hadn't faded at all.

Rose had stared at herself in the mirror that morning. She was
still beautiful at fifty, although she hadn't seen herself that way
since the last time Jacob had looked at her. In his eyes, she knew she
was something special. Without him, she had wilted like a flower
without sunlight.

Fifty years, she thought, looking at her reflection. It was her
birthday that day, but no one knew that. The visa she'd come to
America with, the identity that didn't belong to her, said that she'd
been born two months later, in July. July 16, in fact, an irony she
would never forget, for that was the day her family had been taken
away. She knew that on July 16, Ted and Josephine would have a
cake for her, and a nice dinner, and they would sing "Happy Birthday," and she would smile and play her part well. But today, today
was just for her. It was the day Rose Picard had been born. But Rose
Picard had died in 1942.

Rose did not like birthdays. How could she? Each one took
her farther from the past, farther from the life she led before the
world ended. And for the last few years, she had been consumed
with sadness at the realization that she was growing older than any
of her family ever had. Papa had been forty-five when he was taken
away. Even if he'd lived another two years at Auschwitz, which she
knew was unlikely, he hadn't made it past forty-seven. Maman had
been just forty-one in 1942, the last time Rose had seen her. Rose's
mother had seemed so old to her then, but now, forty-one seemed
youthful. She'd never thought of her mother being ripped away in
the prime of her youth, but she had been. Rose knew that now.

And now Rose herself was fifty. She'd lived longer than her parents and spent almost twice as long in the United States as she had in France. Seventeen years in her native land. Thirty-three in her adopted home. But she had stopped living long ago. The rest had been like a dream, and she had walked through it in a trance, simply going through the motions.

She dressed that morning and walked to the bakery, noting that spring had arrived early. The trees were green, and the flowers around the Cape were just beginning to bloom. The sky was a clear, pale blue, the kind of sky that led to beautiful days, and Rose knew that soon, the tourists would be descending, and the bakery would be doing a strong business. These were things that were supposed to make her happy.

She stopped outside the bakery for a moment and looked through the pane at her daughter, who was busy sliding a tray of miniature Star Pies into the display case. Her daughter's hair was thick and dark, like her father's, and her belly was round and full, as Rose's had once been so long ago. In a month, Josephine would be a mother too. She would come to understand that one's child was the most important thing in the world, that one must protect that child at all costs.

Rose had never been able to bring herself to tell her daughter what had happened. Josephine knew only that her mother had left Paris after her parents died, married Ted, and eventually settled here in Cape Cod. A thousand times, Rose had wanted to tell her the truth, but then she'd pause and look around at the life she had here—her bakery, her beautiful home, and most of all, her devoted husband, who'd been a wonderful father to Josephine. And every time, she'd stop before she ruined everything. She felt as if she were living in a beautiful painting, and that she was the only one who knew it was merely a paper-thin world of brushstrokes and dreams.

And so she'd told Josephine fairy tales throughout her child-hood, tales of kingdoms and princes and queens that were meant to keep the past alive, even if Rose was the only one who knew it.

She imagined she'd tell Josephine's child the stories too, and this would bring Rose comfort, for it was her way of living in her past without destroying the present. Let them believe that the fairy tales were the fiction, and that everything else was real. It was better that way.

Rose was just about to enter the bakery when suddenly, she saw her daughter double over, clutching her midsection, her beautiful face, so like her father's, suddenly twisted in pain. Rose immediately burst through the front door.

"Darling, what is it?" she asked, flying across the room, crossing behind the counter and putting her hands on her daughter's shoulders.

Josephine moaned. "Mom, it's the baby. The baby's coming."

Rose's eyes widened in panic. "But it is too soon." Josephine's due date wasn't for another month and three days.

Josephine doubled over in pain again. "I don't think the baby knows that. It's coming now, Mom."

Rose felt a familiar sick panic rising inside her. What if something happened to the baby? "I will call your father," Rose said. "He will come." Rose knew she needed to get her daughter to the hospital, but she had never learned to drive; there was no need. She lived just a few blocks from the bakery, and she rarely needed to go anywhere else.

"Tell him to hurry," Josephine said.

Rose nodded, picked up the phone, and dialed Ted. She told him quickly, carefully, what was happening, and he promised he'd leave the school and be there within ten minutes. "Tell her I love her and can't wait to meet my grandchild," Ted said before hanging up. Rose did not convey the message, although she wasn't sure why.

While they waited, Rose pulled one of the bakery chairs over for Josephine to sit in, and she flipped the Closed sign around on the front door. She saw Kay Sullivan and Barbara Koontz pause outside and give her a strange look, but she merely gestured to Josephine, who was breathing hard, her face pink and gleaming, and they understood. They did not offer to help, though; they merely averted their eyes and hurried away.

"*Chérie*, it is going to be all right," Rose said, pulling a chair up beside her daughter and putting a hand on her knee. "Your father will be here soon." She wished she could do more, bring her daughter more comfort. But there had been a gulf between them for years, entirely of Rose's own making. She hadn't known how to reach across the coldness of her own heart to reach her daughter.

Josephine nodded, breathing hard. "I'm scared, Mom," she said. Rose was scared too. But she could not admit this. "It will all be fine, my dear," she said. "You are going to have a happy, healthy baby. Everything will be fine."

And then, Rose said something she knew she would regret, but it had to be said. "My dear Josephine," she said, "you must tell the baby's father."

Josephine's head shot up, and she looked at her mother with blazing eyes. "It's none of your business, Mom."

Rose took a deep breath, imagined the life this baby would have without a father, and couldn't bear it. "My dear, your child must have a father. Like you did. Think how important your father has been to you."

Her daughter glared at her. "Absolutely not, Mom. He's not like Dad. He doesn't want to be part of this baby's life."

Rose's heart hurt. She put her hand on her daughter's belly. "You never told him you were pregnant," she said softly. "Perhaps he would feel differently if he knew."

"You don't know what you're talking about," Josephine said. She paused and doubled over, another contraction racking her slender frame. She straightened up, her face red and pinched. "You don't even know who he is. He walked away from me."

Rose's eyes filled with unexpected tears, and she had to look away. This was her fault, she knew. Despite all the things she had tried so hard to impart to her daughter, the lessons she had tried to remember from her own mother, she had really only succeeded in imparting coldness, hadn't she? Her heart had simply ceased to exist on that dark, empty day in 1949 when Ted returned to tell her that Jacob had died. Josephine had been just a little girl then, too young to know she had lost her mother that day.

And now, Rose realized, she had failed in the most important thing of all. She had raised a daughter who was as closed and cold as she was.

"You need someone to watch out for you, to love you, to love the baby," Rose whispered. "Like your father loved me and you."

Josephine looked at her mother sharply. "Mom, it's not the 1940s anymore. I'm perfectly fine on my own. I don't need anyone."

There was another contraction then, and suddenly, Ted was rapping on the front door, his shirt rumpled and his tie twisted to the side. Rose stood and crossed the room to let him in. He gave his wife a quick peck and grinned at her. "We're going to be grandparents!" he said. Then he crossed the room to Josephine, knelt beside her, and whispered, "I'm so proud of you, honey. Let's get you to the hospital. Just hang on a little longer."

Josephine's labor was quick, and although the baby was born a month early, the doctor came out to report that she was healthy, although a bit underweight, and that she'd be ready to meet her grandparents shortly. Rose and Ted watched the minutes tick by in the waiting room, and as Ted paced, Rose closed her eyes and prayed. She prayed that this child born today, on this, her own fiftieth birthday, wouldn't be as cold as she herself was, or as cold as she had made her own daughter. She prayed that the mistakes she'd made with Josephine would not be passed on to the new baby, who had a blank slate, a new chance at life. She prayed that she'd be able to show the baby she loved her, something she'd never been able to do with her own daughter.

It was another hour before a nurse came to lead them in. Josephine lay in bed, exhausted but smiling, holding her newborn daughter in her arms. Rose's heart melted as she looked at the tiny girl, who was sleeping peacefully, one of her tiny hands clenched in a fist beside her cheek.

"Do you want to hold her, Mom?" Josephine asked. Tears in her eyes, Rose nodded. She came to stand beside her daughter, who handed the tiny, sleeping infant over. Rose took the baby in her arms, remembering at once how natural it felt to hold someone so little who was a piece of you, a piece of everything you loved. She felt the impulse to protect this baby surge through her, just as strongly as it had surged through her the first time she held her own baby.

Rose looked down at her granddaughter, seeing both the past and the future. When the child opened her eyes, Rose gasped. For a moment, she could have sworn she saw something wise and ancient in the newborn's eyes. And then it was gone, and Rose knew she had only imagined it. She rocked the baby gently and knew she was already in love with her. She prayed she was strong enough to do things right this time. "I hope . . ." Rose murmured, her voice trailing off as she stared at the little girl. She didn't know how to complete the sentence, because she didn't know what to hope for. There were a million things she wanted for this child, a million things she'd never had herself. She hoped everything for her.

"Honey, have you decided on a name yet?" Ted asked. Rose looked up to see her daughter staring at her strangely. A slow smile spread across Josephine's face.

"Yes," Josephine said. "I'm going to call her Hope."

Chapter *Twenty*

~

By Wednesday evening, Annie has called more than a hundred numbers from her list of Levys, and she still hasn't come up with even a trace of Mamie's Jacob Levy. I'm feeling more and more like we may be chasing a ghost. I take a dozen of the West Coast names from Annie's list and call them after she's gone to bed, but I don't have any more luck than she's had. Everyone I reach says they've never heard of a Jacob Levy who left France in the 1940s or 1950s. Even an online search of Ellis Island's passenger records turns up nothing.

Annie comes into the bakery a few minutes before six the next morning, looking solemn, as I'm folding dried cranberries, chunks of white chocolate, and slivers of macadamia nuts into a batch of sugary cookie dough.

"We have to do more," she announces, flinging her backpack onto the floor, where it lands with a thud that makes me wonder fleetingly about the damage she must be doing to her back by carrying around several heavy textbooks each day.

"About Jacob Levy?" I guess. Before she can respond, I add, "Can you start putting the defrosted pastries out, please? I'm running a little behind."

She nods and goes to the sink to wash her hands. "Yeah, about Jacob," she says. She shakes her hands off, dries them on the blue cupcake towel beside the sink, and turns around. "We gotta try to figure out how to find him better."

I sigh. "Annie, you know there's a good chance that's going to be impossible."

She rolls her eyes. "You're always so negative."

"I'm just being realistic." I watch as she begins sliding crescent moons carefully out of their airtight container. She unwraps each of them from their wax paper and sets them on a display tray.

"I think we have to investigate more if we're going to find him."

I arch an eyebrow at her. "Investigate?" I ask carefully.

She nods, missing the note of skepticism in my voice. "Yeah. It's not working to just call people. We have to, like, try to search some documents or something. Other than the Ellis Island site, because he could have arrived anywhere."

"What documents?"

Annie glares at me. "*I* don't know. You're the adult here. I can't do everything." She marches into the front of the bakery with her tray full of crescent moons and comes back a moment later to begin putting defrosted slices of baklava onto slivers of wax paper.

I watch her for a moment. "I just don't want you to wind up disappointed," I say to Annie after she's returned to the kitchen.

She glares at me. "That's just your way of avoiding stuff," she says. "You can't just not do stuff because you might get hurt." She glances at her watch. "It's six. I'll go unlock the front door."

I nod, watching her again as she goes. I wonder whether she's right. And if she is, how does she know so much more than I do about life?

I hear her talking to someone a moment later, and I head out to begin another long day of smiling at customers, pretending that there's nothing in the world I'd rather be doing than wrapping up pastries for them.

I round the corner from the kitchen and am surprised to see Gavin at the counter, looking over the pastries that are already in the case. He's dressed more formally than usual, in khakis and a pale blue button-down shirt. Annie is already busy putting slices of baklava into a box for him.

"Hey!" I say. "You're dressed up today." The moment the words have left my mouth, I feel silly.

But he just smiles at me and says, "I took the day off; I'm headed up to the nursing home on the North Shore. I'm just getting some pastries to bring to the folks there. They like me better when I arrive with food."

I laugh. "I bet they like you with or without food."

Annie sighs heavily, as if to remind us that she's still there. We both glance at her, and she hands Gavin the bakery box, which she has tied neatly with white ribbon while we were talking.

"So Annie," Gavin says, turning his attention to her. "How's it going with your search for Jacob Levy?"

"Not good," Annie mutters. "No one's ever heard of him."

"You've been calling the names on your list?"

"Like hundreds of names," Annie says.

"Hmm," says Gavin. "I wonder if there's another way to look for him."

Annie brightens. "Like what?"

Gavin shrugs. "I don't know. Do you know his birth date? Maybe there's a way to search for him online if you have a date of birth."

Annie nods excitedly. "Yeah, maybe. Good idea." I expect her to thank him, but instead, I hear her blurt out, "So you're, like, Jewish?"

"Annie!" I exclaim. "Don't be impolite."

"I'm *not,*" she says. "I'm just *asking.*"

I glance at Gavin, and he winks at me, which makes me blush a little. "Yes, Annie, I'm Jewish. How come?"

"I don't really have any Jewish friends," she says. "And now that I know I'm, like, Jewish, I was just curious about, you know, Jewishness."

"It's called Judaism, not Jewishness," I tell her. "Besides, you're not Jewish, Annie. You're Catholic."

"I know," she says. "But I can be both. Mamie's both." She turns to Gavin again. "So, like, do you go to Jewish church every week?"

Gavin smiles. "It's called temple. And I don't go every week, even though I probably should. Some Fridays, I'm working. And some Fridays, I'm just too busy. That's not very good, is it?"

Annie shrugs. "I don't know. We, like, never go to church or anything either."

"Well, I was planning to go to temple tomorrow," he continues. "You're welcome to come with me, Annie, if you're curious. If it's okay with your mom."

Annie looks at me excitedly. "Can I go, Mom?"

I hesitate and glance at Gavin. "Are you sure?" I ask him.

"Absolutely," he says. "I always go by myself. It'd be nice to have the company. I actually go to a synagogue in Hyannis. If you're going to visit your grandmother tomorrow, I can swing by and pick Annie up at the hospital at the end of visiting hours."

Annie is grinning at me, and I shrug. "It's fine by me," I say. "As long as you're sure you don't mind."

"Not at all," Gavin says. "I'll come by tomorrow evening. Okay?"

"Cool," Annie says. "Thanks. It'll be cool to be, like, two religions at the same time."

I stare at her for a minute. "What did you say?"

She looks embarrassed. "I just mean it's, like, another side of me, you know?" She pauses and rolls her eyes when I don't say anything. "God, Mom, I know I'm Catholic. Don't freak out."

"No," I say, shaking my head. "That's not what I meant. I mean you just gave me another idea for how we might find Jacob."

"How?" Annie asks. She and Gavin are looking at me curiously.

"Interfaith organizations," I say slowly. "If Jacob trusted a Christian friend to bring the love of his life to a Muslim mosque during the war, he's obviously someone who respects other religions, right?"

Gavin is nodding, but Annie looks confused. "So what?" she asks.

"So what if he came to the States and carried on that tradition?" I say. "What if he's part of an interfaith organization somewhere?"

"What do you mean?" Annie asks.

Gavin answers for me. "I think your mother is saying that maybe Jacob joined one of those organizations where people work together for understanding between the religions," he says. "Kind of like the way people from different religions worked together in Paris to help save your great-grandma."

Annie looks unconvinced. "I don't know," she says. "Sounds kinda dumb. But I guess it's worth a try."

"I'll call some interfaith organizations today," I tell Annie.

"And I'll try calling some synagogues," Gavin says. "You guys try to find out Jacob's birth date, okay?"

Annie and I nod. Gavin thanks Annie politely for the pastries, smiles at me, and then turns to go.

"Give me a call if you find out anything, okay?" Gavin says as he heads for the door. "See you two tomorrow!"

"Bye!" Annie chirps, waving at him.

"Bye," I echo. "Drive safely," I add. He smiles once more, turns, and leaves the bakery.

"He's so nice," Annie says once he's gone.

"Yeah," I agree. I clear my throat and go back to setting up for the day. "He is."

Annie is spending the night at Rob's, and since it's been a slow day, I text her and tell her that she doesn't need to bother coming in after school; I can clean up myself this afternoon. She calls me from her dad's house after she gets off the bus and tells me excitedly that he's left a note for her saying it'll just be the two of them that night and asking whether he can take her out to a special dinner.

"That's great, honey," I say. I'm glad; it sounds like Rob is making an effort to make her feel important. Maybe my words the other day meant something after all.

"When you go to the hospital, can you tell Mamie I said hi and that I'll be there tomorrow?" Annie asks. "In case she can hear you?"

"Of course, sweetie," I tell her.

I pick up Alain at home after I close, and we chat the whole way to the hospital. I'm realizing how very much I like having him around; he fits nicely into our life. Some days, he helps out around the bakery; other days he spends at Mamie's bedside; and on days like today, he stays home and surprises me by doing things around the house. I returned a few days ago to find all the framed artwork in my attic hung up on the walls; today, I returned to find my pantry and freezer, which both had been virtually empty, cleared out and restocked with new groceries.

"It is the least I can do," Alain said when I'd confronted him in disbelief. "It is nothing. I took a taxi to the supermarket."

At the hospital, at Mamie's bedside, Alain holds my hand as we both sit with Mamie. He murmurs to her for a while in French, and as promised, I deliver Annie's message, although I don't believe that Mamie can hear me through the fog of her coma. I know that Alain and Annie both believe that she's still in there, but I'm not so sure. I keep this feeling to myself.

I find myself thinking about Gavin while Alain whispers to

Mamie, and I'm not entirely sure why. I think it's just because he's been so helpful, and I'm feeling more alone than ever.

Alain eventually settles back in his chair, apparently done with whatever story he was telling. Mamie continues to sleep, her narrow chest slowly moving up and down.

"She looks so peaceful," Alain says. "As if she is somewhere happier than here."

I nod, blinking back the sudden tears in my eyes. She *does* look at peace, but this just reinforces my idea that she's already gone, which makes me want to cry. "Alain," I say after a moment, "I don't suppose you know Jacob's date of birth, do you?"

Alain smiles and shakes his head, and for a moment, I think he's indicating that he doesn't. But then he says, "As a matter of fact, I do. Rose and I met him for the first time the evening before his sixteenth birthday."

I lean forward eagerly. "When?"

"Christmas Eve, 1940." Alain closes his eyes and smiles. "Rose and I were walking through the Jardin du Luxembourg. She had brought me with her to visit a friend in the Latin Quarter, and we were in a hurry to get home before curfew; the Germans insisted on everyone in Paris being home with their blackout curtains drawn.

"But Rose always loved the garden, and we were passing nearby on our way across the sixth arrondissement, so she suggested we walk across," Alain continues. "We went, as we always did, to see her favorite statue in the park, the Statue of Liberty."

"The Statue of Liberty?" I repeat.

He smiles. "The original model used by Auguste Bartholdi, the artist. Another stands in the middle of the Seine, not far from the Eiffel Tower. Your statue, the one in the harbor of New York, was given to the United States by France, you know."

"I remember that from school," I say. "I just didn't know there were similar statues in France."

Alain nods. "The statue in the Luxembourg Garden was

Rose's favorite when we were young, and on that evening, when we arrived at the statue, it had just begun to snow. The flakes were so tiny and light, it was like we were in a snow globe. Everything was very still and peaceful, even though we were at war. In that moment, the world felt magical."

His voice trails off, and he looks at Mamie. He reaches out to touch her cheek, where so many years of life without him are etched across her face.

"It was not until we drew close to the statue," he continues after a long pause, "that we realized we were not alone. There was a boy with dark hair and a dark coat standing just across. He turned as we were just a few feet away, and Rose stopped instantly, as if she'd lost her breath.

"But the boy didn't approach us, and we did not approach him," Alain continues. "They just stared at each other for a very long time, until finally I tugged on Rose's hand and said, 'Why did we stop?' "

Alain pauses for a moment to gather himself. He glances at Mamie and then settles back in his seat.

"Rose bent down and said to me, 'We stopped because it is very important for you to understand that the place where the real Statue of Liberty stands is a place where people can be free,'" Alain says, a dreamy look in his eye. "I did not understand what she was saying. She looked me in the eye and said, 'In the United States, religion does not define anyone. They only look at it as a piece of you. And no one is judged for it. I will go there someday, Alain, and I will bring you with me.'

"That was before the days of the worst Jewish restrictions. Rose, she was very knowledgeable, and so I believe she already knew of the Jews being persecuted elsewhere. She saw the problems coming, even if our parents did not. But I, at the age of nine, did not see what religion had to do with anything.

"Before I had a chance to ask her, the boy approached us. He'd been staring at us all along, and I could see, as Rose straightened up to talk to him, that her cheeks had gone very red. I asked her, 'Why is your face so red, Rose? Are you getting sick?' "

He laughs at the memory and shakes his head. "This only made her turn redder. But the boy, his cheeks were red too. He looked at Rose for a long time, and then he bent down to my eye level and said, 'Your friend here is right, monsieur. In the United States, people can be free. I am going there someday too.' I made a face at him and said, 'She's not my friend! She's my sister!'

"They both had a good laugh over that," Alain continues, smiling faintly. "And then they began to talk, and it was as if I was not there anymore. I had never seen my sister like that before; the way she gazed into his eyes, it was as if she wanted to disappear into them. Finally, the boy turned to me again and said, 'Little monsieur, my name is Jacob Levy. And what is yours?' I told him I was Alain Picard, and my sister was Rose Picard, and he looked at her again and murmured, 'I think that is the most beautiful name I have ever heard.'

"They talked for a long time, Rose and Jacob, until it began to grow dark," Alain says. "I was not listening to them very closely, for their conversation bored me. At nine, I wanted to talk about comic books and monsters, but they were talking about politics, and freedom, and religion and America. Finally, I tugged on Rose's hand again and said, 'We must go. It is getting dark and Maman and Papa will be angry!'

"Rose nodded, seeming to come out of a dream," Alain continues. "She told Jacob we had to leave. We began to walk away, quickly, toward the west side of the park, but he called after us. He said, 'Tomorrow is my birthday, you know! I will be sixteen!' Rose turned and said, 'On Christmas Day?' He said yes, and she paused. She said, 'Then I will meet you tomorrow, here, at the statue. To celebrate.' And then, together, we hurried away, both of us aware that darkness was falling fast, and there would be trouble if we were not home.

"She went alone to the park the next day, and she returned

with stars in her eyes," Alain concludes. "From that moment on, they were inseparable. It was love at first sight."

I sit back in my seat. "That's a beautiful story," I say.

"Everything about Rose and Jacob was a beautiful story," Alain says. "Until the end. But perhaps the story is not yet through being told."

I look off into the distance. "*If* he's still out there."

"If he is out there," Alain echoes.

I sigh and close my eyes. "So Christmas Day, then," I say. "He was born on Christmas Day. Nineteen twenty-four, I guess, if he was turning sixteen in 1940?"

"Correct," Alain agrees.

"Christmas Day 1924," I murmur. "Before Hitler. Before the war. Before so many people died for no reason at all."

"Who could have known," Alain says softly, "what was to come?"

That night, with Annie at her father's, Alain and I sip tea in the kitchen, and after he shuffles off to bed, I sit at the table for a long time, watching the second hand on the wall clock go around and around and around. I'm thinking about how time ticks by without anyone being able to stop it. It makes me feel powerless, small. I think about the seemingly infinite number of seconds that have passed since my grandmother lost Jacob.

It's nearly eleven when I pick up the phone to call Gavin, and although I know it's inappropriately late, I'm seized with the sudden panicky feeling that if I don't tell him about Jacob's birth date now, this very second, it might be too late. It's a silly thought, of course. Seventy years have ticked by with nothing happening. But seeing Mamie slip away in the hospital day after day makes me acutely conscious of the relentless progress of the second hand.

Gavin answers on the third ring.

"Did I wake you up?" I ask.

"No, I just finished watching a movie," Gavin says.

I feel suddenly foolish. "Oh. If you're with someone, I can call back . . ."

He laughs. "I'm by myself, on my couch. Unless you count the remote control as someone."

I'm unprepared for the feeling of relief that courses through me. I clear my throat, but he speaks again first. "Hope. Is everything okay?"

"Yeah." I pause and blurt out, "I found out Jacob Levy's date of birth."

"That's great!" Gavin says. "How did you find out?"

I find myself telling him the short version of the story Alain told me earlier.

"What a great story," Gavin says when I'm done. "Sounds like they were really meant to be."

"Yeah," I agree.

A moment of silence passes, and I look up again at the clock. *Tick-tock, tick-tock.* The second hand seems to mock me.

"Hope, what's wrong?" Gavin asks.

"Nothing," I say.

"I could start guessing," Gavin says. "Or you could just tell me."

I smile into the phone. He's so sure that he knows me. The fact of the matter is, he does. "Do you believe in that?" I ask.

"Believe in what?"

"You know," I mumble. "Love at first sight. Or, you know, soul mates. Or whatever it is that we all keep saying my grandmother and Jacob Levy had."

Gavin pauses, and in the silence, I feel like an idiot. Why would I ask him something like that? He probably thinks I'm coming on to him. I open my mouth to take it back, but he speaks first.

"Yes," he says.

"Yes?"

"Yes, I believe in that kind of love. Don't you?"

I close my eyes. There's suddenly a pain in my heart, because I realize I don't. "No," I say. "No, I don't think I do."

"Hmm," Gavin says.

"Have you ever felt that way about someone?"

He pauses. "Yes."

I want to ask him who, but I realize I don't want to know. I feel a small surge of jealousy, which I quickly push away. "Well, that's nice," I say.

"Yeah," Gavin says softly. "Why don't you believe in it?"

I've never asked myself that before. I consider the question for a moment. "Maybe because I'm thirty-six," I say, "and I've never felt it. Wouldn't I have felt it by now if it was real?"

The words hang between us, and I suspect Gavin is trying to figure out how to answer without offending me. "Not necessarily," he says carefully. "I think that you've been hurt. A lot."

"In my divorce?" I ask. "But that's just been recently. What about before that?"

"You'd been with your husband since you were what, twenty-one or twenty-two?"

"Twenty-three," I murmur.

"Do you think he was the love of your life?"

"No," I say. "But don't tell Annie that."

Gavin laughs softly. "I would never do that, Hope."

"I know."

Silence hangs between us again for a moment. "I think that you probably spent a dozen years with a man who didn't love you like a person deserves to be loved," Gavin says, "and who you maybe didn't love the way you're supposed to love someone. You got used to settling."

"Maybe," I say softly.

"And I think that every time a person gets hurt, there's another layer that forms around the outside of their heart, you know? Like a shield or something. You were hurt a lot, weren't you?"

I don't say anything for a moment.

"I'm sorry," Gavin says. "Was that too personal?"

"No," I say. "I think you're right. It was like nothing I did was ever good enough. Not just with Rob. But with my mom too." I stop speaking. I've never told anyone that before.

"I'm sorry," Gavin says.

"It's in the past," I murmur. I'm suddenly uneasy with the conversation, uncomfortable that I'm telling Gavin these things and letting him into my head.

"I'm just saying that I think the more layers there are around your heart, the harder it is to recognize someone you could really fall in love with," he says slowly.

His words settle in for a moment, and I feel strangely short of breath. "Maybe," I say. "Or maybe when you've been hurt a lot, it just opens your eyes to reality and you stop dreaming of things that don't exist."

Gavin is silent. "Maybe," he says. "But maybe you're wrong. Maybe it does exist. Would you agree that your grandmother's been hurt a lot over the years?"

"Of course."

"And Jacob Levy too, probably?"

"Yeah, probably," I say. I think of all they both lost—their families, life as they knew it, each other. What could hurt more than the entire world turning its back on you while all the people you love are hauled away to their deaths? "Yeah," I say again.

"Well, let's see if we can find him," Gavin says. "Jacob. And we can ask him. And your grandmother."

"If she wakes up," I say.

"*When* she wakes up," Gavin says. "You have to stay optimistic."

I look at the clock. How can one stay optimistic when time keeps marching forward? I sigh. "Okay," I say. "So we'll just ask them if love is real?" I hate that I sound like I'm mocking him, but he sounds silly.

"Why not?" Gavin answers. "The worst they can say is no."

"Yeah, all right," I agree. I shake my head, ready to be done with this futile conversation. "So you think we can find him? Now that we have a birth date?"

"I think it increases our chances," Gavin says. "Maybe he's still out there."

"Maybe," I agree. *Or maybe he died a long time ago, and this is all a wild goose chase.* "Hey, thank you," I say, and I'm not sure whether I'm thanking him for the conversation we've just had, or whether the thank-you is only for helping us try to find Jacob.

"You're welcome, Hope. I'll call a bunch of synagogues tomorrow. Maybe something will turn up. See you tomorrow evening at the hospital."

"Thank you," I say again. And then he's gone, and I'm holding the receiver, wondering what just happened. Is it possible that I've just gotten old and bitter and that this guy in his late twenties knows more about life and love than I do?

I fall asleep that night wishing fervently, for the first time I can remember, that I'm just a big fool and that all the things I've grown to believe aren't true after all.

Chapter *Twenty-one*

Annie and Alain accompany Gavin to temple the next night, while I stay with Mamie past the end of visiting hours, after bribing the nurses on the floor with a lemon-grape cheesecake and a box full of cookies from the bakery.

"Mamie, I need you to wake up," I whisper to her as the room grows dimmer. I'm holding her hand and facing the window, which is on the other side of her hospital bed. Twilight has almost faded to full darkness now, and Mamie's beloved stars are out. They seem to sparkle less brightly than they used to, and I wonder whether they're fading, as I am, without Mamie's attention. "I miss you," I whisper close to her ear.

The machines monitoring her continue to beep away in soothing rhythms, but they're not bringing her back. The doctor has told Alain and me that sometimes, it's just a matter of time, and that the brain heals itself when it's ready. What she didn't say, but what I could read in her eyes, was that just as often, the person never comes back. It's slowly sinking in that I may never look into my grandmother's eyes again.

I didn't think I was a person who needed anyone. My mother was always very independent. And after my grandfather died when I was ten, Mamie was always busy with the bakery, too busy to tell me her fairy tales anymore, too busy to listen to my stories of school and friends and everything that was going on in my imagination. My mother had never been very interested in those stories anyhow, and gradually, I stopped telling them.

I don't need anyone, I told myself as I got older. I didn't talk to my mother or my grandmother about grades, or boys, or college decisions, or anything. They both seemed so absorbed in their own worlds, and I felt like an outsider with both of them. So I created my own world.

It wasn't until I had Annie that I learned to let someone else in. And now that she's right around the age I was when I had to learn to fend for myself, I've realized I'm holding on tighter, in a way. I don't want her drifting out of my universe into one of her own making, like I did. And that, I realize, is what makes me different from my grandmother and my mother.

But as Mamie has regressed through time, turning almost into a child as the Alzheimer's steals her lifetime, I've found her drifting back into my universe too. I realize that I'm not ready for it to just be me and Annie. I need Mamie here a little while longer.

"Come back, Mamie," I whisper to my grandmother. "We're going to try to find Jacob, okay? You just have to come back to us."

Four days later, Mamie's condition hasn't changed, and I've just opened the bakery when Matt comes by with a big packet of papers in his hands. My heart sinks. With all the drama surrounding Mamie's stroke, and the discovery of the existence of Alain and Jacob, I've nearly forgotten the trouble my business is in.

"I'm going to get right to the point," Matt says after we exchange uneasy hellos. "The investors don't like the numbers."

I stare at him. "Okay . . ." I say.

"And I'm going to be honest: you leaving and going to Paris during the time they were considering this investment decision, well, let's just say that was pretty foolish."

I sigh. "Maybe from a business perspective."

"What else is there right now?"

I look down at the tray of Star Pies I've been holding in my hands since Matt walked in. "Everything," I say softly. I smile at the pies for a moment before sliding them into the display case.

Matt looks at me like I've lost my mind. "Hope, they're pulling out. They've run the numbers, and you're marginal, at best. They were on the fence, and I've been doing my best to try to persuade them on your behalf. But realizing you'd closed like that, at the drop of a hat . . . well, that was the final straw."

I nod, my heart thudding. I realize what he's saying to me: that I may have just lost the bakery. And I have a sensation coursing through me that feels a bit like panic. But I'm not nearly as upset as I would have thought, and this worries me a little. Shouldn't I be more upset that my family's business, my entire livelihood, is about to be ripped away from me? Instead, I just have the strange sense that things are going to work out the way they're meant to, whatever that means.

"Are you listening to me, Hope?" Matt asks, and I realize he's been talking while I was thinking.

"Sorry, what were you saying?" I ask.

"I was *saying* that there's not that much more I can do. Do you know how out of my way I went to even get them here in the first place? But they're not going to invest, Hope. I'm sorry."

Matt doesn't say anything as I quietly rearrange pastries in the display case. The door dings, and Lisa Wilkes, who works at the stationery shop on the corner, comes in with Melixa Carbonell, who works at the pet shop on Lietz Road. They were both a few years behind Matt and me in high school, and they come in together at least once a week.

Matt is silent while Lisa orders a coffee and Melixa orders a green tea, which takes me a few minutes to make, because I have to plug in the electric kettle. In the meantime, they argue over whether they'll split a piece of baklava or a piece of cheesecake. In the end, I settle for charging them for a piece of baklava and throwing in a piece of cheesecake for free.

"That's why you're going out of business, you know," Matt says after they've left.

"What?"

"You can't just go giving people free pastries. They were totally playing you."

"They weren't playing me," I respond indignantly.

"Sure they were. You're too generous. They knew if they argued in front of you, you'd be nice and give them both pastries. And you did."

I sigh. I don't even bother explaining that there's no way I'll go through the remainder of the cheesecake today anyhow. "My grandmother always ran this bakery like it was her kitchen and the customers were her guests," I say instead.

"That's not a good business model," Matt says.

I shrug. "I never said it was. But I'm proud of that tradition."

The door dings again, and I look up to see Alain shuffling in. He's taken to walking here himself in the mornings. I worry about him doing so at his age—the walk is more than a mile—but he seems to be perfectly healthy, and he swears that he walks far more than this each day in Paris.

He crosses behind the counter and gives me a gentle kiss on the cheek. "Good morning, dear," he says. He seems to notice Matt for the first time then. "Hello, young man," he says. He turns to me and says, "I see you have a customer."

"Matt was just leaving," I tell him. I shoot Matt a look, which I hope transmits the fact that I don't want him talking bakery business in front of Alain. But of course, he's oblivious.

"I'm Matt Hines," he says, extending a hand to Alain over the bakery case. "And you are . . . ?"

Alain hesitates before shaking Matt's hand. "I am Alain Picard," he says. "Hope's uncle."

Matt looks confused. "Now, wait. I've known Hope since we were kids. She doesn't have any uncles."

Alain smiles thinly. "Yes, young man, she does indeed. In fact, I am her *arriere-oncle*. Her great-uncle, as you would say."

Matt frowns and looks at me.

"He's my grandmother's brother," I explain. "From Paris."

Matt stares at Alain for a second, then turns back to me. "Hope, this isn't making a whole lot of sense. You're telling me you went to Paris on a whim, you're about to lose your business because of it, and you've randomly brought back a relative you never knew you had?"

I feel my cheeks heating up, and I'm not sure whether it's because he's apparently insulting me, or because he's just announced in front of Alain that I'm about to lose the bakery. I turn slowly and look at Alain, hopeful that the words were lost in translation, but he's staring at me with a frozen look on his face.

"Hope, what does he mean?" he asks softly. "About losing the business? Is the bakery in trouble?"

"Don't worry about it," I say. I shoot Matt a look, and at least he has the grace to appear slightly shamed. He clears his throat and turns away, as if to give Alain and me a moment's privacy.

"Hope, we are family," Alain says. "Of course I will worry if something is wrong. Why did you say nothing to me?"

I take a deep breath. "Because it's my fault," I say. "I made some bad financial decisions. My credit rating has totally tanked, and that's tied in to my business credit."

"But that does not explain why you did not tell me," Alain says. He takes a step forward and puts a warm, gnarled hand on my cheek. "I am your uncle."

I can feel tears in my eyes now. "I'm sorry. I just didn't want to burden you. With everything going on with my grandmother . . ."

"All the more reason to lean on me," he says. He touches my cheek lightly with the palm of his hand and turns back to Matt. "Young man!" he calls out.

"Yes?" Matt turns, wide-eyed, as if he hasn't been listening to every word.

"You can go now. My niece and I have some talking to do."

"But, I—" Matt begins. But Alain cuts him off again.

"I do not know who you are or what you have to do with this," Alain says.

"I'm the vice president of the Bank of the Cape," Matt says stiffly. He stands up a little straighter. "We hold Hope's loan. And unfortunately, it's necessary that we call it in. It wasn't my decision, sir. It's just business."

I swallow the lump in my throat and glance at Alain. His face has gone red.

"So that's it, then?" he says to Matt. "Sixty years of tradition? Sixty years of my family baking for this town, and you decide it is all over, just like that?"

"It's not personal," Matt says. He glances at me. "I tried to help, actually. Hope will tell you. But the investors I had interested backed out after Hope went to Paris. I'm sorry, but I guess the legacy has to end."

I look down at the ground and close my eyes.

"Young man," Alain says after a moment. "The legacy is not in this bakery itself but in the family tradition it represents. There is no price tag on that. Seventy years ago, men who did not understand family or conscience, and who only understood orders and wealth, took our first bakery away. And because of my sister, and her daughter, and her granddaughter, the tradition survived."

"I don't understand what this has to do with a loan," Matt says.

Alain reaches over and squeezes my hand. "You and your bank are making a mistake, young man," he says. "But Hope will be fine. She is a survivor. Just like her grandmother. That is our tradition. And it too will survive."

My heart feels like it's going to overflow. Alain takes me gently by the hand and turns me toward the kitchen. "Come, Hope," he says. "Let us bake a Star Pie to take to Rose. I am sure the young man can find his own way out."

That afternoon, armed with Jacob Levy's date of birth, I begin calling the interfaith organizations I'd found using Google. I'd been holding off, because I realize what a long shot this is, and I've reached my limit of disappointment. I'm feeling as if all I hear anymore are no's.

Can I save my bakery? *No.* Do we know that Mamie will ever wake up? *No.* Is it likely that there's still time to turn my messy life around? *No.*

I start with the Interfaith Alliance, then I go down my list to the Council for a Parliament of the World's Religions, the National American Interfaith Network, the United Religions Initiative, and the World Congress of Faith. To each person who answers, I briefly explain the story of how Jacob took Mamie to a Christian, who helped shelter her with Muslims. Then I give them Jacob's name and date of birth and say that I know it's a long shot, but I'm trying to find him and believe there's a chance he may be involved with an interfaith organization here in the States. They all ooh and aah over the story, tell me they'll pass my information to the right people and will get back to me if they find anything.

On Sunday morning at about eight o'clock, Annie and I are alone in the bakery, rolling out dough in silence, when the phone rings. Annie wipes her hands on her apron and reaches for the receiver. "North Star Bakery, Annie speaking," she says. She listens for a minute and hands the phone to me with a funny expression on her face. "It's for you, Mom."

I dust my hands off and take the phone from her. "Hello, North Star Bakery," I say.

"Is this Hope McKenna-Smith?" It's a woman's voice, and she has a hint of an accent.

"Yes," I say. "How can I help you?"

"My name is Elida White," she says. "I'm calling you from the Abrahamic Association of Boston. We are an interfaith council."

"Oh," I say. They aren't one of the groups I called over the last few days. The name doesn't ring a bell. "Abrahamic?" I ask.

"The Muslim, Jewish, and Christian religions all descend from Abraham," she explains. "We focus on bringing together these groups and working from our similarities instead of our differences."

"Oh," I say again. "Right. What can I do for you?"

"Let me explain," she says. "Our organization received a call this week from the Interfaith Council of America, and it was referred to me. I was told about your grandmother and how she was assisted in escaping from Paris by a Muslim family."

"Yes," I say softly.

"I have looked through all our records, and there is no Jacob Levy among our members with a birth date matching the one you provided," she says.

"Oh," I say. My heart sinks. Another dead end. "Thanks for looking. But you didn't have to call."

"I know I did not have to," she says. "But I have someone here who would like to meet you. And in turn, we would like to help you. It is our obligation. Can you come to visit today? I understand that your grandmother is in ill health and time is of the essence. I realize the notice is short, but I see that you are on the Cape, so the journey won't be more than an hour or two. I live in Pembroke."

Pembroke, I know, is just off the highway on the South Shore, on the way to Boston. It would take me just under an hour and a half to get there. But I don't understand why I need to go if they haven't found Jacob Levy in their records.

"I'm afraid today isn't going to work," I say. "I run a bakery, and we're open until four."

"So come after you close," the woman says right away. "Come for dinner."

I pause. "I appreciate the invitation, but—"

She cuts me off. "Please. My grandmother would like to meet you. She is in her nineties. She is a Muslim, and she too sheltered Jews during the war."

My heartbeat picks up. "She's from Paris too?"

"No," the woman says. "We are from Albania. You know, the Albanian Muslims, they saved more than two thousand of our Jewish brothers and sisters. When I told her the story of your Jacob Levy, she was astonished. She did not know that there were Muslims in Paris who had done the same. Please, she would like you to come tell her your story, and she would like to tell you her story in return."

I glance at Annie, who is looking at me hopefully. "May I bring my daughter?" I ask.

"Of course," Elida says immediately. "She is most welcome, as are you. And once we have shared stories, we will help you find this Jacob, okay? My grandmother says she knows how important it is to meet the past, here in the present."

"Hold on," I say. I put my hand over the receiver and briefly explain Elida's request to Annie.

"We have to go, Mom," she says solemnly. "That lady's grandma sounds just like Mamie. Except from Albania instead of France. And Muslim instead of Jewish. We should go talk to her."

I look at my daughter for a moment and realize she's right. My grandmother is lying in a coma, but Elida's grandmother is still able to talk. We may never get the full story of what happened to my grandmother, but perhaps hearing from another woman from the same time period, who was involved in a situation similar to Mamie's, will help us to understand.

"Okay," I tell Elida. "We'll be there around six. What's your address?"

Annie invites Alain to come with us to Pembroke, but he says that he'll stay behind with Mamie instead. We swing by the hospital to sit with Mamie for a few minutes, then Annie and I set off again, after promising to pick Alain up on our way home. He's managed to charm the night nurses at the hospital into looking the other way when it comes to their visitation policies; they all know his story and that he has been separated from his sister for nearly seventy years.

It's a few minutes past six when we pull off the highway in Pembroke. We find Elida's house easily enough, thanks to the directions she gave us. It's a blue, white-shuttered, two-story home in a small, well-kept neighborhood just behind a Catholic church. Annie and I exchange looks, get out of the car, and ring the doorbell.

The woman who opens the door and introduces herself as Elida is older than I'd expected; she looks like she's in her mid-forties. Her skin is pale, and she has thick, black hair that tumbles down her back, nearly to her waist. I've never met anyone from Albania, but she looks like what I'd expect someone from Greece or Italy to look like.

"Welcome to our home," she says, shaking my hand first, and then Annie's. Her eyes are deep and brown, and her smile is kind. "It is just my grandmother and me here tonight. My husband, Will, is working. Please, come in."

I hand her the box of miniature Star Pies I've brought for dessert, and after she thanks me, we follow her inside, down a hallway lined with black-and-white photographs of people I assume are her family members. She tells us that in Albania, the main meal of the day is lunch, but that tonight, they've made a special dinner. "I hope you like fish," she says, turning around slightly. "I have prepared an old family recipe that my grandmother used to make in Albania."

"Sure," I say, and Annie nods. "You didn't have to go to so much effort, though."

"It is our pleasure," she says. "You are our guests."

We turn the corner into a dimly lit dining room, where at the head of the table sits a woman who looks far older than Mamie. Her face is heavily lined, and her snow-white hair has fallen out in places, leaving her with a strangely patchy head of receding hair. She's wearing a black sweater and a long, gray skirt, and she stares at us with bright eyes from behind enormous tortoiseshell glasses that look far too big for her face. She says something in a language I don't recognize.

"This is my grandmother, Nadire Veseli," Elida tells Annie and me. "She speaks only Albanian. She says she is glad you have come and that you are very welcome in our home."

"Thank you," I reply.

Annie and I sit beside each other to the right of the old woman, and Elida returns a moment later with four bowls on a tray. She sets one down in front of each of us and takes her own seat on her grandmother's left side.

"Potato and cabbage soup," Elida says, nodding at the bowls. She picks up her spoon and winks at Annie. "Do not worry. It's more delicious than it sounds. I lived in Albania until I was twenty-five, and this was my favorite food when I was your age."

Annie smiles and takes a sip of her soup, and I do the same. Elida's right; it's very good. I can't put a finger on the spices in it, but it tastes hearty and fresh.

"It's real good," Annie says.

"I love it," I agree. "You'll have to give me the recipe."

"With pleasure," Elida says. Her grandmother says something softly in Albanian and Elida nods. "My grandmother would like to hear the story of how your grandmother was saved, please," Elida translates for us. Her grandmother nods and looks at me hopefully. She says something else to Elida, who again translates for us. "My grandmother says she hopes she is not being rude in asking."

"Not at all," I murmur, although I'm still confused about what we're doing here. But for the next twenty minutes, Annie and I explain what we've learned recently about Mamie's past and how she escaped Paris. As Elida translates our words into Albanian, her grandmother listens, staring at us intently and nodding. Her eyes begin to fill with tears, and at one point, she interrupts Elida loudly and says several sentences in Albanian.

"She says to tell you that your grandmother's story is like a gift to her," Elida says. "And that she is happy you have come to our home. She says it is good that young people like you and your daughter are reminded of the concept of oneness."

"Oneness?" Annie asks.

Elida turns to my daughter and nods. "We are Muslims, Annie, but we believe you are our sister, although you are Christian and come from a Jewish background. I married a Christian man from a Jewish background because I love him. Love can transcend religion. Did you know that? In the world today, there is too much division, but God made us all, did he not?"

Annie nods and looks at me; I know she's not sure how to respond. "Yeah, I guess," she finally says.

"It's why I took a job with the Abrahamic Association," Elida explains. "So that I could work to foster understanding between religions. In the years since World War Two, it seems that much of the brotherhood we once shared has vanished."

"But what does that have to do with us?" I ask softly.

Elida's grandmother says something and Elida nods, then turns back to me. "Your call for help came to me," she says. "In our culture, that means I now have the obligation to assist you. It is a code of honor called *Besa*."

"*Besa?*" I repeat.

Elida nods. "It is an Albanian concept that derives from the Koran. It means that if someone comes to you in need, you must

not turn them away. It is because of *Besa* that my grandmother
and I have asked you here tonight. It is because of *Besa* that my
grandmother and her friends and neighbors saved many Jews,
at the risk of their own lives. And it is likely because of *Besa* that
your grandmother was saved too, even if the Muslims in Paris
did not call the concept by the same name as we do in Albania.
And now, my grandmother would like to tell you her story."

Elida's grandmother smiles at us in silence as Elida rises to
clear our soup dishes. Annie offers to help, and a moment later,
the two of them return with plates full of fish and vegetables.

"This is trout baked with olive oil and garlic," Elida explains
as she and Annie sit down. "It is a common dish in Albania. There
are also baked leeks and Albanian potato salad. My grandmother
and I wanted you to have a taste of our homeland."

"Thank you," Annie and I say in unison.

"Ju lutem," Elida's grandmother says. "You are welcome," she
adds in English.

Elida smiles. "She knows a few words of English." She pauses
as her grandmother says something else. "And now, she would
like to tell you about the Jews she sheltered in our hometown of
Kruje."

Elida's grandmother begins to tell us, with Elida translating,
that she was a newlywed when the war began and that her husband was a very well-known, well-liked man in their small town,
where everyone knew everyone else.

"In 1939, the Italians occupied our country, and then in September 1943, the Germans came," Elida translates as her grandmother speaks. "Right away, it became clear they were hunting
the Jews who lived among Albanians, my grandmother says.
Albania, you see, had become a refuge of sorts for Jews fleeing
from Macedonia and Kosovo, and from as far away as Germany
and Poland.

"In 1943, several Jewish families came to our small town of
Kruje, seeking refuge," Elida continues as her grandmother tells

her tale in her native language. "My grandfather was one of the townspeople who offered to take in refugees. The family who came to stay with them, my grandmother says, were the Berensteins, from Mati, Germany. She can still remember them."

Elida pauses then, and her grandmother says in slow, careful English, "Ezra Berenstein, the father. Bracha Berenstein, the mother. Two girls. Sandra Bernstein. Ayala Berenstein."

Elida nods. "Yes. The Berensteins. The girls were very young, just four and six. The family had fled at the start of the war and had been gradually making their way south, in hiding."

Elida's grandmother begins to speak again, and Elida resumes her translation. "My grandmother says that she and her husband were poor, and provisions were very low because of the war, but they welcomed the Berensteins into their home. The whole town knew of it, but when the Germans came, no one betrayed them. Once, the Germans came to the house, and Mr. and Mrs. Berenstein hid in the attic, while my grandmother and grandfather pretended Sandra and Ayala were their own children, Muslim children. After that, they dressed all the Berensteins in peasant clothing, and my grandfather went with them and helped them move into the mountains nearby, to a smaller village. After a time, my grandmother followed. They lived there with the Berensteins, helping to protect them, until 1944, when the Berensteins again began to move south, toward Greece."

I realize there are tears in my eyes as I listen to the story. I glance at Annie and see that she looks equally moved.

"What happened to them?" I ask. "The Berensteins? Did they make it out safely?"

"For a very long time, my grandmother did not know," Elida says. "She and my grandfather prayed for them every day. After the Germans were defeated in late 1944 in Albania, the country was taken over by Communists, and Albanians were not allowed to communicate with the outside world. It was 1952 when my grandparents received a letter from the Berensteins. They were alive, all four, and living in Israel. They thanked my grandparents for what they had done, for extending *Besa,* and Ezra Berenstein wrote that he had sworn an oath to repay my grandmother and grandfather, should they ever need help. My grandparents were not allowed to respond, and they feared the Berensteins would think they had died, or worse, that they would think they had not remembered them."

Elida's grandmother says something else and Elida smiles and replies to her in Albanian. She turns back to Annie and me. "I told my grandmother I know the rest of the story, and so I can tell you," she says. "I was twenty-five when Communism fell in 1992, and our country was once again open to the world. But Communism had destroyed us, you see. We were very poor. There was no future for us in Albania, but there was no money to leave. I lived with my grandmother and my parents. My grandfather had died years before. One day, there was a knock at our door."

"Was it Ezra Berenstein?" Annie interrupts eagerly.

"No, but you are close," Elida replies with a smile. "Mr. Berenstein had died some years before, as had his wife. But the daughters, Sandra and Ayala, had never forgotten their time in my grandparents' home. They were in their fifties by then, and they had been working to get my grandparents declared Righteous Among the Nations, which is a title given to those people who helped save Jews at the peril of their own lives. Now they were at our door, nearly fifty years after they first came to Albania for shelter, wishing to repay what my grandmother and grandfather had given to them.

"My grandmother explained to them that *Besa* isn't to be repaid," Elida continues. "Not on this earth, anyhow. She told them that it was her duty to help them, her duty to God and to her fellow man, and that she was very glad they had lived and gone on to happy lives. Ayala lived in America by then, and she had married a very wealthy man, a doctor named William. She had converted to Christianity, and they'd had two sons, she told my grandmother. She said she owed my grandmother every-thing, because without their help, she and her family would never have survived. She told my grandmother that she wanted to help us get out of Albania and bring us to America. And a year later, after securing visas for us, that is exactly what she did. My parents decided to remain in Albania, but my grandmother and I moved here, to Boston, to begin a new life."

"Do you still see Ayala and her family?" Annie asks.

Elida smiles. "Every day. You see, I married Ayala's oldest son, Will. And now, our families are one forever."

"That's incredible," I breathe. I smile at Elida's grandmother, who blinks a few times and smiles back. I think about how many lives she changed when she and her husband made the decision to shelter a Jewish family, despite the fact that they could have lost their lives because of it. "Thank you so much for telling us your story."

"Oh, but the story is not finished," Elida says. She smiles, reaches into her pocket, and withdraws a folded piece of paper, which she hands to me.

"What is this?" I ask as I begin to unfold it.

"It is *Besa,*" she says. "You are looking for Jacob Levy, and your request came to me. My husband, Will, the son of Ayala, who my grandmother saved nearly seventy years ago, is a police officer. I asked him to do this favor, and he found your Jacob Levy, born in Paris, France, on Christmas Day 1924." She nods at the piece of paper in my hand. "That is his address. As of a year ago, he was living in New York City."

"Wait," Annie interrupts. She grabs the piece of paper from me and stares at it. "You found Jacob Levy? My grandmother's Jacob Levy?"

Elida smiles. "I believe so. His information matches the details your mother provided." She turns to me. "Now you must go find him."

"How can we ever thank you?" I ask, my voice trembling.

"There is no need to," Elida says. "*Besa* is our honor. Just promise us that you won't forget what you learned here today."

"Never," Annie says right away. She hands the piece of paper back to me, and her eyes are wide as saucers. "Thank you, Mrs. White. We'll never, ever forget. I promise."

Chapter Twenty-two

Cinnamon Almond Cookies

INGREDIENTS

2 sticks unsalted butter
1½ cups packed brown sugar
2 large eggs
1 tsp. almond extract
2½ cups flour

1 tsp. baking soda
1 tsp. salt
1 cup cinnamon sugar (¾ cup
    granulated sugar mixed with
    ¼ cup cinnamon)

DIRECTIONS

1. In a large bowl, beat the butter and brown sugar until smooth. Add the eggs and almond extract and beat until well combined.

2. Sift together the flour, baking soda, and salt, and add to the butter mixture, approximately ½ cup at a time, beating after each addition, until well combined.

3. Divide the dough into 5 parts and roll into logs, wrap each in plastic wrap, and freeze until firm.

4. Preheat oven to 350 degrees.

5. Spread cinnamon sugar in a shallow dish. Unwrap logs and roll them in the sugar until liberally coated.

6. Slice the logs ¼-inch thick and place slices on greased baking sheets. Bake for 18–20 minutes.

7. Cool for 5 minutes on baking sheet, then transfer to racks to cool.

Rose

Once, very long ago, when Rose was four years old, her parents had taken her, along with her sister Helene, to Aubergenville, not far from Paris, for a week in the countryside. Her mother was very pregnant that summer of 1929; Claude would be born just six weeks later. But for those glimmering summer moments in the sun, it was just Rose and Helene, four and five years old, the objects of their parents' attention and affection.

Helene had been charged with watching her younger sister, while her parents sipped white wine on the back deck of the small home they were renting from friends for a week. They were not watching when Helene took Rose around the corner of the house, to the little creek that babbled by.

"Let us go in the water," Helene said, taking her sister by the hand. Rose hesitated. Maman and Papa would be angry, she thought. But Helene insisted, reminding Rose of the stories their mother read them at bedtime about the family of ducks who lived along the banks of the Seine. "The ducks go swimming all the time, and it is fine," Helene told her. "Do not be such a baby, Rose."

And so Rose followed her sister into the water. But the calm surface was deceptive; there was a current running underneath, and as soon as Rose stepped in, she felt it sucking at her toes, pulling her under, taking her away. She did not know how to swim. She was suddenly underwater, thrust into another world, where there was no air, almost no sound. She tried to scream, but the water only filled her lungs. It was dark beneath the surface, dark and unfamiliar. She could see light far away, far above her, but she couldn't seem to get to it. Her limbs were heavy and wouldn't move, and in these strange, watery depths, she felt that time was suspended. Until the moment her father pulled her to the surface, called there by her screaming sister just in time, she had been sure she would disappear into the murky, muted world forever.

That was how Rose felt now, under the surface of the coma she'd been in for two weeks. She was aware that there was a surface—voices and sounds, distant and muffled; light and motion very far away. Her limbs felt heavy, like they did that day in the creek in Aubergenville, and she knew that her father was long gone; he would not pull her out of this frightening underworld. She was on her own, and she still didn't know how to swim.

On that day in Aubergenville, she had wanted to be saved. She had wanted to find the surface, to return to life. But now she wasn't sure whether she wanted that at all. Maybe it was time to let go. Maybe it was time to drift away. Maybe the murky deep held more for her than the bright surface that she could just barely see.

Hope was up there, she knew. And Annie. But they would be well. Hope was strong, stronger than she gave herself credit for, and Annie was growing into a fine young woman. Rose could not stay with them forever, protect them forever.

Maybe it was finally her time. Maybe *he* was here, somewhere beneath the depths, somewhere in this hazy world that seemed to exist between life and death. She missed seeing the stars, *her* stars, and without the sky to shelter her each night, to remind her of the people she'd loved so much, she felt cold and alone.

Rose was sure she was dying now too; she was beginning to hear the ghosts of her past. And that is how she knew her life was nearly over, for she recognized the voice of her brother Alain, grown up and deep now. It was how she'd always imagined he'd sound if he had survived during the war and had the chance to grow into manhood.

"It is you who saved me, Rose," the distant voice kept repeating over and over in their native tongue. "*C'est tu qui m'as sauvé, Rose.*"

The voice in Rose's mind screamed, "I did not save you! I let you die! I am a coward!" But the words would not come to her lips, and even if they had, she knew they would be lost in the depths of this shrouded world. And so she listened, as the voice of her dear brother went on.

"You taught me to believe," he whispered again and again. "You have to stop blaming yourself. It was you who saved me, Rose."

She wondered whether this was the absolution she'd spent her life searching for, although she was sure she did not deserve it. Or was it simply one more result of the dementia that she knew nibbled at her mind? She didn't trust her own eyes, her own ears anymore, for they often didn't match reality or recollection.

And when he began to whisper to her, "You have to wake up, Rose. Hope and Annie may have found Jacob Levy," she knew that her mind was entirely gone, because that was impossible. Jacob was gone. Long gone. Hope would never know him. Rose would never see him again.

Were it possible to shed tears in the deep, murky sea, Rose would have cried.

Chapter *Twenty-three*

On the way home from Elida's house, I can see Annie's eyes shining in the darkness, glinting with reflected light.

"You have to go to New York tomorrow, Mom," she says. "You have to go find him."

I nod. The bakery is closed on Mondays anyhow, and even if it weren't, I know I can't wait another moment. "We'll leave in the morning," I tell Annie. "First thing."

Annie turns to look at me. "I can't go with you," she says miserably, shaking her head. "I have my big social studies test tomorrow."

I clear my throat. "That's responsible of you." I pause. "Have you studied for it?"

"Mom!" Annie says. "Of course! Duh."

"Good," I say. "Okay. We'll head down to New York on Tuesday, then. Can you miss school on Tuesday?"

Annie shakes her head. "No, you gotta go tomorrow, Mom."

I glance at her, then refocus on the road. "Honey, I don't mind waiting for you."

"No," she says instantly. "You have to find him as soon as possible. What if we're running out of time and we don't even know it?"

"Mamie's stable now," I tell Annie. "She'll hang in there."

"C'mon, Mom," Annie says softly after a pause. "You don't believe that. You know she could die any time. That's why you've got to find Jacob Levy as soon as you can if he's out there."

"But Annie—" I begin.

"No, Mom," she says firmly, as if she's the parent and I'm the child. "Go to New York tomorrow. Bring Jacob Levy back. Don't let Mamie down."

After swinging by the hospital on the way home, staying with Mamie for a bit, and getting Annie into bed, I sit in the kitchen with Alain, sipping decaf coffee and explaining what we learned from Elida and her grandmother.

"Besa," he says softly. "What a beautiful concept. The obligation to help our fellow man." He stirs his coffee slowly and takes a sip. "So you will go tomorrow to New York? Alone?"

I nod. Then, feeling foolish, I add quickly, "I was thinking about seeing if Gavin would want to come with me. Just since he helped us out a lot at the beginning of this search, you know?"

Alain smiles. "It is a wise idea." He pauses, then adds, "You know, there is nothing wrong with falling in love with Gavin, Hope."

I'm so startled by his bluntness that I choke on the sip of coffee I've just taken. "I'm not in love with Gavin," I protest through coughs.

"Of course you are," Alain says. "And he is in love with you."

I laugh at that, but my cheeks are hot and my palms suddenly sweaty. "That's crazy!"

"Why is it so crazy?" Alain asks.

I shake my head. "Well, for one thing, we have nothing in common."

Alain laughs. "You have many things in common. I see the way the two of you talk with each other. The way he makes you laugh. The way that you can talk about anything."

"That's just because he's a nice guy," I mumble.

Alain folds his hands over mine. "He cares about what happens to you. And whether you admit it or not, you care about what happens to him too."

"Those still aren't things we have in common," I reply stubbornly.

"He cares about Annie," Alain adds softly. "You cannot tell me you do not have that in common."

I pause before nodding. "Yeah," I admit. "He does care about Annie."

"That is not something that comes along every day," Alain says. "Think about how he helped her when we were in Paris and Rose was brought to the hospital. He was there for her. And he was there for you."

I nod again. "I know. He's a good guy."

"He is more than that," Alain says. "Tell me, why do you not believe in this?"

I shrug and look down. "He's seven years younger than I am, for one thing," I mumble.

Alain laughs. "Your grandmother married a Christian man, although she is a Jew. And you just came from the home of a woman who is happily married to a Christian Jew, although she is Muslim. If something as important as religious differences can be surmounted, do you really think seven years make a difference?"

I shrug again. "Fine. But I also have a child."

Alain just looks at me. "Of course. But I do not understand why this is an excuse for you."

"Well, for one thing, he's only twenty-nine. I can't ask him to take on the responsibility of a teenage kid."

"It seems to me that you have not asked him," Alain says, "and yet he is already here, taking on the responsibility. Is that not his decision to make?"

I hang my head. "But my mother always put men first, you

know? I always felt like I didn't matter to her as much as they did. Her life revolved around whomever she was dating at the time. I promised myself I would never, ever make my child feel that way."

"You are not your mother," Alain says after a moment.

"But what if I turn into her?" I ask in a small voice. "What if now that I'm divorced, that's exactly what I do? I can't let myself go down that road. Annie has to come first, no matter what."

"Letting someone else in does not mean leaving Annie out," Alain says carefully.

I can feel tears rolling down my cheeks and am surprised to realize I've started crying. "But what if he hurts me?" I blurt out. "What if I let him into my life, and he breaks my heart? What if he hurts Annie? She's been through so much with her dad; I don't think I could bear it if I hurt her too."

Alain pats my hand. "It is true, that is a risk you take," he says. "But life is about taking risks. How can you live, otherwise?"

"But I'm happy enough now," I tell him. "Maybe that's enough. How do you know Gavin won't change all that?"

"I don't," Alain says. "But there is only one way to find out." Alain stands and grabs my cell phone from the counter, where it's charging. "Call him. Ask him to go with you tomorrow. You do not need to make any decisions right away. But open the door, Hope. Open the door to let him in."

I take the phone from him and draw a deep breath. "Okay."

Annie wakes up with me at three in the morning, and as I sip coffee at the kitchen table and read yesterday's newspaper, she eats Rice Krispies and drinks a glass of orange juice while staring at me.

"So Mr. Keyes said yes?" she asks. "He's gonna go with you?"

"Yes," I say. I clear my throat. "He'll be here at four."

"Good," she says. "Mr. Keyes is really nice. Don't you think?"

I nod and look down at my coffee. "Yes, he is," I say carefully.

"He's good at fixing things."

I give her a funny look. "Well, obviously. He's a handyman."

She laughs. "No, I mean, like, he fixes people and stuff. Like he likes to help people."

I smile. "Yeah, I guess he does."

Annie doesn't say anything for a second. "So, like, you know he likes you, right? You can see it, the way he looks at you."

I can feel a flush creeping up my neck. I'm not ready to discuss this with Annie. "Like your dad looks at Sunshine?" I make a lame attempt at a joke.

Annie makes a face. "No, not like that."

I laugh. I'm about to say something else in protest, but Annie beats me to it.

"Dad looks at Sunshine like he's scared, I think," she says.

"Scared?"

She thinks for a minute. "Scared of being alone," she says. "But Gavin looks at you different."

"What do you mean?" I ask softly. I realize I really want to hear her answer.

She shrugs and looks back down at her cereal. "I don't know. Like he just wants to be around you. Like he thinks you're great. Like he wants to do stuff to make your life good."

I'm silent for a minute. I don't know what to say. "Does that bother you?" is what I finally settle on.

Annie looks surprised. "No. Why would it?"

I shrug. "I don't know. It's been hard for you, watching your dad move on so quickly. I guess I just want you to know that I'm not going anywhere. You're my number one priority. Now and always."

I look closely at her as I say this. I want her to know I really mean it.

She looks embarrassed. "I *know*," she says. "But that doesn't mean you can't, like, go out on a date with Mr. Keyes."

I laugh. "Honey, he hasn't asked me on a date."

"Yet," she says. She pauses. "For real, he probably hasn't 'cause you act like you don't like him. But you can't, like, be alone forever."

My thoughts from last night come flooding back in. "I'm not alone," I say softly. "I have you. And Mamie. And now Alain."

"Mom, I'm not going to be here forever," she says solemnly. "I'm going to go off to college and stuff in, like, a few years. Alain's probably going to go back to Paris, right? And Mamie's going to die someday."

I draw in a sharp breath. I hadn't known how to broach the subject with Annie. "Yes, she will. But I'm hoping we'll get a little more time with her first." I pause. "Are you okay with that? With the idea that we'll probably lose her soon?"

She shrugs. "I'll just miss her a lot, you know?"

"Me too."

We're silent for a long time. My heart aches for my daughter, who has already had to experience too much loss.

"I don't want you to be alone, Mom," Annie says after a while. "No one should be alone."

I nod, blinking back tears that I didn't expect.

"Just find Jacob, okay?" she says softly. "You have to find him."

"I know. I want to find him too. I promise, I'll do my very best."

Annie nods solemnly and stands up to pour her milk out in the sink and to put her bowl and juice glass in the dishwasher. "I'm gonna go back to bed. I just wanted to get up and say good luck," she says. She walks toward the door of the kitchen and pauses. "Mom?" she says.

"Yes, honey?"

"The way Mr. Keyes looks at you . . ." She trails off and looks down. "I think maybe it's kinda how Jacob Levy used to look at Mamie."

When Gavin picks me up at four in his Jeep Wrangler, he has a cup of gas station coffee waiting for me.

"I know you're used to getting up before dawn," he says as he waits for me to buckle my seat belt. He hands me the coffee cup and says, "But I had to stop for coffee, because in my world, I'd still be sleeping right now."

"Sorry," I mumble.

He laughs. "Don't be silly. I'm happy to be here. But the caffeine's helping."

"You don't have to drive, you know," I say. "We could take my car."

"Nah," he says. "This baby's already gassed up and ready to go. I'll drive." He pauses and adds, "Unless you really want to. I just figure it's easier this way. You can navigate."

"If you're sure you don't mind," I say.

We're quiet for the first thirty minutes, except to make small talk about the route we'll take down to New York, and the possibility we'll hit traffic just outside Manhattan. Gavin yawns and turns the radio up when Bon Jovi's "Livin' on a Prayer" comes on.

"I love this song," he says. He sings along with the chorus so enthusiastically that it makes me giggle.

"I didn't even know you knew this song," I say when it ends.

He shoots me a glance. "Who doesn't know 'Livin' on a Prayer'?"

I feel myself turning red. "I just meant you seem young to know it."

"I'm twenty-nine," Gavin says. "Which means I was just as alive when you were when this song came out."

"You were what, three?" I ask. I was almost eleven in 1986. Worlds away.

"I was four," Gavin says. He shoots me a glance. "Why are you being weird?"

I look at my lap. "It's just that you're so young. A lot younger than thirty-six."

He shrugs. "So?"

"So, don't you think I'm kind of old?" I ask. I resist the urge to add *for you.*

"Yeah, you should be getting your AARP membership card in the mail any day now," Gavin says. He seems to realize I'm not laughing. "Look, Hope, I know how old you are. What does it matter?"

"You don't feel like we're from two different worlds or something?"

He hesitates. "Hope, you can't go through life living by all the rules and doing what people expect of you without thinking for yourself, you know? That's how you wake up at the age of eighty or whatever and realize life has passed you by."

I wonder whether this is how Mamie feels. Did she do the things she was expected to? Did she marry and become a mother only because that was the prescribed plan for women in those days? Had she regretted it?

"But how do you know?" I ask, trying to slow my racing heart. "I mean, how do you know which rules you're supposed to live by and which you're not?"

Gavin glances over at me. "I don't think there are really supposed to be rules. I think you're supposed to figure it out as you go, learn from experience, and try to correct your mistakes moving forward. Don't you think?"

"I don't know," I say softly. Maybe he's right. But if he is, that means I've been living my life incorrectly all these years. I've tried to do things by the book at every turn. I married Rob because I was pregnant with his baby. I moved home to the Cape because my mother needed me. I took over the bakery because it was our family business and I couldn't let it die. I abandoned my own dreams of being an attorney because it no longer fit under the heading of what I was supposed to do.

Now I'm realizing that by always choosing the safe road, the one that was expected of me, I might have given up more than I ever understood. Had I left behind the person I was supposed to be too? Had I lost my real self somewhere along that road of doing everything right? I wonder whether there's still time to figure things out and start playing by my own rules. Can I salvage the life I'm meant to have?

"Maybe it's not too late," I murmur aloud.

Gavin glances at me. "It's never too late," he says simply.

We're silent as we drive across the arching Sagamore Bridge, which spans the Cape Cod Canal. Dawn is still a couple of hours away, and I feel like we're all alone in the world as we cross to the mainland in the darkness. There's not another car on the road. On the inky surface of the water beneath us, lights from the bridge and from the homes on either shore reflect back up toward the sky, pointing toward the stars. Mamie's stars. I don't know that I'll ever be able to look at the night sky without thinking of my grandmother and all the evenings she has spent waiting for the stars to come out.

It's not until we're on I-195 heading toward Providence that Gavin speaks again.

"What's happening with the bakery?" he asks.

I look at him sharply. "What do you mean?"

He glances at me and then turns his attention back to the road. "Annie told me that she thinks something's going on. She heard you and Matt Hines talking."

My heart sinks. I hadn't realized Annie knew anything was amiss. I didn't want her to know. "It's nothing," I say, avoiding the subject.

Gavin nods and stares straight ahead. "I don't want to pry," he says. "I know you like to keep stuff to yourself. But I'm just saying I'm here if you want to talk about anything. I know how much the bakery means to you."

I gaze out the window as we begin to pass through Fall River, which looks like an industrial ghost town in the morning mist.

"I'm about to lose it," I say to Gavin after a while. "The bakery. That's why Matt keeps coming by. There was a chance that

some investors were going to save the place, but I guess I screwed
it up by going to Paris."

"Is that what Matt said?"

I nod and look out the window again.

"That's ridiculous," Gavin says. "No legitimate investor
would give up a promising business opportunity because someone has to leave for a few days due to a family emergency. If Matt
told you that, he's an idiot. Or he's trying to guilt-trip you."

"Why would he do that?"

Gavin shrugs. "Maybe he's not such a great guy."

"Maybe not," I murmur. It seems that the men I've chosen to
let into my life over the years all fall into that category.

"How do you feel about the possibility of losing the bakery?"
Gavin asks after a while.

I think about this. "Like I'm a failure," I reply.

"Hope, if you lose the bakery, it's not because you've failed,"
Gavin says. "You work harder than anyone I know. This isn't a
failure. It's just the economy. That's beyond your control."

I shake my head. "The bakery's been in my family for sixty
years. My mother and my grandmother kept it afloat through lots
of ups and downs. Then it gets passed on to me, and I destroy it."

"You haven't destroyed anything," Gavin says.

I shake my head and look down at my lap. "I destroy everything."

"That's crazy, and you know it." Gavin clears his throat. "So is
this what you've always wanted to do? Run your family bakery?"

I laugh. "No. Not at all. I was planning to be an attorney.
I was halfway through law school in Boston when I found out
I was pregnant with Annie. So I left school, married Rob, and
eventually moved back to the Cape."

"Why did you drop out of law school?"

I shrug. "It felt like the right thing to do."

Gavin nods and seems to consider this for a minute. "Would
you go back?" he asks. "Do you still want to be a lawyer?"

I consider this. "I feel like a huge failure for dropping out," I say. "But at the same time, I have this weird feeling that maybe I wasn't really supposed to be a lawyer at all. Maybe I was supposed to run the bakery. I can't imagine my life without it now, you know? Especially now that I know what it means to my family. Now that I know it's basically all my grandmother brought with her from her past."

"You know, I don't think you're going to lose the bakery," Gavin says after a minute.

"Why do you say that?" I ask.

"Because I think that in life, things tend to come through when you most need them to."

I look at him. "That's it? Life works out the way it's supposed to?"

Gavin laughs. "Okay, yeah, I sound like a Hallmark card."

I'm silent for a moment. "Annie thinks you're some kind of Mr. Fix-It of people," I say in a small voice.

He laughs again. "Oh, does she?"

I glance sideways at him. "You know, you don't have to fix me. Or save me. Or whatever."

He looks at me and shakes his head. "I don't think you need me to, Hope," he says. "I think you're underestimating your ability to save yourself."

His words wash over me, and I stare out the window so that he can't see my sudden, unexpected tears. Maybe this is what I needed all along. Not Matt's money or his investors. Not someone to rescue me. Just someone who believes that I can do it on my own.

"Thanks," I whisper, so softly that I'm not sure Gavin will hear me.

But he does. I feel his hand on my shoulder, and as I turn to face him, he squeezes once, gently, and then puts his hand back on the wheel. My skin tingles where he touched it.

"It's going to be okay, you know," he says.

"I know," I say. And for the first time, I really mean it.

Chapter *Twenty-four*

We stop at an exit off I-95 in Connecticut so that we can fill up the gas tank, grab some breakfast, and use the bathroom. As I come out of McDonald's, juggling two coffees and two orange juices on a tray as well as a bag full of various McMuffins, I glance across the street and notice a big, printed sign in the dim morning light, advertising a Bible study class called "Tracing the Old Testament Family Tree." I'm about to look away, but then a familiar name catches my eye, and something suddenly slips into place in my mind. My jaw drops.

"What are you looking at?" Gavin asks. He screws the gas cap back on and joins me beside the car. He takes the McDonald's drinks and bag from me and sets them on top of the car. "You look like you've seen a ghost."

"Look at that sign," I say.

"'Tracing the Old Testament Family Tree,'" he reads aloud. "'From Abraham to Jacob to Joseph and beyond.'" He pauses. "Okay. So?"

"Joseph was the son of Jacob in the Bible, right?" I ask.

Gavin nods. "Yeah. Actually in the Torah too. And in the

Koran I think. I think all that stuff tracing back to Abraham in the Old Testament is the same in all three religions."

"The three Abrahamic religions," I murmur, thinking of Elida's words. "Islam, Judaism, and Christianity."

"Right," Gavin says. He glances at the sign again, then down at me. "So what's up, Hope? How come you look so spooked?"

"My mom's name was Josephine," I say softly. "Can that just be coincidence? That she's named after the son of Jacob?"

Realization dawns on Gavin's face. "In the stories, Joseph became the one to carry on his parents' legacy. He had to be protected for that reason." He pauses. "You're saying you think your mom might have been Jacob's daughter after all?"

I swallow hard and stare at the sign. Then I shake my head. "You know what? No, that's crazy. It's just a name. Besides, the years don't add up. My mom was born in '44, long after my grandmother last saw Jacob Levy. There's no way."

I glance up at Gavin, feeling silly, and I'm surprised to realize his face looks completely serious. "But what if you're right?" he asks. "What if your mother was actually born a year earlier? What if your grandmother and grandfather bribed someone to falsify her birth certificate? That couldn't have been uncommon in those days. It was during the war. Some low-level clerk could have easily changed the paperwork, destroyed the originals. Easy to do before things were computerized."

"But why would my grandparents do that?"

"So that it looked like your grandfather was the father," Gavin says. He's speaking quickly now, his eyes shining. "So that your mom would never think to doubt it. So that your grandmother would never have to explain Jacob to anyone. You say they didn't move to the Cape until your mother was five. But at that age, it would have been nearly impossible to tell if they'd cheated by a year, especially if they said she was just tall for her age. What if she was really six?"

I feel suddenly short of breath. "This can't be possible," I whisper. "My mom even looked like my grandpa. Straight brown hair, brown eyes. Same kinds of expressions."

"Brown hair and brown eyes are pretty common features," Gavin points out. "And we don't know what Jacob looked like anyhow. Right?"

"I guess," I murmur.

"You have to admit, your mom being Jacob's daughter would explain a lot. Like what happened to the baby. And why your grandmother moved on so quickly after losing Jacob."

"But why *would* she move on so quickly?" I ask. I don't understand that part.

"She must have believed that Jacob was dead already. Maybe your grandfather was a kind man offering her a chance to survive, and a chance to give her daughter a real life. And maybe she took that chance, because she believed it was the right thing to do."

"Do you mean that she never really loved my grandfather?" I ask. It hurts my heart to think that. "That he was just the means to an end?"

"No, I bet she loved him," Gavin says. "Maybe differently than Jacob. But he gave her and your mom a good life."

"The kind of life Jacob would have wanted for them," I say.

Gavin nods. "Yeah."

"But if that's true, what did my grandpa get?" I ask, suddenly overwhelmed with sadness. "A wife who never really loved him the way he deserved to beloved?"

"Maybe he knew all along that that's what it would be," Gavin says, "and he loved her enough that it didn't matter. Maybe he hoped she'd come around. Maybe it was enough to have her there, to know he was protecting her, to be a father to her child."

I look away. I wish I could ask my grandfather what he'd felt, how he'd rationalized it all, if Gavin was right. But he's long gone. I wonder whether the answers and the secrets they'd kept would forever remain buried. I know they will if Mamie never wakes up. In fact, even if she does awaken, there's no guarantee she'll remember anything.

"Do you think my mom ever knew?" I ask. "*If* this is true," I'm quick to add.

"I would be willing to bet she didn't," Gavin says softly. "It sounds like maybe your grandmother just wanted to leave everything behind forever."

As we get back into the car, I realize I'm crying. I'm not sure when I began, but the hole in my heart seems to keep growing bigger and bigger. Until recently, my grandmother had been merely a slightly sad woman who happened to hail from France and run a bakery. Now, as I peel back layer after layer of who she really was, I'm realizing that her sorrow must have gone far deeper than I'd ever comprehended. And she'd spent her lifetime pretending, wrapped up in secrets and lies.

I want now more than ever for her to wake up, so that I can tell her she's not alone, and that I understand. I want to hear the story from her own lips, because at this point, so much of it is conjecture. I realize I no longer know where I came from. At all. I've never known my father's side of the family—I don't even know who my father is—and it's turning out that everything I knew of my mother's side was a lie.

"Are you okay?" Gavin asks softly. He hasn't started the car yet; he's just sitting there beside me, watching me cry.

"I don't know who I am anymore," I say after a pause.

He nods, seeming to understand this. "I do," he says simply. "You're Hope. That's all that really matters." And despite the awkwardness of the center console between us in the car, when he pulls me into his arms and holds me tight, it's the most natural and comfortable thing in the world.

When he finally lets go, mumbling, "We should get on the road before it gets too much later," it feels like only a few seconds have passed, although the clock tells me he's been holding me for several minutes. It didn't feel like enough.

It's not until we're on the highway, and I see a tray of cups fly by the window, that I realize we left the food from McDonald's on the roof. The laughter between us breaks the sad tension.

"Eh, I wasn't hungry anyway," Gavin says, glancing in the rearview mirror, where I imagine the remainder of our uneaten breakfast has distributed itself on the road.

"Me neither," I agree.

He smiles at me. "On to New York?"

"On to New York."

It's just past ten by the time we finish fighting traffic and pull off FDR Drive onto Houston Street in Manhattan. Gavin's following his GPS now, and I look around as he weaves in and out of streets, narrowly avoiding pedestrians and stopped taxis.

"I hate driving in New York," he says, but he's smiling.

"You're really good at it," I say. I did a summer internship here in college and returned a few times since then, but it's been more than a decade since I visited, and everything feels different now. The city looks cleaner than I remember it.

"According to the GPS, we're almost there," Gavin announces after a few more minutes. "Let's just find a place to park."

We find a garage and walk to the exit. As Gavin gets the ticket from the attendant, I nervously shift from one foot to the other. We're just a few blocks away from the last known address of Jacob Levy. We could be face-to-face with him in ten minutes.

Gavin hands me a map he's printed out from the Internet. It has a star marked toward the south end of Battery Place, and I realize with a start how close Jacob lives to Ground Zero. I wonder whether he'd been here to witness the tragedy of September 11. I blink a few times and steady myself. I look north toward the hole in the skyline where the World Trade Center used to be, and I feel a pang of sadness.

"This used to be my favorite area of the city," I tell Gavin as we begin to walk. "I worked here for a summer when I was in college, for a law firm in midtown. On the weekends, I used to take the N or the R train down to the World Trade Center, get a Coke in the food court there, and then walk down Broadway to Battery Park."

"Oh yeah?" Gavin says.

I smile. "I used to look out at the Statue of Liberty and think about how big the world was out there beyond the East Coast. I used to think about all the choices I had, all the things I could do with my life." I stop talking and look down.

"That sounds nice," Gavin says softly.

I shake my head. "I was a dumb kid," I mumble after a moment. "Turns out life isn't as big as I thought it could be."

Gavin stops walking and puts a hand on my arm, bringing me to a halt too. "What do you mean?"

I shrug and glance around. I feel foolish standing in the middle of a sidewalk in Manhattan, with Gavin looking at me so intently. But he's staring down at me, waiting for an answer, so finally, I look up and meet his eye. "This isn't the life I thought I'd have," I say.

Gavin shakes his head. "Hope, it never is. You know that, right? Life doesn't ever turn out the way we plan."

I sigh. I don't expect him to understand. "Gavin, I'm thirty-six, and none of the things I wanted in my life have really happened," I try to explain. "Some days I wake up and think, *How did I get here?* It's like one day, you just realize you're not young anymore, and you already made your choices, and now it's too late to change anything."

"It's not too late," Gavin says. "Ever. But I know what you mean about feeling that way."

"How do you know?" My voice is sharper than I intend it to be. "You're twenty-nine."

He laughs. "There's no magical age when all your options shut down, Hope," he says. "You have just as many chances to change your life as I do. What I'm saying is that no one's life turns out the way they expect it to. But it's how you roll with the punches that determines whether you're happy or not."

"You're happy," I say, and I realize it sounds more like an accusation than a statement. "I mean, you seem to have everything you want."

He laughs again. "Hope, do you really think I sat around as a kid and dreamed of being a handyman?"

"I don't know," I mumble. "Did you?"

"No! I wanted to be an artist. I was the dorkiest kid in the world; I used to insist my mom take me to the Museum of Fine Arts in Boston so I could look at the paintings. I used to tell her I was going to move to France and be a painter like Degas or Monet. They were my favorites."

"You wanted to be an artist?" I ask incredulously. We begin walking again, toward the address we have for Jacob Levy.

Gavin chuckles and glances down at me. "I even tried to get into SMFA."

"SMFA?"

"Ah, you're not a big art fan, I see." Gavin winks at me. "The School of the Museum of Fine Arts in Boston." He pauses and shrugs. "I had the grades, and I had the portfolio, but I didn't qualify for enough scholarships to pay for it. My mom couldn't afford it, and I didn't want to take out tons of loans and be in debt for the rest of my life. So here I am."

"So you just didn't go to college?"

Gavin laughs. "No, I went to Salem State on scholarship. I majored in education, because I figured if I couldn't be an artist, I'd be an art teacher."

"You were an art teacher?" I ask. Gavin nods, and I add, "But what happened? How come you're not anymore?" I bite my tongue before I add something about him being just a handyman.

He shrugs. "It didn't make me happy. Not the way that working with my hands does. I realized that if I couldn't be an artist in the traditional sense—let's face it, college or not, I'm no

Michelangelo—I could create art in some form if I could make things for people. And that's what I do now."

"But you fix pipes and stuff," I say in a small voice.

He laughs. "Yeah, because that's part of the job. But I also build decks and paint houses and install windows and shutters, and renovate kitchens. I get to make things beautiful, and that makes me happy. I think of it as making the town one giant piece of art, one house at a time."

I stare at him, incredulous. "Are you being serious?"

He shrugs. "It's not what I dreamed of when I was a kid," he says. "But I've realized that I never really felt like *me* until I wound up on the Cape. Life doesn't work out the way we plan, but maybe it works out the way it's supposed to after all. You know?"

I nod slowly. "I think I do." He made a decision to find himself, and he's happy with what he found. I wonder whether I'll be able to do the same someday. I've come to look at life as a series of closed doors; it hasn't occurred to me until this moment that in some cases, all I have to do is open them. "I never knew all that about you," I say softly, after a pause.

Gavin shrugs again. "You never asked."

I look down and swallow hard.

We finally arrive at the address on Battery Place. I look up at the building, which has an older-looking brick facade and appears to be a dozen stories tall. It's dwarfed by the buildings to the north of it, but there's something about it that seems charming and traditional to me. I'm startled a moment later to realize it reminds me a bit of France.

"We're here," Gavin says. He smiles down at me. "Ready?"

I nod. My heart is beating a mile a minute. I can hardly believe we might be finding Jacob at any moment now. "Ready."

According to Elida's note, Jacob lives in apartment 1004, so we try buzzing that unit first. When there's no response, Gavin shrugs and begins randomly punching units until the front door buzzes.

"Voilà," he says. He holds the door for me as I enter.

Inside, the foyer is dimly lit, and there's a narrow staircase straight ahead. I look around. "No elevator?" I ask.

Gavin scratches his head. "No elevator. Wow. That's weird."

We begin walking up, and by the time we get to the fifth floor, I'm ashamed to say I'm breathing hard. "I guess I should work out more," I note. "I'm huffing and puffing like I've never climbed a staircase before."

Gavin, who's behind me, laughs. "I don't know. Huffing and puffing aside, it doesn't look to me like you're in need of a work-out."

I look back at him, my face on fire, and he just grins. I shake my head and continue climbing, but I'm flattered.

We finally reach the tenth floor, and I'm in such a rush to see whether Jacob still lives here that I don't even bother catching my breath before knocking on the door to 1004.

I'm still breathing hard when the door swings open, revealing a woman about my age standing there.

"Can I help you?" she asks, looking back and forth between Gavin and me.

"We're looking for Jacob Levy," says Gavin, after apparently realizing I can't get words out.

The woman shakes her head. "There's no one here by that name. I'm sorry."

My heart sinks. "He'd be in his late eighties? From France originally?"

The woman shrugs. "Doesn't ring a bell."

"He used to live here, we think," Gavin says. "Until at least a year ago."

"My husband and I moved in in January," says the woman.

"Are you sure?" I ask in a small voice.

"I think I'd notice if some old dude was living with us," the woman says, rolling her eyes. "Anyhow, the super lives in apartment 102 if you want to check with him."

Gavin and I thank her and head back down the stairs.

"Do you think we came all this way for nothing?" I ask as we descend.

"No," Gavin says firmly. "I think Jacob moved somewhere else and we're going to find him today."

"What if he's dead?" I venture. I hadn't wanted to consider the possibility, but it's foolish not to.

"Elida's husband didn't find a death certificate," Gavin says. "We've got to believe he's still out there somewhere."

When we reach the ground floor, Gavin knocks on the door to apartment 102. There's no answer, and we exchange looks. Gavin knocks again, harder this time, and I'm relieved to hear footsteps coming toward the door a moment later. A middle-aged woman in curlers and a bathrobe opens the door.

"What?" she asks. "Don't tell me the plumbing on the seventh is broken again. I can't handle it."

"No ma'am," Gavin says. "We're looking for the super."

She snorts. "That's my husband, but he's mostly worthless. What do you need?"

"We're looking for the man who used to live in apartment 1004," I say. "Jacob Levy. We think he moved out about a year ago."

She frowns. "Yeah. He did. So what?"

"We need to find him," Gavin says. "It's very urgent."

She narrows her eyes. "You the IRS or something?"

"What? No," I say. "We're . . ." And then I don't know how to continue. How do I tell her that I'm the granddaughter of the woman he loved seventy years ago? That I might even be his granddaughter?

"We're family," Gavin fills in smoothly. He nods at me. "She's his family."

The words make my heart hurt.

The woman scrutinizes us for a moment more and shrugs. "Whatever you say. I'll get you his forwarding address."

My heart beats faster as she shuffles back into her apartment. Gavin and I exchange looks again, but I'm too excited to say anything.

The woman reappears a moment later with a slip of paper. "Jacob Levy. He fell and broke his hip last year," she says. "He'd been here twenty years, you know. There isn't no elevator, and when he got back from the hospital, he couldn't make it up them stairs, what with his hip and all, so the landlord, he offered him the vacant apartment at the end of the hall here. Apartment 101. But Mr. Levy, he said he wanted a view. Picky, if you ask me. So the movers came, end of November."

She hands me the slip of paper. On it, there's an address on Whitehall Street, along with an apartment number.

"That's where he asked us to send his final bill," the woman says. "I got no idea if he's still there. But that's where he went from here."

"Thank you," Gavin says.

"Thank you," I echo. She's about to close the door when I reach out my hand. "Wait," I say. "One more thing."

"Yeah?" She looks perturbed.

"Was he married?" I hold my breath.

"There wasn't no Mrs. Levy that I know of," the woman says.

I close my eyes in relief. "What . . . what was he like?" I ask after a moment.

She regards me suspiciously then seems to soften a little. "He was nice," she says finally. "Always real polite-like. Some of the other tenants here, they treat us like servants, me and my husband. But Mr. Levy, he was always real nice. Always called me ma'am. Always said please and thank you."

This makes me smile. "Thanks," I say. "Thanks for telling me that."

I'm about to turn away when she speaks again. "He always seemed sad, though."

"Sad?" I ask.

"Yeah. He went out for a walk every day, and he always came back at night, after dark, looking like he lost something."

"Thank you," I whisper, sorrow flooding through me as we turn away and head out the door. It seems that all those nights Mamie sat waiting for the stars to come out, Jacob was out looking for something too.

It takes us fifteen minutes to cross east to Whitehall Street and head south to find the address the super's wife gave us. It turns out to be a modern-looking building that soars above the others around it. There's no doorman, which I'm relieved about; we won't have to explain our mission to yet one more person.

"Apartment 2232," I say to Gavin as we head for the elevators. The doors slide open and I punch the number 22, tapping my foot impatiently as the doors close.

"C'mon, c'mon, c'mon," I murmur as the elevator begins its slow ascent.

Gavin reaches for my hand and squeezes. "We're going to find him, Hope," he says.

"I don't know how to thank you for everything you've done to help me," I say, pausing long enough to look into his eyes and smile. For a frozen moment, I'm sure he's about to kiss me, but then the elevator dings and the doors slide open. We're here.

We race down the hall, right and then left, to apartment 2232. It's the last apartment on the right-hand side of the hall, and as Gavin knocks, I glance out the window at the hall's end. It's a beautiful view, out over the southern tip of Manhattan and across the water. But I can't focus on that now. I turn toward the door and will it to open.

But there's no answer, no footsteps from inside.

"Try again," I say. Gavin nods and knocks again, more loudly this time. Still nothing. I'm trying not to feel entirely deflated. But what now? "Again," I say weakly. Gavin raps on the door so loudly this time that the door across the hall opens. An old woman stands there, staring at us.

"What's all the racket?" she demands.

"I'm sorry, ma'am," Gavin says. "We're trying to find Jacob Levy."

"And you can't knock like normal human beings?" she asks. "You have to beat down the door?"

"He's not answering," I tell her miserably. I take a deep breath. "Does he still live there? Is he still . . . ?" My voice trails off, but what I'm meaning to ask is whether he's still alive. It's a terrible thing to wonder.

"Calm down," the woman says. "I don't know where he is. I don't even know him. Now if you could kindly keep it down, I'm trying to watch my shows."

The door slams before we can say anything else. I feel weak in the knees, and I lean against the wall for support. Gavin settles in beside me and puts his arm around my shoulder. "We're going to find him, Hope. He's here. I know it."

I nod, but I can't bring myself to believe it. What if we've come all this way, only to find that we're mere months too late? I glance out the window at the end of the hall again, taking in the beautiful view as tears cloud my vision. Below us stretch a few short blocks of Manhattan, ending in the green tip of Battery Park. Beyond that, across the deep blue water of New York Harbor, lie Governors Island to the left and Ellis Island to the right. I wonder whether that's where Jacob and my grandmother first arrived in this country. Just beyond Ellis Island is Liberty Island, where I see the Statue of Liberty, holding her torch high. It gleams in the sunlight, and I think for a minute about the freedom it represents. What must it have been like to enter into this country for the first time, via Ellis Island, passing such a strong symbol of everything this nation stands for?

And then, just like that, something clicks into place and my jaw drops.

"Gavin," I say, grabbing his arm. "I know where he is."

"What?" he asks, startled.

"I know where Jacob is," I say. "The queen. The queen with the torch. Oh my God, I know where he is!"

Chapter *Twenty-five*

Overnight Meringues

INGREDIENTS

2 egg whites
½ cup white sugar

1 tsp. vanilla extract
½ cup chocolate chips

DIRECTIONS

1. Preheat oven to 350 degrees.

2. In a large bowl, beat the egg whites on high speed with a hand mixer until soft peaks form.

3. Add the sugar, ⅛ cup at a time, beating continuously. Continue to beat until peaks are stiff and stand up on their own.

4. Reduce mixer speed to low and beat in vanilla.

5. Fold in chocolate chips gently with a wooden spoon.

6. Drop by the teaspoon onto baking sheets covered in parchment paper. Try to make sure each mound has at least one chocolate chip. Mounds should easily hold their own shape.

7. Place pan in oven and immediately turn off heat.

8. Leave overnight. No peeking allowed! When you wake up the next morning, open the oven; the meringues will be done and ready to serve.

Rose

It was July of 1980, and Rose sat, eyes closed, in the living room of the home Ted had built for her. It was hot outside, so hot that even the salty sea breeze wafting in through the windows wasn't enough to cool her off. On days like this, she longed for Paris, for the way that even in the heat, the city seemed to sparkle. Nothing sparkled here but the water, and that just seemed to Rose a cruel temptation. It taunted her, reminding her that if she only got into a boat and headed east, eventually she would be home, on the distant shores of the country of her birth.

But she could never go back. She knew that.

She could hear raised voices in the front room. She wanted to get up and tell them to stop fighting, but she could not. It was not her place. Josephine was thirty-seven now, old enough not to be told what to do by her mother. Rose had already failed in protecting her daughter, in instilling in her the things a good mother should. If she had it all to do again, the choices she would make would be different. She hadn't realized when she was younger that fate could be decided in a moment, that the smallest decisions could shape your life. Now she knew, and it was too late, too late to change a thing.

Ted came into the room then. Rose heard his heavy, confident footsteps and smelled the faint, sweet odor of the cigars he liked to smoke on the front porch while listening to Red Sox games on the radio.

"Jo is at it again," he said. She opened her eyes to see him staring down at her in concern. "Don't you hear her?"

"Yes," Rose said simply.

Ted scratched the back of his head and sighed. "I don't understand. She loves to fight with them."

"I did not teach her properly how to love," Rose said softly. "It is my fault." That was why Josephine pushed the men who loved her away, Rose knew. Because Rose had kept her at arm's length.

Because Rose had been terrified of relying on the one person she loved the most. Because Rose knew that the people you loved could be taken away one day with no warning. Those were not the lessons she had meant to impart to Josephine. But she had.

"My dear, it's not your fault," Ted said. He sat down beside her on the couch and pulled her to him. She breathed in deeply and let him hold her. She loved him. Not in the way she had loved Jacob, or her family in France, for she had loved them all with an open heart. When one's heart closed, it was impossible to feel the same. But she loved him in the best way she knew how, and she knew she was loved deeply in return. She knew he longed to reach across the invisible divide that separated them. She wished she could tell him how, but she herself did not know.

"Of course it is my fault," Rose said after a moment. They were quiet for a moment as Josephine screamed at her boyfriend that he would only leave her one day anyhow, so why should she bother giving him another chance? "Listen to her," Rose said after a moment. "The words she is speaking could have come from my mouth."

"Nonsense. You never pushed me away like that," Ted said. "That is not the example you set for her."

"No," Rose said simply. But what she wanted to say was that she had never pushed him away because she had never let him in to begin with. She was a castle surrounded by many defenses. Ted had only made it to the grassy knoll beyond the first moat; there were many more walls to be scaled and many more battles to be fought in order to reach her heart. But Ted didn't know that. It was better that way.

They both watched through the window as Hope came toward the house from the backyard, where she'd been playing in the sand at the edge of the dunes. Rose had been keeping an eye on her— she was just five—and hoping that she'd stay out of earshot long enough for her mother to finish arguing with the latest man she'd brought into Hope's life.

"I'll go keep her occupied," Ted said, starting to rise.

"No," Rose said. "I will go." She kissed Ted on the cheek and headed toward the door. Hope turned and her eyes lit up when her grandmother walked out onto the back porch. For a moment, Rose was too choked up to speak. Hope looked so much like Danielle had looked all those years ago, and sometimes, it was hard for Rose to look at her without seeing the past, without seeing the baby sister whose fate she could not bring herself to fully imagine.

"Mamie!" Hope called out excitedly. Her brown curls, so similar to the flowing curls Rose herself had sported in her youth, danced in the sea breeze, and her extraordinary green eyes, the color of the sea flecked with gold, shone with excitement. "I caught a crab, Mamie! A big one! It had pinchers and everything!"

"A crab?" Rose smiled down at her granddaughter. "Oh my! Whatever did you do with it?"

Hope grinned and blinked up at her grandmother. "Mamie, I let him go! Just like you told me!"

"Did I tell you that?"

Hope nodded just once, confidently. "You told me not to hurt anyone or anything if I could help it. And the crab's an anyone."

Rose smiled. She bent to give Hope a hug. "You did the right thing, my dear," she said. Inside, she could hear the voices of Josephine and her boyfriend rising as they yelled at each other. She cleared her throat, hoping that it would block the sound. "Let's stay out here for a little while," she said to her granddaughter. "How about I tell you a story?"

Hope grinned and hopped up and down for a minute. "I love your stories, Mamie! Can you tell me the one about the prince teaching the princess to be brave?"

"Of course I can, my dear." Rose sat down in a deck chair facing the ocean, and Hope scrambled up onto her lap, slinging her tanned legs over the side of the chair and snuggling into Rose's bosom. Soon, she'd be too big to do this. Rose wished these moments could go on forever, for as long as she could hold her granddaughter in her lap and tell her stories, she could keep her safe and protected.

"Once upon a time, in a faraway land, there lived a prince and a princess, who fell in love," she began. As her mouth moved with the familiar words, her heart ached and threatened to overflow. This, she knew, was why she'd done what she'd done. This was why she'd run, why she'd fled Paris, why she'd turned her back on everything. This little girl in her arms wouldn't be here now if Rose had stayed and accepted her fate. And in that, she knew she'd done the right thing. It was just that in life, there were no clean decisions. Not the big ones, anyhow. To give life to Josephine, and then to Hope, she'd had to trade other lives away. There was no way to justify a tariff like that, no way at all.

"Tell me more, Mamie, tell me more!" Hope demanded, bouncing up and down on her grandmother's lap, as Rose paused in the familiar story.

Rose ruffled her granddaughter's hair and smiled down at her. "Well, the prince told the princess that she must be brave and strong, and that she must do the right thing, even if it is difficult."

"That's what you always tell me, Mamie!" Hope interrupted. "To do the right thing! Even when it's hard!"

Rose nodded. "That's right. You must always do right. The prince told the princess that he had to save her, that it was the right thing to do. But in order to save her, he had to send her far, far away, to the shores of a magical kingdom. Now, the princess had never been to this magical kingdom, for it was far, far across the great sea, but she had dreamed of it often. She knew that in his great kingdom, there reigned a queen, who shone her light over all the world."

"Even at nighttime?" Hope asked, although she'd heard the story a hundred times.

"Even at night," Rose assured her.

"Like a night-light," Hope said.

"Yes, very much like a night-light," Rose said with a smile. "For the light kept everyone feeling safe. Just like your night-light keeps you feeling safe."

"The queen sounds nice."

"She was a very kind queen," Rose assured her granddaughter. "Very good and just. The princess knew that if she could make it to the kingdom of the queen, she would be safe, and that one day the prince would come to find her there."

"Because he promised," Hope said.

"Yes, because he promised," Rose said softly. "He promised he would meet her just across the moat from the queen's great throne, where the light shone down. So the princess went across the sea to this kingdom of the wise queen. And there, she was finally safe. While the princess waited for the prince, she met a strong and kind wizard, who recognized her as a princess, even though she was dressed as a pauper. He told the princess that he loved her and that he would protect her all the days of his life."

"But what about the prince?" Hope asked. "Is the prince coming?"

Rose knew to expect the question, for Hope always asked it. Hope was being raised in a country that believed in happily ever after. And five years old was far too young to learn that happily ever after existed only in fairy tales. But this *was* a fairy tale, Rose reminded herself. And so she answered the question the only way she knew how, because every now and then, she needed to believe in fairy tales too.

"Yes, my dear," Rose said as she blinked back tears and pulled her granddaughter close. "The prince is coming. Someday, the princess will see him again."

Chapter *Twenty-six*

⸺

"Where are we going?" Gavin asks as he follows me out onto the street. I break into a run down Whitehall, attracting curious stares from passersby. One couple, tourists with "I Love New York" T-shirts on and cameras slung over their necks, point and begin taking photos. I ignore them all and dart right on State Street. Gavin comes up alongside me. "Hope, what are you doing?"

"Jacob's in Battery Park," I say without slowing. We pass a brick colonial building on the right, and I notice that it's a Catholic church. I wonder fleetingly whether Jacob could have imagined that Mamie took on a Muslim skin, and then a Catholic one, that all her images of God had become wrapped together in one beautiful entanglement.

"How do you know that's where he is?" Gavin asks. We stop and let traffic pass before we dart across State into the brilliant green space of Battery Park.

"It was in my grandmother's stories," I say. I'm itching to run across the street, but Gavin, perhaps sensing this, puts a hand on my arm until there's a gap in the flow of cars.

He looks confused, but he leads me across the street, and then he slows to follow me as we jog past strolling tourists, sketch artists, and food vendors, toward the thick black guardrail that separates the edge of the island from the water. I put my hands on the cool metal and stare across the choppy harbor to the Statue of Liberty, who faces southeast toward the entrance to New York Harbor. Hers would have been the first face immigrants saw as the island of Manhattan came into view.

"Jacob was in my grandmother's stories all along," I murmur, staring out at the queen with her torch, the one I'd stared at so many afternoons during my summer in New York, never once realizing that I should recognize her from Mamie's tales.

I tear my eyes away from the Statue of Liberty and scan the length of the railing, first to the left and then to the right. The sidewalk is filled with a sea of tourists, even on this chilly autumn day with the wind whipping in from the water. For a moment, my heart begins to sink. Perhaps it will be impossible to find him in the midst of all these people.

Gavin isn't saying anything; he seems to realize that I'm lost in my own world. As I begin to panic, though, to think that I might be wrong, I feel his hand fold gently over mine, and I hold tight with a fierceness that surprises me. I don't want him to let go.

I'm just about to say "Maybe I'm wrong" when I see him. Without releasing Gavin's hand, I begin moving to the right, down the row of benches, down the gleaming rail. I don't know how I'm suddenly so confident that it's him, that it's Jacob, but I'm sure of it even before I can see his face. There's a cane propped beside him, and he's drumming the fingers on his left hand rhythmically against the rail, just like my daughter often absentmindedly does. "That's him," I say to Gavin.

The man is facing the Statue of Liberty, staring out at her as if he can't look away. His hair is snow white, balding on the top, and he's in a long, dark overcoat that somehow looks regal to me. "The prince," I murmur, more to myself than to Gavin. When we're just a few feet away from him, he turns suddenly and looks right at me, and in that instant, any remaining doubt disappears. It's him.

He freezes, his mouth falling open just a little. I freeze too, and we stare at each other. He looks just like Annie; all of her features whose origin Rob once questioned are displayed on his face. Same narrow, beaked nose. Same dimpled chin. Same high, regal forehead. And as we stare at each other, I recognize something else: behind his dark-rimmed glasses, he has my eyes, the sea-green eyes flecked with gold that Mamie always used to tell me were her favorite thing in the world to look at.

"Jacob Levy," I say softly, and it's a statement, not a question, for I already know. Beside me, I can feel Gavin's hand tighten around mine, and I know he's realizing, a minute later than I have, how much Jacob looks like my daughter and what this means.

Jacob nods slowly, still staring at me.

"I'm Hope," I tell him gently. I take a step closer. "Rose's granddaughter."

Tears fill his eyes. "She lived," he murmurs. I nod slowly, and Jacob steps closer, his eyes locked on mine. I pull my hand away from Gavin and step toward Jacob, until we're just a foot away from each other. He reaches out and slowly, tentatively, reaches for my face. I step closer until I feel his hand on my cheek, rough and gnarled, but as gentle as anything I've ever felt. "She lived," he repeats.

And then his arms are around me, and I can feel him shaking as he begins to sob. I hug him back, and I can feel my tears coming too. I feel like I'm holding on to a piece of the past, the one piece that makes everything complete. I'm holding on to the love of my grandmother's life, seventy years too late. And unless I'm crazy, unless I've imagined my daughter's features and my own eyes on this man, I'm holding on to the grandfather I never knew I had.

"Is she still alive?" he asks, finally pulling away from the embrace. "Is Rose alive?" There are traces of a French accent in his words; he sounds a lot like Mamie. He continues to hold tightly to my arms, as if he's afraid of falling if he lets go. There are tears streaming down his face now. My own cheeks are damp too.

I nod. "She had a stroke. She's in a coma. But she's alive."

He gasps and blinks a few times. "Hope," he says. "You must take me to her. You must take me to my Rose."

Chapter *Twenty-seven*

~

Jacob won't let us stop at his apartment to pack him a bag; he insists we get to Cape Cod as soon as possible, without wasting another moment.

"I must see her," he says, looking urgently back and forth from Gavin to me. "I must see her as soon as I can."

I wait with him while Gavin jogs away to go retrieve the Jeep; with his reconstructed hip, Jacob can't walk very quickly. As we wait on the northern end of Battery Park, along the street, Jacob stares at me as if he's seen a ghost. There are so many things I want to ask him, but Gavin should be here to hear the answers too.

"You are my granddaughter," Jacob says softly as we wait. "Are you not?"

I nod slowly. "I think I am." This all feels so strange; I can't help but think of the man I spent my life calling Grandpa. This is all so unfair to him. Then again, he obviously knew all along; he had to have made a conscious choice to take my mother in as his own flesh and blood, even though she wasn't. "You look so much like my daughter," I admit.

"You have a daughter?"

I nod. "Annie. She's twelve."

Jacob reaches for my hand and looks into my eyes. "And your mother or father? The child Rose had? Was the child a boy or a girl?"

It hits me for the first time how tragic it is that my mother died before meeting Jacob, probably without even knowing that he existed. It breaks my heart to realize that Jacob, in turn, will never see the child he lost everything to save.

"A girl," I say softly. "Josephine."

The child of Jacob, who had to be saved in order to carry on. I think back to the sign at the church off I-95, and I shudder. The truth was there all along.

"Josephine," Jacob repeats slowly.

"She died two years ago," I add after a moment. "Of breast cancer. I'm so sorry."

Jacob makes a sound like a wounded animal and hunches forward a little, as if something invisible has punched him in the gut. "Oh dear," he murmurs after a moment, straightening up again. "I am so sorry for your loss."

My eyes fill. "I am so sorry for yours," I say. "I don't know how to tell you how sorry I am." The seventy years lost. The fact that he never got to meet his child. The fact that until this moment, he hadn't even known she'd lived.

Gavin pulls up then and hops out of the car. We exchange looks as we help Jacob into the backseat. I climb in beside Gavin, and after checking his mirrors, he pulls quickly away from the curb.

"We're going to get you back to the Cape as soon as possible, sir," Gavin says, glancing in the rearview at Jacob, who looks up to meet his eye.

"Thank you, young man," Jacob says. "And who are you, exactly?"

I laugh then, a release of tension, as I realize I haven't even introduced Gavin. I do so quickly, explaining how he was the one who set all of this in motion in the first place and helped me find Jacob today.

"Thank you, Gavin, for everything," Jacob says after I finish explaining. "You are Hope's husband?"

Gavin and I exchange awkward looks, and I can feel myself blushing. "Um, no sir," I say. "Just a good friend." I glance back at Gavin, but he's staring straight ahead, focusing on the road.

We ride in silence until we've made our way up the West Side Highway, through the north side of Harlem on I-95, and across the bridge to the mainland.

"Can I ask you something, Mr. Levy?" I ask, turning around.

"Please, call me Jacob," he says. "Or, of course, you may also call me Grandfather. But it is likely too soon for that."

I swallow hard. I ache for the man I spent a lifetime calling Grandpa. I wish I'd known the truth while he was still alive. I wish I could have thanked him for whatever it was he did to save my grandmother and my mother. I wish I'd understood earlier how much he had probably lost in the process.

"Jacob," I say after a pause. "What happened in France? During the war? My grandmother has never spoken of any of this; we didn't know until just a few weeks ago that she was even Jewish."

Jacob looks startled. "How is this possible? What did you believe?"

"When she came over from France," I tell him, "she came under the name Rose Durand. For my entire life, she's gone to Catholic church."

"Mon Dieu," Jacob murmurs.

"I never knew about what happened to her in the Holocaust," I continue. "About her family. About *you*. She kept it all a secret, until a few weeks ago, when she gave me a list of names and asked me to go to Paris."

I tell him briefly about my visit to Paris, about finding Alain, about bringing him back with me. His eyes light up.

"Alain is here?" he asks. "In the United States?"

I nod. "He's probably with my grandmother right now." It occurs to me that I need to call him and Annie, that I need to tell them we've found Jacob. But for now, I'm desperate to hear his story. "Please, can you tell us what happened? There's so much I don't know."

Jacob nods, but instead of speaking, he turns to look out the window. He's silent for a long moment, and I stay twisted around in my seat, staring at him. Gavin glances over at me.

"You okay?" he asks softly.

I nod and smile, then I return my attention to the backseat. "Jacob?" I say softly.

He seems to snap out of a trance. "Yes, I am sorry. I am just overwhelmed." He clears his throat. "What do you wish to know, dear Hope?"

The way he looks at me is so warm that it floods me with sadness and happiness at the same time.

"Everything," I murmur.

And so Jacob begins to tell his story. He tells us how he met my grandmother and Alain in the Jardin du Luxembourg on Christmas Eve 1940, and that he knew at first sight that my grandmother was the love of his life. He tells us that he became involved with the resistance early, because his father was involved, and because he believed that it was up to the Jews to begin to save themselves. He tells us that he and my grandmother used to speak of a future together in America, where they could be safe and free, where people were not persecuted due to religion.

"It seemed a magical land," he says, looking out the window. "I know that now, in the world today, young people take freedom for granted. All of the things you have, all of the freedoms you enjoy, they are things you were born with. But during the Second World War, we had no rights. Under the German occupation, those of us who were Jewish were considered the lowest of the low, vermin to the Germans and to many French too. Rose

and I dreamed of living in a place where that would never happen, and to us, America was the place. America was the dream.
We planned to come here together, to raise a family.

"But then that terrible night happened. Rose's family would
not believe us, would not believe the roundup was taking place.
I insisted she must come with me, that she must keep our child
safe. She was two and a half months pregnant. The doctor had
confirmed it. She knew then, as I did, that the most important
thing was to save our child, our future. And so Rose made the
most difficult choice of all, but it was, in truth, the only choice she
could make. She went into hiding."

I can feel myself beginning to tremble, for in Jacob's words, in
the French lilt of his voice, and in the emotion of the story, I can
almost see it playing out before me like a movie. "At the Grand
Mosque of Paris?"

Jacob looks surprised. "You *have* done your research." He
pauses. "It was the idea of my friend Jean Michel, who worked
alongside me in the resistance. He had already helped several
orphaned children escape through the mosque, after their parents had been deported. He knew that the Muslims were saving
Jews, although it was mostly children they were taking in. But
Rose was pregnant, and she was still very young herself. So when
Jean Michel approached the leaders there and asked them to help
her, they agreed.

"The plan was to deliver her to the mosque, where they
would conceal her as a Muslim for a time, maybe a few weeks,
or a month, until it was safe to move her out of Paris. Then, she
would be smuggled, with money I had given to Jean Michel,
to Lyon, where l'Amitié Chrétienne, the Christian Fellowship,
would provide false papers and send her farther south, possibly
to a group called the Œuvre de Secours aux Enfants, the Children's Relief Effort. They mainly helped Jewish children get to
neutral countries, but we knew it was likely they would accept
Rose and assist her, because she was only seventeen, and she was

with child. But beyond that, I do not know what happened, or how she escaped, exactly. Do you know how she got out?"

"No," I tell him. "But I believe she met my grandfather when he was in the army, in Europe. I believe he brought her back to the United States."

Jacob looks wounded. "She married someone else," he says softly. He clears his throat. "Well, she would have believed me dead by then. I told her that no matter what, she needed to survive and protect the baby." He pauses and asks, "He is a nice man? The man she married?"

"He was a very nice man," I say softly. "He died a long time ago."

Jacob nods and looks down. "I'm very sorry."

"And what happened to you?" I ask after a long pause.

Jacob looks out the window for a long time. "I went back for Rose's family. She had asked me to do it, but in truth, I would have gone anyhow. I dreamed of a day when we could all be together, without the shadow of the Nazis. I believed that I could save them, Hope. I was young and naive.

"When I arrived, it was the middle of the night. The children were all asleep. I knocked softly on the door, and Rose's father answered. He took one look at me, and he knew. 'She is gone already, isn't she?' he asked me. I said yes, that I had taken her somewhere safe. He looked so disappointed in me. I can still remember his face as he said, 'Jacob, you are a fool. If you have led her to her death, I will never forgive you.'

"I tried in vain, for the next hour, to tell him what I knew. I told him that the roundup was to begin in just a few hours. I told him that the *l'Université Libre* newspaper had reported that records of some thirty thousand Jewish residents of Paris had been handed over to the Germans a few weeks earlier. I told him about the warnings issued by the Jewish Communists, who spoke of the exterminations, and how we needed to avoid capture at all costs.

"He shook his head and told me again that I was foolish. Even if the rumors were true, he said, it was only men who would be taken away. And likely only immigrant men. Thus, his family was not really in danger, he said. I told him that I had heard it was not just men this time, and not just immigrants. And besides, because Rose's mother had been born in Poland, some authorities would consider her children non-French too. We could not take that chance. But he would not listen."

Jacob sighs and pauses in his story. I look at Gavin, and as he glances over at me, his face is pale and sad. I can see tears in his eyes too. Before I can think about what I'm doing, I reach over and take his right hand, which is resting on his thigh. He looks surprised for an instant, but then he smiles, threads his fingers through mine, and squeezes gently. I blink a few times and turn back to Jacob in the backseat.

"You couldn't have done anything more," I tell him. "I'm sure my grandmother knew you'd try. And you did."

"I did," Jacob agrees. "But I did not do enough. I believed that the roundups would happen, but I was not so confident that I was able to convince Rose's father. I was only eighteen, you see. I was a boy. And in those times, a boy could not make an older man see his point of view. I often think that if I had tried harder, I could have saved them all. But the truth was, I knew there was a chance that the rumors were wrong, and so I did not speak with the conviction I should have. I will never forgive myself for not trying harder."

"It's not your fault," I murmur.

Jacob shakes his head and looks down. "But it is, dear Hope. I told her I would keep them safe. And I did not."

He makes a choked sound then, and turns to look out the window again.

"The times were different," Jacob continues after a long pause. "But I had the responsibility to do more." He sighs, long and heavy, and continues with his story. "After I left Rose's home,

I went to my own home. My parents were there, and my baby sister, who was just twelve years old. My father knew, as I did, what was coming, and so he was ready. We went to a friend's restaurant in the Latin Quarter, where the owner agreed to hide us in his basement. I could have taken Rose there too, but the risks were too great; she would begin showing her pregnancy soon, and I knew that if she was ever captured, she would be sent straight to her death. So I had to get her out of France, get her somewhere safe where the Germans could never find her.

"My father and I agreed, at the same time, that the safest solution for our family was to wait out the roundup in hiding, and then to go on with our lives, always keeping our ears to the ground so that we were aware when the Germans were coming. That night, and long into the next day, and the day after that, we hid in a cramped room in the basement of the restaurant, wondering if we would be found out. At the end of the third day, we emerged, hungry and exhausted, believing the worst was over.

"I wanted so very much to go to the Grand Mosque of Paris, where I knew Rose had been taken. But my father stopped me. He reminded me that I would be putting Rose and everyone there in danger if I went. And so I managed to get word through my friend Jean Michel that she was still safe. I asked him to tell her that I was safe too, that I would join her soon, but I don't know if word ever reached her. Just two days later, the French police showed up at our door to take my father and me away. They knew we had been part of the resistance, and this was the payment.

"They took my sister and my mother too, and at Drancy, the transit camp outside of Paris, we were separated, taken to different barracks. I never saw them again, although I found out later that they were deported to Auschwitz, just like my father and I."

We're all silent for a moment, and I notice that outside, the sun is casting long shadows over the fields on either side of the interstate. My stomach swims as I think of Jacob and his family being hauled away to a death camp. I swallow hard.

"What happened to your family?" Gavin asks Jacob softly. He squeezes my hand again and glances at me with concern.

Jacob takes a deep breath. "My mother and sister did not survive the initial selection at Auschwitz. My mother was frail and weak, and my sister, she was small for her twelve years and would have been considered unfit for work. They were taken directly to the gas chamber. I pray that they did not understand what was happening. But I fear that my mother, at least, knew enough to be aware. I imagine she must have been very frightened."

He pauses to collect himself. I can't seem to formulate words in the interim, and so I wait.

"My father and I were both sent to the barracks," he continues. "At first, he and I buoyed each other's spirits as best we could. But soon, he grew very ill. There was an epidemic at Auschwitz. Typhus. For my father, it began with chills in the night, and then weakness and a terrible cough. The guards made him go out to work anyhow, and although I and the other prisoners tried to make work as easy for him as possible, the disease was a death sentence. I sat with him on his last night as fever ravaged his body. He died sometime in the autumn of 1942. It was impossible to tell the day, the week, the month anymore, for in Auschwitz, time ceased to exist in any normal sense. He died before the snowfalls, though, that much I know."

"I'm so sorry," I finally manage to say. The words feel woefully inadequate.

Jacob nods slowly and looks out the window for a moment before turning back to us. "In the end, he was at peace. In the camps, when people died, they looked almost like sleeping children, innocent and unworried at last. For my father, it was the same. I was happy to see my father's face that way, because I knew he was finally free. In Judaism, the idea of heaven is not well defined, as it is in Christianity. But I believed, and still believe, that in some way, my father found my mother and sister again. And this brings me comfort, even to this day. The idea that they reunited, that they were together again."

He smiles, a bitter, sad smile. "There is a sign at Auschwitz that says, 'Work makes you free.' But the truth was that only death made you free. And at last, my family was free."

"How did you manage to survive?" Gavin asks. "You must have been in Auschwitz for what, more than two years?"

Jacob nods. "Nearly two and a half. But the fact was, I did not have a choice. I had promised Rose I would come back for her. And I could not, would not, break that promise. After the liberation, I came back to find her. I was so sure that I would be with her again, that we would be reunited, that we would be able to raise our child together, that perhaps we would have more children and somehow escape the shadow of the war."

Gavin and I listen raptly as Jacob tells us about coming back to Paris, about looking desperately for Rose, about believing in the depth of his soul that she had lived. He tells us of his despair upon not finding her, of the conversations he had with Alain, who was alone and adrift after losing his whole family and who was being cared for by an international refugee organization.

"I finally came to America," he says, "because this is where Rose and I had promised to reunite. I was trying to fulfill my end of the promise, you understand. And so every day for the last fifty-nine years, I have waited at the tip of Battery Park. It is where we agreed to meet. I always believed she would come."

"You were there every day?" I ask.

Jacob smiles. "Nearly every day. I had a job, of course, but I would go before and after work. The only days I missed waiting in the park were the day I broke my hip and the days after, as well as the days following September 11, when it was impossible to go to the park. I was standing in the park, in fact, when the first plane hit the World Trade Center." He's silent for a moment and adds softly, "It was the second time in my life I'd watched the world fall down before my eyes."

I absorb this for a moment. "How were you so sure that my grandmother would come for you? Didn't you start to believe that maybe she had died?"

He considers this for a moment. "No. I would have felt it. I would have known."

"How?" I ask softly. I don't mean any disrespect; it's just that I can't imagine hanging on for seventy years because of a feeling.

Jacob stares out the window for a moment and then turns to me with a small, sad smile. "I would have felt it in my soul, Hope," he says. "Do you understand? It does not happen very often in life, but when two people find that sort of connection, the kind of connection your grandmother and I have, they are forever tied to each other. I would have felt a piece of my soul missing if she was gone. When God joined us together, He made us two halves of the same whole."

Gavin's hand suddenly tightens on mine, and he looks over at me with wide eyes.

"What?" I ask him.

Instead of replying, he glances in the rearview mirror. "Jacob?" he asks. "What do you mean by that? By God joining the two of you?"

And in that moment, before Jacob replies, I understand what Gavin's getting at, and I know what Jacob is about to say.

"The day Rose and I were married," Jacob says. "We became one in God's eyes."

I swallow hard. "You and my grandmother were married?" I repeat.

Jacob looks surprised. "Of course," he says. "We did so in secret, you understand. Her family did not know, nor did mine. They believed us to be too young. We longed for the day we could have a ceremony in front of them, to celebrate with the people we loved the most. But we never had the chance."

I'm struggling to understand, and I suddenly realize what this means; if my grandmother was married to Jacob, her marriage to my grandfather had never been real. I feel another pang of sadness for him, for the losses he never knew.

Or had he? Had my grandfather realized in 1949, when he went to Paris, that Jacob Levy had survived, that Jacob's very existence annulled his own union with my grandmother? Had he, for this reason, told my grandmother that Jacob had perished? The thought makes my stomach swim uneasily, and I realize I may never know the answer.

"Did you marry my grandmother because she was already pregnant?" I venture.

"No." Jacob shakes his head vehemently. "We married because we loved each other. We married because we feared the war would tear us apart. We married because we knew we were destined for each other. The baby, I believe, was conceived on the night of our wedding, the first time we were together in that way."

I close my eyes and absorb this. My mother hadn't been the product of an affair between teenagers; she'd been conceived in marriage. She'd been the result of the consummation of the love between Mamie and Jacob. She, and then I—and then Annie— were all that remained of the ill-fated union between two soul mates.

"Don't you see?" Jacob asks after a long silence. "I was right all along. Rose has been alive. I knew it in my heart. And now, finally, I will see her again."

Jacob falls asleep just after we pass through Providence, and in the waning evening light, Gavin and I sit in silence, each lost in our own worlds.

I don't know what's going through Gavin's mind, but his face looks sad. It's how I'm feeling too. I'm not sure why, mere hours away from a reunion that's been nearly seventy years coming, I feel emptiness instead of jubilation. I suppose it's because all that was lost seems to overwhelm what was gained. Yes, Mamie had a life of freedom and safety. Yes, she gave birth to my mother, who gave birth to me, carrying on the family she'd promised Jacob she'd protect. And yes, Jacob had survived all these years, all these miles. But they had each carried their burdens alone, when they didn't have to. Because of misunderstandings, or perhaps lies, they had each lost the kind of love that I'd never believed in before.

But now I do. And it terrifies me, because I know I've never known that kind of love. Not even close.

Gavin pulls over for gas just past Fall River, and as Jacob continues to sleep in the backseat, I step away from the car and call Annie. I tell her we've found Jacob and are on the way back with him in the car. I smile as she squeals and goes to tell Alain. I can hear his exclamation of excitement in the background too. I assure her we'll be there in two hours or less and that Jacob will tell her the whole story then.

"Mom, I can't believe you did it," she says.

"It wasn't just me," I say. "It was you, honey. And Gavin too." I glance over to the car, where he's pumping gas, his back turned to me. He reaches up absentmindedly to scratch the top of his head, and I smile. "It was Gavin too," I repeat.

"Thanks, Mom," Annie says anyhow. There's a warmth in her voice that I haven't heard in a long time, and I'm grateful for it. "So what's he like, anyways?"

I tell her about finding Jacob in Battery Park, and about how he's kind and polite and has loved Mamie all these years.

"I knew it," she says softly. "I knew he'd never stopped loving her."

"You were right," I say. "See you in a few hours, sweetheart."

I hang up, and as I walk slowly back to the car, I look above me, where the first stars of twilight are beginning to poke holes through the sky. I think of all the nights I saw Mamie sitting at the window, waiting for the same stars, and I wonder whether this is what she's been looking for, the love of her life, who'd been here all along.

As I come up beside Gavin, he looks down and smiles gently at me. "You okay?" he asks. I watch as he removes the nozzle from his gas tank, replaces it back on its lever, and screws the cap back on.

"Yeah," I say. I glance into the backseat, where Jacob is sleeping soundly. I'm suddenly overwhelmed, and there are tears streaming down my cheeks. "It's real," I say. "All of it." I don't expect him to understand me, but somehow, he does.

"I know," he murmurs. He pulls me into an embrace, and as I rest my head against his chest and wrap my arms around him, I can feel myself letting go. I cry as he holds me, and I'm not quite sure whether I'm crying for Jacob and Mamie, or for myself.

We stand there for a very long time without speaking, for no words are needed. I know now that the prince is real, and that the people who love you the most *can* save you, and that fate might have a bigger plan for all of us than we understand. I know now that fairy tales can come true after all, if only you have the courage to keep believing.

Chapter Twenty-eight

Star Pie

INGREDIENTS

3 cups flour

1 tsp. salt

3 Tbsp. granulated sugar

1 cup shortening

1 egg, beaten

1 tsp. white vinegar

1 cup plus 4 Tbsp. water, divided

1 cup dried figs, chopped

1 cup dried prunes, chopped

1 cup red or green seedless grapes, sliced and divided

6 Tbsp. brown sugar

1 tsp. cinnamon

½ cup slivered almonds

1 Tbsp. poppy seeds

Cinnamon sugar for sprinkling (3 parts sugar mixed with 1 part cinnamon)

DIRECTIONS

1. Prepare crust by sifting flour, salt, and granulated sugar together. Using two knives or a food processor, cut in shortening until mixture has the consistency of thick crumbs. Add egg, vinegar, and 4 tablespoons water to dry mixture and mix with a fork, then with floured hands, until dough forms a ball.

2. Cool dough in refrigerator for 10 minutes, then divide into two halves. Roll one half into a circle and press into a 9-inch pie pan. Put other half aside.

3. Preheat oven to 350 degrees.

4. Mix figs, prunes, ½ cup sliced grapes, brown sugar, cinnamon, and 1 cup water in heavy medium saucepan. Stir over medium-high heat until sugar dissolves and mixture boils. Reduce heat to medium low, cover, and cook for 20 minutes. Remove cover and cook, stirring constantly, 3–5 minutes more until most of the liquid has evaporated and mixture is the consistency of thick jam. Remove from heat.

5. While filling cools, spread almonds in a thin layer on a baking sheet and toast in oven for 7–9 minutes, until slightly browned.

6. Remove toasted almonds from oven and mix into fruit mixture. Add poppy seeds and remaining ½ cup sliced grapes. Stir well to incorporate.

7. Pour fruit mixture into prepared bottom piecrust. Roll remaining dough into 10-inch-by-10-inch square. Cut into ½-inch-wide strips and arrange them in a star pattern, crisscrossing across top of crust. Sprinkle liberally with cinnamon sugar.

8. Bake for 30 minutes, or until top crust is golden brown. Remove from oven and cool completely. Keeps in the refrigerator for up to 5 days. Serve cold or at room temperature.

Rose

The water Rose was swimming in had begun to turn colors now—muted, milky colors that reminded Rose of the paintings by Claude Monet that she'd loved so much as a girl. There were water lilies and weeping willows in the murky deep, and sometimes poplars casting shadows across the surface, far above her too.

When she was a girl, Rose had always longed to go to Giverny, the place where Monet had painted many of his famous works; she had believed it must be the most beautiful place in the world.

It was only when she was older that she'd understood the place itself wasn't more beautiful than anything she'd seen; it was the way Monet had captured it with his paints and his canvases. Once, she and Jacob had gone to Argenteuil, just outside Paris, where Monet had lived and painted for a time, and Rose had been disappointed to realize that the town, while beautiful, was not as extraordinary as Monet had made it seem.

Beauty, she had realized then, was all in the perception. After the war, she'd found, with a bit of shock, that she was no longer able to perceive that sort of beauty in anything. Although she was dimly aware that the world was still beautiful, it was as if the edges were suddenly blurred, and all the light was gone.

And now, as the silken colors swirled around her in these mysterious depths that she couldn't seem to escape from, she floated and listened. There were voices again, far away, above the surface of this great and gentle sea. She tried to will herself toward the surface; it suddenly felt very important to know who was there. Had she heard something different this time?

As she floated slowly up, closer to the surface, cradled by the soft waters, the colors suddenly reminded her of the dress she'd made for her secret wedding day. April 14, 1942. A Tuesday, a date she would never forget. She'd gotten the fabrics from her friend Jacqueline, the only one who knew what she and Jacob were planning. But Jacqueline had been taken away the first week in March, arrested for daring to be foreign and Jewish. It was just a sign of the horrors to come, but Rose hadn't known that yet. Not on the beautiful day of her marriage.

The dress was many layers of gauzy material, and it had taken her more than a month to sew it in the darkness of her room at night. When her sister Helene would ask what she was doing, she would hide the dress beneath her blankets and make an excuse. She'd always believed that on some level, Helene knew. And although Helene's tight-lipped disapproval of Jacob bothered her, Rose also felt that in the blacked-out darkness of night, Helene was glad that one of them, at least, had found an escape from the sadness that swirled around them.

Rose had not wanted to wear white to her wedding, although she was, of course, still pure. But white represented innocence, and there was nothing innocent in Paris anymore.

And so she had arrived in her dress of many colors, all of them shades that reminded her of the sky at dawn, which was then her favorite time of day. Milky blue. Soft rose. Buttery yellow. Pale apricot. Foggy lavender. A thousand layers, it seemed, that swirled around Rose with a lightness that reminded her of clouds.

"You are the most beautiful thing I've ever seen," Jacob had told her when she entered the room. And from the way he'd looked at her, she'd known he meant it with all his heart. Their eyes had met then, and in his gaze, she could see everything that lay ahead of them: a life together somewhere far from Paris, and of course children, many children. They would laugh and tell stories and grow old in each other's arms. Life stretched before them, endless and happy in that moment. And Rose allowed herself to believe in it.

"I love you," she'd murmured to him.

And now, as she floated in this sea, she realized it wasn't a sea at all, in fact, but rather the thousands of sheer layers of her wedding dress, cradling her in their softness. She saw the colors she'd painstakingly layered together, and she realized that she could see through each of them, just a little bit. They were soft against her skin, just as they had been on that April day, so long ago.

She listened harder as she floated slowly up through the layers. And then, suddenly, she knew. She must be dead already. She was surprised she hadn't realized it before; it was so obvious. Of course that was why she'd been hearing Alain's voice for days; he was calling her home, showing her the way through the milky strangeness, the way to where her family had been all along. They hadn't been in the sky; they'd been in this strange, layered world. But perhaps this *was* the sky after all. How was she to know what the clouds really felt like? Maybe this was sunrise.

Maybe any moment now, the strange sea would be illuminated from within.

And then, Rose knew for sure that she had died, and that heaven was real, for she could hear the voice of her love calling for her.

"*Reviens à moi.*" Jacob's voice drifted down from above. "*Reviens à moi, mon amour!* Return to me, my love!"

Rose wanted to reply. She tried to call back, "I am coming, Jacob!" But the sounds died in her throat.

But then she felt his hand encircle hers. She knew at once it was Jacob; she would know his touch anywhere, although it had been nearly seventy years since she'd last felt it. His hand wrapped around hers the way it always used to: warm, strong, familiar. It was the hand that had saved her, so long ago.

She knew that he was pulling her to him, after all these years, and that this must mean he'd forgiven her for sending him back to his death. Her heart overflowed, and in her eyes, she could feel tears. It was all she'd hoped for over the years.

She took a deep breath and realized that the sea smelled like lavender, the same scent she'd breathed in on her wedding day. She was home, finally home. She held tight to Jacob's hand and began, at long last, to swim toward the surface.

Chapter *Twenty-nine*

❦

It's Annie who notices first.

"Mom!" she hisses, tugging frantically at my arm as I watch Jacob leaning over Mamie, whispering to her in French. We'd arrived at the hospital an hour ago, and Jacob has been bent over Mamie ever since.

"What is it, honey?" I ask, unable to look away from the scene, which feels futile and sad.

"She's moving, Mom!" Annie says. "Mamie's moving!"

I realize with a start that she's correct. I watch in awe as Mamie's left hand twitches a little and closes around Jacob's. He continues to whisper to her, more urgently now.

"Is she . . . ?" Alain begins, trailing off as he stares.

"She's waking up," Gavin murmurs from beside me.

We all watch as her eyelids begin to flutter and then, unbelievably, open. I know that one of us should go get a doctor or a nurse, but I find myself rooted to the spot, unable to move at all.

She exhales loudly, like someone who's been holding her breath for a long time, and her eyes dart quickly around the room, until they alight on Jacob and widen. She says something unintelligible, in a voice that doesn't sound like hers. It's as if she's trying to remember how to use her mouth.

"My Rose," Jacob says, "I have found you."

She moves her lips for a moment, makes another moaning sound, and then says, "You . . . here," in a voice that is raspy and hoarse, but unmistakable. She stares up at Jacob, who is crying now as he leans down and kisses my grandmother once, lightly, on the lips.

"Yes, I am here, Rose," he murmurs. They stare, drinking each other in.

"We . . ." Mamie trails off and tries again. "We . . . in heaven?" Her words are slow like molasses, but she seems determined to speak.

Jacob draws a shuddering breath. "No, my love. We are in Cape Cod."

Mamie looks confused for a moment, and then her cloudy eyes scan the room, alighting first on me, then on Annie and Gavin, and finally on her brother. "Alain?" she whispers.

"Yes," he says simply. "Yes, Rose. It is me."

She looks back to Jacob in stunned disbelief. "Alain . . . alive? You, Jacob . . . you are alive?" she whispers to him.

"Yes, my love," Jacob says. "You saved me."

Mamie's eyes fill and tears begin to run down her face in rivers. "I did not . . . I did not save you," she whispers. "How can you say . . . ?" She pauses, drawing a shuddering breath. "I asked you . . . to go back. It is . . . my fault."

"No," Jacob says. "None of it was your fault, dear Rose. I lived because I always believed I would see you again. It is you, for seventy years now, who has kept me alive. I have never stopped looking for you."

She continues to stare at him.

"Someone should go get the doctor," Gavin whispers beside me.

"Uh-huh," I reply vaguely. But none of us make a move to go.

After a moment, Mamie turns her head slightly until she focuses on me. "Hope?"

"Yes, Mamie," I say, taking a step forward.

"Why . . . you crying?" she asks haltingly.

"Because . . ." I find I cannot explain myself. "Because I've missed you so much," I conclude, realizing in that moment how true the words are.

She looks back at Jacob. "How . . . ?" she asks.

He nods, understanding her. "Hope found me," he says. "Hope and Annie and their friend Gavin."

"Gavin?" she asks. She looks over at us again with some effort, and she scans Gavin's face in confusion. "Who Gavin? You?"

"Yes, ma'am," Gavin replies. "We've met a few times. I'm a handyman in the area. I'm . . . I'm friends with your grand-daughter."

"Yes," Mamie murmurs. "Yes, I know now." She closes her eyes for a moment, and when she opens them again, she stares at Jacob for a long time before looking back at me.

"How . . . how you find my Jacob?" she whispers.

"It was the list you gave me," I say. "The one that sent me to Paris."

She looks confused, and I realize she doesn't know what I'm talking about. In the drama of the moment, I'd almost forgotten about her Alzheimer's.

"But it was the fairy tales," I add as she stares at me. "It was your fairy tales that finally led us to him. I didn't know they were real."

"They are real," Mamie murmurs. But she's looking at Gavin as she says it. "Of course. Always real."

Her eyes shift to Alain and fill with tears again. "Alain?" she says softly.

"How do you recognize me after all these years?" he asks.

"You . . . my brother," she says clearly. The tempo of her speech is picking up a little; it's as if the words are coming back as she wakes up. "I would know you . . . anywhere."

"I'm sorry I did not find you sooner," he says. "I did not know . . . I did not know you were alive. All those years wasted."

Mamie closes her eyes briefly. She's crying again. "I believed . . . you dead," she says. "In Auschwitz. That place. I imagined . . . many million times."

"I believed you were dead too," Alain murmurs.

Mamie turns her gaze to Annie next. "Leona?" she asks.

Annie's shoulders slump, and my heart breaks a little for her; I know it hurts her when her grandmother doesn't recognize her.

"No, Mamie," Annie says. "Who's Leona?"

But this time, it's Jacob who answers. "Leona was my little sister." He's looking intently at Annie now. "My God, Annie, you look so much like her."

Annie looks back at Mamie, her eyes wide. "You've been calling me Leona for months," she says. "That's who you meant?"

Mamie looks confused.

Annie turns to Jacob. "What happened to Leona?"

Jacob glances at me, and I nod slightly. Annie's old enough to know. "She died, my dear," he says. "At Auschwitz. I believe she did not suffer very much, Annie. I believe that she went peacefully."

Annie's eyes fill. "I'm sorry," she murmurs to Jacob. "I'm really sorry about your sister."

He smiles at her gently. "I can see her in you," he says. "And that makes me glad." He turns back to Mamie and bends toward her again. "Rose, Leona died many years ago. But this young lady here is Annie. Your great-granddaughter." He pauses and says, "*Our* great-granddaughter."

Annie looks at me sharply, and I realize that I haven't told her yet. I haven't told her that Jacob married Mamie long ago and was the real father to my mother. I reach over and squeeze my daughter's hand. "I'll explain everything later," I whisper. She looks confused, and a little alarmed, but she nods.

Mamie is studying Annie now. "Annie," she says finally. I can see recognition dawning in her eyes. "The youngest."

"Yes, ma'am," Annie mumbles.

"You are . . . good girl," Mamie says. "I am proud . . . You have . . . spirit in you. It reminds me of . . . something I lost. Never let go . . . of that."

Annie nods hastily. "Okay, Mamie."

Finally, Mamie turns back to Jacob, who is still bent over her. "My love," she says softly. "Do not cry."

I realize that Jacob's body is shaking with sobs, and that tears are streaming down his cheeks.

"We are together now," Mamie continues. "I have . . . waited for you." They stare at each other in silence, and it takes me a while to realize I'm holding my breath.

I watch as Jacob leans forward, slowly, gently, and kisses Mamie on the lips, pausing there with his eyes closed, as if he wishes never to move again. In that frozen moment, I'm powerfully reminded of yet another fairy tale. He looks very much like the prince kissing Sleeping Beauty, awakening her after a hundred years of slumber. I realize with a start that in a way, she's been asleep for nearly that long; for seventy years, she's lived a sort of half life.

"Forever, my love," Jacob says.

Mamie smiles at him and stares into his eyes. "Forever," she murmurs.

Chapter *Thirty*

~

J ust past three in the morning, just a few hours after Annie, Alain, Gavin, and I left her alone with Jacob, Mamie slipped away peacefully in her sleep.

Jacob sat by Mamie's bedside for the next few hours, and just after dawn, when he stepped out of a cab outside the front door of the bakery Mamie had founded so many years ago, he seemed a different man. I had expected that he would be sad, defeated, for he'd waited seventy years only to watch the love of his life slip away. But instead, his eyes shone differently than they had when we'd first seen him in New York, and he seemed a decade younger.

The nurses told me afterward that Jacob had talked to Mamie long into the night and that when they finally came to check on her, and realized she had died, she was smiling, and Jacob was still holding her hand, whispering to her in a language they didn't know.

Gavin called his rabbi, who came to meet with Jacob, Alain, and me, and together, we planned a burial according to Jewish customs. I understood now that Mamie had always been Jewish; that had never changed. Perhaps, as she'd said, she'd been

Catholic and Muslim too. But if one could find God everywhere, as Mamie had once told me, it seemed to make the most sense to send her home along the same road she'd entered upon.

We took turns sitting with Mamie—Gavin explained to me that in the Jewish faith, one is not supposed to leave the deceased alone—and a day later, she was buried in a wooden casket beside my mother and grandfather. I had struggled with what to do about that, having just learned that her marriage to Jacob in effect annulled Mamie's marriage to my grandfather. But Jacob had wrapped his hands around mine and said gently, "God does not mind where you are put to rest. I think Rose would want to be buried here, where she lived her life, alongside the man who gave her a new life, and alongside her daughter. *Our* daughter."

For the next several days, I went through the motions of running the bakery, but my heart wasn't in it. It felt like a great hole had opened in my life. It was just me now, against the world: me responsible for this bakery; me responsible for my daughter; me responsible for carrying on a family tradition I was only beginning to understand.

On the sixth night after Mamie died, Alain takes Annie out for a walk, and I sit by the fire with Jacob, listening as he talks haltingly of the years after the war.

"I am so sorry, Hope, that I was not there to see you grow up," he tells me as he squeezes my hands. I can feel his hands shaking. "I would give anything to have been there. But you are a fine woman, a good woman. You remind me so much of Rose, of the woman I always knew she would grow to be. And you too have raised a fine daughter with a fine heart."

I thank him and stare into the fire, wondering how to ask him the question that has been gnawing at the edges of my mind since I'd met Jacob. "What about my grandfather?" I finally ask softly. "Ted."

Jacob bows his head and looks into the fire for a long time.

"Your grandfather must have been a wonderful man," he says finally. "He raised a fine family, Hope. I wish I had gotten a chance to thank him for that."

"None of this is fair to him," I say softly. "I'm sorry," I add after a pause. "I don't mean to offend you."

"Of course not," Jacob says quickly. "And you are right." He pauses and stares into the fire for a long time. "He will always be your grandfather, Hope. I know that. I know you will never love me the way you love him, for you have known him your whole life."

I open my mouth to protest, for this isn't fair to Jacob either. But he holds up a hand to stop me. "I will always regret that I was not here for the things he was here to see. But that is the hand that life has dealt us. And we must accept it. You can only look forward in life. You can change the future, but not the past."

I hesitate and nod. "I'm sorry," I say, but the words feel lame and ineffectual. "Did my grandmother say anything about him?" I ask. "To you? Before she died?"

He nods and looks away. "She explained everything as best she could," he says. "I think she believed she had to make me understand, but the truth is, I have always understood, Hope. War tears us apart, and there are some things that cannot be put back together."

"What did she tell you?"

He turns to look at me. "She made it to Spain in the late autumn of 1942. It was there that she met your grandfather. He had been in a U.S. military plane shot down over France, and like your grandmother, he had been smuggled into Spain, through channels in France that helped the Allies. He and your grandmother were hidden in the same home, and that is how they met. He fell in love with your grandmother, who was due to give birth soon. It was around that time that there was an influx of Jewish people who escaped from Paris, people Rose had known in her former life, and they told her I was dead. She did not believe it at first, but some of them claimed to have seen me die in the streets of Paris. Another said he had seen me taken to the gas chamber at Auschwitz."

"My God," I murmur, not knowing what else to say.

Jacob looks out the window, where ice has begun to creep over the pane, obscuring our view into the darkness outside. "She did not believe it at first," he says again. "She said she did not feel it in her soul. But the more people who told her I was gone, the more convinced she became that I had, in fact, died, and what she was feeling was due to the fact that I lived on through the child growing inside her. She knew then that she had to protect our daughter at all costs. And so when Ted proposed to her and told her he would bring her back to the United States before the baby came, she knew it would give our child the chance to be born an American, which is what we had always dreamed of together. It would give our child a chance to grow up in a land where she could always be free.

"She went back to the United States with your grandfather, who married her," Jacob continues slowly. "They listed him on the birth certificate as Josephine's father, so there would be no complications. Later, they paid to have the year changed so that no one would do the math and doubt the story. Your grandfather asked just one thing of your grandmother: that she permit him to raise Josephine as his own, that Josephine never be told of my existence."

"So she never told my mother about you?"

Jacob shakes his head. "It was, she said, one of the greatest regrets of her life. But Ted was a wonderful father, and she felt she must keep the promise she made to him. She had traded one life for another, and she never forgot the bargain she had made. But Rose said she tried to keep me alive for Josephine in other ways."

"In her fairy tales," I murmur. "You were there all along in the stories she told my mom and me." I pause and suddenly remember something Mamie told me. "But my grandfather went to Paris in 1949, didn't he? To find out what happened to you and my grandmother's family?"

Jacob takes a deep breath and nods. "That is the one part of the story your grandmother could not explain," he says. "And I did not have the heart to tell her that Ted may have known all along. I was listed in the records then. I had not yet moved to the United States. Not until 1952. I was doing everything in my power to make sure I would be found, because I did not believe that Rose had perished. I believed she survived and that we would find each other again.

"I suppose we will never know what happened," he continues. "But if your grandfather came home and told your grandmother I was dead, I assume he knew he was telling a lie."

"To protect the life he'd begun with her," I say, feeling a sudden chill. I lean closer to the fire.

Jacob nods. "Yes. I believe so. But can I blame him? He loved Rose and loved Josephine, who had become his daughter. He had built a good life with them. If Rose had known I had survived, perhaps he would have lost everything. He did what he could to protect his family. And I cannot fault him for that. In fact, I did the same, did I not? I made choices to protect the people I loved most. We all make choices, sacrifices, for what we believe to be the greater good."

I swallow the lump in my throat. "But if that's what happened, he prevented you and my grandmother from being together. He kept you apart for seventy years."

"No, my dear," Jacob says. "It was the war that kept us apart. The world went mad, and your grandfather was no more responsible for the outcome than I was, or than Rose was. We all made our choices. We all had to live with our regrets."

"I'm so sorry," I say. I feel I'm apologizing to Jacob for what my grandfather did, and for the terribly unfair hand he was dealt. But he merely shakes his head.

"Do not be," he says. "Your grandmother asked me, just

before she passed, to forgive her; she felt she had betrayed me by marrying Ted. But I told her there was no need for forgiveness, for she had done nothing wrong. Nothing. She acted as she did because she believed it to be the right thing for our daughter. The important thing is that Rose lived. As did Josephine. As did you and Annie. Regardless of what happened, Rose saved the child we had created together, the greatest declaration of our love, and gave her the life we had always dreamed of, a life of freedom."

"But you spent your life waiting for her," I say.

He smiles. "And now I have found her. I am at peace." He reaches for my hands again and looks into my eyes for a long time. "You are our legacy. You and Annie. You must honor where you came from, now that you know."

"But how?"

"By following your heart," Jacob says. "Life gets complicated. Circumstance tears us apart. Decisions guide our fate. But your heart will always show you true north. Your grandmother, she knew this always."

I hang my head. "But how do I know what I'm supposed to do?" I don't know how to explain that my heart has never led me into anything more than trouble.

"You will know," Jacob says. "Just listen. The answers lie inside you."

The next morning, as I'm getting ready to leave for the bakery, I come into the living room to find Jacob staring out the window, just where I'd left him the night before. I wonder whether he's looking at the stars, the way Mamie always did.

"Hey, Jacob," I say as I grab my keys from the kitchen table. "I'm headed out. If you feel like it, come by the bakery later. I'll bake you a Star Pie."

When he doesn't respond, I go over to the chair and kneel beside him. "Jacob?"

His eyes are closed, and there's a small, peaceful smile on his face, as if he's in the midst of a dream he doesn't wish to leave. I wonder whether he's thinking about my grandmother.

"Jacob?" I say again. I touch his arm lightly, and that's when I know. "Jacob," I murmur softly, tears beginning to run down my face. His arm is cold, and so too is his cheek, when I reach up to touch it gently. He's gone. And somehow, I'm not surprised at all. He has spent a lifetime trying to find Mamie. And now he has eternity to make up for all those lost years.

I don't disturb him. I don't wake Annie or Alain. I don't leave for the bakery. I just sit beside him, this man whose courage gave me life so many years ago, long before I was ever born, and I cry. I cry for everything lost and everything found. I cry for my grandmother, and for my mother, who never knew the story of her birth. I cry for Annie, because she's had to endure far more loss than one should have to at such a young age. And I cry for myself, for I don't know the way. I don't know how to find the answers Jacob seems to believe I carry in my heart.

After much careful thought, Alain and I decide to bury Jacob beside my grandmother. After all, he has no family left else-where, and we can't imagine anywhere in the world he'd rather be than beside the love of his life. *I have found her,* he told me on his last night. *I am at peace.*

Elida White and her grandmother drive down from Pem-broke for the funeral, and we all stand together—Muslims, Christians, and Jews—and listen to the words of the rabbi at the grave site. I look east, in the direction Jacob's tombstone will face, once it's delivered. Mamie's will face that way too. In a few hours, the first stars of evening will begin to poke through the sky, just like they always have, just like they always will. For as long as there are stars in the sky, I realize, Jacob's promise to love Mamie will live on. The stars she once looked for will keep watch silently over her, and over the love of her life, who has, at long last, returned to her side.

Chapter *Thirty-one*

Winter on Cape Cod is long and lonely, and this year, it feels as if time has frozen in place, as I wait to lose the bakery. There are no prospective buyers, for who would want such a place in the dead of winter? But the bank intends to take it from me all the same. Matt does nothing to stop it, and I do not ask him to. Every morning, as my breath hangs in the air like puffs of frozen smoke, I wonder whether today will be the day that the last of Mamie's legacy will disappear. Until then, I will keep running the bakery, because it is all I know how to do.

One might think that this season would be my least favorite time of year, because of the slow desolation and the lack of business. But I've always found peace in the winter months. The evenings are so still, just before the sun sets, that when the caw of a single seagull sounds over the sea, I can hear it from inside the walls of my cottage. When I walk on the beach, frozen ice sometimes crunches beneath my worn boots. And Main Street feels like a ghost town before the holidays; on the mornings when I arrive at the bakery, sometimes I believe I'm the only person in this wintry wonderland, and I imagine what I'd do if no one else could see me.

The third week of November, Gavin asks me to go to dinner and a movie with him, and although I say no, he comes by a few days later and invites Annie, Alain, and me to his family's house near Boston for Thanksgiving. I'm missing Mamie more than usual that day, and I'm on edge about the bakery, so I explode at him without meaning to.

"Look, I appreciate everything you've done for me and my family," I tell him, as my stomach tightens into a knot. "But I can't do this to Annie."

He looks baffled and wounded. "Do what?"

"Take a chance on someone like you."

He stares at me. "Someone like me?"

I feel terrible, but just like Mamie had put her child's life first, neglecting her own needs, I know I need to do the same. I owe it to my daughter. "You're wonderful, Gavin," I try to explain. "But Annie has lost so much lately. She needs stability now. Not someone else who might disappear from her life."

"Hope, I'm not planning on disappearing."

I look down. "But you can't promise me today that you'll be here forever, can you?" I ask. He doesn't answer, so I go on. "Of course you can't. And I would never ask you to. But I can't let anyone into my life if there's even a chance they'll hurt my daughter."

"I would never . . ." he begins.

"I'm sorry," I say firmly, hating myself.

I watch as his jaw clenches. "Fine," he says. He walks out without another word.

"I'm sorry," I murmur again, long after he's gone.

Hanukkah overlaps with Christmas this year, and Alain decides to stay so that we can celebrate the holidays together. Annie is with Rob during the first two weeks of December, but I have her for the second half of the month, while Rob and his girlfriend travel to the Bahamas. That allows Alain to teach Annie about the Jewish holiday traditions, and we exchange gifts and light the candles of the menorah as Mamie must have done seventy years before, when she believed that a life of happiness with Jacob stretched before her. The sadness of her death has remained, a fog wrapped around us, although some days, I wonder whether it's her life we're mourning instead of her death. For she died with a smile on her face and was joined soon after by the one person capable of completing the puzzle we never knew she was trying to piece together.

It's been over a month now since I've heard from Gavin. It's better that way, I tell myself. Annie and I are just finding our footing again. She's just beginning to trust me. I can't bring a man into that mix, not now. I want her to know that she will always come first.

Alain tries to talk to me about this on the last day of Hanukkah, the day before he returns to Paris, but he doesn't understand.

"Gavin cares for you," Alain tells me. "He helped you find me, and Jacob. He has been kind to your daughter. He did not have to do those things."

"I know," I reply. "He's a wonderful guy. But we're fine without him."

"I know. But do you *want* to be without him?" Alain asks, looking at me carefully in a manner that assures me he already knows the answer.

I shrug. "I don't need anyone. I never have."

"We all need people who love us," Alain says.

"I have Annie," I reply.

"And me," he says with a smile.

I smile back. "I know."

"Do you not believe in love?" he asks after a long pause. "Did you not see it, plain as day, between your grandmother and Jacob?"

I merely shrug in reply.

The truth, which I cannot explain to Alain, is that I do believe in love now, the kind of love that can exist between a man and a woman. I have Mamie to thank for that, and I will forever be grateful, because it is a lesson I never expected to learn. I suppose I am my mother's daughter in that way.

But my heart is as surrounded by ice as the bird feeder that has frozen solid on our back porch. Just because love exists does not mean that I am capable of it. Sometimes, in the darkness of night, I wonder whether I'm even capable of loving Annie in the right way or whether I've forever inherited my mother's coldness. Annie is my child, and I know I would lay down my life for her in a heartbeat, or give up anything in my own life to make her life better, but is that love? I have no way of knowing. And if I can't be sure of my ability to love my daughter the right way, how could I possibly believe I could love someone else?

Besides, it seems to me that Mamie hung on to her love for Jacob like a rope that could save her from drowning. But over the years, the rope that saved her became a noose that tightened more and more with each passing year. I'm afraid that's what love can turn into, if you let it.

Gavin was right; there are layers upon layers of defenses surrounding my heart, and I don't know how someone could get past them. I don't believe anymore that there's anyone out there willing to try. It only took one conversation to push Gavin away, and he disappeared entirely, proving to me that he'd never really cared that much in the first place. How foolish I was to think any differently. How foolish that this breaks my heart.

On December 30, the day after Alain has left to return to Paris, Annie appears at the door to the bakery at two in the afternoon, when she should be home, hanging out with her friend Donna, whose mother had agreed the girls were old enough to be trusted alone in my house for a few hours.

"Is everything okay?" I ask instantly. "Where's Donna?"

"She went home." Annie smiles. "You got a call."

"From who?"

"From Mr. Evans," she says, naming the town's only estate attorney. "Mamie left a will."

I shake my head. "No, that's not right. We would have known about it already. Mamie died last month."

Annie tilts her head to the side. "So I'm lying now?" I open my mouth to reply, but she keeps going. "He said that, like, Mamie didn't want him to call you 'til December 30, 'cause there's some letter she didn't want you to have 'til New Year's Eve."

I stare at my daughter. "You're kidding."

Annie shrugs. "That's what Mr. Evans says. Call him if you don't believe me."

So I call Thom Evans, one of the many men in town who'd dated my mother on and off when I was a kid, and he tells me in his stiff, careful tone that yes, there is a will, and yes, there is a letter, and I can come over any time the next day to pick them up, even though it's a Saturday, and a holiday to boot. "The law never sleeps," he tells me, which makes me have to stifle a laugh, because the whole town knows that if you stop by Thom Evans's office, you're as likely to find him passed out at his desk with a bottle of scotch in his hand as you are to find him actually working.

The next afternoon, I close the bakery early and head over to Thom's office, which is just a few blocks down Main. The sun is shining brightly, although I know that in just a few hours, it will disappear into the sea for the last time this year. Annie is spending tonight with her father, who has agreed to take her, Donna, and two other friends over to the big First Night celebration in Chatham, and I plan to spend the evening alone at the beach, even though I'll need several layers of thick wool to steel myself against the cold wind blowing in from the bay. I've been thinking lately of all the nights Mamie spent searching the heavens, and it seems right to see the year off doing the same thing, from the place where the view is the clearest.

I take off my coat and hat and peek my head into Thom's office, where he appears to have nodded off at his desk, although there's no liquor bottle in sight. I pause before knocking. He must be nearly seventy now; I know he graduated high school the same year my mother did, and for a moment, seeing him brings back the past, making me long to see my mother.

I rap lightly on the door, and he wakes up instantly. He shuffles some papers and clears his throat in an apparent attempt to pretend he wasn't just sleeping. "Hope!" he exclaims. "Come in!"

I step into his office, and he gestures toward one of the chairs facing his desk. He stands and riffles through his file cabinet, while we make small talk about how quickly Annie is growing up and how much his own great-niece, Lili, liked the gingerbread cookies he'd picked up from my bakery on Christmas Eve on his way to Plymouth, where Thom's sister and her family live.

"I'm glad they were a hit," I say. "That was one of my grandmother's favorite things to make every holiday." When I was Annie's age, I'd taken my job as the bakery's official gingerbread froster quite seriously; I'd dress all the little figures up with sugary hats, gloves, and sometimes even Santa outfits.

"I remember," Thom says, smiling at me. He finally extracts a folder from the cabinet and comes back to sit at his desk. "Lili asked me to make a request for next year. She wants to know if you can make the gingerbread men with ice skates."

I laugh. "She's into ice skating now?"

"In the last year, she's been obsessed with horseback riding, ballet, and now ice skating," he says. "Who knows what it'll be this time next year."

I smile. "You know," I say gently. "I'm afraid the bakery probably won't be here next holiday season."

Thom arches an eyebrow at me. "Oh?"

I nod and look down. "The bank's calling in the loan. I don't have the money. It's been a rough few years with the economy and all."

Thom doesn't say anything for a moment. He puts his glasses on and studies one of the papers he's pulled out of the folder.

"You know, if this were *It's a Wonderful Life,* this would be the part where I'd tell you all the townspeople will pitch in to help save the bakery."

I laugh. "Right. And Annie would be running around telling everyone that every time a bell rings, an angel gets its wings." The movie is my favorite; Annie and I had watched it on Christmas Eve, with Alain, just last week.

"Do you actually *want* to save the bakery?" Thom asks after a moment. "If you had a choice, would you prefer to be doing something else?"

I think about this for a minute. "No. I do want to save it. I don't know that I would have said that a few months ago. But it means something different to me now. I know this is my legacy." I half laugh and think back to the movie again. "Where are the generous townspeople when you need them, right?"

"Hmm," Thom says. He studies the document in his hands for another moment and then looks up at me, the hint of a smile playing at the corners of his mouth. "What if I told you that you didn't need the townspeople to save the bakery?"

I stare at him. "What?"

"Let me put it this way," he says. "How much money would you need to cover all the costs and get it back up and running again?"

I snort and look away. From anyone else, the question would have been rude. But I've known Thom forever, and I know he's not being intrusive; this is just his way. "Much more than I have," I say finally. "Much more than I'll ever have."

"Hmph." Thom slips on a pair of reading glasses and narrows his eyes at the page. "Would three and a half million do it?"

I cough. "What?"

"Three and a half million," he repeats calmly. He peers at me over the top rims of his glasses. "Would that solve your problems?"

"Geez, I'd say so." I laugh uneasily. "What, did you buy me a lottery ticket for Christmas or something?"

"No," he replies. "That happens to be the amount that Jacob Levy had in savings and various investments. When you contacted me about the arrangements for his funeral last month, do you remember me getting in touch with his attorney in New York? The one whose name was on his property documents?"

"Of course," I murmur. Although Jacob had never remarried and didn't have any relatives that we knew of, I knew we had to notify someone of his death, particularly if we planned to bury him here on the Cape. Gavin had helped me track down an attorney listed in some of his old records.

"Well, it just so happens that Jacob Levy's will leaves everything to your grandmother, or to her direct descendants," Thom continues. "He apparently always believed she had lived and that he'd find her. That's what his attorney said."

"Wait, so . . ." My voice trails off as I try to piece together what he's telling me.

"You're the next direct descendant of Rose Durand McKenna, who we now, of course, know was initially Rose Picard," Thom goes on. "Jacob's estate is yours."

"Wait," I say again, struggling to understand. "You're telling me Jacob had three and a half million dollars?"

Thom nods. "And now I'm telling you that *you* have three and a half million. After a lot of paperwork, of course." He peers at the papers again. "It seems that after he came to the United States, he worked his way up from being a busboy in a hotel kitchen, to managing a hotel, to eventually becoming a partial investor in a hotel. That's what his lawyer explained. Apparently, he was a millionaire by 1975 and started a charity for Holocaust survivors at that point. He turned that first hotel into seven successful properties, and he sold his shares three years ago. Part of his fortune is going into an annuity to fund the charity. The remainder—three and a half million—has been earmarked for you."

"But he never said anything," I say.

Thom shrugs. "His attorney said he was very modest. Always lived well below his means. Used his money to hire private detectives to try to find your grandmother. But he never knew the assumed name she'd taken on. He was never able to find her."

"My God," I murmur. The news is still sinking in.

Thom nods. "There's more," he says. "Your grandmother also leaves behind a small estate. Of course the assisted living home drained most of her funds, as you know, but there's a little left. About seventy-five thousand after everything. Enough to pay off the remainder of the loan for your mother's house."

I shake my head. "Unbelievable," I murmur.

"And," Thom adds. "There's a letter. Your grandmother sent it to me back in September. The letter's sealed," he continues. "In the note your grandmother sent to me, she asked me to give it to you on New Year's Eve at the end of the year she died."

The lump in my throat is preventing me from replying. I blink back tears as Thom slides a narrow envelope across the desk to me.

"Do you know what it says?" I ask after I find my voice.

Thom shakes his head. "Why don't you head home and read it? I just need your signature on a few things here, and I'll get your grandmother's money routed into your account. Jacob Levy's attorney is already working to get his money to you too. You should have it soon. In the meantime, I'll talk to Matt at the bank, if you want me to."

I nod. "Let him know I'm buying the bakery outright," I say. "No more payments to the bank. I want it to belong to my family forever."

"Ten-four," Thom says. He pauses. "Hope?" he asks tentatively.

"Yeah?"

He sighs and looks out the window. "Your mom would be proud of you, you know."

I shake my head. "I don't think that's true," I say. "I was

always a disappointment to her. I think she wished she'd never had me."

I've never said those words before, and I'm not sure why I'm saying them now, to Thom Evans.

"That's not true, Hope," Thom says softly. "Your mom was a tough woman to deal with. You know that. But you were the center of her life, whether you knew it or not."

"No I wasn't," I say. "You were. And all the men who came in and out of her life. No offense."

"None taken," Thom says.

"It was like she was always looking for something she couldn't find," I say.

"At the end of her life, I think she found it," he says. "It may have been too late for her to communicate that to you properly, though."

I look up. "What do you mean?"

He sighs. "She was always talking about how she was too cold to care about anyone."

"She said that to you?" My mother hadn't seemed that self-aware. And in fact, I hadn't known she was communicating with Thom at all. I thought that once people were out of her life, they were gone forever. It startles me to realize that she'd let him back in.

He shrugs. "We talked about a lot of things. Especially at the end. I think that with your mother slipping away, she had a lot of regrets. It wasn't until the end of her life, Hope, that she realized what she'd been looking for had been right in front of her."

I blink. "What do you mean?"

"She loved you," he says. "More than she'd been able to truly understand as a young woman. I think that she spent her life searching for love, doubting her own ability to love, and at the end, she realized it had been there all along. In you. And if she'd recognized that sooner, maybe everything could have been different."

I just stare at him. I don't know what to say.

"Go read your grandma's letter, Hope," Thom says gently. "And if you learn anything from your mom, let it be that you don't have to search as far as you think for what's already there, right in front of you."

That night, I call Annie to tell her about the inheritance from Jacob, which will be enough to cover the bakery and pay for her college costs—with plenty left over. As I listen to her whoop and holler on the other end of the line, I smile and promise myself that I'll try harder with her. Things will be better. She's a good kid, and I know that I need to keep trying to be a better mom. Maybe I can be better at this than I think.

I tell Annie to have fun at the First Night celebration, and she promises to call me after midnight, when Rob is driving her and her friends back to his house for a New Year's Eve sleepover.

It's just past eleven when I finally settle down in front of the fire with Mamie's letter. My hands are trembling as I open it up; I'm aware that this is the last piece of her. It could be Alzheimer's gibberish, for all I know, or it could be something I'll treasure forever. Either way, she's gone. Jacob is gone. My mother is gone. Annie will be grown up and out of the house within six years. I pull a blanket around me, a blanket my grandmother knit when I was a little girl, and try not to feel so very alone.

I pull the letter out. It's dated September 29. The day we took Mamie to the beach. The day she gave me the list of names. The first night of Rosh Hashanah. The night everything began. My heart skips, and I take a deep breath.

Dearest Hope, the letter begins. For the next ten minutes, I read. I skim the letter once, and then, with tears in my eyes, I go back to read it again, more slowly this time, hearing Mamie's voice in my head as she forms each of the words with her careful, lilting accent.

Chapter *Thirty-two*

Rose

Dearest Hope,

As I sit here today to write to you, I know this may be the last chance I have at clarity. I know my days are waning. You will receive this letter after I am gone, and I want you to know that I was ready. My life was long, and many parts of it were wonderful, but in my twilight, the past has returned to me, and I can bear it no more.

Tonight, if I can manage to stay lucid, I will give you the list of names that have been burned into my heart, and written on the sky. By the time you read this letter, then, you will know that most of my life was a lie. But it was a lie I had to tell, at first to protect your mother, and then, to protect myself.

I do not know if you will learn the truth on your own. I hope you do. You deserve to know it, and I should have told you long ago. I knew I had to keep the promise I made to your grandfather as long as he was alive, but after that, to have told you or your mother felt to me like it would have been a great betrayal of him. And he was a wonderful man, a good husband, a loving father and grandfather. I do not want to betray him. But in the last few months, as more of the past has come to visit me in the darkness of my memories, I know that I cannot take my secrets with me. You deserve to know who I am, and who you are.

I am a coward. That is the first thing you must know. I am a coward because I ran from the past. It took less courage to become a new person than to face the failings of the person I once was. I am a coward because I chose to lose myself in this new life.

If you went to Paris, you know by now that I am a Picard. That is my family. I was raised in a progressive Jewish home. My father was a doctor. My mother was a Polish immigrant whose parents ran a bakery, just like you do now. I had two sisters and three brothers. They all perished. All of them. I have come to terms with that, but I blame myself for not saving them. That blame is with me every day.

There is also a man you must know about, a man named Jacob Levy. I have not spoken that name since 1949, the year your grandfather returned to tell me that Jacob had died at Auschwitz. Every day since then, I have searched the sky for him. But I cannot find him.

Jacob, my dear Hope, was the love of my life. I loved your grandfather too; I do not want you to doubt that for a moment. But in life, I believe we can have but one great love, and Jacob was mine. Most people do not find even that. And I have realized, as I have gotten older, that by closing my own heart off, I have perhaps taken away your chance at finding that kind of love, as I took from your mother her chance. If one isn't taught how to love, it's hard to find the way on one's own. Do not let that be my legacy to you.

I know I did everything wrong. I closed my heart after I learned Jacob was gone, and I did not know how to open it again. Perhaps I did not want to. But because of that, I did not love your mother the right way, and that changed the course of her life, and the course of yours. I can never fully tell you how sorry I am for that. I failed both of you. I only hope that it is not too late for you to correct those mistakes in your own life.

Jacob died before he had a chance to meet your mother or you or Annie, and in that, I believe we were all cheated by fate. Your mother, you see, was his daughter. You are his granddaughter. Ted, who you always knew as your grandfather, knew this all along and raised both of you as his own. He knew already when he met me that he could never have children of his own, because of an injury he had sustained in the war. He gave me a new life, and I gave him a family. It was a trade we both knew we were making, and I have never regretted it. He was a wonderful man, a better man than I ever deserved. Please do not let this revelation make him mean any less to you, because if that is the result, I will have failed at my last important task. He was, and will always be, your grandpa.

I did not know for sure until 1949 that Jacob had died, although I had been told by many people, before I married your grandfather, that he had been killed at Auschwitz. Still, I did not believe it. I refused to believe it. I believed I would have known in my soul, and I did not. So, you may wonder, how could I have married your grandfather, if I believed Jacob would still come back?

It is the cruelest thing I have ever done. Your grandfather never knew that Jacob and I had been married in secret, just months before I left Paris. He never knew that your mother had been conceived on our wedding night. When your grandfather asked me to marry him, he did not understand that if Jacob had returned, it would annul our marriage. I was prepared to do that to him, to your grandfather, and that is something I must always live with. I would have left him in a heartbeat if Jacob had come back, and that, of course, was terribly unfair to him. But marrying Ted before I gave birth to your mother meant that she would be born an American. She would have freedom. No one could take her away to a concentration camp. And this, above all else, was my greatest responsibility. I did not have the luxury to say no to a proposal from an American. I had to save your mother, both because she was my child, and because she was the last piece of Jacob I had left.

Your grandfather and I had a good life together, and I loved him deeply, although in a different way than I loved Jacob. I loved him most of all for the kind of father he was to Josephine, and later, for the kind of grandfather he was to you. He showed both of you the kind of love I was incapable of. I believe that my heart would have broken each time I saw him with you, had my heart not frozen solid so many years ago. Without meaning to, I withheld my love from him, and from your mother, and from you, and from Annie.

And that, I am afraid, is the legacy I will leave behind——that of a cold heart.

I know that is the only way you have ever known me. But I want you to know that I was not always that way. There was once a time when I was happy and free, a time when I loved without reservation, because I didn't know how much love could hurt. I wish you had known me then. And I wish you had known Jacob, for he would have loved you with that sort of depth too. He would be very proud of you. Instead, I made all the mistakes I could have made, and in the end, I leave this world with nothing.

My deepest wish for you is a fate different from mine. I wish that you learn to open your heart. I kept mine closed for all these years, because I was frightened, and that was a mistake. Life is a series of chances, and you have to have the courage to seize them, before the years pass you by and leave you with nothing but regrets.

Your life still lies before you, as does Annie's. Learn to let people love you, my Hope, for you deserve that love. Learn to love freely. Love is so much more powerful than you realize. I know that now, but it is too late for me.

What I wish for you, dear Hope, is a life lived fully. A life lived freely in this country that lets you be what you are. A life lived knowing that God exists everywhere you are; he lives among the stars. And I wish you a life lived happily ever after, just like in the fairy tales I told you when you were a little girl. But you must go after that kind of life with all the strength of your heart. For it is only by loving, and having the courage to be loved in return, that you can find God, who exists most of all in your heart.

I will love you always,
Mamie

Chapter *Thirty-three*

I'm crying by the time I finish reading the letter. I put it down, and with the blanket still wrapped around me, I pad to the back door and walk out onto the deck, breathing in the cold night air. I pull Mamie's blanket tighter around my shoulders and imagine that it's her arms, enveloping me in one last hug.

"Are you up there?" I murmur into the nothingness. In the distance, perhaps carried across the bay a block away, I can hear the faint sounds of people celebrating the last hour of the year that's about to end. I think about all the things that can be started over, and all the things that can never be undone.

I look up at the sky and try to locate the stars, the ones Mamie was always looking for. I find them now—the stars of the Big Dipper—and follow the line formed by two stars in the bowl, just like she'd taught me, until I see the North Star, Polaris, glimmering overhead, due north. I wonder whether that's the direction to heaven. I wonder what she was searching for all those years.

I'm not sure how long I've been looking at the sky when I notice a tiny motion somewhere between the Dipper and the North Star. I squint and blink a few times, and that's when I see them.

Against the inky backdrop, so faint I can barely make them out, two stars are moving across the sky, just past Polaris, making their way deeper into the heavens. I've seen shooting stars before; after all, the nights on the Cape are black and deep enough that you can see farther into the darkness than most people along the East Coast. I spent many nights during my teenage years counting stars and wishing on the ones that fell from the sky.

But these stars are different. They're not falling. They're making their way across the blanket of night, shimmering and brilliant as they dance side by side across the darkness.

My jaw falls as I follow their flight. The sounds of the earth—the distant laughter, the faint babble of a far-off television, the lapping of the waves on the beach—fall away, and I watch in a bubble of silence as the stars grow smaller and smaller, and finally disappear.

"Good-bye, Mamie," I whisper when they're gone. "Good-bye, Jacob." And I believe somehow that the wind, which is whistling around me now, is taking my words up to them.

I search the sky for another minute, until the cold begins to seep into my bones, then I go back inside the house, where I pick my cell phone up from the kitchen table. I dial Annie first and smile when she answers.

"Everything okay, Mom?" she asks, and in the background, I can hear the sounds of celebration in Chatham. There's music, laughter, happiness.

"Everything's fine," I say. "I just wanted you to know I love you."

She's silent for a moment. "I know," she says finally. "I love you too, Mom. I'll call you later."

I tell her to have fun, and after I hang up, I stare at the phone for thirty seconds before scrolling through my phone book and hitting Send again.

"Hope?" Gavin's voice is deep and warm when he answers.

I take a breath. "My grandmother left me a letter," I say without preamble. "I just read it."

He's quiet for a minute, and I curse myself for not being better at this.

"Are you okay?" he finally asks.

"I'm okay," I say, and I know it's the truth. I'm okay now, and I know I'll be okay. But there's still something missing. I don't want to wait a lifetime to put the pieces back together, the way Mamie did, the way my mother never had a chance to. "I'm sorry," I say in a rush. "I'm sorry about everything. For pushing you away. For pretending you didn't mean something to me."

He doesn't say anything, and in the silence, my eyes fill with tears.

"Gavin," I say. I take a deep breath. "I want to see you."

I can hear him breathing. In the pause that stretches between us, I'm sure that I've lost him.

"I'm sorry," I say finally. I look at the clock: 11:42 p.m. "It's late."

"Hope," Gavin says finally. "It's never too late."

I hear his Jeep in my driveway fifteen minutes later, and he's at my door just before the clock strikes midnight. I'm already waiting for him, with the door wide open, not caring that the coldness of the night is pouring in. It doesn't matter anymore.

"Hi," Gavin says as he comes up beside me in my doorway.

"Hi," I reply. We stare at each other, and Gavin reaches for my hand. He's not wearing gloves, and neither am I, but there's a heat between us, and every cell of my body feels like it's on fire, despite the iciness outside. From somewhere in the distance, we can hear the faint strains of a countdown, and then a muffled cheer as the New Year begins.

"Happy New Year," Gavin says, taking a step closer.

"Happy New Year," I murmur.

"To new beginnings," he says. And before I can reply, his arms are around me, and his lips are on mine.

Above us, the stars twinkle and dance, winking down at us from the endless sky.

Acknowledgments

This is the book I've been wanting to write for years, and seeing this come to fruition has taught me some important lessons about following my heart and surrounding myself with wonderful, decent people whom I truly trust and cherish. My agent, Holly Root, and my editor, Abby Zidle, are both incredibly kind, hardworking, wise, and talented, and I can't even begin to sufficiently express how much I appreciate all their effort, insight, friendship, and encouragement. I think I'm the luckiest girl in the world to be working with them.

Agent Farley Chase has been an absolute rock star of foreign rights, and the lovely Andy Cohen has my West Coast calendar full. I'm also very grateful to Lindsey Kennedy, Beth Phelan, Parisa Zolfaghari, Jane Elias, Susan Zucker, Jennifer Bergstrom, and Louise Burke for the roles they've all played in making this novel a reality. I don't think it would be possible to find a kinder, more supportive team.

Novelist Wendy Toliver has been an incredible sounding board, friend, early editor, and brainstorming partner; I also want to thank Anna Haze—who died far too early, at the age of nineteen—for bringing Wendy and me together. What a wonderful gift. Henri Landwirth, the first Holocaust survivor I ever met, was a great inspiration. Lauren Elkin, my close friend and old Paris roommate, once again put a roof over my head during a research trip to the City of Light; her first novel (*Cités Flottantes*) came out in April 2012 in France, and I couldn't be happier for her.

I'd like to thank the many people who have gone out of their way to answer questions about factual points in this book. Darlene Shea of Brewster Fire & Rescue helped with an early draft, and Danielle Ganung helped answer bakery question. Karen Taieb from the Mémorial de la Shoah in Paris was incredibly helpful with my Holocaust research in France. Bassem Chaaban, the director of operations for the Islamic Society of Central Florida, and Rabbi Rick Sherwin of Congregation Beth Am in Orlando, were kind enough to help me fact-check some of my religious and cultural references. Any errors are my own.

Big thanks also to Kat Green, Tia Maggini, Vanessa Parise, Nancy Jeffrey, Megan Crane, Liza Palmer, Sarah Mlynowski, Jane Porter, Alison Pace, Melissa Senate, Lynda Curnyn, Brenda Janowitz, Emily Giffin, Kate Howell, Judith Topper, Betsy Hansen, Renee Blair, GK Sharman, Alex Leviton, Kathleen Henson, Anna Treiber, and Jen Schefft Waterman, who have been great sources of professional inspiration, brainstorming, and friendship over the years! Thanks also to the *Daily Buzz* crew, especially Brad Miller, Andrea Jackson, Andy Campbell, Mitch English, Kia Malone, KyAnn Lewis, Michelle Yarn, and Troy McGuire.

Thanks to my many, many other wonderful friends, including: Marcie Golgoski, Kristen Milan Bost, Chubby Checker (and his wonderful wife and kids), Lisa Wilkes, Melixa Carbonell, Scott Moore, Courtney Spanjers, Gillian Zucker, Amy Tan, Lili Latorre, Darrell Hammond, Krista Mettler, Christina Sivrich, Pat Cash, Kristie Moses, Lana Cabrera, Ben Bledsoe, Sanjeev Sirpal, Ryan Moore, Wendy Jo Moyer, Amy Green, Chad Kunerth, Kendra Williams, Tara Clem, Megan Combs, Amber Draus,

Michael Ghegan, Dave Ahern, Jean Michel Colin, John and Christine Payne, Walter Caldwell, Scott Pace, Ryan Provencher, and Mary Parise. I'm incredibly lucky to have such wonderful people in my life.

A special thank you to Jason Lietz—for everything.

I'm also blessed with the world's greatest family, including my mom, Carol (the most supportive person in the universe); my sister, Karen; my brother, Dave; and my dad, Rick. Thanks also to my brother-in-law Barry Cleveland, my aunt Donna Foley, my stepmother, Janine, my cousin Courtney Harmel, my grandparents, and everyone else, including Steve, Merri, Derek, Janet, Anne, Fred, Jess, and Greg. I love you all so much.

The Sweetness *of* Forgetting

KRISTEN HARMEL

INTRODUCTION

To say that Hope McKenna-Smith's life hasn't turned out quite the way she planned would be an understatement. At thirty-six, she's a law school dropout, a divorcée, the owner of a nearly-bankrupt bakery in a Cape Cod tourist town, and the caretaker of her beloved, Alzheimer's-stricken grandmother, Mamie. When Mamie suddenly presents Hope with a list of names and urges her to travel to Paris to find these mysterious strangers, Hope nearly dismisses the request as yet another one of her grandmother's delusions. But when she decides to take a chance on the unknown, Hope embarks on a trip of a lifetime; one that will take her both through Mamie's haunted past and through her own journey of self-discovery.

TOPICS & QUESTIONS FOR DISCUSSION

1. Readers first encounter Mamie when she is sitting by her window at *l'heure bleue* waiting for the stars to come out as she does every day. Why is it so important for Mamie to gaze at the stars every evening, and what do the stars come to symbolize? Why does she name her bakery after the North Star?

2. Describe Hope's relationship with her daughter Annie at the beginning of the novel. How are they similar? How are they different from one another? How does their relationship change over the course of the novel? How does their quest to discover Mamie's past affect their relationship?

3. In contrast to Mamie and Jacob's belief in love at first sight, Hope has resigned herself to the idea that she will never find true love. How and why does Hope's attitude to love change throughout the novel? How do her interactions and conversations with the men in the novel—Gavin, Alain, and Jacob—serve to change how she feels about love? Do you believe in love at first sight?

4. How does food serve as a bridge between cultures and characters throughout *The Sweetness of Forgetting*? What memories and traditions are baked into Hope's creations, and how does baking help her preserve the past? What does Hope gain when she learns about the unexpected origins of her creations, particularly the Star Pie?

5. Describe Mamie's belief in God, prayer, and religion. How difficult do you think it was for her to hide her true religion over the years, and how does it change her as a person? How was she was able to maintain her Jewish faith while practicing as a Roman Catholic for so many years? Of the differences between religions, what do you think Mamie means when she says: "It is mankind who creates the differences. That does not mean it is not all the same God"?

6. As Mamie struggles to remember her past, Hope meets people like Olivier Berr who help fill in the ever-expanding holes in her grandmother's memory. How does Hope's new-found understanding of Mamie's past help her make sense of her own upbringing and family troubles? Why do the people

in the end? How does their reunion personally impact each character? What does Hope learn from Mamie's final letter, and how does it allow her to move forward with her life?

ENHANCE YOUR BOOK CLUB

1. Bake a treat for your book club using one of the North Star Bakery recipes . . . or make something that reflects your family's heritage! If you have Irish ancestors, make soda bread, or if your family is from Greece, try your hand at baklava! For more ideas and recipes, visit www.world-recipes.info

2. Test your memory skills by playing a game of "Memory" with your book club members. All you need is a standard fifty-two deck of cards. Shuffle the cards and lay them on a flat surface in a square pattern face down. On each turn, a book club member must select two cards. If the cards match, the player keeps the set and takes another turn. If the cards do not match, return the cards face down and move on to the next book club member's turn. Visit boardgames.about.com/od/ca .games/a/concentration.htm for the full rules and suggestions for how to make the game more challenging! Discuss with your group how it felt to actively try to remember when playing the game. Were you ever frustrated?

3. Consider attending a religious or spiritual service that differs from your own beliefs with your book club members. Discuss what was similar to what you are accustomed to, and what was different. Did you learn anything from your visit? Did it raise any questions about your own beliefs?

that Hope meets feel compelled to preserve such a painful history? What do you think would be lost if Hope was not able to find the people who played a role in Mamie's story?

7. Do you think that Mamie should have told Josephine about her past (or told Hope earlier)? Why or why not? What would you have done if you were Mamie? What impact does keeping such a monumental secret have on Mamie, and on future generations?

8. Elida White introduces Hope and Annie to the Albanian word *besa*, the act of taking care of those in need. In addition to the Muslims who took in Mamie during World War II, how do the characters of the novel practice *besa* toward one another? Why is it so difficult for Hope to accept that others want to take care of her, particularly Gavin?

9. How does Hope's relationship with her mother influence how she raises Annie? What does it mean for Annie and Hope to grow up with such strong and independent women as their mothers, and fathers who are largely absent from their lives?

10. Why is it so important for Hope to keep the North Star Bakery in business? What would be lost if the bakery closed?

11. Hope grew up listening to Mamie's fairy tales, but she never imagined that the stories were anything but fantasy. What purpose and meaning do the stories serve for the storyteller— Mamie—and the listener—Hope, and later Annie? How does Hope's understanding of the stories shift as the novel progresses? How do these stories impact Hope's views on love and fate?

12. Discuss the ending of the novel. Were Mamie and Jacob's sacrifices for one another worth the suffering that they endured